THEY SAID

THEY
SAID

A Multi-Genre Anthology of Contemporary Collaborative Writing

EDITORS SIMONE MUENCH
DEAN RADER

ASSISTANT EDITORS
SALLY ASHTON
JACKIE WHITE

Black
Lawrence
Press

Black
Lawrence
Press

www.blacklawrence.com

Executive Editor: Diane Goettel
Cover Design: Richard Every
Cover Art: "I Amplify in Silence" by Jim Tsinganos
Book Design: Amy Freels

Published 2018 by Black Lawrence Press.
Printed in the United States.

CONTENTS

INTRODUCTION

One story, many voices~

What is the appeal of creating a story or a poem in cahoots with another writer—or even a group of writers? Why would a writer abandon their own particular voice for a mutant expression they can't quite control? Perhaps the allure lies in the challenge of having a puzzle to solve. Or a conundrum to cause. A contest. A love fest. Surely there are as many reasons as there are practitioners. But for whatever reason, enthusiasm for collaborative writing is on the rise. Everybody's doing it. Or so it seems.

Not that there's anything particularly new to communal narrative from an historical perspective. From what we know, the origins of storytelling began in the collaborative milieu of oral tradition when the collective knowledge that formed a culture's identity was memorized and performed. Within orality, many voices shaped a common story, a mythos passed from generation to generation. Story making was participatory, enacted through song and dance, the members embodying and partaking in the narrative together, individual identities submerged in a communal experience.

With the advent of writing, orality gradually faded, over time relinquishing narrative as public song and performance to the silences of solitary scribe and to paper. Written works could be signed, sealed with wax, their authority established, even assigned some value. Words became permanent things to be owned that could be transferred across space and time versus words as notes in a shared aural experience, inseparable from communal exchange and the transient moment.

Evolving writing technologies continue to shape our writing practices and our ideas about what literature is. The printing press led to the need for the copyright, the right to make copies of a printed work for distribution and profit, further locating story-making as the work of an individual, if not a gifted, writer, one who not only creates but who necessarily protects their authorship—the creative process—and subsequent rights to their work from plagiarism. And while it might surprise a

Western reader to realize that the concept of plagiarism, of "stealing" words from another owner, isn't universally held across cultures, the idea decisively shapes our Western, capitalist literary tradition. It's what the publishing industry depends on, making current-day literary collaboration a somewhat transgressive act.

And yet it can be argued that the collaborative enterprise never really left us. In 2015, *Salon* ran an article on Gavin Kovite and Christopher Robinson's collaborative novel, *War of the Encyclopaedists*, in which the authors suggest that collaboration is a natural form of writing—we already edit each other's work, we make suggestions, we write in the margins, we alter wording—we are all already collaborating. And of course most writers recognize and revere the thought that our writing is to some extent in conversation with all of the storytellers who have come before us, one begun before pen and paper.

Collaborative writing as an intentional pursuit came into wide practice in Western literature in the late nineteenth century under the Surrealists' influence and then again as postmodern experiment mid-century. For instance, a collaborative sonnet form, the bouts-rimés, supposedly begun as early as 1648, was made popular in 1864 when Alexandre Dumas issued an invitation to numerous French poets to create sonnets by using a provided set of rhymes. When this collaborative sonnet call was sent out, hundreds of writers responded, and Dumas published the poems in 1865. But the Surrealists gained greater notoriety. A special issue of collaboration, *Ralentir Travaux (Slow Under Construction)* is a famous surrealist collection of collaborative poems by Andrè Breton, Renè Char and Paul Eluard written as an *exquisite corpse* and published in 1930. *Locus Solus* was a literary journal named after the 1914 French novel by Raymond Roussel, and edited by John Ashbery (Issue 3/4), Kenneth Koch (Issue 2), and James Schuyler (Issue 1 and 5). The late Harry Matthews published the magazine in France. *Locus Solus II* is the collaborative issue edited by Koch in 1962.

Other cultures have long practiced a collaborative approach to writing. One lesser-known tradition is the dialogic and animist orality that inform Native American literature. Kenneth Lincoln calls this "dialogic oratory" in which any given text is never really the words of one individual human writer but a fusion of the language of the land and a "reciprocal tribalism among plant, animal, spirit, and human" (xv, xviii-ix, 3).[1] Miwok-Pomo Greg Sarris further includes listeners as collaborators

---

1. Lincoln, Kenneth. *Sing with the Heart of a Bear: Fusions of Native and American Poetry, 1890-1999*. Berkeley: University of California Press, 2000.

such that with each retelling, the story itself is remade.[2] Anishinaabe poet Kimberly Blaeser—whose collaborations with her tribal colleague, Margaret Noodin, appear in this volume—notes that an "intricate weaving of Native traditions and consciousness with individual experiences and identities" means that their poetry carries—collaborates with—not only a pan-Indian legacy but also functions as "a response to perceived expectations of Native American literature" (414-15).[3]

Perhaps further afield but more familiar, a very early form of collaborative Chinese linked verse, *lián jù*, developed in the Qin Dynasty, 221 to 206 BC, is cited by various sources as a likely precursor to the still-practiced Japanese *renga*, a series of linked poems written between poets who follow a codified pattern of syllabic verses. Much like *haiku*, the *renga* has clearly established itself in American poetic practice. *They Said* features one such renga by poets Leslie E. Hoffman and Pushpa MacFarlane, as well as "renga essay"—a lyric essay written in "a renga-like mode of oblique linking" by Gillian Parrish and Jennifer Atkinson. You'll also find an example of *somonka*, a pair of love letters composed using two *tankas*—five-line syllabic poems that have been a part of Japanese tradition for 1,000 years—in a formal epistolary exchange between Tom Barlow and Diane Kendig.

Another ancient Chinese practice of collaborative composition possibly familiar to western readers appears in "The Wang River Sequence" by renowned Tang dynasty poet Wang Wei, written back and forth between Wang Wei and his friend, poet Pei Di, using classical codified forms. *Chang-he,* literally "chanting and echoing in response," is still practiced among Chinese contemporaries using less formal, vernacular structure often accompanied by drinking wine. According to Professor Balance Chow of San Jose State University, who confesses to having recently participated in one such prolonged poetic exchange at a party in Hong Kong using text messaging, such *chang-he*—oral and written—becomes part of the social experience, composed between participants "on the spot" to commemorate aspects of the event. As such, the practice continues the community-enriching functions of early orality while embracing contemporary writing technologies and language structure.

---

2. Sarris, Greg. essay "The Woman Who Loved a Snake: Orality in Mabel McKay's Stories." from *Nothing but the Truth: An Anthology of Native American Literature*. John L. Purdy and James Ruppert, eds. New Jersey: Prentice-Hall, 2011.

3. Blaeser, Kimberly. "The Possibilities of a Native Poetics." from *Nothing but the Truth: An Anthology of Native American Literature*. John L. Purdy and James Ruppert, eds. New Jersey: Prentice-Hall, 2011.

It is the Western tradition, enthralled with the Romantic and democratic notions of the individual, that has missed out. In its embrace of singular authorship and the primacy of an "original," distinct voice, Western literature abandons the unifying function of the shared voice, leaving it to ecclesiastical tradition and to song, but losing the generative community-building capacities of collaborative practice.

While contemporary stage and cinema continue to offer a type of communal experience of story, as do public readings and slams, it is perhaps our suddenly interconnected digital world with limitless communal forums for sharing news and narrative of all sorts that has taken intentional collaborative writing viral. As reading and sharing becomes once more communal and interactive, so too does creation. And while the rise of social media initially led to serious social isolation, and more so for writers who already work to a large degree isolated, these virtual platforms have ironically enabled new modes for connection and collaboration. Writers have found new writing relationships online, and we are reveling in the experience.

To collaborate is to abandon, if only for a while, the guise of the solitary writer. To surrender one's authority, identity, one's autonomy. Maybe collaboration provides some sort of relief. To experience, if for a brief time, creative partnership and for that time to be freed from the pressure of working alone within our hyper-competitive industry is to be revived at the core of who we are. We draw back to the primal, to the community of griots and poets, of minstrels and tricksters. We tell a story together.

Many stories, one voice~

They Said is an innovative collection of recent collaborative writing drawn from domestic and international writers. Our anthology includes poetry, fiction, cross-genre work, and creative nonfiction, each piece having more than one living writer as the primary author. While some works feature an alternating perspective, others are co-authored or group authored so that it is impossible to tell which of the named authors actually "wrote" or "created" any particular portion of the final text. Though we value works of *ekphrasis*, and works written "after" other pieces, as well as those written in essential conversation with dead authors, we've chosen to focus on the creative wrestling implied in living exchanges and what this give and take produces.

While *They Said* isn't the first collaborative anthology, it has been a decade since the significant and comprehensive collaborative poetry anthology *Saints of Hys-*

teria: A Half-Century of Collaborative American Poetry (2007), edited by Denise Duhamel, Maureen Seaton, and David Trinidad, came into existence. As fans of their project, we felt that it was time to produce an anthology that would also include fiction, creative nonfiction, and cross-genre works to further highlight what's being created in this rapidly expanding field of collaborative writing.

We have ordered the offerings by genre, though such classifications can easily be contested. Therefore we simply let the authors assign their works themselves. Their choices and the process pieces they've written reveal the widening parameters of genre in contemporary writing. While we celebrate the transgressive tangos with traditional poetry forms offered here, such as the sonnet and sestina, as well as a variety of *exquisite corpse* and epistolary pieces, we also revel in the seeming abandon of innovative approaches that move us across the page, across genre, across identities.

In her introduction to *The Best American Poetry 2017*, guest editor and former US Poet Laureate Natasha Trethewey noted that "any anthology could serve as an autobiography of the mind of the anthologist." With four practicing writer-editors reviewing submissions for this collection, it is clear that the "mind" behind this anthology represents just as much a collaborative hive-mind as do the individual works.

All four editors have diverse histories with literary collaborations. Lead editors Simone Muench and Dean Rader have both collaborated with other authors for previous books and collaborated with each other for their 2017 collection, *Suture*, recently published by Black Lawrence Press, enlivening a traditional form through their process. They subsequently put together a panel on collaboration for the 2016 AWP conference. The panel was a huge success, so much so that some audience members suggested they put together an anthology of such writing to fill a major void.

While Dean and Simone had already been thinking along these lines, the audience's enthusiasm toward the possibilities of a collection of collaborative writing proved hard to ignore. Assistant editor Sally Ashton, who attended their panel, was one such enthusiast who jumped at the opportunity to work on the project having enjoyed her own collaborative forays with visual artists, musicians, and other writers. While assistant editor Jackie White has also collaborated with visual artists and musicians, most recently having a poem set to acoustics and dance, most of her collaborative writing has taken the form of translation and cento experimentation. We are each avid practitioners and enthusiastic supporters.

One story, many voices~

Writing with a partner isn't just about the process, about a shared experience, or even simply about the finished piece. To work collaboratively engenders a more playful approach to your personal practice once you return to it. Collaboration encourages greater risk-taking and deeper trust in the power of language to come through for us. It's exhilarating, revelatory, satisfying, and ultimately, just plain fun.

After all, from the amount of collaborative writing gathered here and what's continually being produced, writers, it seems, are having *lots* of fun. For readers, however, the appeal of some literary work can often be the "voice," and among the pieces in *They Said* are collaborations of correspondence, call and response, and linguistic *pas de deux*. What strikes us are the amazing ways in which differing minds are able to converge and negotiate terrains to create a seamless point of view which is neither one person or the other, but a new entity—a third voice that goes beyond the ancient melding of individual voices to create something original and unique.

The art of the collaboration lies in creating this voice, whether a singular voice from several or a conversation to which we're compelled to eavesdrop. Listen in. We hope, and suspect, our project will inspire new modes of collaborative creation, and maybe a round or two of *chang-he*!

—by Sally Ashton with contributions from Simone Muench, Dean Rader, and
  Jackie K. White

POETRY

Kelli Russell Agodon and Martha Silano

I DON'T BLAME YOU

for the toxins in the mango,
for the fireplace being less fire,

more ash, for the French-fry-begging gulls,
their ubiquitous laughter. Ashes that congregate

like coal dust on our country's black lung.
I want to tell you a story about a woman

who became a pond, but instead I'll hand you
an umbrella for your woes, for your worry

about the lack of snow in the mountains,
the mudslide in your soup, the funeral

for your child, water darkened by millions
of bodies—the aching Atlantic, the pleading Pacific—

this disjointed union like a broken kitchen plate.
Someone throws a mango at a wall. It's easy

to be angry at the uselessness of ruin,
but a broken ceramics piece is a stepping stone

mosaic. Though it may be overripe, though it may
need to be washed three times, don't throw away

the mango. When you've eaten every bite,
suck on the giant pit. *All clear, all clear* they insist,

hoping you won't notice the ash-gray sky.

Kelli Russell Agodon and Martha Silano

FIELD TRANSMISSION OF TULIP VIRUS IN PATRIOTIC COLORS

Tell me a story with a tulip
included, a frilly red tulip
splattered with mud, a tulip
with certainty, a century
of long lines and not enough
food. It's easy to be hungry
for what we're serving, terrific
tulip leaning towards
a baby holding a tulip
bomb in a field of forgotten
veteran tulips, white blossoms
blooming in the dirt. Our flags forget
to be warm, become doors, tulips
the color of grieving, 300 million,
like icicle stems dropping
at our feet. Tulip as travel ban,
the flowers of so many
countries forbidden, restriction
of movement like a fenced-in field
of American Dreams. It's hard to miss
what you've never seen, the road
outside the park leading to a landscape
of springtime, tulips with sasquatch,
some bearish curiosity, some
staggering hairy beast mostly
out of focus, but moving
closer on a moonless and foggy
evening. We're all holding telescopes,
I mean tulips none of us need.
Tell me a story, you say,

but when I try to speak,
it only comes out in grunts,
so we neanderthal our way
through the tulip fields
of these United States, arms open,
sometimes trusting, knuckles dragging
along the frost-heavy ground.

Kelli Russell Agodon and Martha Silano

JOINTLY RESPONSIBLE

What does a gesture hold?
What of the body, its let and go?
What if you offer, instead of a house,

a housing project, a promise or a lie,
whether the alarm is armed, not knowing
by way of a gaze, a glance—the eyes severed

from status. I nod at the soldier because
I have no words, though I know I am more
than my Garamond, my Times New Roman.

When he died he died the way a leaf dies,
a birch leaf, how it sticks to the shoes
of all who pass by.

Like playing Clue,
Colonel Mustard with the rope
in the parlor. Miss Scarlet with the knife.

Sometimes I need my secret decoder
to know if you're grieving, to comprehend
the library of your pain, my losses tallied by wind.

What grows in the ice is null,
but the dirt adds up, the soot from the sky.
I know what a handshake returns. Tripping,

we pretend we are dancing.
Absolution, like absolute. Adding
the salty unknown, stirring toward a solution.

The soldier speaking quietly in the field.
The hand, we say, lend a hand, the part
standing in for the whole. Therefore, stars

and stripes, the men in blue,
a podcast of weeping, the YouTube
channel of wincing. Searchbox grief.

How can we judge time when time
reminds us of church bells? Who's gone
down a rabbit hole? *Wintry mix.* Crust you must

break through. She entered the house.
Fetched a plastic tub. Labeled it *March 4th.*
Filled it with snow. Simplicity of a woman holding the cold.

Kelli Russell Agodon and Martha Silano on their process:

I approached Kelli in early 2017 about trying our hands at writing collaborative
poems together. She was enthusiastic, so the next time we got together to write I
presented a prompt where I'd read one sentence of Wislawa Symborska's poem
"Questions You Ask Yourself," which appears in her book *MAP, Collected and
Last Poems*, and then set a timer for two minutes and write off that sentence. We
did this all the way through the poem, and then we went back to our respective
writing desks and revised what we'd written. Then Kelli emailed me her lines, and
I mixed them in with mine, cutting what didn't fit and rearranging as I saw fit. For
the other two poems, "I don't blame you," and "Field Transmission of Tulip Virus
in Patriotic Colors," Kelli devised a prompt called The Accordion Method. This
method involved taking a piece of paper and writing for a minute or two (Kelli
started), folding over (and thus hiding) all but the last line written, and passing
the folded paper back and forth until we got to the bottom of the page. Then
we unfolded the paper and Kelli took home to revise what would become "Field
Transmission of Tulip Virus in Patriotic Colors," and I took home what would
evolve into "I don't blame you."

Maureen Alsop and Hillary Gravendyk

BALLAST

In the veiled light, the chest is a shroud
    for what used to linger, powdered wing
      and circle of flames   destination
mapped my understanding—
gaps at the waterfront where the ships slowed
to listen to the gulls' song bodies

O, this close to the sea
   The salt covers everything
   like a stuttering glass garden
   at the turn of winter

The women crouch in the sand
  wrestling shells from the insistent shoreline

My pocket flooded with charms
Dusk drawn dawn, moth hour—
venerated faces balance outside the window—

The day's failed confession
   A black stone on the tongue.

Maureen Alsop and Hillary Gravendyk on their process:

I sit up straight ask for space within her congenial grove. Before pain's absence moth's infected the gloam. Her vessel came, low twilight. No sea. No city. No man's sky. Starred with damage the body what was left to tell. A mirror shone a refused language, the last moon slipped. As to the dreaming craft lightened one moment then another left.

But if it troubles you this scratch across the eyelid, lark's skeletal procession. She wanders now in gladness the moss lit edge, fates resolute placebo where yesterday we carved statues for the gods.**

**this process piece was written in collaboration with Matteo Lexa

Maureen Alsop and Brenda Mann Hammack

THE CORPSE IS NOT EXQUISITE

when it rots and, yet, the skeleton inside,
washed clean by centuries' rain,
is cultured pearl.

We ask where would we find him,
how we would remember
his name. Green

frost under the sun. As we enter
the quarry, as if gazes, sieving,
might unearth Tintagel

pot shard, fossilized nest, he hid
above the pasture, stood, in fact,
open

in the presence of his lover,
while in the next century, the room
filled with brine,

and we cleared the table.
We did not save scraps
for compost.

We did not praise or even thank
our ancestors. We did not pray.
We did not read

April's breath within our own
even as we watched the rise
and fall of breastbones.

Spendrift voices do not clot
into souls. Lovers quiver
resurrection. Alone.

Maureen Alsop and Brenda Mann Hammack

THE CORPSE IS NOT EXQUISITE

when it rots and, yet, we do not look
for bodies in turf the shade of verdigris.

We do not survey the quarry, sieving
through grey to unearth [   ]

We try not to imagine flesh rippled, veins
varicosed. Bog bodies turned compost.

We do not save nail pairings. We do not praise
or thank ancestors, complacent in our faith.

We do not believe April only a breath's rush
away. We watch the fall of breastbones.

We will to forget maggots before Resurrection:
earth turned with flies, luminously blown.

—Brenda Mann Hammack

Maureen Alsop and Brenda Mann Hammack

THE CORPSE IS NOT EXQUISITE

At the old house we mulch grey pachysandra & peony—atremble of sticks, stasis, sandalwood-scented cinder. We ask where we would find him, how

we would remember his name. Green frost under the sun as we enter the aborted orchard. Spared bees earn a circadian pattern—afterlife's adaptation, or a passive threat.

He hid above the pasture. Stood, in fact, open, in the presence of his lover; while

in the next century the room filled with brine and we cleared the table. I hold then what I never loved—shadow grass lodged in the lung, nightingale's spate noon. But we did not read April's breath within our own.

I stood within sound's aura and watched a pale architecture exit fern's undergrowth. Spindrift voices. Kestrel's counsel followed us like firebombs through the grove.

—Maureen Alsop

Maureen Alsop and Brenda Mann Hammack on their process:

When I tripped across the bones in the dry creek bed I imagined the border, a space without sinew or stench—as when the elements polished the doe's skull, sternum, vertebrae to disclose beauty's articulate—as if a body's infinity lay in suspension among autumn's yellow enclosures: chinaberry, poisoned ash, cape lilac. Perhaps this was a postwar confession, as when you wrote: never am I again. The only channel between civilizations, violet wired fences, failed the town and the twelve fragrant dreams of the other. How did you answer the question. Where a girl and a sword forget the rattle-box measure of sky, twilight heron's iodine-colored feathers lingered at the gate. A pack-sled over sleep's rocks, I sent you a round. How did you answer the question. Night, neither a shadow's guess, his dust, nor the pond's red curdled seaweed. O wicked Sailor, the mixing water is ice-broken. Nevertheless you'd said he was not familiar. Was he the same being? When I constructed the second message there was no more ledger. He was very sick by then. He never wanted to die. Savior to unequal reason. I recall death's best face. A surrealist's parlor game. The angle by which dead visualize you.

Maureen Alsop and Joshua Gottlieb-Miller

HEIRLOOM, STEREOGRAPH

Someone hammers,
dirt habitations. Not the sun
but the beginning
of a windless distinction.
A sail on my back
to attract a mate,
an ink black smear
in light's seam.
Like you this prototype,
a satin river,
time held in the palm,
dusk dust, downy drifts, sky
skin. Photos on leaves
using photosynthesis,
old evergreen trees
imprinted in rock
a formation well-known
for preservation.
Guitarfish, dragonflies,
a meadow, unclear
whether the shark
is pained or hungry,
open-mouthed.

Maureen Alsop and Joshua Gottlieb-Miller

EIR

When I was brought up to the trench

I disassociated the slaughter into three systems:
medical, warrior, and borderlands. I dispatched
healing as some violent gift. Some

curse the living for borrowing time. Some curse time
for borrowing the living. Fireweed compress
over glass splinters. The last stitch of cotton,
thumbed gauze. Ice pasted, cool as milk,
over the right eyes.

Some would think it good to waken the dead,
alone under the sweep of a single gull. I spoke

three languages of dead: gristle between toes, blue
wisps of hair, vats of honey stilled
in fire light. Conversations

slanted and warped through long
hours of the night. Until each world
trembled at the sight of the living.

I, among the dead, the ones
time loves most, impractical

healer, stitched the yellow
trance between plane trees; shaved my face
in the infected gloss of an amputee's tibia
pool of after-hope. Waited
bed-side of earth.

Maureen Alsop and Joshua Gottlieb-Miller

SONG, MARY

I don't even believe in desire
sometimes. Like the artist from Israel
I didn't want to sleep with—

she painted Vermont's green mountains.
There weren't any bombs in her paintings, so
her paintings must have taken place

in those fifteen seconds
between belief and desire,
the air raid sirens   and shelter,

grace and God.

Night aspens, weeds wink. I am
kept by this rifle. I am spared.

I drink in the lips of thee, sleep
in the pasture. Speak dear shadow thee

quelled air is folded, felled.

Death, little desert, mine
forsaken uneven   swoon. One
of my horses leans a long time
into the scent of juniper; there is a bridge
light will not cross.

Maureen Alsop and Joshua Gottlieb-Miller

0909_FAR_50

Rather than any foretelling, my words
were solitary. I walked from one horizon
to another, ankles brushing the empress-green
underpinnings of sweet grass and nameless
gateways. There was never a solution
for the immortals. Only the red hawks stirring
imperial clouds, a gathering hindsight

of swallows. Bob Hass doesn't remember
me, but I hit a softball into his chest at a conference
in California. Lazy pop fly, the sun
rounding first. It dinked to the ground.
If I had been legging it out I'd probably pull
a double. A sacrifice fly, we say, because
the runner on third tags up. But I round first. Nobody

ever knows anything for a fact. I had passed Bob Hass
on a path in the woods and he flinched like a sway of seaweed
at high tide. I didn't know to call him Bob. The body holds
its own memory: pop-fly balls, subtle mis-position of the feet, glove
shielding the eyes, accumulative effects of the lupine's shadow,
the lily-flecked green of the meadow where behind together,
the cellular repetitive closeness recalls a wider knowledge, beams
like the moon's mirrored door, as the heartbeat, golden, sun-blinded.

Maureen Alsop and Joshua Gottlieb-Miller on their process:

Maureen Alsop and Joshua Gottlieb-Miller began writing collaborative poems almost a decade ago. These four poems came from different methods and eras: themed groupings, constant back-and-forth, ekphrastic response, divide-and-conquer. The only constant was our continued, mutual interest in trying new methods; the collaborative act is inherently dynamic, the continuation of collaboration is challenged by the necessity of evolving as poets separately and together. In other words: "The only constant in a decade: We walked as if we followed. Yet, nothing led us. Breath, painted over. Prayers, draft and spill. A park, eyed suspiciously. I like poems better than explanations."

Maureen Alsop and Lissa Kiernan

APHRODITE'S THIRST

You spread salt over the map so the body might
continue as a trajectory—lantern and water
succumb to snow.

I stood in the civility of language. Fog
scaffolding the latticework, pigeon's linden-lined paths.

Over the past five centuries no one remembered
the threat the hand made of progress. The wooden steps
leading upward to mist.

I stood at your door. The way fog
scaffolds the latticework, the staunch stump
stands in solid light. My shadow, a splintered wind-
mill, a chapel in the round.

Civility, the language
we speak when we speak
with the maturity of the dead, at ease
in cloud where the overlooked beauty
of pigeons ripple
the linden-lined dirt paths.

The wooden steps
my shadow splinters spreading salt
over the last five threats.

Maureen Alsop and Lissa Kiernan

PERHAPS IT WAS A CLEARING,

Ironwood doubled beyond switchback. West's silvering
notation scrimmed a buck's skull blanched and sculpted

clean by the late season's lake-effect snow.
Had the buck ranged on a tuft of turf-tall fescue,

sipped from the rivulet's intoxicating trough?
Perhaps it was the buck's own rippling reflection,

window within window, that caused it to look twice
at its own mirage—two tapering velvet sabers

straining to reach new heights? Did they distract the buck
from seeing his own conclusion approach sideways

or from behind? Was there no hint, no whiff of pine
or shift of wind to trouble the buck's languid white

under-tipped tail? Had he not overheard the sedge grass
whispering, or did the creek's incessant utterance mask

the stealth of predator closing in? Or was there no wolf,
no coyote, no cougar, nor hunter to harvest the trunk

and consider trophying the head, before declaring
the antlers atrophied, even as they grew heavy

on the buck's young head? Perhaps this heaviness
was his demise, or was it not something borne down,

but rather something inborn? Or was it invisible,
lacing the water, glazing the grass? Was it fast

and clement, or did it—the dying—go on for some time?
And had a raptor carried a limb to another

clearing, black alder stooped over dwarf pine?
And did the soul come with its heart-

half or stay behind? And how long before the skull's
stunted antlers, become bleached so driftwood light?

—Lissa Kiernan

Maureen Alsop and Lissa Kiernan

JANUARY ITINERARY, PARENTHESIS

Perhaps it was a clearing, ironwood doubled beyond switchback. One drawer
after another opened: adolescent compositions, train ticket stubs; west's
silvering notation scrimmed a buck's skull blanched and sculpted by the grove's
indistinct spires. What question was I, not who, not kindness. But a physical
concentration, late season's lake-effect, snow—

—Maureen Alsop

Maureen Alsop and Lissa Kiernan on their process:

We stood at the bar, etched with initials almost discernible—drank through
each wave's precipice. Pain's mysticism held an errant earring. We read the cur-
rent between mantelpiece portraits, the falling other in the other's song. Were our
eyes able to ascertain what horizon arrived in the fold where each night the brigade
planted a line of elms orphaned side by side? "What question was I…" She and I
never told. The gates closed. And heat threaded each ventricle.

James Ardis and Maggie Woodward

SCRIPT NOTES FOR *NEKROMANTIK*

SCENE I

they opened the body bag like a christmas present
do you recall what I was wearing? / *we are fucking,*
learning new things[i] / transitioning from cum to blood
crunching hard candy till it severs our tongues
transitioning from fur to the strata below / if I've said
anything that inspires you
let me know

SCENE II

Our protagonists Betty & Rob absolutely for certain met at German Denny's
because at German Denny's (much like Denny's Classic) you pay your bill at the
front & you tell your waiter aloud how much you're going to tip them. Betty &
Rob are absolutely for certain both really into this.

SCENE III

now Betty jabs a pipe into the dead man's groin / now Betty
slides a condom on the metal / Betty won't catch any dead man diseases
don't worry, the dead man's wife is dead too / our manifesto
is of transgression: *we propose to break all the taboos of our age*
by sinning as much as possible. there will be blood, shame,
pain & ecstasy / there will be body bags
opened like christmas presents

SCENE IV

Remember when Dr. Pepper used to talk about their secret recipe of 23
ingredients & made a really big deal about those 23 ingredients? In high school

I called corporate Dr. Pepper toll-free from a booth at German Denny's &
pretended I was having an allergic reaction to Dr. Pepper[ii]. I demanded that
they list off all 23 secret ingredients. I started taking it seriously. I drank too
many iced cappuccinos. My body oozed an angry sweat that never left that
booth in German Denny's.

SCENE V

you stupid dead man,
how could you get your stupid ass killed
                    & your stupid eyeball impaled by part of a car
                    & cheat on your wife who is not as dead as I implied earlier
                    & how could you let them open your body bag like a christ-
                    mas present

SCENE VI

Our manifesto says *there is no afterlife*, our manifesto says *the only hell is the hell
of praying*. I pray while I smoke cigarettes in a movie theater. I don't even smoke
but I saw a dipshit do it once & now I wanna do it too. Buying both your ticket
& your Dr. Pepper Ten at the box office at the same time is brilliant. The dead
man's stagnant eye is brilliant. I smear Cholula[iii] & melted cheese across my
face in my booth at German Denny's. I tongue the stagnant eggs below.

SCENE VII

Betty is able to collect her thoughts
                    she's collected all the viscous fluid
Betty is very unsure of where she'll be accepted
with her corpse lover
                    I mean, can you imagine

SCENE VIII

Betty, there are lines that just cannot be crossed
like when you opened the body bag

        & why you opened the body bag

        & where you opened the body bag

        & how you knew that the body bag

was your christmas present

when you type it out it's pretty clear what the reason is

SCENE IX

the porn theater industry was still slightly in vogue

~~they could afford larger theaters complete with couches~~

        & leather chairs

        & beds

        & *What lives that does not live from the death of someone else?*[iv]

let me know if I've said anything

SCENE X

                that inspires you

our manifesto knows that *the only hell is the hell*
of obeying laws & debasing yourself
before authority figures

our manifesto thinks we can't fully love
until we understand mortality

under our manifesto I am certain
my consumption will become violent

do you know what I mean, Rob?
when I say / I want to *be* a word

COMMENTS FROM PRODUCER:

[i] we need to credit nick zedd & underground film bulletin for the quotes if under copyright

[ii] get permission from DP to use brand name before shooting

[iii] is this brand name too? if so need permission

[iv] maybe could use for marketing tagline?

James Ardis and Maggie Woodward on their process:

About two years ago, Maggie challenged herself to watch every film on Complex Magazine's list "The 50 Most Disturbing Movies of All Time." Their selection for #2 is the aptly described "love story for necrophiliacs," Jorg Buttgereit's *NEKRO-MANTIK*. Naturally, Maggie became obsessed with this disgusting & delightful movie & it didn't take long to convince her fave fellow weirdo poet to watch with her. Then, they took to Google docs to discuss their favorite images & scenes. What you see is a happy merging of their personal styles. Maggie will always be grateful to James for lending his voice to this absurd poem & premise.

Horror movies are not really James's thing, so he had a lot of fun fitting them into his personal aesthetic. He never would have written lines like "cheat on your wife who is not as dead as I implied earlier" if it wasn't for Maggie and he thanks her. Even sections four and six, which are very much in James's comfort zone, only work because Maggie tightened them up perfectly.

Cynthia Arrieu-King and Ariana-Sophia Kartsonis

FOX SHOOTS HUNTER IN BELARUS[1]

The red weeds crinkling, a back taken up mountainous,
air burnt, sky wrinkled, a mountain backing up.

What is smoked but intention, feral quips, a fox
laying a delicate nose to the gun

a crack, the earth slides sideways,
gunpowder and fur collar, a momentary

level to the injured and injuring. A hunter
shot by his animal, what else can the sky laugh on?

Clap its blue to our surprise. What color
chosen for our ability to endure; to miss a shot,

to remiss, to be remiss. One awkward feeling
altered with talk and love and instantly

another awful feeling springs up.
We forget ourselves—the beasts of us

and what feasts on our amnesia;
the color of sundown and mistake,

the rusting slyness, the true aim
untrue, then too, the good things of accident.

---

1. *A wounded fox shot its would-be killer in Belarus by pulling the trigger on the hunter's gun as the pair scuffled after the man tried to finish the animal off with the butt of the rifle, media said on Thursday. The unnamed hunter, who had approached the fox after wounding it from a distance, was in hospital with a leg wound, while the fox made its escape, media said, citing prosecutors from the Grodno region. "The animal fiercely resisted and in the struggle accidentally pulled the trigger with its paw," one prosecutor was quoted as saying.*

Cynthia Arrieu-King and Ariana-Sophia Kartsonis

WINDSHELF

A kite broad as a red square hung in a gold painting
and you listening.

The space between petals of the turbine,
he-loves-me-not and moving.

A soft thought opening my mouth to cold and its
improvements.

The underside of bluejays and jets.
Feeling buoyed up, in fall, the maple leaves a library

that dandelion spores pause against
before starrily descending

to where you are sitting. I lean to kiss your hair:
The air stands still for this.

Cynthia Arrieu-King and Ariana-Sophia Kartsonis on their process:

Collaborating with Sophia: Ideally it's Christmas, we're surrounded in our respective homes by a lot of cookies, half-paying attention to the news, then hearing something so full of pathos, some headline so geared on exemplary loneliness or mishap, that we tell each other about said headline and start to laugh tea/milk/coffee out our noses. It also helps that we have our volume and prosody and detail etc. levers all at complementary settings. We play and I still feel astonished by what happens when we do.

Amy Ash and Callista Buchen

BUILDING AS CRADLE

support, frame, structure, framework,
underpinning, foundation, crib, hold

At the base, knees and shins, what isn't bruised
or wounded, the slightest movement of sling or swing
carves breath, breath, breath. What contains
this small frame, spindle and spine
long like spirals of pulled glass, the distance
splayed before you, and reaching. Embrace
each sharp point, walls sweated into elbows, embers
burrowed into floorboards, ambered into ash.
Suspended between root and lift, you and heat
this shadow, this shelter, this drift. Only after
do you realize the shadows are pilgrims, the columns
rows of ghosts. Hollow ribcage, welcome them
with buffered pulse, crowd out the echo
that sounds, then splinters against bone
fragments of ritual, journey. What protects
this home, what breaks, what we build and build again.

Amy Ash and Callista Buchen

FLIGHT AS CONVERSATION

trip, journey, voyage, hop,
tour, talk, exchange, natter

"I wanted to ask you about flight or fracture,

what the wing articulates with its dip and lift."
"I imagine thermals as crowds, fluxes followed

and ignored, the rutted path to height."
"These crest clouds below, gristled cartilage, they stretch

and connect. The compacted vertebrae of the mountains."
"Everywhere, body. What of the hollow bones?"

"And the dark shape that glides over the backs of clouds?"
"The bones, narrow, not marrowless, infused with air,

that dark bird circling. It hovers, hungry."
"Even static, I lilt, absorbing the swoops and dives,

at sparrows dodging between branches, hungry, too."
"What are we to do, then, open-mouthed and grounded?"

"Let's unravel our voices like kites. Wingless, we walk
still connected to sky."

Amy Ash and Callista Buchen

FOREST AS STORY

> woodland, jungle, plant, floor
> landing, tier, untruth, account

Beside the mosses, chanterelles burst in gold flourishes over some other season's oak leaves. We don't know what to crush. Shoeless, our toes touch padded ground, plush carpet. We kneel at a tree trunk, split open like a storybook. Inside, we bury hands in rotted bark. We think softness, we think quiet, as if we can read the flood of insect song, scuttle and mumble in the alburnum. Wings, legs, antennae, fragile as eyelash. Blink and the sky slides between branches, flutters in the wind. What we think we hold is slippery. Shadows, shapes, until we can't tell time. Hunger hovers like fog. Behind us, the wolves breathe.

Amy Ash and Callista Buchen on their process:

We write by alternation, usually choosing to write alternate lines, stanzas, or so many words. Together, we choose a title and general form, and then we decide who begins the piece (an honor/challenge we also alternate), each leaving the other a phrase or turn to finish, over and over. We have no idea how the poem will shift, where a line might lead. We are constantly surprised. Most often, we compose in Google docs. While we like to be in the same space while we're writing, we don't really talk about what we're doing as we trade lines, conferring aloud only once we have a sense a poem might be finding its end. We view collaboration as a space for possibility and trust, an act of listening. As we write, we often lose track of who wrote what, the language evolving into something different from our own voices. We think of our writing self as a chorus or as a collage, something new and whole emerging from our individual contributions.

We value what collaboration can offer writers, what the experience can teach. We believe that collaboration is a way to explore this increasingly divided world, and can help us better engage with the social implications of voice, authorship, and identity, creating a dialogue that plays an important role in our lives as writers and global citizens.

"Building as Cradle" is our first collaborative poem. We have been writing together for over three years.

Devon Balwit and Jeff Whitney

LETTING BONES SPEAK

I don't ask for much—a little weather,
a little wonder, a brief reprieve.
Like a cicada, I've grown accustomed

to chrysalis, comfortable in my self-made
sepulcher, scorpions outside lifting claws.
The rats of any alleyway are not rats,

but the flitting souls of whatever leaves us
in the end, the cars of the funeral cortege
pulling away. Once we had maps

as full of yearning as a dog waiting
by the window for the departed
to come home. Now, everyone I know

has an answer they can't recall, red tape
over the mouth of the imagined. Let this
be permission to fail, to lose the war

we never signed up for. Let the water
drain from the globe, joining the history
of broken things, clockworks exposed.

I arrange bones to have something to talk to.
They retail lost cities, ruins loud with singing.
I am ready to believe almost anything.

Devon Balwit and Jeff Whitney

THE LIGHTNING STRIKE

I am one of those people who orders bibles
just to have someone to talk to.

Whatever it is, I stand ready to believe:
That duck shadows are bombers, that

my grandfather fell off the roof singing.
That all the planets in the universe

were scattered by a single hand like toys
in a child's bedroom. Professor Seagull

spends his nights reading the newspapers
he's wrapped in, changing every proper noun

to marble. President Marble promises
to pull his troops from the Bay of Marbles.

He's happy in one way & miserable
in another. He's as independent as the sun.

Sometimes he howls for no reason.
There are times I think I see him.

Near water, walking a bride down the aisle:
every place somewhere he rages against,

full of marbles that rattle right through him,
scattering and regrouping like pond scum.

Yes, tell me the history of broken cities,
of lucky slots, of a baseball diamond

cleared of people but for two wrestling
on second base, of a civilian with a refrigerator

tied to his foot to show the heaviness of life
without virtue. When he lifts his arms

like a praying mantis in wind, loose-jointed,
hollering to the watching seven thousand,

he can't know that lightning is coming,
but once struck, he is satisfied, like a rat

in a pot of warm butter doing the backstroke,
the butterfly. Singed, he intones my own mantra:

I am ready to believe almost anything.

Devon Balwit and Jeff Whitney on their process:

Jeff and I operate quite differently as poets. His mode is imagistic, and his pace is blistering. My mode is narrative, and I tend to go to write from a slow, deep place. Collaboration for each of us meant abandoning our comfort zones. We wrote side by side in a public cafe, which I usually never do, preferring the quiet calm of my studio for composition. He would email me a huge block of text, jam-packed and evocative, before I'd even settled into what story I wanted to tell in my own slight poem. From his piece, I would tease out a thread, suture connections, breaking the block text into stanzas. I would send this back to him, and he would tee off from a line to create another dense block of new text that I would, in turn, thin out and structure. We each went home with the four or five poems we created in this fashion with full permission from one another to edit and use them as we saw fit. Here are two born from this encounter.

Tom Barlow and Diane Kendig

IN 2005 WE FIND THIS SOMONKA WE SENT BY USPS IN 1975

> *"Whom then are there now,*
> *in my age (so far advanced)*
> *I can hold as friends?"* —Fujiwara no Okikaze

The sky is full. Where
is your face? Not here, in this
drop of moonlight. Yet
once it was. Will you return
with the solstice of winter?

Every thirty years
I arrive: Basho reading
old mail in new light
of moons and stars. Look, Tom, our
words become burnished with age.

Tom Barlow and Diane Kendig on their process:

We have known each other since birth, our parents being friends in Canton, Ohio who had us, their first-borns, in the same year. After college, living in separate cities, using real mail (stamps, envelopes, waiting for days), we set up a writing exchange in Japanese forms, including the somonka, originally a collaborative poem exchanged through letters. That year (1976), our chapbook of those poems was accepted for publication in a series on collaboratively-produced manuscripts. However, in that small press now-you-see-it/now-you-don't way, the press folded, and the book was never published. Life went on.

Fast forward to 2005 when Diane found the poem "Somonka: a Decade Embraced," but wasn't sure if Tom would be willing to revise. She phoned to find him writing fiction enthusiastically again after decades of not. He had just attended the Clarion workshop and was keeping a writer's blog. He was game. In the latest round, mostly the second stanza and title changed. Having actually read Japanese poetry in the good translations more available in the intervening years, we were able to replace "Odysseus" with Basho and add the Okikaze epigraph, for thematic connections, we think, and not just a tag-on. We decided to make the poem reflect what it (and we) have been through, for example replacing the futuristic final lines of our youth, "till words/burnish clear with age" with what we hope has happened, no "till" about it. If there can be a moral to a process, ours is hold onto drafts and friends and keep reading.

Molly Bendall and Gail Wronsky

CRYSTAL ON A ROPE

```
                        dive in transparence
        crystal blue persuasion

                        more tales
            to live by
                    Kris Kringle/Kristeva
                my new age angel/angle

        directionality                    cut glass

            critique/Lalique
        facet
                                turn it     off
```

aftermath of culture/suture

sharp. razor

stage looking glass

lucite (bang)les

light up sheerness

wear it around my neck

Molly Bendall and Gail Wronsky

EYES/FAUX LEOPARD

You were   looking at me

w(hen)   my   girl-group   p(lay)ed

       Club   (Linger)ie   *ce soir*

we were   so   *Monique*   so

       (Wii)ng   in our   see-through

s(pots)   our   (Gap)   jeans

     you   per(used)   me   bad   *primitivo*

   s(ur)f-boy   you   duded me

deluded   me   with   your   m(I'm)e

    r(out)ine   your   Geek

        élégance   *Monsieur*   Medusa

s(lay)   me   I   mean   f(lay)   me

     in   y(our)   temple-tomb   lift up

mine skin   YOU ARE: Paul de Man:

     RuPaul: *demain*

       man

Molly Bendall and Gail Wronsky

TOKYO, MY POODLE

Hello Kitty
            and my plastic hair

        (God)zilla me Issey Miyake
                    the sound of

    Sailor Moon
Who's your favorite designer?

            Sayonara

B(ash)o
my sign/your sign
we all sign for
asymmetry
metallic
bullet
toy dog
girly bubble
con(mod)ification
pa(god)a
empire

Molly Bendall and Gail Wronsky

STARS/KNOTS

Walpurgis   knot   a little   naught
        music oh   my   ent(angle)ments
dis-cussioning   and   fistfuls   of disco dollars in
        the belly of   some Revlon-elation   I'm
all   tied   up   with   now(here) to
        self-fashion   Masseuse me
Zeus!   my hair is so tangled I can't even   kill you
        the   flower-net   of   intentionality
is   falling   out   the knots   the
        fathers   the   feminisms   ooh   sweet *fascista*

k(no)tty heaven   k(not)ty women   n(aught)y pine

Molly Bendall and Gail Wronsky on their process:

M: We initially thought of this collaboration as a "conversation," and that we'd write poems back and forth to each other. We wanted to talk about fashion, pop culture, and "fashionable" language, particularly what was fashionable in poetics and academia.

G: Yes, I definitely saw it as a conversation about trends—in fashion, speech, poetry, academia—our shared interests. I found that our friendship animated my involvement with the project, made it more energized and immediate. In the same way that poetry can sometimes seem like a secret language among friends, these poems try to take that idea and have fun with it. Girl talk, but with an intellectual and aesthetic spin.

M: I do like the sense that we shared inside jokes and gossip. Also, I enjoyed how much we challenged each other verbally and, most of all, made each other laugh with our own subversive touch and punning and innuendo.

G: Play was indeed our main m.o. when writing these poems, but I also think that we were exploring the idea of a female sentence, or female sensibility—mock serious about masculine discourse but within that mock seriousness a real questioning of the logos and a kind of urgent and energetic examination of the possibilities of language.

Mary Biddinger and Jay Robinson

THE CZAR

The Czar declares it is too early
to be speaking German. He declares
this in German. He ransacks

his study for an illuminated
manuscript on the tenuous nature
of our attachments. One day

you're sitting in a dull literary
theory class, the next touching
the man across the room from you

in a dull literary theory class,
and no dull literary theory has ever
ventured to explain this. Maybe

he'll become your new Czar, or
at least the Czar of the week. You
voted against the partial-Czar-

abortion bill, but then took hard
showers in the town plaza and ate
the berries from questionable

bushes. You lecture your own
literary theory students on nothing
but *Das Unheimliche*, because who

needs the same thing twice. Unless
the same thing isn't the Czar
and rejects the Czar, his affinity

for corks from the finest wines
possible at the Circle K. Something
Derrida would never deconstruct.

Something never so dull as
the feel of the non-Czar's fingers
on your latest manuscript.

Mary Biddinger and Jay Robinson

THE CZAR

has nicknamed himself Frankie
Machine. He has heavily annotated

my copy of *The Man with the Golden
Arm*. What an asshole! Lou Reed

is dead at 71. Why go on? Everyone is
riddled with shrapnel from war.

You know the type: hop a wrong train
and next thing you're a novel

away from a spry Italian bookie and
a woman lighter than her own

shawl. Sometimes I think my sexuality
would make a great libretto

for street opera. Enter Czar, literally
dripping with potential. He

can wear harem pants into the twenty-
first century. The woodwinds

start up like a stampede of ants
at a picnic we didn't plan on because

we wanted to eat lunch. The Czar
then holds a press conference

in his bedroom. Only he was the one
asking questions. Slowly, I

dissected his rhetorical strategy.
Pathos is a character I'd undress,

I said, as if the kingdom were a novel
and I couldn't hear the flute solo.

Mary Biddinger and Jay Robinson

THE CZAR

is a little worried about how much he loves the novel *Wuthering Heights*. In private, he whispers, "I am _____" then sends himself to un-heaven. Who is the naughtier child, Catherine or Heathcliff? And why doesn't the weather in Czarland Heights vacillate like a northern place with moors and hillocks? He can't say that heaven wouldn't want him, as he invented the concept. Why did it have to involve heaps of coconut? Why was his movie in black and white, and replete with ringlets, the dogs dead for decades? In a less probable world, the Czar would have also been a Czar. Yes. In a less probable world, though, Edgar wouldn't have died. And the peasants would have feasted nightly on more than limburger cheese and half-stale crackers. Before the Brontë sisters, he considered books an accelerant. Like his mistress's faux bridal lace teddy. Or the Lady Czar's culinary renderings of aimless heft. At night he stares out the castle windows. A low, accusatory moon in the Czar-like sky. Stray cats in an alley and a pail of warm milk. Low water level in the moat. He sips Glenfiddich by the gallon, tells his mistress he will stay up all night until he finds the right word. But he never does.

Mary Biddinger and Jay Robinson on their process:

The idea behind these poems took root in a conversation in Mary's University of Akron office in September of 2013. We joked about a fictional Czar. At the time, every societal ill seemed to warrant its own Czar. We jotted on sticky notes, in text messages, on the backs of envelopes. We realized we should attempt a collaborative poem when we planned to write a poem a day the following month. But we are obsessive people, so we decided to write a bunch of poems. We drafted The Czar using a shared Google doc in October of 2013 through the first week of November 2013. One of us would start a poem; the other would finish it. Sometimes you could open the document and literally watch the other person writing the piece you would endeavor to finish later that day. These poems were written in libraries, or in our heads while driving, with cats at our feet, or kids playing in the background. They were written in Ohio or New York or wherever we traveled. In rereading these poems, it's not at all certain who wrote what. Both of us have experienced the sensation of not knowing whose words are whose. We mirrored each other's aesthetic in an aesthetic that's solely the book's. We never analyzed the character of the Czar or the collective narrative of the book. It felt like putting together a puzzle with our eyes closed, which sounds exactly like a parlor game the Czar would play.

Kimberly Blaeser and Margaret Noodin

TRANSFORMATIONS: *ZIIGWAN*

Crane calls vibrate across March skies
ajijaak's elongated body stretching from winter to spring.
I am clan struck—longing.

Aandeg answers the pouring chorus
of melt, then rain, *baashkwanakwad* from sky to earth.
I am a draining constellation.

Beneath star stories *omagakii* inflates his pouch—
the trill of marshland songs rise in the night.
I am a holy bellows.

Kimberly Blaeser and Margaret Noodin

UNDOCUMENTED

Ink a left-handed bridge, *manjininj azhegan*, reaching—
I am the spilled water of old hearts,
I am the tiny hook in search of an eye.

Story a right-handed river, *michiziibi*, tracing belonging—
With *gete-nibi* I baptize tomorrow's shore,
With the curve of my silver I pierce expectations.

Night travelers, *Niibaashkaa,* now gather in dark becoming
We are land's own descendants—we cross in safety,
Our bundles are not burdens.

With dawn we rise out of our dreams, *mooka'am*
To inscribe *wiigwaasabakoon*, tell anew this citizen science—
Tempestuous climate, its turns: *Nishwanaajakiing.*

Kimberly Blaeser and Margaret Noodin on their process:

We have collaborated in the past and always it is a dynamic experience, for both the texts and the authors. Perhaps this is why our titles, "Transformations: *Ziigwan*" and "Undocumented" both circle around movement—between languages, between generations, between ways of thinking and writing. The turns in language often created new perspectives or turns in the poem.

As we wrote, both of us were conscious of the process of continual exchange, perhaps as students of Gerald Vizenor we were attempting to include what he calls the "natural motion, or visionary transmotion" of literature and poetic construction. We exchanged both the emerging poem and short commentaries on what we or the other person had written. The poems, written in this way, lifted us away from the starting point in unexpected ways: "Undocumented" may have opened with ideas of citizenship, migration, ancestry, or historic land theft, but came to suggest as well the unrecognized sustainable ecological practices of Native peoples.

Very specifically, our poems developed in layers. Kim would send Margaret an opening stanza, Margaret would add another. But, in each exchange, we both also fiddled with various phrases/lines in what had already been written—in both English and Anishinaabemowin. Lines that began in English took turns in Ojibwe, while lines that began in Ojibwe built bridges to English that had not previously been crossed. We created echoes that were more harmony than equations of exact equality. The collaboration—a criss-crossing of language and ideas—cracked open new spaces and reverberates yet.

Sarah Blake and Kimberly Quiogue Andrews

THE SEA WITCH MOVES TO LAND

There, through the wall
of cleaned, stacked bones:

a naked body, striated, variegated,
many small, shifting horizons.

All movements are the wreckage
of preconceived notions of poise.

When she does not move,
she's a pause flush with breath,

a pulse visible due to the
terrible redundancy

of the bones. It's easy to confuse
one line for another. What

does she reach for? What does
she bring to her mouth?

Our jaws such that we may speak
of eating, of watching witches eat.

Sarah Blake and Kimberly Quiogue Andrews

THE SEA WITCH IN HEARSAY

AAAAAAAAAAAAAAAAAAAAAAAA
AAAAAAAAAAAAAAAAAAAAAAAA
AAAAAAAAAAAAAAAAAAAAAAAA
AAAAAAAAAAAAAAAAAAAAAAAA
AAAAAAAAAAAAAAAAAAAAAAAA
AAAAAAAAAAAAAAAAAAAAAAAA
AAAAAAAAAAAAAAAAAAAAAAAA
AAAAAAAAAAAAAAAAAAAAAAAA
AAAAAAAAAAAAAAAAAAAAAAAA
AAAAAAAA she is made AAAAAAAA
AAAAAAAA of eels AAAAAAAAAA
AAAAAAAAAAAAAAAAAAAAAAAA
AAAAAAAAAAAAAAAAAAAAAAAA
AAAAAAAAAAAAAAAAAAAAAAAA
AAAAAAAA she will turn AAAAAAA
AAAAAAAA your skin to eels AAAAAA
AAAAAAAAAAAAAAAAAAAAAAAA
AAAAAAAAAAAAAAAAAAAAAAAA
AAAAAAAAAAAAAAAAAAAAAAAA
AAAAAAAAAAAAAAAAAAAAAAAA
AAA she is also lonely AAAAAAAAA
AAAAAAAAAAAAAAAAAAAAAAAA
AAAAAAAAAAAAAAAAAAAAAAAA

Sarah Blake and Kimberly Quiogue Andrews

THE SEA WITCH TAKES A WALK

How long does it take to work through a new linguistics of breathing?
In the ocean, each particle is inhale, exhale.

Now this. She feels weightless, and she read Kundera once.
She knows the absence of a crushing force can feel like sadness.

She could propel herself to the top of a house.
Instead, she wraps herself around a neighbor's porch railing,

allows the terrible horizontality of movement to shift her hair, slightly.
A small dog yips at her and the eels hiss. She stands

in her god-form for only a second: in a back yard, a few houses away,
a boy tastes salt water; everything looks wet, threatens to exude.

She corrects herself so dry it won't rain for weeks.

Sarah Blake and Kimberly Quiogue Andrews

WHY THE SEA WITCH LIVES IN BONES

Isn't the sea filled with skeletons?

And all the whales and their car-sized hearts.

a house of one—a lung of two—a bolt of three

This is a wonderful neighborhood.

What we'll call deaths.

You can see all the cages I'm imagining.

The tunnels and their liquid language.

In the heat and sun, the tongue is a useless thing.

an anchor of four—a finger of five—a tooth of—

Why not approach her yourself?

She sits with her back to a bone that holds her.

Sarah Blake and Kimberly Quiogue Andrews

THE SEA WITCH AS A FIGURE OF WAR

Dermal eels. Mutliply prehensile. In the pit, the math of limbs and limbs.

Not girl shark. An error: boy shark, too. But rows of regenerative rend.

The horseshoe crab, the octopus, the starfish, the sea urchin—mouths tucked away—and peripherals closing over the words *to scuttle, to swim.*

What lies near to the mouths of rivers breaks the banks of the branches and sows salt into the fields so that they wish they grew the seas, had already

been growing them, had a long history of being them, the seas, the seas.

An error: witch. When in fact: witch.

Sarah Blake and Kimberly Quiogue Andrews

THE SEA WITCH NEEDS A MORTGAGE FOR THE LAND, IF NOT FOR THE HOUSE OF BONES

The man at the bank says, *I don't want to be depressing*

In her kelp dress   In her seashell dress
In her dress of ink, here is the problem,

a persistent sartorial illegibility,
what do you do when your face has borne no true witness—

I mean, we offer a variation on life insurance,
such that, if you were to,   he clears his throat

She looks at him in the manner of putting
makeup on a fingertip

such that the mortgage would be paid off in full and not
be a burden   *on your kin*

She devours her children like she devoured all the songs
invented to wish her a mortal, a fish, an innocent

If she could die maybe men would be necessary
As it stands   there will be no relief

Sarah Blake and Kimberly Quiogue Andrews on their process:

Our process is a bit like a very friendly tennis match wherein one of us starts by making the ball. One of us will write a draft of a poem, as complete as we can get it, and then we send it to the other, who has free reign to add, cut, rearrange, etc. We go back and forth for as many rounds as the poem needs, sometimes quickly, but sometimes taking years in between bouts of editing. We mostly avoid discussing the intent of any single draft in the beginning, though at this point the major themes of the collection are pretty clear to both of us. So a few drafts in, we'll talk about how the piece we're working on fits into the larger narrative of our sometimes be-tentacled protagonist. We want all the poems to feel like a single voice as we tell the story of the Sea Witch.

CL Bledsoe and Michael Gushue

HOW TO LICK A THOUSAND STARS

Start with a dependable work ethic. Sleep
enough but not to excess lest you become
lost in a dream. Stretching is important.
Remember that butter is nature's way
of saying you're too healthy. So slather it
on at each meal, repeating the following
phrase: "Though they shot the shoe-man,
they won't shoot me." A man will come
to your door claiming to be from the ministry.
Do not believe him no matter how well-
groomed his nose hair. Instead, ask, "Why
do the stars burn my tongue when all
I want is to love them?" "This is love,
the burning," he should say, "Stars are always
hungry, always eating themselves. They're
just not that into you." But this is a lie.
The truth is, there is no ministry, no stars,
the shoe-man survived. That'll be him, now,
knocking at your door, trying to wake you
from his dream. He'll have every shoe
you've ever dreamed of, but not in your size.

CL Bledsoe and Michael Gushue

KODACHROME

I'm just a shadow in your mind, but you
are Kodachrome in mine. The flicker
is so much more appealing than staring
at the darkness, hearing the rustle of coats
against seats, the odd cleared throat. A hand
brushes mine and zips away. A whiff
of popcorn or perfume. It seems as though
everyone is comfortable, and I can't find
an empty seat. It's my own fault for being
so transparent, for trying to enjoy the film.
A movie screen hides something by showing
something else. You look like a person made
of light, but the wagon wheels turning backwards
tell the truth. I made up those colors,
used a filter that turned day into you.

CL Bledsoe and Michael Gushue on their process:

We never consciously tried to develop a process. One of us will toss the other a
few lines, or a stanza, sometimes just a title, by email. The other adds a few lines
or more and tosses it back. It may go back and forth many times, gaining a few
lines each time or losing a few. Eventually, it starts to look like a poem; sometimes
it doesn't. Mostly, we try to discover something surprising or crack each other up.
Both of us have a free hand to cut, revise, find a better word, jigger, and move stuff
around without argument or complaint. It's a bit like a game of exquisite corpse
except both of us are cheating all the time. At some point, we both decide that the
end seems like an ending, then go back and see if we can make any of it better, or
weirder, or funnier, or sadder. It works because we respect each other enough to
let the poem happen.

John Bloomberg-Rissman and Anne Gorrick

SONNET 1 – MY BEAUTY SOUNDS LIKE ITSELF

My beauty is not a story. My beauty is not free speech. "Twenty-three, with black, straight, shoulder-length hair / and tight T-shirt and jeans, my beauty looked / like it could be a Ramone, the bartender / thought so; before the show, he kept / serving it free drinks." My beauty is a Last Chance Beauty Queen. She's restless for an Ikea rodeo, wears sushi bar sandals, stale green light, Styrofoam skin care products, government faucets, formaldehyde iPhones, my beauty is reading this to find out how you can get free stuff, Evanescence edits my beauty. You lied about the number of atoms in other elements. Go photograph a deck of cards and separate them from your other nouns. I'm injecting my eight-year-old son with Botox. 'Tis ma belle (mah bel), my beauty, an indexical. The night I met Einstein. Ah, Whitney, après la deluge! My beauty sounds like itself. Is my beauty base or superstructure?

John Bloomberg-Rissman and Anne Gorrick

SONNET 9 – HE SAID, "I'M DRINKING THE BEAUTIFUL SCOTCH."

My beauty has a Black Friday velocity. My beauty has the attributes of the Number 8, men and women who dance like birds and salmon herds, the South West Wind, *The Maltese Falcon* and *Farewell, My Lovely*. My email account had a dark and twisted fantasy about Walmart and a diary mask ammo kit. The moon is enough for us in Spanish, even when death goes undetected by Beauticontrol.™ His everythings were shallow, not a cough in a carload. But there were shy violets, birds—skylit, scarlet. It's so beautiful there and the trout are great. Why waste money on fire prevention when prayer rallies can generate actual cash? When Cocteau was asked what he would rescue if his house burned with all his precious objects inside, he said he'd rescue the fire. My beauty burned on April 16, 2007. A fire came near my parents' house once. My mom was in Florida, so I called my dad and asked him what he'd packed. "How do you pack a life?" he said. "I'm drinking the beautiful Scotch." Good lord, he was drunk!

John Bloomberg-Rissman and Anne Gorrick

SONNET 29 – IN CONTRAST, KLEE CUT ANALYTICAL TRENCHES

In the months before her grotesque death, Vickers had made calls not to cowboys, who set off to explore a seemingly endless frontier likewise traded away, but to a man who roams the seemingly endless corridors and salons of a luxurious hotel. In contrast, Klee cut analytical trenches from one mode to another to construct a seemingly endless labyrinth. "It is a somewhat heretical view that this viscosity should not matter." Grocery shoppers in northwest Kansas and Queens, NY, might not know it, but they have a lot in common. In the struggle over memory and meaning in any society, some stories just get lost. Insanity, reductionism, slavery, a "beautiful, dangerous, red-headed croupier," love always, mom. Good afternoon friends, family, and supporters! We pray all of you are well. We're super excited to let you know that Naz's case is a true, personal story. I am splashing stone, the only truth there is. My beauty begins to show his faultlines. Coders determined whether his stories were mostly positive, or mostly negative. I am a member of the Swiss family called Robinson. Except that I'm not really Swiss. The susceptibility of this story to rewriting suggests the difficulty that plagues perception and interpretation.

John Bloomberg-Rissman and Anne Gorrick on their process:

The "source text" for this sequence is Lynn Behrendt's chapbook *This is the story of Things that Happened.*

Alternating lines, we took the nouns from each and processed them via one of two computing techniques. The first involved wetware and the hidden algorithms of the imagination. The second involved Google. Neither of us consulted or inquired as to how the other was engaging with these techniques. The only other compositional constraints were that this was a poem revolving around the phrase "my beauty," the "who" in "my" never being specified, and thus floating between personae and pronouns, and that each time we hit fourteen lines we called it a sonnet and went on to the next one.

We turned these sonnets into titled 'prosed sonnets' when we finished the project. We did this in order to lose track of who originated what. We are both gladly responsible for all of it.

A number of the titles are derived from another collaboration, this being "Crisscross," by Jack Collom and Lyn Hejinian.

Andrea Blythe and Laura Madeline Wiseman

A GATHERING OF BABA YAGAS

I. First Sister, Sister Winter Snake

I didn't know what choked me in the Russian courtyard,
amid the drifting jeweled wisps. I came to drink our history
hidden behind iron gates, to interpret the flag fluttering
its sickle and hammer, to witness one lone cottonwood
bright in the golden-red light. *Myth,* our sister said, *Revolution.*

A weight of fingers, again, around my throat in the sunset's glow,
luminescent and ghosting. I could neither speak nor breathe,
my tongue clamped by the past's vice-grip. When the server asked,
Coffee black? I shook my head, eyes watering, hands quaking.

We know her, are her, our sister said. *We are ancient as babble—*
a language withered by family truth. Who had I believed
we were for? I held the fairy book of Baba Yaga, the one gilded
with her image—long nose, mouth to suck, teeth to cut
a heart—open in my lap. *Why do I hunger?*

II. Second Sister, Sister Moon

My little babuschka, my mother whispered to my wrinkled face,
squeezing pruny fingers and toes, mussing my hair, knowing
the cold, sharp edges of Moscow streets, how they would scour me,
how they would whet my teeth to points and shear my leg to bone,
shaping me into yet another. *Baba Yaga,* they called me in school,
skinny girl with bony shanks, hawkish nose, birdlike fingers
carving horns to cull songs. I shaped a firebird charm to wear.
Classmates stared where it jiggled, dropping feathers of ill-luck.
My name means horror, fury, torture, pain. *Baba Yaga,* we're called,
a name I was born into, grew into, am. I wobble on chicken legs,

build fences like rotting bones, live in a home on stilts that turns
in wind. My days feel mundane—cook, sweep, grind herbs to spell,
curse, and hex, warn so many away, tend to my sisters. Snuffling,
I nestle candles in skulls. Lift my nose, sniff for Russian men.

III. Third Sister, Sister Death

One of us was naive, the good girl men would sing-speak pop songs to
over vodka, "I Will Survive" a humming drunken mumble in July sun
as music warbled from the Black Sea boardwalk of flapping tents.

One of us was compliant, letting fate grind and mash her
like dreamspells of herbs worked by mortar and pestle,
she licking the limbs of men, cracking and sucking them down,
men of marrow and bone. *Are we here of our own free will?*

What answer isn't a lie? One of us was fierce, riding out the night,
a shadow's specter, refusing her mother's latching warmth,
the sweet suckle of milk-tit beyond babyhood. I cast my voice
to the moon, snarl, be the wolf bitch for the world. Who doesn't

consume to escape? I ride the pig. I dance the old men, pull
them down. *Give me secrets,* I say, *Give me your babes.*

Andrea Blythe and Laura Madeline Wiseman on their process:

"A Gathering of Baba Yagas" was one of the first poems we wrote collaboratively. To write this poem, we alternated writing lines, composing them one or more at a time. As we began the draft, we decided to add the constraint of working with fourteen-line sonnets to retell a folk story of Baba Yaga by exploring the various ways she was represented. During the composing, and later the revising process as well, we researched the stories for inspiration. Three separate point of views evolved out of our initial draft, which were honed through separate revision sessions over a period of several weeks. We communicate via email and social media and work primarily in synchronicity on google docs, which enables us to follow along as we compose and revise, engage in discussions, and plan next steps. Generally, we meet weekly for one-hour collaborative sessions, though we live in different time zones and over 1,500 miles apart. Technology like the internet makes our collaborations possible. Our collaborative work has become a vital part of our writing practice, inspiring and sustaining our individual work.

Traci Brimhall and Brynn Saito

THE WATCHTOWER

You could guard the city if you could bear
your own loneliness. The night could offer you
wildflowers and moonlight and your bright face

in the waters below. But how will you rise
if I continue to seduce you? Look at the sea,
the bereft immensity. No ships approach.

But don't confuse that with safety—absence
is the heaviest tide. Watch for the sea wind,
and for the wildest enemy within you.

Once sunrise shows its unmerciful beginning,
you will know you must save yourself more
than once. Count the sails of continuing departure

and the cut tongues in the blood coral. Come
with your torn heart and bright ring to the bottom
of the reef. The shipwreck you find hides in its hull

a rusted rapier, whalebones, and a trunk full
of compasses. Beware the gleam of forgotten gold.
Beware the dark bite of sought pleasures.

Cut your hair and climb through the swaying.
Then open your body to the windless night. The light
inside you will guide the burning ships to shore.

Traci Brimhall and Brynn Saito

THE LIBRARY

Standing in the book aisle like a broken tulip,
searching for a history. What has happened
to your self from six years ago, and why

can't you remember the title of the book
that says a word once divided land from sea,
light from shadow? Every story is a door.

Run your fingers over the dusted spines
holding stories of wolf-hearted gods and glorious war.
How can you believe there are answers here?

Here, where villains teach you about heroes.
Here, where the usual angel betrays the Lord
for the sake of a boy's beauty. You know all

the names for god, but you've forgotten how
to speak. Tonight, when the light goes, place
your two hands over your heart. A sadness

exists there that existed before language.
It will outlast you. It will outlast every page here.
Dusk comes, like a wise man. The library

is stone quiet but your mind is a storm
in August. In the half-light, a hand appears
to write on the wall—*Here is your sorrow and here*

is how to survive it. Rising waters will one day
spare nothing, not even the word. Not even
your hunger—the only sign that you are living.

Traci Brimhall and Brynn Saito

THE CEMETERY

This is where it begins, with a mouth
full of ashes and a stone with a name.
The lost children waiting for paradise

beg with splendor from the middle skies.
They see you as I see you, rocking
on your knees, not in prayer

but overcome by what you read
in the book left out in the rain.
Now you know what your father knows

and what his father before him felt
when he came here asking
for a mystery big enough to hold

the universe within. It's yours now—
the stars' bright message and the ache
inside the sycamore beside you.

What will you do with soil and stone?
Who will you bury if you refuse to love?
Return to me when your body hurts

the way a magnolia hurts in the April dark,
and I'll show you how to be as still and resilient
as a gravestone choked by midnight.

I'll reveal every name if you return with
moonshine and a difficult faith. I'll show you
how to go to your death like a god.

Traci Brimhall and Brynn Saito

THE BRIDGE

One day you will leave. I will try to understand this.
I've built you a wide road spanning the ocean's waters.

Beyond it, the world we came from, the one dreamers
enter at night, the one we all return to in new bodies.

One day I will say, *Cross over me*, and you will begin to fear
your own heart. I'll offer my back as a testament

that nothing lasts, nor was it meant to. Every morning
when the waters move under me, I think of you,

still asleep, the shadows of the buildings pulling
away from you as the sun rises. Wake and remember.

Once, you were young—you weren't afraid of anything.

Traci Brimhall and Brynn Saito on their process:

Years ago, both of us were writing about ruins, so we decided to write the story of a ruin together. Early on we knew it would be the story of a girl wandering through an abandoned city, and the city would speak to her. That allowed us one easy and direct way to begin each poem: it would always start in a new location with that location addressing the girl. Whoever chose the location would also start—and end—the poem. If that person started in couplets, the other person would write the next couplet and so on. And, since the person who began the poem had larger creative control of the poem, the other person would become the editor, so that each poem had an equal amount of creative input from both of us. We used Google Docs so that we could always see each other's contributions, which kept us writing and exchanging fairly quickly. Every time we went to check the document it was as though we'd written into the abyss and the abyss answered. Soon, we had enough co-written poetry for a chapbook and *Bright Power, Dark Peace* was published by Diode Editions in 2013.

John F. Buckley and Martin Ott

IF POETS HAD CONQUERED AMERICA

The voyage would have started with meted
rigging, papyrus sails, iambic rowers,

two dozen arms beating hexameter couplets
past Skyllas, krakens, their parents' distaste

for "the airy trade." They would have landed
on shores expanding freely with verse, each

tongue a new state, newly forgotten zeppelins
tethered to clouds. The first winter would be

the easiest, inaugurated by an impromptu salon,
voices teeming with game and fresh rhymes,

all tribes' verbal missiles striking dear hearts
cleanly in the back of a log-beamed cafe.

That was before the seven-year cycle
of cicadas, poison berries, wolf howls,

before they mistrusted freedom, sought
out Petrarchan sonnets. Factions grew

into factories, formalists on the workshop
line grinding out sestinas in sausage casings.

Others fled ivory forts, running woodsward,
darning leatherstocking Language in camps.

A second generation of bards and lyricists
emerged via Atlantean tubes and purgatorial

paths, erecting concrete poems into freeway
obelisks and tame topiary dragons. Aiming

up and out, astropoeticists scanned the ether,
recasting each constellation as a sudoku haiku.

They powered their nation with chant-propelled
windmills and learned that words were a force

that could bring buds bursting forth or fill
rockets with Beowulf, Inferno, annihilation.

Every syllable a crossroads, they sang forth
a national anthem Mahabharatan in scale,

a stanza per citizen, a continent in constant
renewal, something to write home about.

John F. Buckley and Martin Ott on their process:

Our collaboration arose out of John's consternation, the reasons for which we
needn't delve into at this moment. He sent Martin two lines of poetry and chal-
lenged him to write the next two lines. Martin returned the serve and demanded
lines 5 and 6. We kept playing poetic volleyball, two lines at a time, until we had
finished the first draft of "Chiron in Los Angeles." It was a lot of fun, so Martin
started us off with a second poem, "Bee Lust in Manhattan." On and on, taking
turns, until we had our first manuscript of fifty poems about two years later.

Playing together has taught us both the value of combining divergent voices into
a somewhat harmonious whole. It's taught us the value of sharing, of improvisa-
tion, of not being greedy with the turns we take. No extended solos! We take turns
playing the bass line or the guitar. And aside from the musical analogies, playing
together has afforded us both an opportunity to create poetry that combines the
political, societal, and humorous—to get out of the "I" voice, that sometimes dark,
sometimes limiting well of ego.

Michael Burkard, Erin Mullikin, and David Wojciechowski

WHAT WE FOUND IN THE WOODS

By the time the lilies fail and the lights stay on longer,
something feels totally obliterated for me.
A sense for how the deer will edge up against the line of woods,
how they will freeze then bolt. So I am startled
when I see them, when their white hooves crash through the pines.
You see splinted houses made from barks, circles,
the strongest of houses. If there is a frightened tree in this neighborhood
no one would suspect it. Many of the neighbors do seem
fearful, but who knows?—it isn't uncommon to be afraid of
something, especially when studies have now revealed
that by the age of two—two!—all children have learned how
to lie, and do so. I'll tell you something: by the age of four,
forget about the feeling of truth—remember how it holds.
That red bird on the black branch, there is your holding,
and it doesn't matter one iota that the branch is dead,
the tree is dying, but the red bird can warble a melody
around death, or dying, or the knotted systemic leaves
which remain but are misunderstood entirely by everyone
except for the birds, the worms, the spiders.

Michael Burkard, Erin Mullikin, and David Wojciechowski on their process:

We're in the same room. That's important to mention. Every poem we've written together begins in the same room. We almost always have a title in mind when we start; we keep a list of titles to pull from whenever we need. This title rarely, perhaps never, makes the final draft. The rest of the process is deceptively simple: we pass a laptop back and forth, adding one line, maybe two or three, as we go, until one us decides the poem has ended. It's usually in that spontaneous ending that we realize what the poem was trying to say. The editing process is done individually. One of us goes through the first draft and might make a few cuts or substitutions, change the form from couplets to prose or from prose to a lineated poem, suggest new titles, etc. Then the other person reads this edited draft and might make a few tinier changes; might not. And so on. Each poem is made in the same room, but it doesn't exist there. It becomes something distinctly *not* in the room. But the atmosphere of the poem remains, like smoke clinging to the layers of air. And our guides—old cartoons, Gumby reruns, David Bowie's narration of *Peter and The Wolf*, a few Russell Edson or Vasko Popa [not exhaustive] poems, the remnants of a Death Door's gin bottle—weave around each poem as if to say *the same room the same room the same tomb*.

Elizabeth-Jane Burnett and Tony Lopez

SEA HOLLY

I.

mudstone crumbs	salt
shell	marsh
fragments	shallow
finest sand	soil
tidal	shingle
grind	marram
every day	grass
every	fescue
night	grass
a medium of	tidal
crawling	path
life	creek
compressed	of
baked,	pollen
lifted	falls
blown away	in whispers

in the clay in the loam in the top of the soil
in the sand in the molt of the sea

in the light sand the light sound of shift in the swash
zone waves burrow for release

in the bend of the body
I balance my current only takes me back
when seawards seawards is the call of my curve
& no turning

2.

Two large cormorants flew rapidly and very low across the water heading directly towards Langstone Rock, where Dawlish Warren joins the coast just beyond the western edge of the Exe estuary. Their wing tips were almost touching the choppy water. This must have been about 7:45 on Friday morning; I was thirty yards or so out in the sea, only my head visible between the waves that the cormorants flew in among as they powered along one behind the other. I had come down the concrete lifeboat ramp and taken just a few steps on wet sand scattered with various shells, little gleaming stones, and scraps of seaweed, getting quickly into the cool water. The sky was piled up with dark grey cloud overhead but clear and bright at the horizon. The two birds passed close by and continued on their way indifferent to me watching them from the water and they gave no indication if they saw anything unusual.

she swam
only at night
on the spring tides

in the silk light of water
slipping her over
the mud flats

when they studied why she did it
drifted far beyond her limits
though it made her vulnerable to prey

several theories came
but none swam
at night in a spring tide

in the silklight unsure
of itself
becoming only what is left
after breaking

3.

herring gull
black-headed gull
arctic tern
oystercatcher
turnstone
sanderling
carrion crow
jackdaw
white wagtail
rock pipit
peregrine
kestrel
buzzard
brent goose
cormorant
kingfisher
farther out
gannet

stomach of fur
coughed up at low tide
stranded

snowfall of fur
dusting the mouth
sanded

out of this
worms fall
soft as whispers

coiling into faun-
ing "Aphrodita"

& out of her hair come the corpses
of a swallowed sea

4.
mussel
shell
oyster shell
clam
shell
cockle shell
whelk
shell
limpet shell
winkle
shell
razor shell
crab shell
lobster
shell
prawn shell
sea
lettuce

she
       windblown sand
       seashell sand
       shifting sand
she
       sea sandwort
       sea rocket
       sea holly
she
       half sand
she both sea
       she half sea
she both sand
she is a both-formed thing
she

```
        wool sand
        cotton sand
        wood sand
she
        sea leather
        sea crystal
        sea skin
she
        half wool
she both skin
        she half skin
she both wool
she is a woollen skin

she
        asphalt soil
        nylon soil
        sandy soil
she
        landscape
        escape
        seascape
she half soil
        she both scape
she half scape
        she both soil
she escapes
```

5.

And swimming my slow breast stroke out to the channel I saw a dark-winged butterfly come flying in above the waves, moving with the breeze, heading for the dunes. Was this a migrant painted lady, third generation, from Africa?

drifter   on the surface
upside   down dead
                   water

            floater   upper   sheltered
                on the littoral fringe
                          lower   very sheltered

                swimmer upward   of hundreds   of thousands
                                      of hundreds   of thousands
of hundreds   of thousands   of hundreds   of thousands   of hundreds
    of thousands   of hundreds   of thousands   of hundreds   of
thousands   of hundreds   of thousands   of hundreds   of
thousands   of hundreds   of thousands   of hundreds   of
thousands   of hundreds   of thousands   of hundreds   of
thousands   of hundreds   of houses of   hundreds   of
houses of   hundreds   of houses   of hundreds   of
houses of   sands   of houses   of sand   of
houses of   sand   of hums   of sand   of
hums   of sand   of hum   of sand   of
humming

Elizabeth-Jane Burnett and Tony Lopez on their process:

This was a kind of poetry 'blind date' collaboration; we were partnered by the organisers of the South West Poetry Tour in England, and asked to make a new piece for a performance at Schumacher College on the Dartington estate. Each pair of poets had six minutes for their gig. "Sea Holly" came from a common land/seascape in Devon—where Tony lives now and where Elizabeth grew up. Elizabeth sent some research notes for her work-in-progress, "The Grassling, A Geographical Memoir," and Tony replied with a sea swimming piece. Elizabeth found a report of 39 invertebrates recorded near the site of Tony's swim and began writing and sending invertebrate-swimming poems. Tony responded with his own pieces on seashore creatures and shells. We met in person just a few minutes before the reading at Dartington, which was great fun. The Schumacher reading was recorded and can be found at https://www.youtube.com/watch?v=iem9j7OBEuA. The poem was first published in *Poetry* (Chicago), December 2016.

Tina Carlson, Stella Reed, and Katherine Seluja

LEDA'S PETITION TO LILITH

I'm afraid of this air
beaten by shadow,
its collision with skull
and thighs, wishing an owl's head
to see cleanly over my shoulder.
Even now the pressure
of the river rises
between my shoulder blades.
Wings and water terrify,
how they fit together
in ways my body won't allow,
one floating on the dark
depths of the other,
even the moons are black and blue,
smell fearful, like slaughter
houses.
I know where you are
by your silence:
in harrowed earth,
poisoned wells, the back of my throat
filled with fingers. I sense
you spidering forgotten canyons,
in black leaves lifting
on seasick air.

Soon it will be January
and the river empty of swans.
Still I press fingertips together
like a temple. Someone must
staunch the bleeding.
I know the choice is there

to evaporate, become air
for my children to breathe.
Don't let them find me
with braided rope around
my throat, twined river grass
once hollowed in swales
where the animals lay
with each other.

Tina Carlson, Stella Reed, and Katherine Seluja

DEAR LEDA

I wish I could tell you I left the garden on my own. That he put his bone hands
on me and I didn't break into pieces, that he was gentle, that I was willing.
Instead the garden was a grave I didn't consent to. I wish I could say I heard
your call across the centuries, that your lost cries found me in my wild forest
underground. All these wishes did not stop the death, alone in your story.
Instead might I have climbed the stalk of your undoing, tendered that rope
from your neck, carried you to the lit ground, my eyes a sky for a while. Wash
you in mud, take the feathers from your mouth. Together our throats could
spill, wordless, ancient, splitting all the sound that has come before into the
other side of slaughter. Dear Leda, that first garden was a grave. I have lived but
wild, like the hanging bats that found you first.

Lilith

Tina Carlson, Stella Reed, and Katherine Seluja on their process:

x epistles + urgency = seeds

~~Linear~~   ~~logical~~   ~~controlled~~

R e a c h i n g   a c r o s s   t i m e & m y t h o l o g i c a l   ////
barriers

A force at the base
               of the spIne
                    N
                    I
                      L
                    A
                    D
                    N
                    U
         Not labor: easier—K

Who wrote this?

Anders Carlson-Wee and Kai Carlson-Wee

DYNAMITE

My brother hits me hard with a stick
so I whip a choke-chain

across his face. We're playing
a game called *Dynamite*

where everything you throw
is a stick of dynamite,

unless it's pine. Pine sticks
are rifles and pinecones are grenades,

but everything else is dynamite.
I run down the driveway

and back behind the garage
where we keep the leopard frogs

in buckets of water
with logs and rock islands.

When he comes around the corner
the blood is pouring

out of his nose and down his neck
and he has a hammer in his hand.

I pick up his favorite frog
and say If you come any closer

I'll squeeze. He tells me I won't.
He starts coming closer.

I say a hammer isn't dynamite.
He reminds me that everything is dynamite.

—Anders Carlson-Wee

Anders Carlson-Wee and Kai Carlson-Wee

SLEEP

In downtown Chicago the vendors are folding
their boards up, tossing the left-over scraps in the trash.
Dogs in the alleyway sniffing a drainspout.
Cars headed home and the sun sinking down
like a fiery coin in the lake. My brother says maybe
the shelter will take us in. Maybe we ride on the El
up to Evanston, camp on the grounds of a fancy estate.
A pale light burns in the Sears Tower windows,
sparking electric, as if there were pieces of diamond
being shattered inside. A few lonely sailboats search
the dividing line, turning their rudders in,
slacking the jib-lines for shore. We ask for directions,
a few bucks for nachos. Whatever sounds easy
for someone to give. The night is beginning
to stretch out its dark wing. Carry us into
the wind. We name a few friends we can barely
remember. Search through our Facebook accounts
at the mall. Our calls go unanswered. A thin rain
is starting to darken the sidewalk around us,
forcing us under a ledge. With nothing to guide us,
we slide through the open emergency door on the El.
Ride down to Ashland and Sixty-Third,
pick out some pears from the corner-store dumpster.
Most of the Southside deserted at midnight.
Burn barrels flash in the doorways of recent foreclosures.
Can-pickers dig though recycling bins on the curb.
We follow the track-line, hop a few chainlink fences.
Set up our bags in a back-alley entrance where truckers
deliver supplies to a bar. No one in earshot.
We lean on the bolted door, whispering down at the shadows
between us now. Taking our turns with the knife.

—Kai Carlson-Wee

Anders Carlson-Wee and Kai Carlson-Wee

TO THE RAIL COP AT RATHDRUM

You knew you had me for trespassing,
and probably for vandalism, but you weren't sure
how to charge me for the fire still burning
under the train bridge in the railyard you patrolled
nightly, the flames throwing a shiver-glow
on the tagged girders, the rusted tracks, the plastic
unblinking eyeball on the seeable side
of your otherwise unremarkable face.
Arson, you thought, but you knew the word
wouldn't hold up in court. You unbuckled my pack,
hoping for more—dope, or a fingerprinted weapon,
or a scale for weighing and selling. You ran
your flashlight over the bushes, needling the beam
through the barest branches, shocking
the dry leaves with the raw bleached-out colors
of themselves. With your one good eye you caught
my brother's duffle among the torqued shapes
of your shadow-show and realized
I wasn't alone. You cuffed me to a piling.
Tiptoed a search of the firelight's perimeter.
Asked me who it was out there in the dark.
Asked me why he was hiding. Said my silence
couldn't protect him, and only made it worse
for me. You radioed for backup, widened
your circle, your boots glissading the sloped beds
of the railroad tailings. You offered to cut me
a deal for a name. Said the cold truth
was my buddy wouldn't protect me, not once
he was caught, not once he was facing the law.
You'd be surprised, you said. You asked how well
I knew him. Said I should think about that

before I threw myself on the tracks.
Think about that: Who was it out there
in the cold dark hiding? How well did I know him?
As if you needed those questions
half as much as I did, as if you had any stake
in this. And sure enough, after the sky tipped
the dipper into the iron wash of dawn
and my coals smoldered on
in the ritalin moods of the wind, and after failing
to find any ID tucked in the socks
at the bottom of the duffle, you gave up—
drove home, and left me with the day shift.

—Anders Carlson-Wee

Anders Carlson-Wee and Kai Carlson-Wee

MINNESOTA ROADS

Dawn-light and I'm driving the back-country dairies
and hayricks on North 64, my brother asleep
on the window beside me. The radio tuned
to an alt-country station they stream
out of Walker-Laporte. Fog over everything.
Wheels and ditch-grass. Broken machinery
rusting away in the yards. Satellites shine
now and then in the lifting dark. Headlights align
with the fences and trail off, haunted
like fishing boats trolling the point.
Everything stalks to the edge of the morning
and waits. Even our car seems to slide
on the cusp of a barely invisible screen.
Hinting at some kind of wilder country the silos
have always kept hidden from view—
squatting an open-air flatcar in Portland,
opening tin cans of stewed prunes and tunafish,
fireworks blooming the eastern Montana sky.
Thinking of Olaf alone in the mountains now.
Kerri-Ann living off food-stamps in Bellingham.
Severson army-bound. Zeidlhack dead.
Somewhere near Wilmar the sun hits the trees
and my brother wakes up to the glare. Townes
on the radio. Crows on the power-lines passing beside us
in waves. I dreamt of a mutated cowboy,
he tells me. A man without fingers, but still
having hands. I pass him the rest of our Zig-Zags
and shaker. He takes out the rumpled-up atlas
and rolls down the window to let in some air.

—Kai Carlson-Wee

Anders Carlson-Wee and Kai Carlson-Wee

THE RAFT

He baits the hook with an Indian Paintbrush petal,
lets out the line, reels, traps it with his thumb-pad.
October. Powder on the peaks. We float on a raft
lashed together with a loose weave of duct-tape and rope.
I paddle us forward with a cottonwood branch,
my leg in the water for a rudder, trying to hold us close
to the darkness of the drop-off where the trout go
to stay cool in the afternoons. Later we'll make a fire
and cook our catch with blueberries gathered frozen
from the cirque above the tarn. We'll blow on the coals.
We'll check for tenderness. We'll add ash in place
of salt. But for now I'm watching the sunlight
bounce off the surface and shimmer in the shadow
under my brother's hat. The way he plays the line.
The way he lets it troll behind us. The way the trout
cloud our wake and flick their rainbowed sides.
I'm torquing my leg underwater. I'm turning us back
toward the darkness we've drifted away from.

—Anders Carlson-Wee

Anders Carlson-Wee and Kai Carlson-Wee on their process:

As brothers, we grew up traveling together. Our family took excessive road trips
across the country, stopping at roadside attractions along the way. Later on, when
we were skaters, we spent countless hours driving around the Midwest and South-
ern California to skate the best spots we could find. We've hopped trains together,
hitchhiked, and backpacked throughout the Northwest. Our collaborations on
poetry projects have centered around these trips, and these experiences have served
as a nexus for our work. We don't write poems together, but we tend to write about
similar things, so the poems develop a back-and-forth conversation, offering two
different sides to shared stories.

Brittany Cavallaro and Rebecca Hazelton

NOT, FRIENDS, HIS WORST IDEA

He lay by the main of the field, and flailed.
More depressants for Paris,
seraphim (most) and down here as he is,
without earnest words to bite open
and insults afresh and refresh,
his memory is indifferent to him.

—You never read *novels*. We are so transfixing,
hissed Edward R. Murrow.
—In seconds I can ignore the short story,
hissed today a consumer hot as a Ritalin capsule,
because you know everyone is in us,
the dead ones especially.

The intelligentsia applaud him, to ignore writing on vine leaves,
and this is, probably, his lowest feeling.
Terse Sappho, at the end, said *nothing*
and Plath did the reverse at the beginning,
and Anne Carson
said: —They are reproducing your organs in latex. So they lose.

Brittany Cavallaro and Rebecca Hazelton

NOT, FRIENDS, HIS WORST IDEA

She stood at the edge of the room, and stilled.
Less caffeine for Helen,
demon (all) and up there as she was,
with cloying letters to lick shut
and compliments to replay and replay,
her forgetfulness loves her.

—We never read *newspapers*. They are so boring,
yawned the Lowest Muckraker.
—In an hour I can watch the long film,
yawned yesterday a producer cold as a sleeping pill,
because I know no one is in them,
the live ones especially.

The unthinking scorned her, to agree to watch films,
and that was, surely, his best idea.
Longwinded Homer, at the start, said *everything*
and Eliot did the same at the end,
and John Berryman
said: —We are using our own skins as wallpaper and so we win.

Brittany Cavallaro and Rebecca Hazelton

IN US WE TRUST

Sky clouds at noon, Oconomowoc storms rage
as the land discharges the peaceful
like a jack-knifing car. More, now, more ravines,
more river-basins, at the lowest point
they are on guard. Distrustful underneath
even their stone houses,

those we don't want. Sundance and pause,
rain and fall, these days we pray
for all to burn out, shine
while they do. Years from now on holiday
the tar pits uneven and insistent
as an attraction.

At this moment, the air breathes them
like lung-coal, and they stand leagues beneath
and they keen. There is no war
and so there are no stars, there is
the reeling notion
that now they are worse than dead.

Brittany Cavallaro and Rebecca Hazelton

IN US WE TRUST

Dirt clods at midnight, Vidalia weeps love
as the sea sucks in the pugilists
like an open-mouthed boat. Less, then, less river,
more canyon, at the apex
the watch falls to sleeping. Naïve on the rim
of a glass teacup,

the one I desire. Nightshuffle and run,
parch and rise, in the dark we curse
for some to wick, snuff out
when we do. Just then on leave without pay
the skyscrapers regularized and quiet
as disgust.

Later, not now, the dirt coughs us up
like nitrogen, and we sit miles above
and we laugh. There is peace
and there are stars, there is
the solid fact
that now we are better than the dead.

Brittany Cavallaro and Rebecca Hazelton on their process:

We were neighbors, and we were poets, and so we met every day to write together. Brittany had the idea of writing an opposite imitation of a John Berryman Dream Song, and suggested that Rebecca write an opposite of that opposite. It was a strange game of literary telephone, and by the end, it was hard to know who'd written what.

We've since seen this process called antonymic translation, a term which nicely encapsulates the first pass. We don't have a term, however, for what happens when you perform the process more than once. Certainly, we didn't end up where we started. These poems are an homage to Berryman's singular syntax and diction, and our own engagement with it.

Travis Cebula and Sarah Suzor

from **LAST CALL**

the last call
was the call no one answered.
an unheard question of
spent breath was left

hanging.
in better times
an exhalation was only
hanging up

there in the ether—
where
the long hair and whispers had
gone. as always

Morning had no idea
where
the darkness went
while the sun was boring

in. another day loaned to loneliness.
without other words,
Morning had no idea why.
in that here, in that then,

Morning was a mess.
silence became the bridge
to a tune widowed
from its lyrics and bliss—

in formless sound
a mourning dove moaned
around this empty house
while

in better lines
an us shined and
the song of a phone
meant a chorus.

And it was only right
Morning sabotage Morning.
The crumbled bridge,
its hinges resting in a bed
of borrowed garbage.

She dreamed desperation:
a voice screaming from the other end,
"If I had your number,
I'd call you tomorrow."

Without another way,
they didn't.

The last call was calculated.
Scientific, not spoken.
It lay in a letter
sealed by the sorry water
of the river. It lay
consumed.

And it was only right
Nocturnal listen
as the percussion of concrete
took it all from his fingers.
A structural rhythm.
A last chance.

Nocturnal's stance
on last   chances
                    evolved
with every one he missed.
for example, he missed   Morning's

call   while he was watching
            a barge of   garbage
slip through the hinges of
this failing bridge,   for example.
a thinking   that and a fridge

full of cheap beer,   for example.
            he knew
Morning would say,   "nice view"
and   "thinking of you" while
he trampled   old light bulbs like sabotage—

oh his feet to ribbons   in the dark.
oh he didn't even   need
to answer, so
            over and over
                        the stark bell shrieked

            and on and on. he missed
his answering machine—
            he missed the clean break. the click and tone.
it floated by   with all the other sick and
bloated   corpses of things he loved.

and the sight impaled him
where   he stood—
his last chance   to make good
on promises memorized
and   a throat sore from singing

old love songs.
so long,   so gone—
most of the time he hated   last chances.
most of the time
he wanted   a few more.

And Morning had chalked it up to bad luck.
There was no choice in that.
No chance.

Her mind was a tape
on constant rewind,
no buttons,
just fingers shoved
in tiny grooves,
re-raveling a line
the length of a noose.

She figured dreams were worse than silence.
The fox fluttered back for one last kiss,
again and again,
to prove it all meant nothing more
than...

that story was over.

She saw Nocturnal
sitting at the shore
screaming at all the things
she had stolen.

"Good riddance," she thought. "Decent view."

The last straw was an easy swallow.
And without another choice,
his things became her promises.

They broke
just as easily.

"Couldn't even call me," she had said smashing.
"Couldn't come to terms,

to the table,
        but, oh, how he'd write about legs and
                walking through the dry desert
                    just to find me.
                         Me."

And how that never happened,
and, strange how,
each time it didn't, like clockwork,
the fox would flutter by for one final kiss.

Travis Cebula and Sarah Suzor on their process:

There is really no substitute for laughter. Over the years we've learned to more or less collaborate constantly and to have fun doing it. Collaboration is, at its core, a relationship. It takes time to develop any real depth. You work on it. When the two of us talk, hang out, travel, give readings or listen to music together, we are always mindful of the other person's flow of thought. You can track a lot about a person through their sense of humor. Collaboration is also an exploration. Really knowing a person and, most particularly, the way they relate to language, enables you to improvise with them and pursue new thoughts at any moment. So, once the minor detail of an email back and forth happens (or a few hours in New York with a notebook, or Facebook comments, or…), the groundwork for interesting poetry has already been mapped out for years. Things just flow from there.

Christopher Citro and Dustin Nightingale

AND ME WITH ONLY A BOTTLE OPENER IN MY POCKET

Since I was a little boy, I wanted to be the alcoholic in *Fried Green Toma-toes*. A movie I've seen over and over again is an old woman alone in her kitchen, the windows open, and starlings come to settle on the emerald bottles. There are 18 crows circling above my eyelids. They are fighting over a piece of meat. My dogs won't stop worrying with their shallow bellies. Every animal is doing what they're supposed to automatically. Some people pick the wrong heroes and they're great at this. They're like watching an athlete or a trained bear with a cage on its face prance around until it double knows it is trapped. People like to watch. And after, when it's time for dreams, they'll line up to pass and remark, How childlike he looks sleeping there. Behind my eyes, the lions let loose into the arena.

Christopher Citro and Dustin Nightingale

STARING OUT A WINDOW ECHOING THE ACTUAL MOON

You made a hole in yourself and now you can see things clearly. The eye doctor is confused when you say it all looks the same. He wants to go home, like the rest of us, drink and forget he has to get up in the morning to do the same thing. You should see a tear duct specialist, weeping at a picnic because it's all so perfect. The onion Kaiser rolls are not perfect. Not enough to cry over. There is this missing comma in a book you read and you can't remember which book, though it made you feel superior. Or it wasn't a book, but something someone said to you recently. Not a comma at all, not a bear or a fish but a pause enough to think what could have flown to the stratosphere and then fallen back. Your mouth a fleshy O, a pit, for what might make it in. The moon you never see anymore. I mean, why would you even look?

Christopher Citro and Dustin Nightingale

I FEAR WE HAVE MADE A TERRIBLE MISTAKE

I'm sorry, despite the beauty of the first tulip under my flashlight all I can see is this darkness pressing in on us. You're upstairs asleep in bed, but I know you're feeling it too. A satellite's passing over us and I'm sending it wishes it makes it across the sky without falling in love with what it records. The words of a radio DJ floating above a lake. Let them go. Uppermost leaves of a beech tree. Allow that to sway away. You roll over, crushing a breast slightly beneath you. Rain clouds. Owl sounds in your birth town travelling over the water, through the leaves and in your window. It's silly really, the way we pretend to hold hands with earth and time. Yet still, my heart is filled with this lonely migration. The distant boiling of a dog bark, the soup of an even further wind chime, our necks still hot with yesterday's sun.

Christopher Citro and Dustin Nightingale on their process:

We are generally very intuitive poets, and we like to be as free as possible in our collaborations, staying open to the unexpected, getting purposefully lost in a forest just to see that happens next. When we look back on completed poems it's often impossible to remember who wrote what. We work in groups of four at a time, emailing the drafts back and forth as each makes additions or deletions. Titles are introduced along the way. Whatever we would do with the poems if they were our own drafts, that's how we treat the collaborations. Sometimes things can get quite drastic. If one of us notices a poem is just coming out dead in the water, he hacks it to pieces and we start fresh from the remains. It can be brutal, but after years of doing this we're still friends.

We never have preconceived plans of where our collaborative poems will go, and we don't discuss drafts while they're in process, preferring to let them develop entirely through the writing alone. We have found that one of the reasons this seems to work for us is that we share a sense of the internal shape of a poem. When to create tension, when to leap, when to release, when to run on, when to call it a day and lick our wounds. When to introduce the distant boiling of a dog bark, 18 crows, or some onion Kaiser rolls.

Ben Clark and GennaRose Nethercott

from DEAR FOX, DEAR BARN

DEAR BARN,

Everything is a prayer, out here in the flatlands.

Billboards made mirror in the night rains. Moon

ballooning over the interstate. Rest stop bodegas

with the proud posture of chapels, creaking in the heat.

Cornfields & copperheads & the tumult

of my own claws chattering against asphalt.

I am enthralled with travel's gospel.

With the way my body hums when it moves.

If you could see me now, you would not see me at all.

You would find smoke pluming from an empty bed.

You would find my shadow like a sundial

loping across the earth. You would find my silhouette

lingering in silos & attics where I paused only to doze

or eat or consult the atlas, before passing through,

as I once passed through you. A footprint. A trace.

A trick of the eye.

Ben Clark and GennaRose Nethercott

DEAREST FOX,

Again I lumber into the prairie grass,
though bluebirds badger my rafters,

protecting their nests from even
my hushed voice, whispering

a song you taught me long ago.
You said then to befriend the birds,

the spiders, the mosquitoes even,
but my hands, big as they are, are bound

to find them. It's why I'm here, to pray
beneath the storm clouds.

It's why you should come home Fox.
If not, who'll stop me from bartering your only quilt

for a jug of backwoods whiskey, or trade
the box you held shut with a smooth river

stone for dusty records
I have no means of playing?

Who'll stop me from offering up this leaning frame,
that you have passed through, slept in, and left?

Ben Clark and GennaRose Nethercott

DEAR BARN,

I am hungry

I am a bullet

I am a sign of rapture—a two-headed birth, blood from the faucet

I am fog-built

I am searchlight

I am nothing when not in motion,

I am fed on new earth

I am a wild animal bowing to my nature

I am tuliping open, ears sharpening to points against alien sky

You are the last door I closed

You are still on my teeth, even now, as the train belays me west

You are phantom, no longer in your body

You are in my body

You are the boxcars, rattling like tin cans

You are Orion & the bow & the arrow that finds me beleaguered in the dark

You are more than yourself

You are the myth of you

You are smudging around the edges

You are quicksand

You are the tollbooth, static in the midst of movement, ever-witnessing speed

You are my shadow

You are the cannon that the cannonball of me once called home before I flew

Ben Clark and GennaRose Nethercott

BARN,

Steady yourself. Let quiet settle
on your tongue, or hummingbird
into familiar song. If you must,
let what you remember of her
paws fill the hollow of your hand
and warm you. The vast sky
has no use for your sad bones
leaning into it. The dirt no
interest in you repeating: fox,
fox, fox. Handmade candles
and offerings of flame will
go unnoticed. Fox is gone,
night skips shamelessly after day,
elsewhere things are far worse.

Ben Clark and GennaRose Nethercott

DEAR BARN,

Foxes have many tricks for throwing hunters off course.
We tightrope along fence rails & dry ridges where wind
tugs the thread of our scent & unravels it.
We cloak ourselves in sheep, perfumed in the flock.
We retrace our own steps, then leap sideways,
& the hunters follow the straight path to ruin.
We build masks. Coat ourselves in soot & milkweed.
Burn our maps. Burn our luggage. Burn our paw prints slick.
At dusk, we find track dogs asleep & crawl into their mouths
& possess them & bark false orders to the pack.
We shape shift into hunters' wives & lie with them.
We jam muskets with goose bones. With cake flour. With wax.
Whittle the barrels into flutes so the rifles, when fired, sing
so sweet the hunters & their dogs waltz amongst the trees—
onetwothree, onetwothree—until they've forgotten us,
& their names, & the path home
which is the one thing a fox never, never forgets.

Ben Clark and GennaRose Nethercott

DEAR FOX,

I forget most everything these days, and wander out to the pasture, then back,
        then out again. The weather inconsequential. Storms move through me,
but the haunting never sticks. I find myself further and further away,
        leaning over a hole I've dug, or will fill with damp earth.
I try to make a list of all the things you would do with your mouth,
        cruel or otherwise, all you would shake from your fur
after weeks away. I can't remember anymore
        whether you were truly a fox, or a fallen tree, or a mountain
goat, or a column of orange light balanced through the gut of me. I can't remember
        why this place is so silent. Has every creature left, or were they never here?

Ben Clark and GennaRose Nethercott on their process:

"Dear Fox, Dear Barn" was born in the liminal otherworld of the Midwestern expanse, June 2015. We were spending a month at the multi-disciplinary residency Art Farm Nebraska. Mornings began with cold coffee sweetened with condensed milk, and an hour of pulling nails out of boards. In the evenings, we read fortunes by candlelight while raccoons screeched in the walls. Fox and Barn must have been haunting that land far before we arrived—for when we first tucked into rafters with pens in hand, a thunderstorm blooming around us, they arrived. We became them, writing back and forth in-character, a new epistolary poem slipped under the other's door each dusk, until at last, Fox and Barn had told us their story.

Brian Clements and Maureen Seaton

YOUR LOVE IS GONE

A blues

There's always a white woman dancing drunk as fuck on the boardwalk near my
  house.
*There's always a white woman dancing drunk as fuck on the boardwalk by my
  house.*
I don't mean to start off negative. (Let's delete *always*, then delouse.)

Or we could delete *fuck*, but I like a short "u", so *nuns* might work. Or *guns*.
We could delete a word or three, but, *fuck*, I like a short "u" as in *nuns* or *guns* or
  Gus.
Or let's delete *white* and thereby solve all Floridas but wipe out Connecticuts.

Because one word can change everything. (Wait for the jury to reveal its
  crackers.)
We're waiting for one word to change everything from the mouth of some cracker.
The jury might also reveal some results regarding *thereby* and demographics.

No matter how you feel about *thug* music, a spark near the wrong molecule will
  cause some problems.
It doesn't matter how you *feel*. The wrong spark at the wrong time is going to
  cause some problems.
It only takes a word for the catalyst. Careful what you say to the vagrants,
  dancers, pilgrims.

For protection we could bring in a gun moll and hug her (not slug her) in an
  offbeat kind of way.
What I'm saying is we could bring in your soccer mom valley girl baby mama
  and love her in an unusual way.
I'm not talking about the boardwalk. I mean not sacrificing babies to Disney or
  horse or NRA.

Almost everyone loves Elvis. Or, to put it another way, I may walk it back re: crackers.

But he took that photo with Nixon and shot out all his TVs. He is us: a culture of crackers.

Arkansas Mississippi Tennessee Texas James Byrd, Jr. Emmett Till Medgar Evers

And why should Elvis walk backward? Why hug him (not slug him)? Why not hipstep (fast swivel) (slay)?

That could be Elvis right there spacewalking into the Robot in a syncopated dangle and sway

in the middle of a bunch of kids like starfish or man o' war or land crabs dancing sideways.

But I'd rather wear a hoodie than some giddy lapse of nostalgia lapelled on Old Glory pins.

I'd rather dress like a thug on the boardwalk than wear a flag funeral pin.

The jury marches out of the box to some anthem, single-file, like prisoners, the way kids pretend.

Don't sit down in an SUV. Don't walk home in the rain. Give the boy a kiss
the way you'd kiss the lamb or this projectile as it slides between your lips.
Your love is gone. Kiss the holes the way you would kiss his fingertips.

Brian Clements and Maureen Seaton on their process:

2/9/14   Brian (in CT): 12/14 happened and I haven't finished a poem since.

2/12/14   Maureen (in FL): I'm sending you something. You can treat it linearly or write something before it even. I put it into both renga and a prose stanza. Choose either or both (or, truly, none—and send me something else altogether).

2/19/14   B: Spent much of the last several days shoveling snow. What if we both, separately, played around with it?

2/20/14   M: Here's something by Melvin Dixon that reminded me of you up there.

              ...My blood/is southern laterite, my cradle/Connecticut, and my skin/the color you've kissed before. (from "Hands," *Love's Instruments*)

              B: Right when I read your message, I was listening to a Son House song, which seemed fortuitously southern.

              M: Listening to "Death Letter Blues" I realized the shape of those lyrics is similar to our collab.

2/24/14   B: I kinda went crazy on this. See if there's anything you like about this at all. If not, ignore it. If you want to riff off of this, or totally change it, that's fine with me. It has a lot of problems, but it was good for me.

              M: I can really feel a coiled anger and a sad sad blues in there and I love it.

3/16/14   B: Happy St. Paddy's! Sorry this took me so long this time. I was thinking about how blues and rap lyrics are often written out in long lines, so I thought I'd give that a try, in verse triads, to see how it works. See what you think.

3/22/14   M: Wow. And Happy belated St. Paddy's to you!

Cathryn Cofell and Karla Huston

I CLING TO

a man
who will not cling to me
I imagine he
imagines me
a sock
stuck
inside his pant leg
to be rid of me
he has to strip down
pull the electric eel
of me loose
only to catch to his
sleeve and clasp as if
greeting
that first meeting
shocking as the last

a woman
stuck like static
wants me
close to her
one that's lost
and wandering
the quick strokes
to her sticky bidding
O, I want to explode
the alarm and crawl free
but captive still
fingers sinking,
unbutton(ed), fly, my
fist uncoiling,
this, tryst over text
grip, thumbs on fire

Cathryn Cofell and Karla Huston on their process:

Karla and Cathryn began collaborating in 2000, on a six-hour road trip with no music, one bag of licorice and far too many cups of coffee. Since then, their collaborative poems have been published in *Rhino, Indiana Review* and *Quiddity* and anthologized in *Saints of Hysteria* and *Wingbeats: Exercises & Practice in Poetry.* Their collab chapbook, *Split Personality,* was published by *sunnyoutside* in 2012. Like several of their poems, "I Cling To" came to life while Cathryn and Karla worked across from each other at Karla's kitchen table. Cathryn had a partial poem, but was stuck. She emailed her lines to Karla, wondered what could be done with them. While Cathryn sipped her wine and worked on another collaborative poem, Karla added her own lines (and wine) to the abandoned piece. Instead of writing between and around, Karla worked across the page, trying to mirror what Cathryn had done. They emailed various versions back and forth, offering revisions and suggestions, working toward a final one-voice version that could be read both vertically and horizontally.

Mackenzie Cole and Tony Ruzicka

NAME_____CLASS_____
DATE_____SCORE_____

MEMORY

Read the directions carefully and in their entirety. Cursive blue, blue or black ink only.

1.   _____ or reliving what was again. To repeat experience. An acute kind of suffering.

2.   List and describe and be clear and concise.
      a.   As you touch me our skin fuses.
      b.   When you touched me the first time I thought our skin had fused, that we would never be apart.
      c.   It's been three weeks since you put your hand on my hip.
      d.   I was in the back seat of the station wagon, the window was down and my cousin was crawling in. I was in one of those child safety seats and she tried to use my hair to drag her hips through. Her face was in front of mine so I chomped her nose.
      e.   I remember not remembering biting my cousin's nose. But after my mother, my grandpa, my aunt and my dad told me about it whenever she came around, I remember starting to remember.

3.   Harry Potter had this thing called a seeing stone, I think. And he'd take a stick and suck your _____ out of your head, squeeze them into that stone and dunk his face in them. With his head in there, that's how he made whores crux and started to live forever.

4.   MATCHING I remember starting to write this and what potential it had.

a. I remember thinking of Harry Potter.

A. _____

b. I was sitting here at a purple table in Minneapolis, at the Second Moon.

B. _____

c. There were sprinkles from a donut on a plate. I was alone except

C. _____

d. For all the people around me, also staring at their computers.

D. _____

e. I'd just talked to the barista for a while about when he was in Glacier

E. _____

f. Across a stream a mother Lynx lead three kittens up a patch of snow.

F. _____

5.   Define stability:

6.   People say: Memories are you. You're what you remember. But when that goes away, you're still out here, breathing. Taking and putting to the wind.

7.   _____ (the police) found my grandmother in a patch of willows, her sweater caught on a branch. The snow at her feet wasn't pounded flat. She had wandered into the trees and stopped, standing still until the cop came. The darkness, the cold, they didn't scare her. We'd known _____ she was lost for hours, but being lost no longer meant anything to her.

8.   You trust your memories, I'll pass on mine. Forget about _____.

Mackenzie Cole and Tony Ruzicka on their process:

One night we got drunk. We said things and took notes. We holed up for days without seeing other people. Frantic. Trying to create poems out of notes. Then I drove to Minneapolis, almost died. I sat in coffee shop. Wrote that poem out of the noes, sent it to Tony. He rewrote it. It aged deep in my computer, and then after a few years, I let it out.

Mackenzie Cole and Alicia Mountain

WHEN YOU HORSE AROUND, HOW DO YOU HORSE?

Do you Trojan, hiding inside the other?
Do you bridle? Do you rein?

> I walk beside him with a hand
> on his shoulder.

Do you wrestle other boys,
boisterous, and call it horseplay?

> I touch the sole of his foot, I bow,
> I ask him to give me a kiss.

Do you slapbox empty-handed?
Do you headlock (halter)?

> I try to be warm enough for a kind
> of watered down wanting. I haunt him.

Do you pin him to the field floor,
straddled to feel the heft of a body?

> I remember what the smell of nothing is.
> I become aftertaste. I praise.

Do you know you can love
something without spitting in its mouth?

> I know the drought has broken
> like a fever, the fear has gone transparent.

Mackenzie Cole and Alicia Mountain

TIDE PULL

I, too, am reworking this haunting.

For example: the watermark left by a coffee mug vase of poppies; where you walked casually through the bonfire; where I also believed. Have the cherry blossoms come back into bloom under the Burnside bridge?

There's no conciliation in canyons.

Therefore, I see you in the sideview mirror at the corner of Pine and Greenough. Not unflinching. In fact, very much flinching.

Hello is out of place here.

Therefore, I turn to you as I am waking, a kind of aftertaste, as if in your arms all noise will quiet, all fear will turn transparent. And I remember what the smell of nothing is. Therefore, we still have long talks about the burning-of-it-down, and the what-will-come-of-this

in the far and away, far and away.

And one last therefore—the long breathing beside each other, with me in Montana cold or on fire, and you there, ankles tided to the beach. Where I am haunted by how the whorls of our hands would have touched. We gesture, nearly reaching out.

Mackenzie Cole and Alicia Mountain on their process:

We started by practicing movements. Me, small movements about the town where we met. You, long movements across the continent.

We had been we for a while I think. Shooting pool, walking dogs, becoming an encyclopedia of data together. I cut your hair. I brushed your horse. We changed things in one another without trying.

I called you my brother, there was never a brother.
I called you my sister, there was never a sister.

Poem in my inbox. Poem in the jacket of a book. Poem the receipt for a transaction I lived and lived again. Poem my god. Poem fish hearts glowing. Poem a carrot and no stick. Poem never a stick.

How much we got smacked around by words. How much we erased and were erased.

We wrote to one another. We wrote to ourselves, by ourselves together. You cut down lines I wrote, I cut down lines you wrote. We needed words that hadn't arrived yet. We made them. We tried.

Michael Collins and Annie Kim

~~Remembering~~ GHOSTS

a baseball barely
out of reach, fingers
blurring swiftly into
field,

payback, a curse, a rose

from a childhood garden or
its thorns,

nothing ~~at all~~, a blindfold,
bills left on a table under
a coffee mug,

stain
on the ~~white~~ milky carpet,

knuckles ~~fumbling~~ never
able to scrub it out

Michael Collins and Annie Kim

~~Tides~~ BEGINNINGS

> Death was exactly how
> we'd imagined it: rush
> of notes, crescendo,
>   one grand pause.

A single cigarette lying on the concrete.

A woman in a white coat ~~chiding~~ forever repeating,

> *Never turn your back.*

> A long white ~~page~~ horizon of silence.

> Darkness we were used to, footlights
> beneath the stage, voices
> floating above us in the pit.

The waves are relentless.
You couldn't see through them
if your life floated back one morning.

—Like a lawn chair in the tide, a black
umbrella, ring of keys.

Michael Collins and Annie Kim on their process:

When we wrote our first poems together, we tried to come up with a lot of rules. It was like going for a walk in a new town when all you have is a very small, very unparticular map. You say, "Let's go right until we get to that building that looks like a library." The only rule we actually stuck to was fairly quick turn-taking. That led to the dialogical feel of our early poems. One of us would start out with a line or two, email them to the other, and then the other person would come back with a line or two. And in these poems, the voice of the collaborator replaces—or maybe triangulates with—the inner voice that usually sparks ideas or expressions. It's kind of like jumping on the same trampoline while building the trampoline—you can do that, right? In other words, what one person chooses to add might change details of the other's response. Each draft, then, began to feel more like a collection of themes, metaphors, images and whatnot coming gradually together, and we each began to notice different elements to bring out or develop.

Juliet Cook and j/j hastain

HOW DO STICKY LEGS HAVE MEANING?

1.

Maybe I can't
quite tell if this spider
has evolved or degenerated.

Maybe I can't
quite tell if this spider is
carrying young or evil;
if it's aiming to give birth
to a new life form
or just packing
a gun to point at me.

I don't even know
if I'm a moon or a mean spider
egg trying to give birth.

Are you willing to wait
or will you run away?
Or will you shoot me,
just in case I might aim
to bite you?

2.

Maybe I can
remember when meanness was not
the first response.

Maybe the spider floats
into outward trajectories
pointed toward North
so the webs won't douse
our house.

Instead they will live inside
the moon
and none of us can
squash the moon.

Which means all of us can
try aiming towards freedom.
Webs sinking peacefully into milk.
Webs rearranging themselves in half and half.

Juliet Cook and j/j hastain on their process:

It's hard to describe our poems in non-poem language. Some of our poems have to do with not fitting in to any one particular place or mind or body. For j/j there's always a strong draw of the ear. j/j feels like Juliet's approach is often a very visual response to the creation of lines. And then j/j ends up hearing something that slant rhymes with that picture, like a sort of synesthesia. Process-wise, we start each poem with a few lines and then the other person adds a few lines, and as we progress, some of the lines might be removed, revised, re-ordered, or otherwise re-positioned.

James Cummins and David Lehman

...AND TURNING FOR HOME, IT WAS SECRETARIAT!

I was supposed to meet Monica, my secretary, at
Three o'clock: where was she? I felt like a ruffian,
Standing in the infield, watching the wind whirl away
Lost tickets. A policeman approached. A citation
Of some sort? No, he tipped his cap. "Sir Barton?"
He inquired, most respectfully. Yes, I affirmed—

What is it? "Just routine," the cop affirmed.
I felt like a low-ranking diplomat at the UN Secretariat
Accused of spying for Belgium. Would the real Sir Barton
Avoid his inquisitor's eyes as I did? No ruffian,
He, but a master of codes, ciphers, and encrypted citations
In fortune cookies. ("Autumn comes, goes, and whirls away.")

I cleared my head...That world was worlds' away
From this one. The policeman's handshake was a firm,
Live thing. He pulled an envelope from his book of citations,
Then blushed. "Sir, I—I spoke with your secretary at—"
Scrawled across pink flowers, in Monica's ruffian
Hand, was what the young man pointed to: 'Sir Barton.'

"Huh," I said thoughtfully. What was Monica doing at Sir Barton,
My estate, where I go to get away from the social whirl? Away—
I need to whirl away. Having no choice but to play the ruffian,
I slugged the cop and ran. My masculinity thus affirmed,
I felt good. But there was still the question of my secretary. At
A loss, I looked up her name in the index. Two citations

For cigar smuggling…Wait, what's this? A third citation—
A monograph! Horrified, I read: "*The Life and Times of Sir Barton*"!
The scamp! The exploiter! Hastily, I cell-phoned the Secretariat.
"Adlai!" I shouted, "Adlai!"—but I watched my words whirl away
As I realized, with a shock, Adlai was dead. I was alone, a firm-
Ament of pain my sole sky. I was, at last, one of the roughs. "Ian!"

I said, catching sight of James Bond's creator. In the rough and
Tumble of life, the man stood erect, in an obvious state of excitement.
What the cop had intimated about Monica was true, he affirmed.
Indeed he had just spent a delightful day with her at Sir Barton.
All of them were in on the plot. It was, well, an LA way
Of doing business. Everything for sale, even the name "Secretariat."

After his recitation of the specials—including orange roughy and
Pepsi—the waiter whirled away. Sir Barton sighed. The rather, ah, *firm*
Haunches of the lad reminded him of that great warrior, Secretariat.

James Cummins and David Lehman on their process:

JC: I'm eagerly awaiting this anthology so I can see what David has to say about process. Because I can't remember exactly how we did "Secretariat." We usually— or maybe this is what we do now, not then—start when one of us sends the other a first stanza of a sestina. I'm thinking of a recent poem about Jack Benny. But maybe we went line by line with this one. I look at it now and I really can't tell who did what. David is usually the urbane, cosmopolitan one, and I'm the crabby Midwestern moralizer. But he kind of freed me up a little with this one, I think. One important note: the book this poem comes from was a complete collaboration: the painter Archie Rand did paintings for each of the approximately 40 sestinas (!), and Beth Ann Fennelly, Bill Wadsworth, and Denise Duhamel also joined in. And of course, Secretariat, that greatest of athletes. The main thing is, it was a lot of fun.

DL: Jim is a maestro of the sestina form, and his book of Perry Mason sestinas ("The Whole Truth") is one of the most dashing and inventive books of poetry written and published in the 1980s. I got to spend the month of May 1995 in Cincinnati and found conversation with him to be as inspiring as it was amusing. Jim and I commenced writing sestinas in mutual affection and with the intent to wow each other. When the idea of a book occurred to us we wanted the whole enterprise to be a collaboration, and I think we succeeded. Jim had the idea of treating the authors as characters in various narratives. It was he who proposed the names of triple-crown-winning race-horses as the generative conceit of a sestina. When we collaborate on a poem or a project our personalities tend to merge, and the author of "Secretariat" was a third party. I can't give you his name, but you should see how he rendered the essence of Jack Benny in thirty-nine lines.

Kristina Marie Darling and John Gallaher

THE PRACTICE

We've each killed someone, but it's been so long ago we no longer remember the details, like what it was over or what we did with the body. That's fine, we think, as forgetfulness is a kind of pardon or fresh innocence. And maybe it never happened. Maybe it's just something we've dreamed up out of guilt for how nice the view is from the patio and infinity pool. There are times though, in our love-making, where our hand will slip, and the thumb will find itself at that little indentation at the base of the neck and it'll feel so familiar, like a reflex. Maybe we shouldn't go through with the renovations to the guest house after all. No, that's safe, we're sure. Maybe we shouldn't sell the rental property or look inside the freezer we keep forgetting we keep in the basement.

Kristina Marie Darling and John Gallaher

A HISTORY OF THE PASTORAL

The only difference now is that the trees are covered in ice. One by one the branches seal themselves off, disappearing into their darkened rooms. Soon the foliage around our house is made of mirrors. Perhaps that's what invited sadness into the yard to begin with. You noticed the flowers looking not quite "morning," not quite "yellow." Still I stutter and try to name them. The naturalist's Latin dead weight on my tongue.

A frozen bird, a branch snapped in two. *Bonjour tristesse,* I say to the meadow. But the landscape no longer remembers me.

Kristina Marie Darling and John Gallaher on their process:

Kristina Marie Darling lives everywhere and nowhere, so cell reception is rarely a guarantee. When her phone rings in the middle of the night, there's never anyone on the other end, only snow and a bit of music in the distance.

John Gallaher spends a lot of time one the other side of the road from a cornfield, though some years it's soy, and now and then, fallow, but no matter how far out he lives, he continues to get all the same TV stations everyone else gets. Radio too.

Kristina Marie Darling and Carol Guess

3-TIERED STEAMER

My pink comes from before. Your house breathes faster. Tonight I'll break
your heart and leave you street corner easy: besotted, best beast. I pick you up
at 8, a little late for a Coke and a candy apple. Your father waves you off, but
he's misplaced your mother, so she comes, too: curled in the backseat, chignon
nonplussed. You've brought your favorite dimestore purse, pleather and calico.
Pink is learning. The vulgar present is calling. I pull you inside out.

Kristina Marie Darling and Carol Guess

SILK FLOWERS, TRUSSED

Strapless, you slip into the suicide seat. We swipe bicyclists and barn doors
barreling detours. The highway knows which way to turn. Forked road, forks,
and a flask for a picnic. I read to you from a cereal box. Here's plastic sushi and
candied lemon, fallen apples and dandelion tea. Your hair covers your eyes. You
twist statements to questions. Confession: I've never kept orchids alive. Down
Main Street, mannequins proffer bouquets: carnations, stitched. Your duct-
taped lips.

Kristina Marie Darling and Carol Guess

{CUPS & SAUCERS}

My tea stains came from your picnic. Now the kettle boils & shrieks.
Tomorrow you'll fasten your diamond cufflinks & leave me disheveled, waiting:
torn dress, wilted corsage, clutching a few dollars for a cab. When I open the
door I feel a little old for a trinket or flowers pressed in a book. But I should
warn you: there are always mementos, & I've only begun my collection. Before
long I'll enshrine you on a red satin pillow. I'll display your former self in a glass
cabinet.

Kristina Marie Darling and Carol Guess

CROCHETED TISSUE BOX HOLDER

Sometimes things go wrong at weddings. Someone steps on the veil or loses the ring. In a "trash the dress" photo on the bank of a river, one bride lost her footing, dead weight in her dress. I can't save you; I can only be careful. For example, my mistress won't help with the cake. For example, we won't get married in Texas, where I'm wanted for something I'll never confess. Don't worry your pretty neck over dresses: tea-colored silk, Rosaline lace. We'll lash our rings to a red satin pillow. Keep the flower girl leashed. Use erasable ink.

Kristina Marie Darling and Carol Guess on their process:

At the heart of this book lies the conflict, so prevalent in American culture, between an understanding of marriage grounded in romantic and sexual love, and an understanding of marriage grounded in commerce, exchange, and debt. Our collaboration[1] allowed us to explore[2] the different[3] myths about weddings we'd each grown up with as white women, one straight, one gay; and as feminine-identified feminists unafraid to admit our own conflicted feelings about the allure of the myths we critique. Like the marriage we depict in *X MARKS THE DRESS*, our poems mutate as they unravel, dragging word trains down the page[4].

---

1. From the Latin *com*, meaning, "to labor."

2. In academic writing, the word "exploration" inevitably functions as a placeholder for what is not known, or cannot be explicitly stated.

3. By "different" she means *divergent*, in much the way a door can open into not one but two hidden rooms.

4. She could see places where the text had been erased and written over. Case in point: gone missing sing sing.

Jon Davis and Dana Levin

A STILL FOG. A FLAT SEA.

1.

Godsmashed—

2.

Tell me, in the days before the end, what did you dream?

> I was paralyzed at the threshold, I felt the wind through the door but I could not look.

How did you recognize the end days?

> Each mast a spine—the rigging made a bone-music when the wind blew, when the sails were down—

How did you travel?

> The way you walk into a room and forget why you entered.

Did you suffer much?

> I didn't believe the Captain when he said the moon was dead.

Is there still hope?

> Beef, coffee, chocolate—didn't we burn the world?

How will this end?

> I'll put on the pig mask and pose against the barnyard back-drop.

When the smoke cleared, what was left?

> Foghorns, their ghost-moan of warning, though the ships were battered and gone.

3.

We danced to the beat of bloggers inventing pseudonyms:
        Anarcho-Grandma, Olive Goil, Pez—Dispenser of Daily Wisdom.

We danced to the beat of The Cutter, on her flowered bedspread, cutting.

We danced to the beat of graffiti exploding from a day-glo eye:
        "Ehyeh asher ehyeh, I am that I am!"

We danced to the beat of people trusting, not trusting, people, to saviors
        debating palindromes.

We danced to the beat of the digital president
        saying remain calm remain calm remain calm—

We danced to the beat of drones floating over the desert,
        technicians nodding at their screens.

We danced to the beat of ragged vigilantes firing RPGs
        from the parapets.

We danced to the beat of dust devils whirling over drought-cracked cornfields.

We danced to the beat of smoke rising from charred bodies,
        tangled limbs, the rib-tented torsos of the starved.

4.

. . . crawling blind in hats of metal—

Everything was ending and still they tried to get it right. But for him, the helmets were a problem. He tried to hint at this in the poem: *the obvious metaphor must be wrong.* But she insisted: the helmets kept *arriving;* he kept turning them away. *Turning away,* as in that coffee shop when the conversation lulled: he'd turned to watch the man in the frayed sweater in the darkest corner open a journal, write a single line, and then scan the shop, eyes wary—

Still, there were moments. She'd written, *the citizens gathered / in little knots at each shipping container.* The echo of Olson in the word *citizens,* the surprise in the word *knots.* He'd written about the lobsterman *hoisting his pots.* That rhyme. She: The waves that *sloshed up the pilings.* The surprise and rightness of that *up.* Then he gave in to the helmets, with a fortuitous bit about *staring into their dark bowls.* As if nourishment. As if mystery. Or, as she wrote, in a turn that would never have occurred to him: *as if scrying for the source—*

5.

What do you remember?

    A still fog. A flat sea.

Were you afraid to be alone?

    We dragged the wrecked boats ashore and salvaged enough to build a raft.

Did you pray?

    Using bedsheets for sails, we made passage.

Did you practice divination?

    Whales groaned and whistled in the harbor's mouth.

Did you believe the signs?

    Terns dipped and swerved off the bow. Dolphins curved alongside.

Who said it was hopeless?

    We kept the bonfire blazing all night. We scoured the horizon for lights.

Why do you keep coming back to the harbor?

    Gunmetal, that horizon, and a crimson-rimmed sea.

Jon Davis and Dana Levin on their process:

Jon is really good at inventing forms; Dana is really good at enlivening them. We offer great thanks to Jeffrey Pethybridge at likestarlings for the call that sparked our collaboration. As for the rest: *My stars shine darkly over me: the malignancy of my fate might perhaps distemper yours* (Shakespeare, *Twelfth Night*).

Matthew DeMarco and Faizan Syed

IN VACUO

When the zip sound rips open the night,
a hole of darker black expands from the seam
torn lengthwise through the dark of the sky,
and the stars bunch as the seam pulls narrow
at its expanding ends, bursts wider in the middle,
the stars bunch on either side of the opening
black eye in the middle of the night, and here
we are. You in a wooden chair in the black kitchen
of air. You sprinkle leaves in your open palm,
cup your hands together, and ask for hot water.
I find a snake of steam and guide it into your hands
with whispers. Your hands must be burning
but your eyelids still half-cover your eyes, and you
are still. Have some, you say. I kneel, and you pour it
down my throat, and it's hot, but nothing burns me.
You ask me to tell you the names of all the constellations
I know. Your eyes are now wide. You need to know.
Your mouth is slack. I know that all the stars are the same
but because we are now sitting in the darkest rip tide
of the night, there are no more constellations.
I know that I must lie. I arch my hand: this arc
is the head of a mallard-rabbit. That ribbon
is known as I-90. And the X above your head
is a crucifix and the start of two loose threads winding
around each other in the initial threading
of a gentleman's necktie. And you say, yes,
I see that.

I once saw the new
moon, risen within
the abandoned bowels

of a night cracked
open, an eggshell
drained.

The hemorrhage sprouted
inside your skull. My hands
are drenched with it,
searching. All it took
was the stiff crook

of a finger. *Click*. Who else's
would it be, but mine?   Your night
creeps into me, a breath, a rigid
neck. The eye's hollow bezel
        penetrates me

until your face is an aurora
bleeding overhead, the ground
threatening to unfold
like a valley carved
deep into the dull
silver of lunar soil. I
can still see it. A shock

of white, tangled wisps. This hideous
cloud inside you. The tremble
in your hands, reaching out
to no one in particular:
            God,
        your pupils
      locked onto me
        as I rest my hand
          on stiff skin,
            lying-
                    "Everything
                    is going
                    to be okay."

Hands on the railing. The ground
stretched out like your body, your
cachectic finger, arrow of night
that watches me. Endless ebony
crawls out my eyes, my throat
brimming. I live inside
the whisper buried
underneath the dulled
edges of dusted gravel
on the rooftop, half
sworn to the ether, every
promise a pebble thrown
into the void, every cold
ember. To kill
is to turn your head
to the sun
and stare.

Matthew DeMarco and Faizan Syed

STORY OF THE YOUNG SPRIGGAN

I was once wood, the kind
of timber that catches
sparks of moisture; a kiss
wrung from the mouths owned
by a sheepish girl in sweatshirts
and dollar-store eyeliner. I was once
a hole in the ground, as fresh
as fabric softener pressed
into sheets, wound into cotton.
I was once cotton. It's true:
the threads wrapped around
pink skin, thin as a needle; I was
once your warmth flickering
off the shadows, the layers
weighing you down, the body,
the knife, the carving
in the tree. My own skin.
I breathed deeply enough
that it seemed as if I was made
of nothing but the scratches left
in the tree I once was:
that I was made of the lock
of your hair that was pinned
by a knife to a knot
in my trunk where the rain rose
beneath the absent clouds,
a thickening shaved clean.
There was an eye watching,
flooded by night, the freshly packed
dirt at my feet, bones
held by the curled, twisted

edges of me, growing, fingering
the taste of sea salt, the savory
ribbons of ornamental sage
(now made less ornamental),
the elegant notes of cedar,
cherries, pears, and precious
pine nuts. I was once crushed
into hummus. Your mouth
found me, spread on burnt
naan, funneled into
your throat, and the acid
burn of you still
eats me alive. I was
two meaty legs
joined at my hips,
and I was the sweat
that I noticed
had pooled
where they sheared me
in my sleep. I could never
evaporate. The sun bored
into me, fused me
to me. I dispersed
into a million directions
and found myself
between
your eye
and my lid.

Matthew DeMarco and Faizan Syed on their process:

When we alternate lines and edit together, as we did for "Story of the Young Spriggan," the process of creating a poem seems to shift. It no longer feels like the poem is an object that we construct. Instead, it feels like the poem already exists and that we simply bring it forward so that we can see it better. It's the act of removing vines from the front of a house to reveal the façade. When we alternate larger chunks of material, as we did for "In Vacuo," we use the poem as a vehicle for a multilayered conversation that dwells in contrasts. Intention and meaning become emergent phenomenon driven by the words themselves as we strive to challenge each other's associations.

These poems were written as part of an ongoing dialogue that we continue to actively develop. Our collaborative process originated from an elliptical collaborative freewriting exercise that we call The Game, which was developed with our friends Daniel Wolff and Erik Allgood when we studied together at University of Illinois at Urbana-Champaign.

Kendra DeColo and Tyler Mills

WHAT TO WEAR TO REPORT YOUR STALKER TO HR

Wear your most earnest look. Wear a watch.
  Wear a shirt that says, *I did not ask*

for this. If you wear a skirt with diamond
  stripes up the seam, the receptionist

will say, *You look cute.* Does this mean
  you look stalkable? Does this mean

if the phone rings and it's him, your
  voice will erupt into a murder

of crows that cloud the halls so
  fluorescent-lit corners push him away

with glossy wings? My friend never reported
  her murder. That's how it works. She left

her husband weeping in their tin-roofed
  shack, the coils of a stove top counterfeiting

a smolder. Her nails were red that day.
  She left him under the tin roof that some would want

to say was punctuated with stars, the metal,
  I mean, not her body, how it buckled

under heavy rain. He wept and then when he wasn't
  weeping, he was a cloud. Do not think

of her body when you grind the pen,
    scratching the letters of your stalker's name

in thin blue ink. Think. That's how it works—you
    see him, write him in the spangled cells

of your neurons, and the cops read
    your face and see you as him. *Keep a diary*

of his movements, one said, and you thought this:
    sunflower fields, the tangle of metal

rusting in the scrapyard, horses gathering
    slowly in the distance like a cluster of silver clouds.

Wear a whistle. Wear a lie-proof coat.
    Wear the wind. The police chief counted my deaths:

first, red roses rotting on my windshield.
    next, the window of my bedroom framing me

in a pilled, sky-blue bra. Then, my house.
    Rape would be next, he said with a catch

in his breath, like a mothy bouquet.
    As a child you waited for the wolf

to turn belly up, expose the jangled
    teeth, a mouth of burnt opals. *This probably*

happens to you all the time, the cop smiles. Unlatch
    your jaw. Let the stones fall to his feet.

The head of HR finally speaks, looking me up
    and down—first my toes mashed into my boots, his eyes

dragging doubt up my legs, then my high-
              necked sweater, my mouth, my eyes. Like a bat

adjusting its wings, he shuffles my list of incidents. *Just look
at this evidence. Who is to say you aren't stalking him?*

Kendra DeColo and Tyler Mills

POEM WITH A MILLION-DOLLAR BUDGET

I. Optical Disillusion

How to film financial risk: nothing
domestic, no three-martini business lunches
or conversations that fractal like snail shells.

The method should be formal, one wide
brushstroke of dark acrylic paint—I won't
even say the color—in a frame. Set up

cameras to catch the last dregs
of daylight squeezed through an alleyway
like a ruptured membrane or softened vein,

the city angelic in the distance
wavering chalky thighs, secreting
an innocence between the knuckles

like someone dotting umlauts over the o's
of English words, a studio technician
snoozing among an ecosystem of knobs and lights.

How to coördinate fraud with the circular saw
of belief—switched on and slicing fast
through the before & after. What is iron,

but change? What is caught in the light,
disappointed by how quickly life returns?
Mare Serenitatis, the empty sea of the Moon.

II. Commission

When the score plumes gaseous-blue
          as a burnt tongue of brass and unstitched
libido. When the cymbals mimic smoke

seeping into the theater, a prolonged
          asphyxiation like winter holed-up
in a cottage whose cracked fireplace

emits a shapeless agony, dying
          a little more each day from the scent-
less fumes. At what point must we

redirect? We asked for music
          to follow the action; seductive, complex
but hopeful. The composer charges us

$2,000 a song. How much does each note
          sleep through the set? How much for the death
a soundwave stretches into a horizon

the sun already splashed red then silvered?
          I want twelve songs, one for each electric
hour before the clock flips everything around.

I want to embarrass the law into giving you
          John Lennon's voice, free, and all *the* happy
birthdays not in *The Jerk*, *Sixteen Candles*,

and *The Birds*—where a girl with a white napkin
          tied over her eyes plays blind man's bluff—the song
evaporated from the actors' mouths into clouds of

psychedelic figure$. The composer who wets
          crystal goblets with the tip of her finger and rims
the transparent lips of the glasses into song

might pay off her credit card now, I hear. Well,
        what do I know about love other than the pixels
of organ dragged out of the synthesizer's throat,

so much warmth and robotics in the conjured
        echo, how my mother must have sang
to me, half from habit as she packed her bags

in the night, not knowing her voice would sear
        me like the pocked face of a planet, the glimmer
of a last note, all the light she left behind.

III. Credits

Give me Al Pacino in HEAT, all flab
and satin. Val Kilmer's pixie-blonde

mane as he fingers the venal riggings
of a bomb. They don't make heist movies

like they used to. I want to be robbed
sometimes, unaware of what's been

lifted, to not understand my own wealth
as the ingénue never realizes her beauty

until it's been siphoned dry. I hired the scam:
pistol at my throat in Venice, my cardigan

knitting my wrists useless. The way swans
attack children in lavender shadows,

I say, *Do it again.* The motorcycles arrive,
a ladder lifts to my window ledge, and all the men

climb in—isn't this what the libido
wants, America? All breasts and no

clit? Let's publish the screen in dollar bills,
act, crazy, and quit. Lights, camera—

Kendra DeColo and Tyler Mills

CHALLENGE IN TV YELLOW

Pulsars look like prisms through the binoculars
you aim at the gaps in power lines. So what.

Your guitar isn't a 1954 Gibson. And the moon's dissolved
edge does not look like mink fur. What matters is the lens:

white glowing like radiation on screen,
mid century, through cuts of static. Your imitation is rubbed down

to wood where the body of it swells
because of the forearms that sweat there, owning

and trading it in, while the instrument waited for the tubes to warm
in the amp and hum a little like a math tutor

reading questions quietly to himself in a cafe.
I'm supposed to say the Beatles played this color

for what it's worth—popping everything black and white.
That a sulfuric undertow reverberated through the frame

as ghosts smoothed their faces against the glass,
but I'd rather imitate Hendrix orchestrating a convocation, licking

his palms before beating the eggshell sheen
of his fender, nacreous as broken oyster shells

illuminating a path to the sea. I'd rather have the reptilian
swagger of a busted Stratocaster peeled

from Slash's burn-out arms. You can't counterfeit
the gag of surrender, or the measurement of the belly

with a fistful of peppermint leaves lined up in a chain
where only the wind can startle them. Do not say, *I am*

the brain—that is my triumph. Feather-headed with swallows,
I have been letting the sun in to settle inside me

like buttercup petals you see in the field only in springtime. TV Yellow,
you put a guitar in a T-Shirt and say, *The past is always better.*

Here comes the thief to rob the grave of its warrior: no more
pears enameled gold, no more lyre the singer lent death.

Give me paint, give me a neck that hands haven't touched,
give me vinyl needled into static stutters in time. So the twentieth century

slipped the nine-volt battery from the smoke detector.
Plug it all in. The house will burn down eight times faster.

Kendra DeColo and Tyler Mills on their process:

In our collaborative poems, the boundaries between authorial voices blur. We leave an image mid-footstep on its journey up a staircase, a line mid-sentence, inviting the alchemy and serendipity of association to guide the poem's logic.

Interruption is not always disruption. Deviation is not always derailment.

We welcome the improvisational. The circular. The fragmented.

Women abandon their sequence of thoughts/inner compositions throughout the day—while caring for a child, standing in line at Dunkin' Donuts, or grading papers on the subway. When the thought is returned to, it has disappeared or taken on a new shape.

Women's lives confront shards: of time, of the self, of the body in its many changes. Our poems engage with these shards, reflecting the violence and vitality that the world brings to our feet daily, monthly, yearly.

In a sense, we are always collaborating with ourselves.

Cat Dixon and Trent Walters

from THE SEARCHERS: A POETRY SUITE

> "We searchers are ambitious only for life itself.... We want
> to live in a relationship that will not impede our wandering,
> nor prevent our search, nor lock us in prison walls; that will
> take us for what little we have to give. We do not want to
> prove ourselves to another."
> —James Kavanaugh

I. Triptych TripTik
by Trent Walters

I want to travel
where to—when to—doesn't matter
I want to use words to get there

to fly farther than I have trudged before
did you think you would surprise
saying death's lawn looked greener
my brother said, as if it were a surprise

*"I have to pee," you say. I say, "I'll pull
over." The gas station's a museum, like those you only
find in the deep South: International House
of Triptychs. A father added a shed to showcase
his daughter's talent. It begins with those she drew
as a precocious toddler to those triptychs as an arthritic senior
on her death bed. You, an artist yourself, never heard of her.*

that I need to buy health
insurance but that assumes
and you know what you do
when you assume

let us go then, you and I,
our patience etherized upon an ass
just like Jesus, Mary and Joseph.

II. My patience is a nervous flightless bird
by Cat Dixon

My patience is a nervous flightless bird
that flaps her wings, steps up to sing,
but cannot make a sound for her beak
is filled with worms and dirt—gifts
she intended to give to you.

This grief that sits on your chest,
like a lead-filled bird building her
nest, searches for a home.

Your home is here, I want to say,
but every time I have, you
fly away.

V. Dystopic Utopia
by Trent Walters

We scuba 5000 feet below the ice
surface of Europa. A vibrant
orange eel-like being
wiggles before our masks.

A klaxon sounds, and a computer
voice bleats, "Simulation
terminated. Simulation terminated."

*In scuba suits, dripping wet, we sit again at the gas
station café, the International House of Triptychs. I spin
on my barstool to face you. "Why'd you turn off
the simulation?" Your face reddens. "Isn't reality
enough? We haven't discovered all there is
here." A klaxon sounds. A computer voice repeats,
"Simulation terminated. Simulation terminated."*

In a moldy basement, my brother dangles the virtual-sim
cord in his hand, gesticulates madly at the wall
of book shelves, arrayed like an army. "Look

at them all. Did you not know that
the DSM-VI lists books, writing, and imagination
as a serious, crippling illness? They cured
Philip Roth and Patrick McLaw. You're next."

VI. Sail
by Cat Dixon

"We have lingered long enough on the shores of the cosmic
ocean. We are ready at last to set sail for the stars."
—Carl Sagan

A fireball of hot gas flashed when
Shoemaker hit Jovian atmosphere—
black scars left three times earth's size.

Some comets lose their way,
but don't focus on unplanned collisions.
Every violent impact schools us.

If you analyze everything,
meteors destined to pockmark
your lineage, will paralyze you.

Like Rhea, we must save our sons,
replacing flesh for rock. Then water
them with a frequent attaboy.

I tire of this game, and I'd like
to hit the reset button.
I'd choose another character to play,
another realm to journey,
a different monster to defeat.

Cat Dixon and Trent Walters on their process:

We collaborated years ago. When we saw an ad for collaborative poems, Trent wrote one, and Cat responded, etc. What emerged were two voices with two different stories—not unlike what emerges in most relationships: two ways of seeing. It became a seed crystal for our collaborative chapbook.

While Cat can write and revise quickly, Trent can take years. He shaped his until each poem mirrored the others yet were separable and matched Cat's (or at least, harmonized). It wasn't until we'd gathered our call-and-response poems that we saw that one piece of our collaborative puzzle didn't fit. Another poem, however, fit perfectly. A second ad called for collaborative poems, and this time we had something ready.

Natalie Diaz and Ada Limón

CARGO

I wish I could write to you from underwater, the
       warm bath covering my ears—
one of which has three marks in the exact
shape of a triangle, my own atmosphere's asterism.

Last night, the fire engine sirens were so loud they
drowned out even the constant bluster
       of the inbound freight trains. Did I tell you, the
R.J. Corman Railroad runs 500 feet from us?

Before everything shifted and I aged into this body, my
      grandparents lived above San Timoteo Canyon
where the Southern Pacific Railroad roared each scorching
California summer day. I'd watch for the trains,
howling as they came.

Manuel is in Chicago today, and we've both admitted
      that we're traveling with our passports now.
Reports of ICE raids and both of our bloods
are requiring new medication.

I wish we could go back to the windy dock,
drinking pink wine and talking smack.
Now, it's gray and pitchfork.

The supermarket here is full of grass seed like Spring might
      actually come, but I don't know. And you?

I heard from a friend that you're still working on saving words.
     All I've been working on is napping, and maybe
being kinder to others, to myself.

Just this morning, I saw seven cardinals brash and bold
        as sin in a leafless tree. I let them be for a long while before I
shook the air and screwed it all up just by being alive, too.

Am I braver than those birds?

Do you ever wonder what the trains carry? Aluminum ingots, plastic,
        brick, corn syrup, limestone, alcohol, fury, joy.

All the world is moving, even sand from one shore to another is
being shuttled. I live my life half afraid, and half shouting at the
trains when they thunder by. This letter to you is both.

                        —Ada Limón

Natalie Diaz and Ada Limón

EASTBOUND, SOON

I am back in my desert after many years.
   The Mohave.
This desert was once an ocean—
      maybe this is why I feel myself drowning most places—now it's
the driest desert on our continent.

Bone dry, we say. Even though one third of the weight of a living
   bone is water. We know nothing
      about ourselves.

I have my passport with me these days too, like you and Manuel.
   Not because of ICE raids, but because I know
what it's like to want to leave your country. *My country*, to say it is
      half begging half joke.

Lately, I settle for an hour instead of a country.
What joy might be in this hour? I ask myself. And there is much—

Two nights ago I watched bedside lamplight rush like a
      metaled bird
to the inside of my lover's elbow, and fall more still, and bright,
   across the soft underside of her forearm,
then disappear quickly into her open and shadowed palm, surging
      again brilliant along her fingers—

a wave of moonlight riding the dusked rails of her arms.
   I was tied there—to the moon, those tracks.
Fasteners, sleepers, ands spikes. Bound in light.
      Unbolted from my sadness by the fast engine of joy.

The Burlington Northern Santa Fe Railway runs our desert. Its trains
cry out into star thick nights,
                    split desert darkness and heat with their own.

In Needles, California, Mojave women sold beads and pottery at the old
          El Garces Hotel, built for the train stop.
Houdini's wife died on our line, on an eastbound train from
     Los Angeles to New York.
                 Her body was removed at the Needles stop.

I'm eastbound myself, soon. For a reading at the Whitney.
    For love or art. For the grime of New York,
and the grime I might make of my body in that splendid city.

—Natalie Diaz

Natalie Diaz and Ada Limón

SOMETIMES I THINK MY BODY LEAVES A SHAPE IN THE AIR

I slipped my hands in the cold salt froth
     of the Pacific Ocean just two days ago. Planet-like and
everything aquatic even the sky, where an eagle unfolded so
much larger than my shadow.

I was struck translucent. A good look for me.

My hands were slick with the water I was born next to,
     and there was a whole hour that I felt lived in, like a room.

I wish be untethered and tethered all at once, my skin singes
    the sheets and there's a tremor in the marrow.

On the way back to the city, a sign read:
Boneless, Heartless, Binge-Worthy.
     Next to it was a fuzzy photograph of a jellyfish.

Imagine the body free of its anchors,
    the free-swimming,
a locomotion propelling us, pulse by pulse,
but here I am the slow caboose of clumsy effort.

When the magician's wife died, how could they be sure he
hadn't just turned her into ether, released her
     like a white bird begging for the sky outside the cage?

Creeley says, *The plan is the body*. What if he was wrong?

I am always in too many worlds, sand sifting through my hands, another me
        speeding through the air, another me waving
from a train window watching you waving from a train window watching me.

—Ada Limón

Natalie Diaz and Ada Limón

ISN'T THE AIR ALSO A BODY, MOVING?

It holds the red jet of the hawk in its
      hand of dust.
How is it that we know what we are?
If not by the air
    between any hand and its want—touch.

This is my knee, since she touches me there.
This is my throat, as defined by her reaching.
    I am touched—I am.

What pressure—the air.
        Buoying me now along a minute the size
of a strange room.
Who knew air could be so treacherous
    to move through? An old anxious sea,

or waking too early in a coppered and
        indigo morning,
or the bookmark she left near the
end of the book—
all deep blues and euphemisms for my
        anxieties.

Sometimes I don't know how to make it to the
other side of the bridge of atoms
    of a second. Except for the air

breathing me, inside, then out. Suddenly, I am still
    here.
Escaping must be like this
for the magician and mortal both—like
    lungs and air. A trick

of bones and leaving any cage—a breath.
    Everything is red this morning,

here in Sedona. The rocks, my love's mouth, even the
    chapel and its candles. Red.
I have been angry this week. A friend said,
Trust your anger. It is a demand for love.
    Or it is red. Red is a thing

I can trust—a monster and its wings, cattle grazing
    the hills like flames.
Caboose cars of trains were once red,
    and also the best parts of the trains.
The heat and shake of what promised to pass—finally,
    the red and the end of them.

Maybe this living is a balance of drunkenness off
nitrogen and the unbearable heaviness
    of atmosphere or memory.

From the right distance, I can hold anything
    in my hand—the hawk riding a thermal, the sea,
the red cliff, my love
glazed in fine red dust, your letter, even the train.
    Each is devoured in its own envelope of air.

What we hold—Creeley knew—grows weight.
    Becomes enough or burden.

What if it's true about the air and our hands?
       That they're only *an extension of an*
outside reaching in?
I'm pointing to me and to you to look out at this
       world.

—Natalie Diaz

Natalie Diaz and Ada Limón on their process:

The series of "poem letters" we wrote to each other gave us a way to connect to a more intimate voice with a specific reader, a real person to write to. To be able to compose to each other—not a wider audience, but only woman to woman, friend to friend, poet to poet, brown girl to brown girl—allowed us to be as honest, as complex, or as dreamlike as we desired. These "poem letters" were a small, intricate house we built out of breath and distance. And at times, that house was the safest place for our minds to live.

Tyler Flynn Dorholt and Joe Milazzo

FROM **TROPOPAUSE**

II.

It was not what we wanted to meddle with, the dethroned CEO, the past-pleasant
dreamer who squandered all years on impulse, ravaged ponies on the side of the
        road
during each Holiday hello, who quoted the Old Testament on conference calls
        with private
fanatics, baiting the debate with canned meat. Channels advertising Air Force
        perfection
aren't much of a panacea, not as long as cell phone spectra are blipping their cicada
        anthem
down columns of random cornfields. It's brown out in the obsolescence of this
        settling rust

so we service the truck to quarantine our advance, crag the tires, and learn from
        how the rust
settles that nothing having been is going over smoothly. As noted: all is below
        pleasant.
The miles you gas limit longer than miles of braking. Now arriving, a soon
        departing anthem
leases a beautiful locker whose keys won't be equaled. Silver ciphers crown a callow
        road
for another road for a road that cuts its sequel. There is echo here, striving for some
        perfection
within the coral reach, yard art and holograms gone lights-out as the voices inside,
        so private,

so bifurcated, so maddened and weaned draw shadows on embers. This instinct,
        fully private,
just a hushful child seating stars at tea parties, it wires us for song. Motes
        hoisting their rust
for perfection as perfection upon repetition need not be repeated but if repeated
        and if perfection
then the high seas, they swoon. They become opportune swaysong, dilettantes
        for the pleasant
refrain that resounds in a thousand and more gloats. A show is hardly a show
        except the road
takes to it, a mutt in the shape of some lanky shine. Freights escort oughts in a
        jangled anthem

for the pool of liberty building within our briefs. It is a degenerate chairperson
        tune, part anthem
part Eurocentric exegesis. It unfolds plexiglass in tatters of rural matter,
        exonerating the private
acres of mummer, hocket and plaint. The ersatz, like chattel, trot doltishly in;
        bridging the road,
the roost, the cock-eyed pitch lots with barbs and crests. Captains bred thin in
        combers of rust
bumble out of bleak avuncular spittle, pubbing it up for fact because in fact
        things aren't pleasant
at all anymore, especially science, especially pleasantries like using reflection as
        perfection.

Compromise haunts every velvet chamber until hearts are halved by a
        legerdemain's perfection
grandpa'ed in short lapels, vested in polite nooses. Always a he fattening whoops
        on our anthem

collapse, making stew. I think it altogether, the lodged mania of families'
      reunion, no bit pleasant
or appropriate for our one earned vacation. You cannot, in fact, bottle the public
      up for private
baffles. Paradox, by virtue, will grind the halt to tinder. Blood has a spark in arid
      channels; rust
has a freedom that kills the common cure for envy. The altogether tragedies van
      this hurried road

and you can expect unfinished sequels dispelling the doggone celibacy myth.
      It'll be another road,
the candidacy, helmeted access to the pantheon of passwords, envisioned torso:
      it's perfection.
When stepmothers man the thrust, brace the begats for a national veer.
      Constellations scour rust
from genealogies as dreamers curtsy to sups of help and saints. A lisp hidden in
      the new anthem
slits from blue blood a booming goodbye to the public hearts because this is
      always private,
this is always, this turning and tanking and holding and yearning, privately so
      privately pleasant.

It is just, this guiding, and it is buggy, this rust, as certain as nominations
      panning this road
for pestles and dittos. Siphon off the pleasant, simmer from the haunches of the
      base anthem,
it is just, this altering bravado, and it is private, but we hear it out, wear it into
      old perfection.

Tyler Flynn Dorholt and Joe Milazzo on their process:

The work that ultimately culminated in *Tropopause* (the manuscript from which "11." is excerpted) began in October 2010 with a series of haphazard, riffing exchanges on and around the phrase: "And it occurs to me I am punctuated by far too many avenues of ingress and egress." The exchanges were generated within emails and as Word documents. What followed was a good two years of correspondence and collaboration fueled by various constraints the authors devised and imposed upon each other. Each section grew without inspection for some time, and each was added onto after each exchange. Much of the writing inhabited the side conversations that were happening within the e-mails. Spanning jobs gained and lost, moves, superstorms, droughts and multiple genres, *Tropopause* is the record of an emerging long-distance friendship, which has grown from the very writing itself to be one of strength today. The writing is also an attempt to pin down what it means to have a discipline—and to be grateful for the nourishment that austerity supplies.

Denise Duhamel and Maureen Seaton

FLORIDADA

When we were out walking that day, our
voices drowned by the sea, we talked
about our bodies in a city of plastic surgery,
how to love them without resenting gravity,
the daytime moon pressing down on us
as we walked side by side, stepping
over dead men o' war, bruised coral, our feet
soft from sand and sea foam. Last year a doctor
told me, "Hmm. Looks like you lost a half inch."
Everybody shrinks. Everybody
masturbates as well. I saw a kid's book
on Amazon that says so and I realized that,
being human, I like to think
we're all the same—although I heard recently
in some countries it's customary to spit
on a child to protect her from the evil eye.
There's a lot of spit in a bird's nest,
that's the way the twigs and feathers
stick together, such an elemental cement. Our
bodies aren't used to tumbling across a gym floor.
Neither are they supposed to fold themselves
into backpacks or keep themselves young as isotopes.
Mr. Google says isotopes are measured
through "radiometric dating," which sounds a lot
like eHarmony for protons, speaking of which,
I keep getting a pop up ad for "SinglesOver50.com."
How rude! I wonder if they're in cahoots
with the crematoria people of South Florida who
send me special rates daily or if
baby boomers really will tip the earth on its noggin
sooner than we think. (Shrink)

(Bloat) (Shrink) (Bloat) You can buy your own
casket at Costco! Jen and Carol just joined
and bought a whole ton of shoes for next to nothing.
I myself own few shoes since moving to Florida.
I also have no raincoat, no wool socks, and I never bake
in a real oven anymore. I don't even use my stove
since the burners are cockeyed and hard to clean.
My favorite "cooking" device
is a microwave which can't compare and those
waves scare me (or is it particles?). Anyway: Florida.
Now there's a little tink tink if ever there was one.
I've got seven more propositions for you
before I let myself watch *The Good Wife* on iTunes
or buy the boxed set of *Friday Night Lights*.
I would like to win just once, something more than luggage,
something like an argument, an argument with myself
which is what Yeats called poetry. My nephew
yells "touchdown" every time he sees a ball,
but I can't think too much about football or my mind
turns into a sock hop. I prefer car chases,
the screeching of brakes, nephews jumping
from monkey bars. (Monkee bars)
O, Davy Jones, sweet teen idol, wanna-be-
Beatle, *Daydream Believer*, years later
raising horses in Indiantown, FL, where
I once went to get my hair cut. I was worried
when I realized my bathing suit made me look
exactly like a penguin or a sea otter, something
a shark would love to eat, which is only one
reason I didn't wear it the day we walked on the beach,
talking and talking, our bodies turning turquoise
in the twilight. I'm glad we donned our hats
and plunged our hands into the surf, our prints
washing away straight to the Sargasso, where the ocean
is a soup of seeds and beans and eels and dreams:
continents that were once connected
stirring a gigantic witchy pot.

Denise Duhamel and Maureen Seaton

EXQUISITE POLITICS

The perfect voter has a smile but no eyes,
maybe not even a nose or hair on his or her toes,
maybe not even a single sperm cell, ovum, little paramecium.
Politics is a slug copulating in a Poughkeepsie garden.
Politics is a grain of rice stuck in the mouth
of a king. I voted for a clump of cells,
anything to believe in, true as rain, sure as red wheat.
I carried my ballots around like smokes, pondered big questions,
resources and need, stars and planets, prehistoric
languages. I sat on Alice's mushroom in Central Park,
smoked longingly in the direction of the mayor's mansion.
Someday I won't politic anymore, my big heart will stop
loving America and I'll leave her as easy as a marriage,
splitting our assets, hoping to get the advantage
before the other side yells: *Wow!* America,
Vespucci's first name and home of free and brave, *Te amo.*

Denise Duhamel and Maureen Seaton

INTERVIEW WITH A COMIC STRIP DIVA

We sat down with Olive Oyl at her home in Chester, Illinois. We were struck by the graceful reserve with which she served us herbal tea, her quiet yet sparkling generosity.

MS: Ms. Oyl, you've been called the skinniest thing in boots. Do you find this interferes with your self-esteem?

OO: Did you ask General MacArthur that? Nancy Sinatra? Betty Boop?

DD: Are you concerned at all about America's obsession with the private lives of celebrities?

OO: I've never had sex with Clark Kent. But that doesn't mean I won't if I get the chance.

DD: Are you saying you've considered a career outside of showbiz?

OO: I am not monogamous. There are millions of monogamous people, but I am not one of them.

MS: In that case, would you like to respond to the *Inquirer?* I'm thinking especially of the front page spread with the picture of you and Bluto caught in an indiscretion.

OO: It's not as though Frank O'Hara was monogamous, right?

DD: Speaking of the New York School, do you align yourself more with them or the Beats?

OO: You can't imagine how boring it gets in all these little boxes, each strip's linear predictability.

MS: I'd heard you were a surrealist at heart.

OO: There are sardines and there are sharks—it depends what you're in the mood for.

DD: Are you as uncomfortable doing interviews as your publicist says?

OO: I believe in performance *and* page. My goal is to bust through genre restrictions—strips, 'toons, feature films.

MS: Oh, are you double-jointed?

OO: Why can't I be it all? Pen and ink legs with human hair or Meret Oppenheim's tea cup covered in fur, the way art has sex with life and vice versa.

Denise Duhamel and Maureen Seaton

CAPRICE

From the day she met you-know-who, Olive Oyl was tortured by spinach.
She'd made a thousand green soufflés before she gave the sap the boot,
whipping eggs with spinach, splashing everything with oil, Cold-Pressed and
        Virgin,
then sliding the pan into the oven with Popeye's stern orders
to make it snappy. Why didn't he like her honey baked hams? He preferred
        skinny
sausages, strung link to link like necklaces. Their lopsided kitchen was no haven

for Popeye's lanky paramour. Still, she was used to the shenanigans of zany
        Sweethaven,
her sailor breakdancing on the linoleum, peeking up her skirt, catching spinach
leaves like wet confetti on his tongue. Only Olive knew the skinny
on Popeye's perversions, the way he loved to spit-polish her big brown boots,
tap his pipe on her bony back, lower his voice a scratchy scale or two, order
her to kiss him. There was nothing Tammy Wynette about Olive—

more than once she'd shrunk his bell bottoms, then sucked the pimentos out of
        his olives.
She beat him at bowling, despite the snickering from his cronies on the
        Sweethaven
League, despite the fact that she sometimes liked all the butch-femme stuff,
        ordering
and submitting, the kinky games they sometimes played with spinach.
He'd wrap her in foil so she looked like a can, arranging spinach leaves around her
        boot-
tops, a few green stems in her hair. He squeezed her silver middle until she
        popped, her skinny

abs twitching and rippling like a filly, all the pencil-sleek and board-skinny
parts of her hardening to attention. Sometimes he called her "Olives"

and she'd slap him, sure he was making fun of her breast size. He'd call her boots
"bootsk" and she'd kick him, waiting to see if he'd smile. Sex was a haven,
something they rowed into after Segar, their creator, died and they could finally
 fuck. Spinach,
on the other hand, lost its slimy appeal during the Bobby London years, the chaos
 and order

of pro-choice battles smudging up the strip.[1] Olive filed a protection order
against iron-enriched greens. No matter what he bench-pressed, Popeye's biceps
 stayed skinnier than the duct tape on Olive's nipples when she marched in
 the pride parade. "Spinach
sucks" read the sign she held over her head with an anarchic gleam in her eye. "I
 love
Sour Patch Kids," gurgled Swee'pea, unused to the protests surrounding the
 usually safe haven
of his basket. Without warning, Olive whipped out her laptop and booted

into space, a full-figured Cyberella-star in the spring sky: Virgo, Boötes,
Ursa Major. She entered the chat rooms of large women, browsed amazon.com
 and placed orders
for every book published by Firebrand Press. Sweethaven now felt like McHaven,
a fat town full of gristle and greasy-bottomed paper bags, where only the French
 fries were skinny
and size fifty-six hips switched charmingly down the boardwalk. Olive
kissed a girl in cyberspace. They both loved Tracy Chapman and despised spinach

in any of its forms. Their boots left deep footprints all over pink clouds' skinny
wisps. They ordered each other around like siblings. "Oh Olive"
bounced along the rooftops of Sweethaven, the heavens sailorless and spinach-
 free.

---

[1] London was fired by King Features after penning an episode in '93 in which Olive was
perceived as pro-choice by the anti-choice owner of Popeye's Fried Chicken.

Denise Duhamel and Maureen Seaton on their process:

All of these poems, except "Floridada," were co-created using our beloved Surrealist games. For "Exquisite Politics," one of our very first collaborations, we used Exquisite Corpse, where half the lines remain hidden until the poem is finished. (We liked the pun of "Exquisite" in the title.) For the sestina, "Caprice," we chose six end words ahead of time and adapted the more traditional form to fit the wilder Exquisite Corpse. And we used the Surrealist Q&A, where questions and answers are hidden from each other and reunited at the end, for "Interview with a Comic Strip Diva." "Floridada" came along more recently. We wrote two lines at a time without hiding anything. (Although Exquisite Corpse will never lose its surprise appeal for us!)

Alicia Elkort and Jennifer Givhan

AUNT LUCY PACKS A SUITCASE

Lose: all dresses save seven

        Sunday's red crinoline dress, shredded

Lose: all addresses save one (away)

        he told me the dress belonged to him, my body—

Lose: a baby's fine cream china

        punched me where the baby lay

Lose: a baby's fine self

        when the bleeding stopped, I cried seven tears

Lose: a milk tooth, a woman's front tooth

        seven in my hand, no baby

Lose: the date Lucy will leave

        no one must know, I leave like death

She will choose other than family

        arise from ashes, a bird, a metaphor

She will choose ocean

        take me to ocean, O God renew me

She will choose shutter (her once fine self)

                I have forgotten who I am

She will spray herself from a bottle like perfume

                distilled to my own putrid essence

Say golden   say burning

                pray forgiveness seventy times seven

Say any other concrete salvage

                & still I reach for tea, a biscuit with butters

Loose: Lucy from the South

                the stranger that dwelleth with you shall be unto you

Loose: the bus from its station

                as one born among you & thou shalt love her as thyself

Loose: the ticket nonrefundable

                my unborn children will know who I am

Loose: the roadmap of shame

                every star laid out against sky love in the hand

& in that Lucy-broken night the owl unable to prey

                will lose / will loose its jaw

Alicia Elkort and Jennifer Givhan

WHY DEATH? WHY MUD?

a cornflower paloma

becomes mama   becomes red chile

bringing monsoons   & pecans suspire melón

suspire winds   & birds

dream

    limón & cures

catch the throat   her throated blood

guava

    & blue

canyons   become house

    becomes land   a yellow moth

flaps sage   & palomas

fly   mama flies

away

Alicia Elkort and Jennifer Givhan

INVENTION OF THE (SHRINKING/GROWING) MYTH OR HOW I LEARNED TO SHIFT & SHIFT AGAIN

when I was the princess I stripped my body rag by rag

unbound planted my feet like hammers

& the pounding & the dance (what cleaves / what scars)

in my glory I tore roots from the rusted earth

if others weren't laughing they fell away & still I shook

& still I loved every ragged edge & sweet corner

it's been years unthroned & I'm thorned joy in the bright

good my map my compass my legs stalwart

cactus barrels my ribcage (I bloom in reverse) & lose

only what their eyes can see what shuttering a window /

what sprouting a rose

Alicia Elkort and Jennifer Givhan

A SMALL METAMORPHOSIS
OR THE POWER OF SEEING

I am a pat of pearl-colored flamingos
        I am a towel fading by the bathroom sink
I am a set of new bed sheets not yet washed
        I am the broken swing set near collapsed
I am crabapple buds swollen on a February tree
        I am a knob of roots waiting for someone to pull
I am a stamp collection in a case
        I am lost letters unsent & yellowed
I am snakeskin dried under a microscope
        I am bundled sage meant to burn for cleansing
I am the doll painted as candy skull
        I am two lanterns one broken & the night watch long—

Two lanterns against the long night
        I am the doll my mother caressed as she lay dying
I am bundled sage a gift a prayer
        I am dried snakeskin remnants of the past
I am lost but found grace in every bruised crevice
        I am a collection of horses in the field
I am a knob on a door to a celestine attic
        I am apple blossoms against the bluest sky
I am broken wounds filling with gold
        I am a bed sheet's pleated shine nightjars of desire
I am a towel wet with dewdrop
        I am pearl & flamingo the sweetest light

Alicia Elkort and Jennifer Givhan

ONE BY ONE

In the damp of rain, I swept leaves rusted with dying
there wasn't peace, there should have been peace—
still in the crevices another too-small child

scurrying across brick & bog. Where do children
rest? I could never answer, never satisfy, I clamped
each child for too long & when one by one they sustained

themselves, how I was held & and how I was broken
& in breaking unchained
each song.

Alicia Elkort and Jennifer Givhan on their process:

Jenn and Alicia have been giving each other feedback on poems since they first met
in an online poetry class. When the idea of co-writing came up, it seemed like a
natural conclusion. Their distinct themes and language offered an opportunity to
create a fresh voice united by their similar understanding of life and beauty. Some
poems were written much like a call and response with one poet responding to the
outline of a poem by the other poet. Other poems were written in a more organic
manner, emailing one line at a time back and forth (Jenn and Alicia live in dif-
ferent cities) and editing as they progressed until they had arrived at the end—a
completed poem. All the poems were given time to settle, then edits would be
made. In some of the poems, themes that are more reflective of one poet or the
other would stand out, and still the poems are relevant for both poets. The synergy
between poets can work like a real time cut-up tool, discovering new expressions,
word choices. On a deeper level, writing together demonstrates how narratives
can coalesce.

Chiyuma Elliott and Michael Peterson

PLEASE PLEASE FOLLOW ME

If you never let reason
          want today,
                    it would follow.

And in my rooms,
          I was justified;
                    nothing more.

And in my rooms,
          nothing more
                    than the original version

                              of this pageant.

Chiyuma Elliott and Michael Peterson on their process:

"Please please follow me" is part of an experiment: collaboratively drafting poems via text message. The challenge here was to write about Agnes Martin's work using only the vocabulary auto-generated by our text programs (the changing three word arrays that our phones' algorithms predicted we intended to use). This process has inspired an evolving set of constraints; the only wholly introduced word we allowed ourselves was "Agnes," but we quickly decided that we could delete words and letters, which helped garner more word options. We also gave ourselves permission to edit offline for lineation—though many of the final versions still behave like epigrams, and fit on an iPhone screen.

Kate Hanson Foster and Paul Marion

STAR GRACE

We are made of burned-out embers,
some Einstein says. But I want to say burned
-in, or burned-on, for the way star grains
don't go out—the way they stay in us,
in the grocery store or outside in the driveway
shoveling snow. Our bodies simply shape—
beehives alive and surviving the replacement.
It's an illusion of permanence, they say, copies
and copies of cells cycling—not human at all,
but just a light-powered pattern of being.
In the town tomb, worms have the last word,
stringing out what's left into the dirt—
some things lost forever while others form
for the first time—the next running round
of movement, a road surfaced many times
over. We can't think about this all the time—
break our mind on the skies with metal eyes
and ears looking for all we can't see, distant
explosions flung back a billion years. We are
gutter, we are canal, a template design
but always different water. Rain and sleet
passing through, hammering the rooftops
in multitude, and this wine running through me—
a stellar death, a piece of dust with my name on it.

Kate Hanson Foster and Paul Marion on their process:

Star Grace is inspired by *Living With The Stars* by Karel Schrijver and Iris Schrijver, and the book's fascinating first line, "Our bodies are made of the burned-out embers of stars that were released into the Galaxy in massive explosions long before gravity pulled them together to form Earth. These remnants now comprise essentially all the material in our bodies." This is an awesome and incomprehensible concept—to think that we operate entirely "by the grace of stardust" when considering our otherwise mundane lives, and our bodies are simply an illusion of permanence when the universe and our existence are constantly in flux. "Star Grace" began as a few lines and ideas passed back and forth, words and phrases cycling in and out until the poem began to form. The irony was not lost on us that the process of revision was much like the preface of the book—the idea that our bodies, our buildings, and even our roads are constantly being rebuilt over time, and the final product lives with us, only briefly, until it is replaced once again.

Elisa Gabbert and Kathleen Rooney

THE ONE ABOUT THE DOG

A poodle walks into a bar. The poodle wants to 1) have fun, 2) make money, 3) meet other dogs who think they're people. She's not poor, so why wouldn't she hold herself to higher ethical standards than those struggling to cling to the base of Maslow's pyramid? A kind of cartography, a dangerous fantasy. Business *is* pleasure. She answers to the name of Fauna. You wouldn't know it from her haircut, but she hates in-group conformism. There's alcoholism, & then there's social dependency.

Elisa Gabbert and Kathleen Rooney

THE ONE ABOUT THE UNHEIMLICH

My doppelganger walks into a bar. He has a nasty disposition, whereas I am merely having a bad day. Does he enjoy watching forest fires? Do the patrons think we're twins? Only a certain kind of man would identify the color as "cyan." Or announce that "Rippling abs don't just appear on your midsection; you have to sculpt them." Hark—a sudden sunshower. Now he is reenacting a classic tourist photo cliché. And now I am surprised to find myself weeping.

Elisa Gabbert and Kathleen Rooney

THE ONE ABOUT THE INCONGRUITY THEORY OF HUMOR

A comedian walks into a bar. At this point, nothing can stop her. Don't call her a comedienne— she's not Lucille Ball. Is sadness a heritable trait, or isn't it? And is it really so terrible? Must every event be one of the heartening glories of the fucking year? Whenever people laugh, she wants to snap, "It's not funny." Like the internet, she just wants to be free. If information has replaced the story, what will replace information? She refuses to cast herself as a sex object, but her defiance just makes her sexier. *The only nonsentient zodiac symbol is Libra— what's with that?* she says, but nobody gets it. If animals are smarter than we thought, maybe humans are dumber?

Elisa Gabbert and Kathleen Rooney on their process:

The two of us began collaborating on poetry via email back in 2006, and for many years we wrote almost daily, working in dozens of fixed and invented forms. For our series of joke poems, we combined the prose poem format with the classic "guy walks into a bar" joke opening. One of us would start by choosing who or what was walking into a bar, then we took turns composing, always leaving a sentence incomplete so the other would have to finish the thought. The end products, we find, are jokes but not: They veer in expected, sometimes awkward directions, like improv sketches; they don't always have happy endings. Are they funny? Who can say?

John Gallaher and G.C. Waldrep

YOUR FATHER ON THE TRAIN OF GHOSTS

Your father steps on board the train of ghosts.
You watch him from the platform:

somehow, he doesn't look as old
as you expected him to be.

You think this must have something to do
with the light, or maybe

how much bigger the train is.
It stretches down the track
a long way, as far as your eyes can make out.

It's like a black bullet
that keeps speeding toward you,
you think, and then:

No, it's like a very long train, that's all.

Somewhere on board the train, your father
is choosing a seat. Maybe

he's already found one, has settled in,

picked up a magazine or newspaper
someone else left lying there,

is flipping through it, idly.
Maybe he's looking out the window, for you
you would like to think, waving,

only you'll never see it
because of the reflected glare.

Or maybe he's not looking for you at all.
Maybe he's watching the hot air balloons
that have just appeared

all over the sky, ribbed like airborne hearts
of the giants Jack killed.

In the stories, Jack has no father.
This would explain a lot, you are thinking

as the train begins to pull away:

his misplaced affections,
stealing the harp of gold that played
all by itself. Around you,

men and women and children
are standing on the platform, shouting, waving,
hugging themselves.
The wind is cold; it must be March.

You would want that kind of music
if you were Jack, wouldn't you?

John Gallaher and G.C. Waldrep

YOUR LOVER, LATER

Your lover is on the roof.
The gray roof. Your lover is sitting on the roof
of that house you remember. Your lover long ago
sitting there
with both hands down. Your lover
sitting there waving
into the pockets of air.

It's an easy idea.

All the people of the town are out
on their roofs. Little people
over their porch lights. Legs over the edges
like many high
and beautiful things.

And one of them is your lover. Remember?
Some of them you can see, and some not.
Call to them. Why not call to them

and then listen all night.
All night the sound of that town.
Your lover on the roof
and a train along the horizon
that's crowded with hotels.

The Ford dealership is setting off
balloons, red and blue and green and
white balloons.

I'd like to climb up there. It would be
such an easy concept. Such an easy way to be.

And what about your lover? It's such a large town,
isn't it? So many roofs
and so many people
with their hands at their sides
in the future. It's easy. It must be.

Tell me again what to do.

John Gallaher and G.C. Waldrep

IDEAL BOATING CONDITIONS

You open the box and see yourself staring back.
"Cool," you think, and then you realize
it's just a mirror at the bottom of the box.

The wind shifts. The little boats go this way
& that in the harbor. You watch them.

Somewhere on board each of the boats
is a mirror, from which you watch yourself
watching the boats. The self you're going to be
sends postcards back to the self you are now,
only the self you are now won't get them
until it's too late, until you're different.

You think the part of you that is out there,
in the harbor, must be happier than you are now.

There's this wedding you're missing,
or this anniversary. The music cycles backward,
past Chopin, Bruckner, Buxtehude even.
See, this city isn't even built yet.

You want to use every word you hear
as a verb: "neon," "medical student," "Talmud."
"Persimmon." "Volkswagen." "Aramaic."

You read the postcards one by one
like cadavers inside of which cloudy coils
of ocean have just gone missing.
A gentle breeze off the water ruffles your hair.

Someone's excavating Troy, someone's
living there—the little shops, the excise tax,
a furnished room near the college,
baskets of blue eggs in the marketplace.
The searchlights launch themselves into the void
music's left, hatchlings on the riprap.

The you that's on the boats misses the you
that's here, with the box. You understand this
much. Someone else's Troy is burning.

John Gallaher and G.C. Waldrep

THE CITY EXPERIMENT

We spent all night on the city experiment,
but the thing barely moved, and now
we're worried. The formula looked good
in the congratulatory lighting, and we had this feeling
we might be able to push through to the other side
and it would turn out to be a movie set,
and you'd be walking the carpet
to an award show. Yes, you immersed yourself
in that role. Yes, you believed you were indeed that person
up there, and thank you, it sure was something,
and of course you're going to miss it
now and then, but next season it'll be a museum
or some people digging in a field.

There were other things we liked, of course,
when it wasn't important to be careful,
and the weather cooperated, with the knowledge
that this moment's going to be repeatable
and more comfortable than the boats
we used to like, but still with the feeling
that maybe it really isn't all that repeatable
after all, or at least not with you. But at that moment
the cocktails arrived, so we crested,
and whatever we said fit, or fit well enough. Yes
to the cocktail, because we're polite.

And wasn't it warm in the sun
through this window in winter,
the snow outside? I'm sure it's something small
we've overlooked. What type of cocktail,
perhaps. Perhaps survival is a state of mind,

in your floating future, there in the city experiment,
past the tennis courts and trees, and an old harmonium
someone put out by the curb, a trace
of broken china, a fleeting study of a figure
in a landscape, until you're writing notes on a napkin
that blows into the lake, and you're hearing the flat echo,
some harbor gone dark into ordinary things.

John Gallaher and G.C. Waldrep on their process:

We began writing what was to become *Your Father on the Train of Ghosts* slowly, by writing poems back and forth, via e-mail, borrowing a lot from each other—reusing images, riffing, quoting, answering back. At a certain point we realized the energy might be right, and we dove in. (Or further in.) Once it got going it really took on a momentum of its own, and was difficult to bring to a close. There were various micro-constraints along the way, for instance the period when one of us would come up with a title and the other the poem to go with the title. (This is how the title poem came into being.) The original writing wasn't difficult—it was fun; it represented a great freedom, not having to start every poem ex nihilo (because we were responding to each other's poems). The editing and organizing of the book was a fairly long process, however, and more work. Some of the cuts were hard, but harder yet was joint revision. Part of each of us always wanted to revise everything back towards a G.C. Waldrep comfort zone or a John Gallaher comfort zone—the urge to revise towards a known voice—but what we were hoping for, what we thought the book wanted, was to evolve towards a third voice, neither G.C. Waldrep nor John Gallaher. Learning to listen for that voice, and to revise towards it, was a new experience.

Ross Gay and Aimee Nezhukumatathil

from LACE & PYRITE: LETTERS FROM TWO GARDENS

SUMMER 2011

I still marvel at all the people who first mapped the summer sky—
the pretty patterns from chalk and string they pulled
across the fresh-swept floor. Every monster wishes their teeth
gleamed louder than Vega, summer's brightest star. Every night
has its own delights: waxwing, paper moth, firefly larvae.
I would drink the red and blue stars if I thought my thin throat
could handle it. Even at the darkest hour, my garden throws
furtive dots of pale light to guide my steps: the bubble of fresh
egg-froth on a frog's back, the secret bloom of moonflowers
when the children have been tucked into their tiny beds.

O teasel bur and grasshopper—how you catch in the hem of my skirt
like a summer cough. It's exhausting, this desire. But I would never
trade it for any shiny marble. Would you? I love the silence
of sweat in these the slow days of summer. All the mysterious sounds
in the trees—like a sack of watches—while I tend to tomato plants
who have only thought to give four fruits this entire month.

—AN

It's true. No golden marble or treasure chest or even tongue
mapping me ankle to the cove behind my ear quells that guttural
tug by which I unwind bindweed from each thorny raspberry
cane, or clip the fish pepper from its scaffolding, or swing my axe
if need be.
With which I hack back the jackass branch
or beg the rampant sunchokes this way, or that.
Or dream beneath the currant's myriad
golden mouths.

Some days I catch glimpse of the hurdy-gurdy path I make
through
this garden: ooh! the gooseberries aglow,
ooh! the lemon balm tufting up, ooh! wasps swilling the golden
florets of bolted kale, and Good Lord the strawberry flowers
are the pursed lips of ghosts
I want to know. Yes, today I am on my belly for that
scant perfume, this invisible parade of dying and
bloom.

                    —RG

AUTUMN

At the onset of fall, there are days full of the need
to exhale without sound around the crispy aquilegia
stalks. One last plume of astilbe is the only shot of pink left,
and even now drifts of unraked leaves threaten to choke
it out. I wouldn't wish this sickness on anyone.

The only sound I remember from that week
with you at summer's end was the terrible toss
of bullfrogs flinging themselves into the pond
when we approached. *Wait.* The only sound
I remember is actually a color, muddy river water

that hides an ancient fish. I never sat up nights
with sick horses and I wonder if that's
the difference: their coughs will never haunt me.
They say frogs are vanishing all over the Midwest,
but I can still hear them.

—AN

And yet, and yet, when the cold
makes brittle what remains—the spent okra stalk,
the few pepper plants that hung on through the first
two frosts, those little gold tomatoes—when it with-
ers even the rogue amaranth, its tousled
mane bent and defeated,
when the silver maple out front has ceased whisper-
ing, and when the bullfrogs nestle into their muddy
lairs, and the peepers go where they go,
and the crows circle,
just down the street, its leaves too mostly blown off,
spindly and creaking in the wind,
while the whole world shimmers with death, hauling
all its sugar into perfect globes
the size of a child's handful, giddy, it seems,
at the sound of ants slurping beneath, at me
joining them, brushing away wood chip and beetle
before burying my tongue
in the burst pulp
dropped on the earth below, the persimmon
gives its modest fruit for yet
a while

—RG

Ross Gay and Aimee Nezhukumatathil on their process:

In the late July swelter and dragonfly buzz of the summer of 2011, we began a poem correspondence, based on no prompts, no assignments—just that we were to send a poem at least once a week, maybe more if we were lucky. No commentary needed. Happy mail.

This selection from our chapbook, *LACE & PYRITE* is how we made sense and record of a full year from our respective gardens. After almost a year of writing to each other, we boarded a train together for the Millay Artist's Colony in the Berkshires in upstate New York. There, we met up with several other writer friends (who were also working on independent projects of their own) and revised and finished this series of epistolary poems.

It is our hope that some of the pleasure and anxiety of tending each of our gardens—which is to say, tending to ourselves, our relationships, our earth—comes through in these poems, written over the course of about a year. There's bounty, yes; but there's loss and sorrow too: like a garden, like a life. But as the leaf buds start swelling, as they start, even, unfurling—right around the corner!—it's time to focus on bounty: sing at the crocuses, get those peas in. Make friends with someone who has a rhubarb patch. See if the community garden has a plot with your name on it.

Benjamin Goluboff and Mark Luebbers

BILL EVANS SOLOS ALONE

"What Kind of Fool Am I?"

The changes are temporal
but he experiences them as space,
as wall meets wall
as the chord resolves
enclosing him in this room
with the instrument.

Here he presses toward a stillness
he cannot achieve,
fails always to answer
the instrument's question.

Benjamin Goluboff and Mark Luebbers

BILL EVANS IS ARRESTED FOR HEROIN POSSESSION AT JFK

"…I have always preferred playing without an audience."
—Bill Evans

Standing beside the shining baggage claim
the pianist wishes for evaporation, as opposed
to flight, since he has just come to ground.
The carousel is empty, still, yet humming in key:
planes of stainless linked in sequence, an endless scale.
Waiting for the valise holding his fix to reach his hand
the marshals are static outside the automatic doors
in sunlight and heat. This is for them a minor affair.
It is early in the decade, but late for absolution.
He has tried again to be honest with his lovers.
He has repaid the money to his friends.
The carpet looks so cool, so broad and smooth
he would like to reach down and feel it with his fingers.
He sees his reflection, jacketed and tied, in the glass,
and the half-note difference between black and white
forms a space in his mind where he rests for a count.
Then, the switch is turned on and the carousel keys slide.
Somewhere inside a beat begins, and so he must play.

Benjamin Goluboff and Mark Luebbers

AFTER THE DEATH OF SCOTT LAFARO

Past midnight the Dodge rolled over
and left the curved pavement
of Route 20 near Flint
in the Finger Lakes.
The old sweet double bass
in the back seat was mostly crushed
but not damaged by the fire.

Back in the city there was a low long
time off through the autumn:
a numb space in which loss
could improvise,
but then the piano
slid over again into the first bars
of that Gershwin tune, as if on its own.

Benjamin Goluboff and Mark Luebbers on their process:

Early last year I started working on a seam of poems about imagined moments in
the lives of famous artists, capturing them when their aesthetic or ethical prin-
ciples were tested or changed. These were short fictional narratives based on bio-
graphical fragments, which presented interesting ambiguities both in the artist's
life, and by extension, my own. There was a little voyeurism in this, I guess, but I
found that creating an important moment in an important life was fertile ground
for language, image and reflective insight.

Then I read an article by Ben on the *Bird's Thumb* blog entitled "Confessions of an
Anti-Confessional Poet." I immediately felt that I'd met my poetic Doppelganger.
He wrote, "Many of my poems have been biographical narratives, which I've writ-

ten, somewhat compulsively, in suites or sequences... These poems combine facts about these people with a good deal of invented detail and circumstance."

Far from jealous of my "territory," or envious that he had published a whole bunch of very scholarly efforts in the same realm, I was relieved, validated, and encouraged. I couldn't help but write to him, and even though we'd never met, and lived and worked hours apart, he was instantly gracious and we immediately conspired to work on several collaborative projects, mostly (to this point) by correspondence.

Ben too, was using historic figures as vehicles. His writing has an element of catalogue: a finely chosen litany of ephemera that populate a constructed moment. His poems are objective, without editorialization or judgement, and they have a deep attention to detail. It has been both liberating and challenging to venture into the minds and actions of these artistic, historic icons, and we both feel grateful that they allow us to do so. Bill Evans struck both of us as an immediately rich subject: his life was one of fascinating and poignant contradictions—like his music. We're continuing to expand this series, but have been distracting each other with various ideas for new ones. Who knows, maybe a chapbook is in the works.

Carol Guess and Daniela Olszewska

THE PASSENGER SEAT OF YOUR CAR, BARRELING DOWN LAKESHORE DRIVE

I am only half-participating in this conversation about the Renaissance Faire strike. Both my brains have been working overtime to make me look like someone you could fall, then stay, in love with. It's exhausting, always gluing glitter animal shapes to my face. Sorry my taste in music embarrasses you. I'll make up for it by trying to look lost like you like. You cut off an undercover law van, swerve against curves, cut corners into paper dolls: long string of high femme or holiday lights eyeing crosshatched lake. I keep pressing the brake like I'm driver-decider. When you screech to a winter halt, you stretch your arm across my chest, more makeshift air bag than making out. I take what I can get while you accelerate, racing late geese and underpaid Santas jostling for the Polar Bear Plunge.

Carol Guess and Daniela Olszewska

THE OTHER CENTRALIA

We packed Aquatic Invasive Species in suitcases and drove through the minor cities changing our safe word. You pasted stick figures to the back of the car:

girl-stick

girl-stick

fish

fish

water-moth

There's an absence of endings in a city of nightlights. Children shake cartoonishly large hands at bad drivers, eyes glazed from the dashboard telly. Two kinds of ashes fall from the sky:

fire-wag

grit-smolder

We end up in Oregon. How did we end up in Oregon again? Here's *A Book of Common Mistakes*:

untying the wrong man's shoe

putting seafeather pillows in the wash.

eating snack foods with someone else's fins

tying purple seafeathers into your rough red braid

This road ends with a gift shop. We're out of cash, but they're willing to take a personal check. So many names we might forge:

Hairspray Jones

Eileen Myles

Onward Christian Soldier

Tom Waits V

Immigrant Trout

Susan

Swimming Thru a Rough Patch

If there's a motel in the back of the gift shop, we'll stay there 'til morning. Not sleeping off the miles, just filling the tub with ice from the machine down the hall.

Carol Guess and Daniela Olszewska

HYPOCHONDRIAC EX-NURSE

This room smells very elderflower and hospice-afternoon. My forehead freckles.
Every time I sass the thermometer, basement mice scurry away the special
blue cheese I was saving for all of our miraculous recoveries. My tote bag's
inscribed with the old Hippocratic oath: *Life is for the loving. First, do no less.* In
school, I was the worst at finding veins. No one volunteered to be my partner.
I punctured lovers, red running from heart to syringe. *Be My Valentine* had
special meaning. My cartoon cards were popular with boys and girls alike. You
haven't seen hunger until you've seen an arm swollen with want in the nick of
goodnight. I lost license to practice due to licentiousness. My secret's safe in
hazardous waste.

Carol Guess and Daniela Olszewska

VINYL-SCENTED NOSTALGIA CANDLE

Glass broke up the punk scene living in my hair, barrettes and bird's nest tangles a tattletale display. Tambourines and coffee mugs and whirligigs: these are all birthday-related. Romance is tidying up my extensive music collection, while boomeranging between Birmingham, Alabama and Birmingham, England. Something in that vinyl tree house growls with its mammal-throat. Tonight, we'll dance until the downstairs neighbors whack the ceiling with their ceiling whacking cane. *Me* is pretty, but *We* is getting stuff done: dogs sniffing the manicured lawn of the safe house. I want to tie you up so no one abducts you and, subsequently, ties you down. It's a myth that vampires need an invitation. Actually, humans have the need to invite. Whoever invented cereal had a thing about mornings. If I were a typewriter, I'd probably misplace my keys, too.

Carol Guess and Daniela Olszewska

YOUR BEDROOM, WHICH USED TO BE A UTILITY CLOSET

I woke up with that doe-dead feeling about you. You reminded me too much. Don't mention nostalgia to a woman holding three different kinds of flowers in her gut. You love ballerinas again. This means you will only ever like one type of rejection at a time. Outside, a January-ish whistle. Ask about how I'll get home again now that I'm too angry to blink. Ask about when you can see where we're at in a month. Don't ask about beach glass in my galoshes. I found a text message in a bottle, sand and broken glass everywhere, okay? I woke up and went missing. You reminded your alarm to chime. Don't mention pirouettes to a pole dancer; jealousy's just reckless nostalgia. You love when the mop falls in love with the broom. Your bedroom blossoms with buckets and gloves.

Carol Guess and Daniela Olszewska on their process:

Sound startles us out of the gate and we're off, racing against the alphabet to finish each line. Like doctors, we swear first do no charm, eschewing sentiment in favor of surgical syntax. Unlike doctors, we are still unsure as to whether or not we want to make your heart sick or to make your heart well. We are still unsure as to whether or not we want to make your heart do anything at all.

We do know that we want you to bend your ear to the page and whisper these lines out loud, even if you're afraid you'll be overheard and mistaken for mad. If someone mistakes you for mad, twist and turn the tables on them: accuse them of ghost thoughts.

Breaks between stanzas just mean we ran out of

A. coffee
B. tea
C. identities

D. time
E. all of the above
F. none of the above

We wrote these poems in safe houses, microclimates, and stolen moments. We borrowed from the sentient and non-sentient voices surrounding us, but only after making sure we had their blessing and a notarized contract clarifying the interest on our repayment plan. Our goal was to keep moving any intelligible goal posts we encountered off the playing field. Our goal was to not leave any words on the bench during the big game. Our goal was to give each letter of the alphabet a participation trophy and a championship ring lined with precious and gaudy jewels.

Shrode Heil

MULTIPLE CHOICE

My source material is always
secondary. So the downward slide
of your lips might refer to mornings

beyond their base. See the flowers
along the hill? Are they irises?
Inside your eyes are many days

of expectation and regret that I match
with vanity and friendship, depending
on the day. I'll see that card with

a Joker on it. How great to be a student
again, eyeing a teacher who is wholly
desirable. We'll choose the discount

provided and reclaim our ideas about beauty
at the picket lines. I find black
Fridays to be media-friendly

but not for us. When I think about
the important people in my life
who are much older than me

being buried, it makes me want
to talk to their younger selves,
or to myself, as I wish us to be,

ever-present oh, vanity. You know I find
our mule-like ways inevitable, that we
are only what we have to be,

that is: us. Us is a frightful pronoun
because it implies a gluey union
past the alphabet we agreed upon.

Shrode Heil

WE ARE DEALING WITH YOUR REQUEST

A foggy lens. A mound of squarish stones. Three windows
lit by sky give off the impish prospect
of stepping into grasslessness.

At Keats's grave we picked up two twigs
of equal length then snapped them in two.

The one bloke we met who'd ever been to Pumpkin Town said
that there there were no quiet Matthews. But

the arms spread across the Jesuit church
in Rome told us otherwise, even
if we waited for someone else
to put a euro in the light box.

The drama of darkness
and rocks. The sound of
mammalian wind chimes.
Who knows why
our wanders get away from us—

suddenly we're living
in what looks like an infernetto
even if its breath is redolent

of paradise. In the Campodoglio they spoke
of strands never materialized as we listened,
uncomprehending. Baby, it's okay if words do

less work than we'd like them to because
they never truly do the work we want—capito?

Let me translate English into English for you
again. On the corner of the coast we fell
like so many anvils made of glass.

The sun reddened our bodies.
Someone put a euro in the light box.
Now

we were reminded of how hard it is
to go home—not because we never do
but since this time, we have to—

Shrode Heil on their process:

To speak about our process is to speak about the accidental genesis of writing
poetry together. We were both living in Fayetteville, Arkansas, at the time, both of
us a bit bored with the town. So we decided one day, tetchy and restless at a café, to
write a poem together. Neither of us can remember who started the poem. A first
line or phrase was penned by one, then passed across the table to be continued by
the other. And so on: back and forth, a poetic conversation, until the last line was
penned and agreed upon (sometimes a point of contention, especially since only
one of us got to end the poem); later, we'd transfer the pocket notebook pages to a
Word document, there deciding on stanzas and lineation. Surprisingly, we rarely
edited the content.

All of the poems we've written together have been drafted this way. We've tried
to collaborate over email, but the lack of mutual physicality—notebook, pen, and
other—essentially sucked the creative gusto out of the process. As such, there is
a very social and situational aspect to our poems. They are composed in a public
place—park, pub, train, coffee shop, etc.—and whether in Arkansas, New York,
London or Italy, the atmosphere and essence of that surrounding space inevitably
bleeds in. In this way, our poems serve as artistic evidence of our time together.

Derek Henderson and Derek Pollard

from *INCONSEQUENTIA*

Vine Street. Midnight. Streetlights.
Yellowing across. Sprung into it,
what it is left in the light—what it is
spilled in through the window—
little tips of water stuck in. Cracks
in the street. Arched windows.
Night blackening, full of fan sound.
Abandoned.

>   Time slips backward and kisses itself
>   on the arch of its own back.

Vine Street. Noon. Greening over.
Old Hannah burning the back into
what is left at the end of the bottle.
The bottle. How green it is. Limning
the edge. The broken edge. The lip
brushed by lacquered sunlight. Moving
slowly across the horizon. Glassed in.

>   *What is left* for *what is yet to become.*

There was a table, there was a rug,
there were flowers woven into the fabric
of found cushions. There was a sense
of lost nostalgia, a tremble of the lips,
a stutter that would try to condemn
the ones who were left over in the places
left behind. A stutter that was stuttering
—that had stuttered and was stuttering.

Vine Street. A new bottle is heated.
The clock reads 1:38 a.m. As the bottle
begins to simmer, I remember when I
was King and had to walk seven times
around the earth before I could die.

Time is turning backward, isolating
another part of itself. Every part kissed
disappears. Parting from the kissed.

The kissed who touch each other and
are lost. The kissed who move across

this poem and make of it something
more than mere words. Is *this* the poem?

These people? The remnant of a kiss?

I wonder about the pressure, the weight,
the exquisite line of your lips—

Is this poem enough?

She asks these questions as dawn breaks
open, paling the cemetery gates and
making of this poem nothing more
than a glance over the shoulder.
The gristle of these words, this poem
which we are writing as if there were
nothing else left for us to do.

In the other room, the baby nuzzles
the bottle close. Out in street, morning
begins to lighten—

Green glass. The horizon.

Vine Street

     Streetlights

What light left

     —Is through—

Of or *in*. The windows
Full of sound

     Slipped kisses—the, its

Noon

What of
The green. Limning

The. The

     By. Across. Glassed
     Is what

Was there
Flowers. The

Was found
Of. Of

     Would condemn
     Who. Over places

Was
Had, was

 Streetlight

     Bottle

_____ a.m.
Bottle

Simmer. When
Turning

      Kissed itself
      From

Who. Other
Lost. Who

This. Make something
Mere. *This*

The wonder

Pressure
Of—

      Poem

These
Paling gates

      Of nothing

Gristle
Of

      Words

Which writing there
Or else us

Begins—
Green horizon

Derek Henderson and Derek Pollard on their process:

Inconsequentia began as a mail art project while Derek Henderson was living in Kalamazoo, Michigan, and Derek Pollard was living in Minneapolis, Minnesota. This was in 1994, years before either of us had our first AOL account. We started by returning to a collaborative poem we'd written with a number of friends and passersby at a house we'd both lived in in Kalamazoo the previous year. Working intuitively under the aegis of Thelemic magick, we imposed various numbers-based constraints on that poem (and years later, on another written with Seth Nehil and William Lee) which resulted in a series of revisions we would mail back and forth to one another. Those poems, splinters and re-imaginings of these first, became the basis of a poetic dialogue between us that stretched over ten years and that eventually led to *Inconsequentia* being published by BlazeVOX Books. The poem here is excerpted from one of the poems in that book and is, as a result of the editors' welcome abbreviation, a fitting example of the ways in which *Inconsequentia* remains an ongoing project, one in which, as the book's first line attests, each reader becomes another author, helping to extend the poems' arc further.

Jeannie Hoag and Kyle McCord

SOMEONE TONIGHT IS KNITTING

Dear Adonic Others,

Know we are cheering you
when your hair falls
or you squeeze
thoughts through a mail slot.
Files can't be recovered,
and your brother is very ill,
and at any minute
this whole deal could go.

Go. And if you become
what is asked,
it was not felicity.
A mother of two
and the two,
who have treated the neighbor's rental
to death by muddy shoes,
love which will not reprimand
it was not. Anything of awe
which saved you.

Dear Adonic Others,

Search for your screws
by one working lamp.
You descend
to the grand disguise party
that is Death.

This clacking of needles
from without or withal.

From your hall,
the light left by two lives
twines in air.

Dear Sweethearts,

Dear Exoskeletons,

Know we want to have wanted for you
what was
best. For you,
the smallest thought
may string
incalculable hours.

Dear Brevities,

Dear Dear and Distant,

Dear Cauldron of Rain,

Jeannie Hoag and Kyle McCord

SELF SEEN AS ART 5

After Edward Hopper's "American Landscape 1920"

And I've tried to think the right things, J.R.

The laggard dream
of summer sloping into the valley.
Returning to see the farmer,
found only his house, his ox.

The ox's hoof slips
as she steps
over the track that parts
the long wheat pasture
from the blackhanded hills.

I imagine the farmer's children.
Their Sundays
of incommunication.

I watch the hands
drawing
them from the dark hill,
their xylem, phloem
hair snipped short.

You quaff the stars
for you believe in them
you have life.

Move out to the porch,
its pillars
so many muscled hands.

And I think on this ivory magic
we've been
wielding, you and I.

These faces in the sheen off the moon
on the truck, and I am tired of dreaming
says the sun to the stars. Of the tiny shapes
who look upon me. And sometimes one will scrape.
And sometimes one will sigh.

Jeannie Hoag and Kyle McCord on their process:

Our project was conceived of as epistolary poems between two voices, Ms. Kim and J.R. We set out a few basic guidelines: one of us would write a poem from the voice of our character and send it to the other, who would write a poem in response.

The poems often have an epistolary quality, but they aren't always letters. At times the response is on a sonic level, or an associative level, and sometimes one voice changes the subject completely. Much of the book is about the breakdown and renewal of communication, and in that way, the poems mirror how people actually communicate.

Getting started, we had a conception of who the two voices were, and we found that writing as specific voices was a way to bring consistency to each round of poems. As the project progressed, these voices developed into stronger and more independent identities.

Ultimately, the poems developed story arcs that we had not planned, and had not anticipated. Our characters' journeys and responses to one another created an exciting tension that left us in very different places from when we began.

Leslie E. Hoffman and Pushpa MacFarlane

FIRE-BORN

Fire-born in winter
embers rain into the sea
Kilauea sighs

Pele born of fire, leaving
a sizzling comet trail

Coconut palms weep
platinum bolts of lightning
set ether afire

Vulcanite—smelting copper,
burning skies—hot summer winds

Phobos and Deimos
draw the chariot of Mars to-
ward the Sirens' song

Agni Aryaman Mit-Ra
Surya Ravi Masai Sol

Leslie E. Hoffman and Pushpa MacFarlane on their process:

Truly, fire-born—a product of friendship and fusion of words.

Writing a collaborative piece with Leslie, a good friend and poet, seemed not only ideal to commemorate our friendship, but also truly ironic.

I've been interested in collaborative writing since coming upon a book of rengas, where several poets across the county participated, writing back and forth. I suggested we try a renga and Leslie was game. She sent me a couple of short stanzas she'd recently written, and I welcomed the challenge. I read her lines and wrote in response to them, thereby, creating a renga.

To create a renga, we started with three of Leslie's lines for the first stanza, totaling seventeen syllables. I responded to her lines with a couplet consisting of seven syllables per line. We repeated this format, alternating a three-line stanza with a couplet, until we had six stanzas in all. Our lines fell in place as if they were meant to be. The irony being how elements of Greek mythology harmonized with nuances of the Kīlauea volcano, Pele, Siren, Masai, and Indian sun gods.

What an example of spontaneous creativity—like having an unannounced visitor staying on for dinner. With no time to cook a fabulous meal, or order from a restaurant, you have to get exceedingly creative and come up with something ingenious. Well, we did. In fact, we came up with something magical!

We're delighted to be in this incredible anthology.

Grant Holly and Rachel Neff

LOST

In the reflection of a mirrored beer sign, this bar, you
snapped on a smile that smears across the silver. Rest
your head against the bricks, hoping that the wall
will provide the gravity and stability the beer sign
takes away with convex contours. Tonight you fuck.
It doesn't matter who. In this moment you are free

of everything. You will lean heavily on someone's arm
and kiss as if consuming them. You will exist
for a moment, then come back to the shell you drag
around the rest of the week. Showering will not take
away the smokeless night's silvered beauty.

Grant Holly and Rachel Neff on their process:

Rachel and Grant have known each other since they were undergrads at Washington State University, drinking pitchers of Pabst, eating $5 burgers, and writing earnest poetry until all hours in a campus bar called The Coug. This project started out nearly a decade ago as a series of flash fiction vignettes and bar conversations, but more recently morphed into a series of poems. Rachel and Grant work simultaneously via Google Drive, first by setting a scene and then building upon a singular moment of focus. Together, they polish the images, language, and scene. They are each other's trusted writing counsel, opening up their veins and letting words pour out into the world.

Ron Horning and David Lehman

THE GREEKS

1.

It pleased Phaedra to be there
When the wrecking ball smashed into the doll's house
She had planned to grow up in
In Manhattan. One of her neighbors played "Eve of Destruction,"
The other favored "The Ballad of the Green Berets."
They could both go to hell. Phaedra played "Get Off My Cloud"
Not because she liked it, but to drown out the noise.
She needed a drink. One strawberry daiquiri coming up...
In her left hand she held a shell, in her right a book
Titled *The Riddle of Gravitation,* which hadn't yet been written,
About the curvature of space, a concept that beguiled her,
But she was finding it hard to concentrate. She kept recalling
How it felt, the adrenalin flow, when they razed
The Manhattan hospital she was born in
While she watched, as though it were being done
At her request, years ago: walls and floors exploding
And sunlight spiking through the dust that kept falling
Upward, to hang in the air, a twisting cloud, long after
The reverberations stopped. Where was that daiquiri?
And where was the Italian painter who had asked her last night
To pose for him this afternoon? Surfing off Sounion, probably,
Their date erased from his brain by dreams of hanging ten
On the Banzai Pipeline, then shooting like a bullet to shore.

"I am mad to surf," he had said. "I wish Greece were Hawaii."
"Done," Socrates had said, promising to pick him up
In the morning and drive to the finest waves in Attica—
Long, low, blue swells that only a winter storm could rile
Into the towering cliffs she'd seen on *Wide World of Sports.*
On the Aegean, though, those cliffs would be killer mean.
They are both mad, thought Phaedra, but no madder than I
To have believed a friend of Socrates. What kind of modeling
Did the Italian have in mind anyway? She'd modeled before.
She loved art, but she was tired of taking off her clothes.
Here came her drink at last. Placing book and shell on table,
She raised the heavy goblet. Yellow, not pink? A sip. Great:
Banana, not strawberry. Couldn't anyone get anything straight?

2.

"I saw Maria Chakonas on the F train today,
Her thick brown hair bobbed short and trimmed close
The way she wore it the summer of '67,
When Jimi Hendrix burned down his guitar at Monterey,
And the way, twenty years later, so many girls
Old enough to be our daughters wear theirs.
The history of fashion is a tale of youth relived,
And sometimes one's own." Socrates looked up
From the novel he had brought to Central Park
To read before his meeting with the casting director
Who thought a real philosopher would lend a special touch
To her company's next epic about aliens, set in Troy
During the war for Helen. He had thanked her
(The cackling overseas connection) and said
There were no philosophers in the *Iliad,* only
Men, women, and gods. She paused. That didn't matter,
The writer had added one for the flashbacks to Athens
And she thought the role perfect for Socrates. Well?
He felt as if he were shadowing her down city streets,
But from in front, using his ears instead of his eyes.
Then she told him he could change the part as he saw fit,
All changes subject to the producer's approval, of course,
And how much money he would make.

                                        Socrates said yes.
He needed the cash, and given that much freedom
He'd take more. Rewrite the script? Not a chance.
He wouldn't even read it, he'd just shoot from the lip
As always. Plato had taken notes for years, promising

To build them into books, but Socrates hadn't seen one yet
And he'd be damned if he was going to bore away
His precious time bent over a desk, so this seemed
An ideal chance to score a few points, albeit on film
Rather than the papyrus Plato had taught him to expect.
What does paper have over film, Socrates reflected,
Watching the forsythia flame past the bicyclers' helmets
In a brilliant wave. He glanced at the sun: still
A few minutes to kill before he was due at the hotel,
So back he went to *The Buried Head*: "But it wasn't
The young woman's hair that reminded me of Maria most,
Or her small round face, her bright smile, dark skin,
Pert nose. More than anything else, it was the way
She wrapped her vivid glance, soft and brown with light,
Around her boyfriend's face, making him invisible
To all who did not feel as strongly about him as she.
To the other riders, then, he existed merely as a hypothesis,
But a hypothesis whose proof was as solid as any of Euclid's."
And likely to stay solid longer, thought Socrates,
Reminded again of his old quarrel with Alcibiades.

3.

Later, the Emperor fell asleep and had a dream
About the history of clothing. "The truth is never
An example, the truth is always a distortion,"
Said the man in the bowler hat after Zeno told him his life story.
He was looking for stereotypes, but these were people,
The kind who sent text messages when friends didn't answer the phone.
Everything was fake, even the boxes—a magician's trick,
Its ability to wow a crowd dependent on their appetite for delusion,
But lovely still, like a landscape of sushi remembered long after
The last snow clouds of shredded daikon float away on the tray.
Superman put down his chopsticks. A compulsive gambler, a citizen
Of the age of innocence (about which he knows nothing),
A celebrity priest, and caddie to the stars, he was an orphan
In search of his double, and couldn't wait until he found him
And a woman stopped them at the corner of Sunset and La Cienega:
"Are you two brothers?" Their no would mean yes. Elegance is refusal,

Which is why the difference between freedom and relativity
Is the same as the difference between action and history—
Less noise, more music, and a philosopher who bets on his brain the way
A pitcher bets on his arm. He can't stand stinginess
And believes the best masks are worn by dancers he wouldn't look at
Otherwise. Their names pull the long train of paintings
Through the eye of the needle. "Things could be worse,"
Insisted Phaedra when Socrates came to her house
And complained about the way Zeno's attention to detail,
Not to mention his well bred bad manners, was driving them all crazy.
"Consider the geisha who compares the red moon to a slab of beef,

Or the bartender who names a cocktail The Road to Fallujah.

Consider the man who prefers the riddles he can't solve to the ones he can.

Consider the woman who banished all the mirrors from her apartment

Before she had the Emperor over for tea. Consider her courage,

And that of her husband, about whom the Emperor knows nothing."

Ron Horning and David Lehman on their process:

The three poems in "The Greeks" are the first poems in a book entitled *The Unex-amined Life*. The book consists of three sequences, all of which, except for the very last poem, were drafted in a single year. There were many revisions, though, and one of us had moved to Los Angeles before we got together two summers later, wrote the last poem, and typed up the manuscript. The book began in the most natural way, as we had been collaborating on poems almost from the time we met in the fall of 1972.

"The Greeks" was written and edited in typewritten exchanges arranged by the US postal service when one of us lived in Brooklyn, on the wrong side of the BQE, and the other lived in upstate New York. Many of the poems that followed were written in the summer of 1987 when we were in the same room at the same time, usually with one of us shelving books while the other used a blue ballpoint pen on a legal size yellow pad. Sometimes while one of us wrote, the other would read aloud a passage from a book. Billie Holiday sang "I Can't Get Started with You." Wine flowed. It was a joyful experience we were happy to repeat when, years later, we started a novel.

Amorak Huey and W. Todd Kaneko

SLASH THROWS HIS GUITAR INTO THE LAKE

A guitar is not a sword the way a rock star is not a king
the way this lake is not an audience. But all our legends

begin in light, end in water. Anyone can fall in love
with drowning. Every song is a quest

to return to music's source, is a gift for the Lady of the Lake,
is the hope that she will reach out to grab what is offered.

There is a liquid grammar to an instrument hurled,
a pattern transcribed in the air that explains everything

just before it's too late. Maybe the distances
between front row and center stage, shore-sand and lake-bottom

are too great to be bridged by the body's impulses—
yet this effort is the premise of rock and roll.

He sets down his hat. Removes his clothes. Walks into the water.

Amorak Huey and W. Todd Kaneko on their process:

We were both separately writing poems about Guns 'N' Roses and Slash, so
decided that perhaps we should write them together. We individually drafted 25
or 30 poems and then started revising them together, with the agreement that we
check our egos at the door, the poems no longer mine or yours, but ours. The hope
was that our collective vision would be larger, more surprising, more complex,
richer than either of our individual visions alone. When we look at the poems
now, it's sometimes difficult to remember their original forms, how they were ever
anything but the result of our collaborative revision.

Megan Kaminski and Bonnie Roy

from SEVEN TO DECEMBER

Dear Bonnie dear nine a.m.
because seven a.m. is not so dear to me
still sleep-soaked in bed warning off early rays
no wonder I say I love to sleep
let's imagine I wake to fields of Kansas wheat
or corn stalks baking barely rustling in wind
anything bucolic really rather than the construction
of parking lots and sorority song practice
it's damp and cool here this morning   my own
coastal longings start a slow slide of earth
westward to you to the city to the sea
perhaps all language is both living and dead
resuscitated in each sentence formed and mutated
in our exchange   a place where we dwell
together   I think of you through cricket-call and refrigerator hum
the grass grows tall and weedy out front
the campanile tolls in the distance

Megan Kaminski and Bonnie Roy

Say I wake to pigeon's groan, suburb's
skylighting. drove one hour and slept
a little higher on our parallel. your Kansas
meets my central valley sunflowers on this
shared band, world's water line,
cold dmz and hothouses of seedlings,
canopied beds of soil down the road
of olive trees I run. dear Megan, the heat
broke last night and comes back again
as dahlias whose signage lists no price
in the plaza market. back home. your campanile,
my hearth clocks strike the hours and halves.
the wall of family portraits, hair plaits and brooches,
halts in symmetry over last week's hydrangeas,
drying their time.

Megan Kaminski and Bonnie Roy

It's hot here too and perfect morning
the cat chasing house flies and sun
a little too bright in coming through
front windows facing the street looking
to lines of girls in their Friday's best
dear Bonnie these last weeks have been
strange and solitary a big wet kiss
from summer with too much tongue
plants grow thick in the yard
basil's wooly overtaking of whatnots
and my legs are heavy soft they carry me
not at all just hours of watch and wait
seeing from darkened window
daily excursion into day and week
and year passing years

Megan Kaminski and Bonnie Roy

Dear Megan, slept in a city. dear Megan,
woke to one thin line of sunlight where fog
carried San Francisco across the bay
where the bridge carries no one this weekend,
long labor day, hurray. now kusodama petals
pinch Cairo close to Norfolk, center marked
in mesquite pods, last season lavender stalks,
and flour jar's four-by glass magnifies all latitudes
and longings to: home. here succulents
bouquet their sea greens and saint pinks
in the done leaves under clotheslines.
black dog's hair draws kitchen's white tile
in detail like bone in the open book
of ancient anatomies. coffee's ice
beads the plastic, diagrams
my desk in Venn of purse and sip.

Megan Kaminski and Bonnie Roy on their process:

The impetus to collaborate on "Seven to December" came out of a desire to think with, rather than in isolation. The poems began like letters, documents of everyday life shared between friends, across a distance. No rules were imposed on their composition, but the process of receiving and returning poems between Megan in Kansas and Bonnie in California shaped the project's form. A sight, sound, or feeling isolated in one poem often found a companion in reply: campanile to clock, coastal heat wave to prairie heat wave. Over the different geographies they represented, the poems made an environment of their own.

Megan Kaminski and Anne K. Yoder

from SIGIL AND SIGH

REFRACTED LIGHT. WEB IN THE CORNER. ARMS ABOVE.

Bass thump and corner turn, rubber on rock, heat radiates from roof from body. Our densities measured by thickness of flesh, scattering of syllables across tongue, diphthong glide into evening. Snow stretch from town to state line. Bear down bare carry back down the hill back down the boulevard. Bending at the knee to carry us all carry us fully from this place and longing. No bird song no calls in this night. Gangrened and lost. Dive and dusk. All this carry all this weight all this labor.

Megan Kaminski and Anne K. Yoder

[AUROLEUS PHILLIPUS THEOSTRAUS BOMBASTUS VON HOHENHEIM]

Auroleus Phillipus Theostraus Bombastus von Hohenheim: alchemist, botanist, palmist, physician. found truth in the solidity of sulfur and mercury. count revolutions of celestial planets; trace cartographies of the to come.

cross-hatched line: a restless heart. jet set across the palmar plane. take the via lascivia to bass lines and Kim Gordon sighs, a future of palm fronds and castanets. cast spells, cast-away. let others tell origin stories.

Megan Kaminski and Anne K. Yoder on their process:

Sigil & Sigh is a collaborative chapbook made for the Dusie Kollectiv. Inspired by alchemical arts, divination practices and long Midwestern winters, *Sigil & Sigh* was born from a period of daily meditations and the process prose/poems that resulted from them. We, the authors, worked separately but in parallel, engaging in practices inspired by palmistry, tarot, and ailuromancy, and communicating frequently, almost daily, between ourselves to discuss ideas, their intersection, and words written. The physicality of the chapbook was important to us, and we collaborated on making those decisions, too. The card stock pages of the original chapbook were intended to physically conjure the tarot. They were left unbound so that resonances between pieces and authorial voices would play out anew with each reading.

Persis Karim and Dean LaTray

HOW MANY BLUES?

How many words for blue
In your language? I answer
As if I know—blue sky, blue
Feeling, blue eye. I want to know
The word for blue in Swahili,
In Russian, in Arabic. I want

To taste and breathe it, drink
From its tenderness and power.
I wonder whether Gaugin understood
Blue differently in Tahiti?
I suspect *that* blue stretched his
Mind and cast him out of the prism
Because he knew the ache of too-blue.

And the Navaho? What does blue
Mean to them? They live in the blue
Light of red, where shadows cannot
Bear the blackness and so—and so,
People of the desert see ravens
In their true color—the blue-
Black of all beginning.

Persis Karim and Dean LaTray on their process:

"How Many Blues?" was written on our first date. We met online and poetry was one of the attracting factors in our email missives back and forth. We had met each other for the first time only one hour before we composed the poem. After a short walk, and sipping on small cups of lukewarm coffee from a thermos, Persis recited an e.e. cummings poem, "I thank you god for this most amazing day." After she finished the poem, she said, "hey let's write a poem together!" She pulled out her small red moleskin notebook and Dean wrote the first line, "how many kinds of blue are there?" We wrote alternating lines, without any discussion of the topic or ideas and finished the poem in a matter of minutes. After we heard the approaching noise of a weed-whacker, we moved to the tall spring grass on a nearby slope and wrote a second poem which remains to be published. This poem was drawn from our experiences, and from the many blues that surrounded us while we sat on a bench atop a small slope facing the Golden Gate Bridge. When we parted from each other, we agreed that each person would take one of the poems home, type it up and email it to the other. The poems were edited a little in the email exchange and arrived the same day in our inboxes; other than that, "How Many Blues?" is almost exactly as it was written on that first encounter as strangers drawn to poetry, to beauty, to sunlight, and the blue of that spring day.

Ariana-Sophia Kartsonis and Stephanie Rogers

READING ANNE BOLEYN'S LIPS

> *After Anne Boleyn was beheaded on the orders of her husband*
> *King Henry VII, her eyes and lips were said to move. Some*
> *medical authorities subsequently believed that consciousness*
> *can continue for an unknown length of time after decapitation*
> *because blood remains present in the brain.*

Last night the skyscape wore itself out trying to warn me.

Who can attend to a skyscape with so much love wedged between us?

When I say skyscape I mean, the kingdom of extreme measures, of course,

When I say so much, I mean what excess makes us do or want to.

When I say wedged, I mean prying. When I say pry, I mean rip.

When I say love, I am not so sure what I mean.

He has what he has. A sharp, bright blade. Someone else to wield it.

Always someone else.

There's a gorgeousness to the severing.

All highways lead to the coliseum of brain and blood.

Memory. Each minute housed in the skull's closed arena.

Each terrible night: Rough grip. His cock bellied-deep.

His face open like a child's afterwards.

Every son might come to this.

Every son might come to this telling. Every beheading is an act of attention.

When I say attention, I mean to say laying claim.

When I say laying claim, I mean that the head is a keeping place.

The blood that feeds the heart gives up the heart first.

The blood that feeds the heart is loyal to the brain.

When I say loyal, I mean willing to kill for.

Like a son, like a warning, like a skyscape arching over.

Ariana-Sophia Kartsonis and Stephanie Rogers

ROPE LADDER RANT FOR ALL OF YOUS

You with the faces to meet the face
that you meet.

You with your leafy promises.

This is so I won't forget

you with your remedial taxonomy,

you with your unfinished novel.

You with your tin singings.

You with your star-fuckers.

You with your shook foil.

You with your Lyn Emanuels.

You with your Andrew
SmackMeIambic! Hudgins.

You with your nothing pretty, your no-love.

You with your blueprints, the
Morton Salt
Girl, (doubt it not) will always be
mine.

You with your saxophone.

You with your little trombone.

You with your coffee and oranges.

Listen up, Lambkins you put the
sad in
sadistic. You with your Phantom
Fireworks.

You with your Fireproof Warehouse.

You with your stingy, sunset city.

You with your frolic and your fancy.

You, you are God's understudy,
aren't you?
(Next to me you're my favorite
narcissist.)

You and your touch-me-not husband.

You with your Wife of Bath. Your
sick little
                    Medieval mind.

You with your foot fetish.

You with your poodle skirt. You
with your
                    one white dress.

Your mother says you take your boys
mulletted and illiterate.

Your mother sets you
up with the dyspeptic.

Listen Lambkin, I don't take tumbles
down the stairs for just anyone.

You. *I miss your broken-china voice.*

You with your saran wrap pressed across
our photograph, wrapped around everything
you know I'll try to touch.

You with your asparagus theories.

You with your riddles.

Your artichoke peel-away
lovesmelovesmenot heart.

You, who actually said I used it all up, like it

                   was cereal—our cereal.

And you! I don't even owe you money!

                   You with your Hartshorn Avenue.

You with your coin purse:
you are exactly that necessary.

                   You with my boyfriend's heart.

You with my crush, his beautiful hair
pressed neatly on your thigh.

                   You with your so-called *smiley-eyes*.

There's a poem that ends
with someone giving a shit.
There's a poem that ends with me
lighting (off) your cigarette. This

                   is not the end. You.

                   You with your piccolo messages left
                   on my voice mail. They call it *voice*
                   mail for a reason, you cruiseship
                   woodwind whore!

You with your portable bad weathers
You with your eight inches of snowfall

                   With you there was never enough
                   atmosphere. With you: never
                   enough doubt.

You are not the end.

                   You with your line breaks

You with your breakups

                   You with your breakdowns

You with your brakelights

Ariana-Sophia Kartsonis and Stephanie Rogers on their process

"Rope Ladder" was written in passed-back-and-forth sections and then shifted around to smooth the overall poem. "Reading Ann Boleyn's Lips" was different: a process of writing in persona. We abandoned the persona and kept Ann Boleyn and a handful of others in that mode.

Collaboration can work really well when the collaborators vary vastly in taste and style. We are the opposite. So much of the same poems move us. We like to write what we like to read. Sometimes we write lines, I think, to give the other a thing she might like to read. Then she replies in kind. Most of our poems, one way or other, go like that.

Mary Kasimor and Susan Lewis

HELD, FOR EXAMPLE

Held, for example, like irons to the fiery tantrum of expansion. So much misdirection. I thought I'd found the North Star, but it was a false glitter in my eye. No one is how they appear. The earth is a simple bowl of clay that strayed away from Venus. Who can blame it for its shame and ugliness? Hurtling blindly in love and war. Mars seething redly, deaf to the gravity of the attraction. Deftly rolling in our credulous orbits. The earth is a seedy place with few surprises. Looking for the fabulous we find the obvious. Today the spider built an empire. I found myself inside its spit and bled myself into the sea. The water was used, so I swam into its cheapened art. Proffering my unwelcome advances, salivating towards salvation on ragged soles. Dimly I recall cresting and crowning like any bloody start. The illusion of warmth as sly as a hungry ferret. The wolf, cold and glamorous, is best trapped with an iron bite although the earth calls for council and refuses to care about life or death. The meat mill survives while the planet revolves. Some days the hues of existence are in the black and white detail found beneath an umbrella as we wait for a bus.

Mary Kasimor and Susan Lewis on their process:

We first became poetry "comrades" via the internet, meeting in person at an AWP conference several years later. By the time we started talking about collaborating, we had established a solid foundation of mutual respect for each other's poetry, as well as a deep sense of personal affinity. But our differences were also a rich and unpredictable source of energy and experimentation. One of us would start a poem by sending a couple of lines to the other, who responded with an equivalent number of lines, and so on, until one of us declared our intuition that the first draft was finished. We took turns on being the "starter," since in some ways each poem's opening ended up setting the terms of that piece. Some of the pieces became prose poems, like *held, for example*, and some were lineated—at first because Gmail inserted line breaks in Mary's text, which Susan assumed to be intentional! After many months, we took turns revising the poems, without regard to which line "belonged" to whom—and gladly discovered that both of us were more interested in making the poems as good as they could be within the context the conjunction of our texts had created, than in protecting the initial poetic impulses which had given rise to it. Happily, by the time we considered them finished, it was difficult for either of us to identify which lines had originated with whom. What delights us most is that these are not Mary Kasimor or Susan Lewis poems, but those of a third poetic sensibility, born of our interaction, in all of its twists, turns, endings—and beginnings.

David Lehman and William Wadsworth

FALSTAFF

"Look at that bum in the corner." "That's no bum, that's Harold Bloom."
If a tragic romance of uncles and aunts is the story of poetic influence,
he's the voice on the phone who talks without listening, a lightning rod of anxiety.
The rest of us are in prison, but the walls are not made of words, and misprision
will not bend the bars that keep us from our freedom, as the new canon
keeps cadets in the dark on the charms of Hamlet or Falstaff.

Some have greatness thrust upon them. Then there is Falstaff,
asleep under a tree, indifferent to the charms of flowers in bloom.
Some dream of glory in combat. But he has heard the cannons
roar. The noise made him cherish the more the influence
of sack in the conduct of man's affairs. Not subject to misprision
is this self-evident truth: that we live and die alone, with anxiety

our common lot. Consider Nym, whose anxiety
was jealousy, a humor his master Falstaff
found humorous. Poor deluded Nym misread
his Mistress, believed her more constant than Mrs. Bloom.
Then under the broken-hearted influence
of too much Eastcheap Sack, he broke the canon-

ic law and robbed the Church (and took a non-
stop flight, anon, to the gallows). Anxiety
is the humor of our age, an influence
for the worse. For Dr. Bloom that old bum Falstaff
is the only cure. To be human, says Bloom,
is to be Hal, not Henry—a king mistaken

for a man by scholarly fools in whose misreading
the play's the site of a battle pitting Jill's canon
against Jack's, with Leo's old vision of a New Bloom-

usalem receding as fast as anxiety
will allow. And therefore do we turn to Falstaff
with our flags at half-staff under the influence

of parents, teachers, and stars. The influence
of Falstaff is the will to live, to escape the prison
of our days, not to praise them. Falstaff
is all men, potentially (except Milton). "Yet the canon's
contradictions may doom it," Jack said, radiating anxiety.
"And well they should!" said Jill: "Doom to Bloom!"

Yet when midnight chimes, 'tis the influence of Jack's canon
that makes Miss Priss unbosom her anxiety
in the giant arms of Falstaff, conceiving Bloom.

David Lehman and William Wadsworth on their process:

Regarding Shakespeare, the marriage of true minds
admits the truth: when lust unites with love,
the world below the waist appears above
reproach as it dances, joining two of a kind.
Like earth and sky, one cannot do without
the other. The two converge and in fusion give
permission to creation; together they thrive
as opposites attract. They never doubt

that doubt will lead the way to faith if not truth,
as endings always are uncertain. But *now*
forever tells us all we need to know:
this poem about a poem contains a myth
of never-ending generation. The heart
is a tango, two minds, two bodies, one art.

Rae Liberto and Molly Thornton

NO

mums wilt and shed
gold drops
like no bad ever happened

november came and went
left the dead

pompon heads faded
dried and stooped asking
no more questions

what was impossible
became simple

the soft thing
pressed itself
to the blade

clarity of force
the answer

clicking bones
dislocating pop
resolved

no

it could be as simple
as unhinging the jaw
to let more in

it could be as straightforward
as the edge of glass gliding
along leaking skin

we could answer no
questions leave no
notes and be buried

two happy bodies
each pretty head resting
on the other's wilting
like no bad ever happened

Rae Liberto and Molly Thornton

MY COUNTRY IS A PARTY

My country is a party
you said I thought you said
make art mean again
exactly what the world needs

You said I thought you said
make slogans fake again
exactly what the world needs
the way it is but keeps coming out wrong

Make slogans fake again
my country is a cake
the way it is but keeps coming out wrong
a sweet soggy sponge in sugar mud

My country is a cake
make words fire again
a sweet soggy sponge in sugar mud
let me open my own cage

Make words fire again
and no one would ever
let me open my own cage
unless it feels good or heals

And no one would ever
make pain go away again
unless it feels good or heals
what everyone has always wanted

Unless it feels good or heals
my country is a party
what everyone has always wanted
watch me open my own cage

Rae Liberto and Molly Thornton on their process:

To create the poems included in this anthology, we worked across 800 miles via shared documents in the cloud and FaceTime discussions to reinterpret and add to each other's visions. "My country is a party" began as two separate poems drafted by Molly and one poem Rae wrote in response to those. The final poem is a conversation between those three poems woven together into a pantoum. "no" began as a poem Rae wrote and Molly responded to in reverse order, with the additional theme of an interrupting marigold. The poems became one, reflecting forward and backward with Rae's piece followed by Molly's response as a mirror of the initial images and actions. In between drafts we discussed words, ideas, and writing processes that inspired the results. Outside of this collaboration, we commonly provide feedback to each other and cover similar themes and perspectives in our individual work, so it was a joyful and rich experiment to build more closely on each other's work and to navigate the creative process together.

Sarah Lilius and Jennifer MacBain-Stephens

from THE WOMEN UNDER THE OCEAN

I.
He sets them up:
hair and thighs like pins
in the front row.
Lips: ironed linens.
Blender the thoughts
together inside a
pretty skull package.

They endure to be false
trees, white birch limbs out of reach.
He grabs the weak ones to put
in his pot.
Heavy wool coat, he sinks
into the Atlantic, salt water
in fungus hair.

Tendrils reach salty surface
wrap around soft calves
reflect in black patent heels.
Make me over a hiss.
Suffocate me a conjuring.
Coat cuffs reach for diamond
laden necks.

Victims, their value in chiffon,
screech, a song with no understanding
rake him from water to sun,
burn pretend wings,

roast him, prime for melting.
Let him know how to be grabbed
by heat, how to die, at the hands

of another.

Sarah Lilius and Jennifer MacBain-Stephens on their process:

We wrote this poem while on a writing retreat at The Porches in Virginia not long after the 2016 election results. We each wrote a line in a separate room and e-mailed it to the other, until we had a series of poems.

Sarah Maclay and Holaday Mason

from THE "SHE" SERIES: A VENICE CORRESPONDENCE

She sees the obsidian. *Seriously—*

you can't really be afraid of the re-arranged height, no I mean, light, he says &
offers lemon,
yes,

pure lemon cake before
guiding her   through

the almost-freezing expanded bright hallways of mirrors
        to the past & into, also,
        the dreams of the mad—
        those
        glaring portraits of the velveteen desert,
        a perfect moon cooling the low-slung spine
        of the singing lion,
        his peaceful breath   a storm.

He leads her hand over
the city.
She observes her hand over
the city
like a finger on a jeweled button (the city)
        & in the palm of his other hand—a stolen marriage bed.

Whistling way down below
in the streets, in the canyons between buildings

(*afraid of heights? You can't see, seriously . . . ? The black-crayon twirling descent of
    potency?*)

she watches the world/no, really, just a single congested street—
so small at the tip

of her boot, which is at the fantastic ledge of the building—
the people, like insects & pebbles,

seem to be all in black & every one without their genitals
& also, she thinks, *without the moon,*
                    without collar bones
                    & without the

                    halo (hallow) moon.

                    —HM

Sarah Maclay and Holaday Mason

And I imagined her lying there, alone, in the cathedral, nearly invisible, in the late light of the afternoon, listening to the mad keys of the organist and his kind hair, strewn, streaming across the enlivened air in a kind of mass of curl—and this is wrong—air, hair, wet hair, wet from the playing, as she lay there, lay there before being discovered—and dismissed. She had loved the trees—the metal trees—of Madison Park, and the metal boulder—thought them beautiful—which I only saw at night. But they were terrifying—I thought of my brother, making them, as he could have, welding them together. Tin woods in a forest-park of fall-plucked trees, like an omen: only metal trees—furious, arguing, held together in their mutually branching dance of rage. Siamese trees. And, beyond them, blue light of the Empire State—and the gold, triangular tower—shorter, closer; far behind us now, churches with names like Grace; the Chrysler with its lights—isolated in their knife-like spire—white light flung like broken piano keys.

—SM

Sarah Maclay and Holaday Mason on their process:

The poems in The "She" Series are not co-written but echo many years of close resonance—workshopping and growth in the fellowship of poetry since 1996. The manuscript is a VERY loose call and response—first composed in a kind of dialogue, then spiraling out like a double helix. Many long sections were written with no mutual contact; others in close proximity. Since we live next door, we got into the habit of sealing the poems in envelopes and sliding them through the cracks, or leaving them around, in odd places, to be found—a bit like that May Day ritual: leaving flowers, running away. The most challenging thing: not to workshop them, since that's been our habit, but just to let them co-inspire us.

We both found that while, for us, poetry rarely comes from a conceit, these began to represent the experience of genderlessness in humanity as well as the very gender-specific concerns of women in the middle (presumably) of life, and the strangeness of identity—the oddness of that, over time, in time: the quotations marks around the "She" feel as important as the pronoun. Both the individual works and the collaboration emerged from a deeply intuitive process depending on trust and delight at the unfolding.

Kevin McLellan and Derek Pollard

THE SKY AS VAULT

And now / throughout
this arcade where once
we embraced / the climbing
nightshade chafes
my upturned hands /
strangles the bent iron
arches / leading me to pause

at that moment when
our fingers first traced
the whitewashed stone
rivered with cracks / and I
must wonder if it is true
that we were here
as I have said / and if
it is / I do not know myself

to remember and can
offer you nothing more

Kevin McLellan and Derek Pollard on their process:

We hadn't met prior to being paired on a panel at the Ocean State Summer Writing Conference that was to focus on collaborative writing, so it seemed necessary for us to get to know one another. Together, we wanted to be able to frame our presentation and to address the questions we anticipated receiving. So, we set out to write a single poem, exchanging emails between Massachusetts and New Jersey before meeting in person on the campus of the University of Rhode Island, where the conference is annually held. Over the course of the next several months, and with an unexpected ease between us, that one poem became several.

We would start each poem by one of us providing a few lines of text, something indeterminate but available to further addition and amplification. We set few if any rules outside of allowing one another to alter the evolving poem in whatever ways each of us saw fit. There was no time limit between emails and no previously arranged constraint in terms of line length. We simply passed the poem back and forth when we could and for as long as it seemed the poem required. Perhaps strangely, this led, even when one of us would erase or significantly alter the other's work, to an enthusiastic, supportive exchange in which our own poetics became plural and each poem benefited from our shared vulnerability and daring. It also led to a lasting friendship, that most tender exchange shared between writers and readers.

Erin Mullikin and David Wojciechowski

DEAR 2012,

the stars don't care whether or not we see them.
Nor do the deer who fail to cross our street
in darkness, but rather, wait for our headlights
to illuminate the way to death.
                    Shadows are an impulse of death.
The stars we see have long since burned out,
and our thoughts come from the shadows of ourselves.
Our thoughts, like deer, don't know the way away from the road.
Star-gazing, our thoughts mingle with the rest, and all of our thoughts
become one energy, lighting the way to the river
where our car hits and sinks into the darkness,
a forever stasis, a hummingbird frozen before a red feeder,
heat lightning petrified on the most familiar horizon.

Erin Mullikin and David Wojciechowski on their process:

We're in the same room. That's important to mention. Every poem we've written together begins in the same room. We almost always have a title in mind when we start; we keep a list of titles to pull from whenever we need. This title rarely, perhaps never, makes the final draft. The rest of the process is deceptively simple: we pass a laptop back and forth, adding one line, maybe two or three, as we go, until one us decides the poem has ended. It's usually in that spontaneous ending that we realize what the poem was trying to say. The editing process is done individually. One of us goes through the first draft and might make a few cuts or substitutions, change the form from couplets to prose or from prose to a lineated poem, suggest new titles, etc. Then the other person reads this edited draft and might make a few tinier changes; might not. And so on. Each poem is made in the same room, but it doesn't exist there. It becomes something distinctly not in the room. But the atmosphere of the poem remains, like smoke clinging to the layers of air. And our guides—old cartoons, Gumby reruns, David Bowie's narration of Peter and The Wolf, a few Russell Edson or Vasko Popa poems, the remnants of a Death Door's gin bottle —weave around each poem as if to say the same room the same room the same tomb.

Isobel O'Hare and Sarah Lyn Rogers

THIS IS NOT MY BEAUTIFUL HELL

This is not my beautiful hell
but I don't know whose it is.

Unlike me, the neighbors were not
surprised by your departure.

Here doesn't feel like a place to end
up—more like waiting for a bus

that never comes, lanterns igniting
along the bridge in the light

of the nearly-gone sun, a shadow
parade of humanoid shapes

crossing that threshold. The resonant
hum of your sleep-breath floats

on the bedroom air. A plaster cast
of your face remains on the kitchen

counter, next to the glass cabbage
your great aunt gave as a wedding

present. They warned us that it was bad
Feng Shui. The day you left I found

a fish spine in the hedges;
oracle bones arrived too late.

Looks like you got up to answer
the phone, take out the mail and never

came back, dirty plates, piles of shoes,
books whose pages turn in the wind—

pieces of some other life
held like a breath I can't let out.

Isobel O'Hare and Sarah Lyn Rogers on their process:

We collaborated on this poem through email, beginning by sharing lines from our poetry notebooks with each other as prompts. This felt like swapping pieces of teenage diaries, or finding each other's public-but-still-secret livejournals. I wrote a prose poem based off of lines from Isobel's notebook, and they wrote one based off of lines from my notebook. Next, I mashed together the most resonant lines from each prose poem into one with line breaks. Isobel sent me more notebook prompts, then mashed up my mashup, making two stanzas or two side-by-side poems out of the two different ideas we were working with, which had a similar mood or voice. I saw a throughline there and mashed them into a single poem, borrowing heavily from the way that Isobel paired and ordered and broke the lines, with some rearrangement on my part. The result is an "I" speaker who didn't spring from either of us specifically. I like to think this makes it more universal, like a radio frequency Isobel and I both heard.

Christine Pacyk and Virginia Smith Rice

NOW, WITHIN REACH (WHICH WILL BIND ME)

Just for a moment, melt the hoarfrost from my skin
and make me feel. Make me
a boat quickened in this cool symmetry of sun.

Lift me from the sweet-seeking insects,
~~barbs sticky and caught in hair~~
as they gather honey simply to salvage
and swell their shrunken abdomens.

Make me again:

A girl waiting to be called upon by name.

A girl reminded of her place (crossed legs, stitched lips,
a floral universe of quiet.)

Make me again my body:

The body a backward slide of memory (stiff-soled Mary Janes
scuffing the oak planks of a living room floor.)

The body a flimsy fabric suddenly recognized as a torn sash,
a single shoe in the middle of a road.

The body retreating like a glacier scouring a mountain into valley.

The body shrinking as cornered things do, as ice
retreats in sunlight, face-down in the reeds.

Christine Pacyk and Virginia Smith Rice

THE INTERNET CONFIRMS HOW THEY BROKE DOWN THE DOOR

Cast a planet into an empty well and listen
as it startles the darkness.
Somehow our world feels heavier now.

Gravity tugs on us,
even in sleep, distorting our bodies;
my weight disfigures your flesh.

In the center of the city, centered in a square,
a voice shouts   *You don't belong.*
Who owns those words? Who emptied the well?

To grow old is to walk with no shadow
early one Sunday morning on a dusty street—
at the corner, a stucco building with gray slate,

red awning over the entrance. Inside, you climb
the wooden hill, and in the hall is a blue threshold
you can step over, and leave again.

And cross over. And leave. Cross over.
Leave. Then suddenly, cannot go back.
Door closed, and you on the other side. Yes,

like that: looking up from the street at a rusted
wrought iron balcony, a geranium
freshly watered and draining onto the red canvas,

a dark stain pooling the sidewalk chalk.
Go to the well and seed it with
worlds that invite us in and transform

gravity into tides, oceans, continents.
It goes dark   then winks.
Keep your eye on the star just now emerging,

the morning fog that lifts and holds us,
the women who gather at the well, the woman
who says nothing and engulfs voice in her silence.

Between her fingers,
a tiny gold key.
Her hand a jagged blade.

Christine Pacyk and Virginia Smith Rice

ABOVE THE FROST LINE (A FULL, CLEAR GLASS)

Thank god the world, too, will end.
We slow together, dragging our feet
through clutter and constellations

tangled in endless fine root hairs.
In winter I don't remember myself.
I exist in those paperwhites, maybe,

sprouting on the sill, or in the siskins
at the feeder, the thistle seed, the sterile
terrain swaddling us all. Maybe

to breathe under tiny white stars
is simply to forget the trumpet flute,
how it pales in the fall,

then folds until there is no flush left,
only frost-withered blossoms feigning
resilience in a fortress of thorns.

Christine Pacyk and Virginia Smith Rice on their process:

To begin building collaborative poems, Virginia sends Christine a short poem to imitate (whenever possible, a poem Christine is unfamiliar with). When Christine completes the imitation, Virginia pulls out individual lines from the imitation and adds them to a 'line bank.' She then adds lines of her own to the bank that seem somewhat related to Christine's, and/or writes additional lines. This process is repeated until there are enough lines banked to start building a poem. Virginia typically writes a first draft, and if Christine agrees that the draft seems promising, then the poem is shared and critiqued back and forth until it feels complete. Christine is gifted at writing the initial imitations and Virginia is good at spotting potential connections between lines, so sometimes the roles are flipped, just to keep the process challenging. One of the great benefits of this type of collaboration is that the resulting poems tend to turn in unexpected ways, and end up in surprising places.

Derek Pollard and Shannon Salter

A FLOWER IN JOSHUA'S ARMS

I.

We are nothing to one another but
The brush of fingertip against wrist
Hummingbird arcing across a field of
Columbine, lily in the desert so
Abundant with bloom that the sun itself
Is yet another flower in Joshua's arms

Here, the sky gone all the way over in
To that other valley, where to believe
Our eyes is to have nothing to say and
To continue saying it

                    The Joshua
Verge toward sacrament, and for them we bend
To the earth, to the quick and lasting calm
That meets us just before the eruption
Of noise, the fretwork of the stars bent to
Breaking, the note held, and held still, as the
Train sluices across the desert plain
Robbed of the violence of its own sound
Our voices, too, given up to the myth
We have longed for for so long it has be
Come our testament

II.

Before us
Two sparrows

Chasing the
Last of
The day's
Cold light

The cactus
Spills over
The wall's
Tattooed brick
Its blossoms
At odds
With the
Quick and
Whitewashed dun
The wavering
Splotches of
The city's
Meanest braggadocio

III.

It is true that green is as good as gold
The shadow the needle's end, our way through
These avenues of glass, the wasp's nest whirring
Against the moldering oak beam, the stucco
Chipped in the honeysuckle dead of morning

We are saying everything that we can
Filling the day even as the song escapes

IV.

Which is
That which
Is

V.

Single pinecone lying open on the forest floor
The almost–motion of winter's last insistence

What matters most is this smallest moment

Wind bending the trees and lifting fallen palm
Fronds against the hurricane shutters

The air a sieve of blossom after the cold–tile winter

The grapefruit just beginning to swell in its tree
The ground beneath paving stone and *cul–de–sac*
Another ounce of bullion added to the sinking
Ship, the Jolly Roger the last clear sight against
The darkening horizon

VI.

All morning we wash
Cherries, and yet the
Grit remains untroubled
By our efforts, glad
Of the cottony
Circles we bathe them
In, each to each, each
The same
                    Our attention
An apostrophe
That blesses us under
The sign of the sun
The sign of the Lion
That is e'er moving
Outward

              What we are
Is this and this alone
The first stem to feel
Its seed, the collapse
Of our closest joy
The most joy we have
For one another
Before we know our
Selves in the morning
Light that then comes up
On us

Derek Pollard and Shannon Salter on their process:

When one looks, one begins to see; and when one sees, vision is afoot. Imagination recedes, giving way to a bold, unmitigated experience of the seeing itself. As with Plotinus, as with William Blake, as with John Cage and Ronald Johnson, this is the territory and activity, perhaps even the Eden, of the poem, which is only ever a seeing through, not with, the eye. In the case of "A Flower in Joshua's Arms," the old playground taunt of "four eyes"—one that Derek Pollard remembers from his own early days—could not have been more energetically turned on its head. Would that all of us were so blessed, and all the more so for the fact that the four eyes in question belong to two people, two people who found themselves, however briefly, in accord and able to write their seeing. That the poem holds up as an aesthetic object seems merely to confirm the great promise in people's willingness to engage in open dialogue and in entrusting their vision to one another.

Ethel Rackin and Elizabeth Savage

SILENT E

If once I had seen
a picture of you
little vowel, baby
bougainvillea—

      more petals
than can be swept
print & all the known
stars

*

Those are stars for looking
she once said
and stars for looking out to
too—or as a wave starts
slowly at first, then
faster, first

*

A wave, a looming
ever after
      And some,
even

with a look out
miss the start

*

As ships at sea
on a cold night
become the twist
in a wave
the wringing out
ever after,
the look—

*

Even after
the return—a twist—
look—keeps
wringing darkness
a ship, once
a wave

*

Once seen, a ship star's
lonely, lost
as if the longer
one looks, the brighter
the stare
baby bougainvillea

how I've missed the chance
to see
you star

*

So long
I have looked through
the falling
into brightness
I knew all along
this brilliant mess
our wash of petals
so I roam
the shore deep
with watching

*

And now a watcher
starstruck stood
perched over the shore
in perpetual
brightness—
in the legend of
the look

once seen
if among loomings—
never could I

have pictured

such a twist

starkest print

struck, startled

      Starts

Ethel Rackin and Elizabeth Savage on their process:

Silent e is the name of the feminist press we began planning when we first met in person in 2013. With Ethel in Philadelphia and Elizabeth in West Virginia and considerable teaching loads, the press itself remains an imaginative work in progress, but the poems we have written evolved out of that readiness to encourage poetry that doesn't fit into lyric categories neatly. The poems formed through a call-and-response, back and forth exchange. We took turns starting a sequence, then conversed through the lyrics, revising as we went, often consulting and citing poets suggested to us through one another's lines, like Riding, Stein, Guest, Wordsworth, Oppen, and Shelley. One poem broke that pattern; one of us wrote two responses in a row, but neither of us remembers which one, so we aren't entirely sure about who wrote what in any of the sequences. That's part of the fun: letting go of the need to mark our own poetic territories, finding where our voices meet, watching as our names collide and speak.

Andrea Rogers and Paige Sullivan

from DUETS

ETIOLOGY

In the beginning there was the shell,
and darkness was upon the surface
of the deep. And the man took the shell
from the woman's quivering fingers,
placing it deep inside his pocket.

Now the man said, "Let the shell
lie here upon the nightstand."
And he never told her that he loved her,
but he let her sleep on his side of the bed.
There was evening, and there was morning.

And when the woman woke, the man
did tend her as one belonging to a flock,
a beast, ruminant and moving,
which he felt compelled to feed,
but which he could not comprehend.

And when the woman slept, she dreamt
all beasts, all size and manner of creatures,
but could not describe what she had seen.
Yet she recalled the shell, how the man
had slipped it, like a trophy, from her hand,

and so each night she turned her face toward it
where it lay. And there was evening, mourning,
sharp-edged. Then the woman said, "Let us be softer."
But the man said, "Let the woman be softer, her face
wild with all that is wild in man." And it was so.

And from that night onward, each time the woman
woke, she rolled onto her left side, arm pointing
toward what would be the nightstand of what would be
the man, and looked for the shell. And she saw
that it was good. And she saw that it was gone.

—Andrea Rogers, from *Duets*: Side A

Andrea Rogers and Paige Sullivan

ETIOLOGY

Ekphrasis of My Grandparents' Engagement Photo

They are clearly posed:
the ring only just cresting the joint
to rest above her knuckle,
her fingers calm tendrils
fitting against and around his soft grasp.

Both gaze at indeterminate points
away from each other and the camera,
pensive, her pin curls frizzing,
his coif sharp as the sloping lines
their noses make in profile.

His suit jacket swallows what must be
a slender body, her silk sleeves balloon
at the elbows, cinch at the wrists—more formal
than their uniforms at the pencil factory,
where my grandfather signs her time cards.

He pawned, repurchased, and resold
his best watch to court her, and she would save
two dozen pencils in a Bell Telephone box
to pass down to me: a relic of the bargain,
this negotiation of time, an inheritance.

—Paige Sullivan, from *Duets*: Side B

Andrea Rogers and Paige Sullivan

MOTHER LESSONS

Ekphrasis: Photograph of my Mother on her Honeymoon in Nassau, 1983

Draped in turquoise and white, she doesn't smile,
but holds, over her growing belly, a woven

tote fresh from the straw market.
Could it be a curse was woven in,

the weft housing that warp of dark hands
moving in shadow, tightened with a crooked

finger, then laid to rest in a mounting stack?
My father may have haggled for it there

that very morning, while she stood, as always,
to the side, eyes half-glazed

like a baby at the breast. *A curse,* she thought,
but didn't say it then, and wouldn't now.

For years, the bag sat at the back of her closet
unchanged by time, until, age ten,

I pushed my way through the stacks of old clothes
and reached out to touch that straw curse,

which, post-divorce, she cleanly deposited into my hands—
It's yours, she said, *you can have it now.*

—Andrea Rogers, from *Duets*: Side A

Andrea Rogers and Paige Sullivan

MOTHER LESSONS

The man who exposed himself
     in the Kroger parking lot was unfortunate,
          but you're a beautiful girl. Sometimes

that's just what happens to women. Don't jog
     at night, or alone, or with a ponytail,
          and never, ever with headphones in.

When you approach your car, look under it
     and in the back seat for anyone who could be
          lying in wait. Always leave behind

your tag number and hotel address just so I know
     where you are, you know that I worry, you know
          how much I love you, please be safe.

I wrote the word *cunt* on a napkin to teach you:
     if a man every calls you this in anger, you
          have the right to shove his balls

down his throat. Marriage is only worth it
     if staying makes sense. Be a Wal-Mart greeter,
          be a doctor. I don't care what makes you

happy, just as long as you are. Talk is cheap.
     Reach quietly for someone's hand
          when you try to tell them something.

—Paige Sullivan, from *Duets*: Side B

Andrea Rogers and Paige Sullivan on their process:

This project came into being during a time of shared grief and self-discovery and was created by utilizing a list of potential poem titles that functioned as small writing prompts. While crafting these poems, we did not communicate to each other what we had written, though the overlapping content matter might seem to suggest otherwise. Further, while interrogating issues like trauma, broken relationships, and womanhood, another common theme surfaced: the unhealthy patterns of behavior women observe and inherit from their mothers, particularly in the South.

This collaborative project evolved into a chapbook manuscript titled *Duets*, and we have since performed these pieces for a segment on Atlanta's NPR station and at a variety of live readings in the Southeast. During these readings, we each perform our version of a title, explaining a bit about the history and context of the piece. We perform our versions back-to-back, switching off to create a layered experience for the audience, an effect we also hope to accomplish for readers during their interaction with the text.

Philip Schaefer and Jeff Whitney

PAGAN ERA

And this is how we lucid dream. I click down the empty street in stilettos with
    an axe over my shoulder. You dig blue fingernails into the piano strings of
    my back, chanting *not today*.

A pair of dogs chasing each other tethered to a toothpick on my chest. So small
they fear houseflies the way Tokyo fears Mothra. We are young again, dousing
    every dollhouse

in gasoline, exploring the bendable corners of our plastic gender. Twin birds
    ruffle
hallelujah from the crown of a tree. Twin boys murder their family. We ask the
    same

question: who is responsible for this? And answer. The way Picasso did when
    called
from his home by the fascist inquisitors and asked to explain Guernica—who'd
    been

responsible for it—and he said: you are. Drowned in the faceless thirst for more
of more. In the comma between days a girl with an accordion will burst into
    flame,

become a country with ninety-seven names. We'll hold her ash like asking for
    smoke.
We say the opposite of *over* is *because of*. I'm leaving out the skyscrapers we tear
    down, the fish

we slit open, so many futures inside. When the cowboy was called out to the
    street to fight
I'd like to think he'd been reading Hawking, and could imagine a million
    versions

of himself having that duel—one of him with pockets of bullets but no gun, one
    in cahoots
with a gambler named Desire. One with a pair of hummingbirds tied to the
    toothpick

only he doesn't call them birds and they look more like trash in a child's drawing
of Paradise, the ash of the girl mentioned above, than birds. This is a dream

in a country where any dream is a danger. Believe we're keeping our teeth
on our sleeves, hungry for hearts. This is a new brand of worship. Get on your
    knees.

Philip Schaefer and Jeff Whitney

BOILED NOISE

Instead of aim, fire, repeat, just give me the gold bullet
to swallow. I want to taste its fingerprints, tongue
the story of those who forged this death, trace
their loved one's names along my gum lines.
Instead, I wear the same bored face through the bright
video arcade, sketch the masks of my enemies
on storefront windows and walk away while the sun waxes
them clean. I'm auditioning to be the worst person
in town by not dying and shouting continually
at clouds. To even say anything is to say I've no idea
what. Didn't friend, in Latin, originally mean one
who walks with you to the edge of water and lifts it for you
to drink? Good news, friend. I'm starting a committee
that I think you'll really love. We kiss the charred wrists
of lost gods. We make it count. You know the joke
where you hold up a naked hand with something awful in it
and say look what I almost stepped in? Yes, the heart
is a sofa licked by flame, wood cutout of a splintered
bison. There are moments that moments have. Silences
between thunder only mice can track. The quiet clown
undressing in a parking lot. I too want to remember
what it was like to breathe arsenic. For the ones who loved me
most to be a row of bones under an overgrown hill. Maybe
I'll make my bed there, sleep with thorns in my mouth,
whisper rumors of war and ruin, let them know I'm alive

begging not to be, beating the earth like whale skin,
hot metal, anything strong enough to echo me back.
I only want to hold a sea horse's heart until its little song
stops, held in a fire no bigger than a period on this page.

Philip Schaefer and Jeff Whitney

TANTRUM PARTY

I'm mapping out a list of all the people who no longer speak to me. Each
    morning
I fingerpaint a new face on the wall, my own private hallway of mug shots. I
    place my ear

like a stethoscope to their chests. Pretend to tongue out their eyes. Sometimes
    it's hard
to be this close to loss. To know I'm only haunting myself. But their mouths are
    beautiful

green birds that turn their silence into language, their hate to envy. Some day
    I'll be one
of those people who orders bibles just to have someone to talk to. Whatever it is
    I am ready

to believe almost everything. That duck shadows are bombers, that my
    grandfather fell
from the roof singing. That he never spent a night reading the newspaper,
    changing every noun

to "marble." That the bees aren't busy dying slowly as a strip mall. Let's say it was
    my fault,
that I never listened close enough. That my hot air balloon head finally caught
    fire. That

at night, when the attic drains its ghosts and the linoleum pools a hundred
  moons,
you are able to talk back. Your cursive lights up the room like airplane smoke,
  your hair

a new kind of Ouija. I've given you the voice you never wanted.
These are my hands, this is my bucket of black paint.

Philip Schaefer and Jeff Whitney on their process:

Jeff & Philip met in Missoula a few years back when Jeff was having an apartment garage sale before moving to South Korea to teach. He'd just finished up his MFA, and Philip was just beginning his. Philip left with wool socks, two copies of Jeff's new chapbook, and a future friendship and partnership neither of them knew would unfold.

After reading Jeff's chapbook, Philip reached out, and the poem exchange began. They quickly realized how similar their interests and voices were, while still retaining individuality. The collaborations began by pairing poems from one writer with poems from the other. Then the poems became more fused, stanzas and chunks and lines from one would sandwich stanzas and chunks and lines from the other. As the years went on, even they couldn't always remember who wrote which line or made the decision to reformat a prose block into couplets. A third voice took over, and it's where they found the most success in letting go, in trusting the process no matter where it took them.

Martha Silano and Molly Tenenbaum

LIKE A SMALL WOODEN DOLL, THREE WOODEN BALLS STACKED UP

Said my three-year-old, falling into sleep, God is a dinosaur,
his thoughts compartments in compartments
like boats. We can fold the end of the alphabet

back to the beginning. We can swivel a creature
of the cretaceous into a *goddamn it* deity,
tuck ourselves in the mechanics, grow to five feet.

Say the word *garden*. Say it while your hair falls out
like a grandmother's dentures. Say error, crack, fault.
The bruise in the fruit while insects gnaw

the tortoise-shell binding off the veneer,
while cascading eyes storm the air. Go pick dill
because [blank needs to go here, the driest, most absent

language] nothing moves but a housefly
rubbing its miserly front legs. Because terminal
equals connection, she was dying, the cures buzzing, seeking

a knob on a black-and-white TV. Because mother didn't
want me to switch my flight [now shine it to work better].
My son who had been in her arms, not

quite crawling. Happy as an equation, happy
as an abstraction. His first plane ride, her last breaths.
Blinking, making *b* sounds in the buffer zone,

revving up to roll over, while my grandmother's body
loaded in the back of a pick-up, revving up
to crawl into a tube, emerge from the smallest opening.

Can almost see the tops of trees. The picnic waits;
ticks crawl up your legs. In the nick of time,
we say, cut on a stick. A kind of zero, a counting

like inadvertent clocks. I would choose
parsley. Parsley with its humanoid roots,
arthritic fingers, but asked me to fetch dill,

a bottle of pills. It was imprecise, didn't come
with a toolkit. There was no face. But engines,
their lift and thrust, doing the laundry, cooling off

the house. The distance between us and the brass shine
from the orchestra pit, the headwaters and the white dress.
A physics problem, a lesson in angles, in scent.

Martha Silano and Molly Tenenbaum

MY FATHER'S BODY, LAID IN THE GRAVE

Ormolu moth, melted man. Sourish oils
lamb at the sweaters of youth—
pet them like memorial programs,
rolled menus of biographers and buns.
Numb my bytes: unbeen. Dirt shirt up and tied.
Yum, he sips like a bee, like an enemy,
says Say, take my imaginary *the*,
my laminae all ant aeration.

Who the soloist, who the omission?
Methyl noun. Aim my mumblebone atoms
at mothballs. The Armagnac can fend
for itself. Make of me a tomb, an I.
Humanely beetle me. Belt me
fifty bow-ties, a drawer of rubles.

Martha Silano and Molly Tenenbaum on their process:

To compose "Like a Small Wooden Doll, Three Wooden Balls Stacked Up," we scheduled a Facetime date wherein I read a line of Wislawa Szymborska's "Prologue to a Comedy," then paused for two minutes while we both free wrote off the line. We did this line by line to the end of the poem. Next, we worked separately, revising our individual results of writing "off" the Szymborska poem. The next step was for Molly to send me her draft, so I could smoosh it together with mine. Finally, we sent the combined draft back and forth, continuing to revise until it felt finished. For the sonnet, "My Father's Body, Laid in the Grave" we each wrote seven lines, and the only rule was that Martha's lines had to contain some words made of the letters of Molly's full name, and Molly's lines had to contain some words made of the letters of Martha's full name. Martha then sent Molly her lines, and Molly took her seven lines and mixed them in with Martha's to make a first draft. Then we sent it back and forth.

Wikipoesis

[THE BODY'S POLITIC]

the body's politic
's more than souls—

[*spoiler alert—here be metaphor*]
[*TFW you've found over-much*]

I was not awake & I,
I was not unsurprised.

I'd heard the words darked-up
and, like I, exasperated.

as if your rants were matter
as if you'd been enough.

o, nothing's unfuckwithable.

'cause, reasons.
'cause, finding's over-rated.

'cause fanfic's always the best fic.

Wikipoesis

[WE TOOK TO EACH OTHER.]

We took to each other. Took time,
took what offered itself, I recall.

You, deep-veined. Me, unlettered.
& the storm came in quickly.

O, TFW you unlike the brimming fanciful.
Like, once our bodies knew what we'd become—

tangles of smoked-glass skin, stretched desire,
& weary, we slept the fever back & dreamt.

You didn't what you couldn't & I hated you for it.

Wikipoesis on their process:

Tell this to your children. Wikipoesis was born continuous, born besotted. Wikipoesis decamped what comes before & Wikipoesis happened here. Wikipoesis wounds that which enters unopposed, displaced and stumbling. Around the ever-confessional remember-mouths, Wikipoesis is the purple mass bloomed and the tongue become tourniquet, a harp-hearted osteotome. Ruing the underside of this commitment, Wikipoesis will sully it good. Wikipoesis keeps and what deigns be kept. Wikipoesis is *The fuck you say?* A snake eating a snake eating its own tail. Wikipoesis shills for words-a-blinding. Wikipoesis will unfist the line, O, charming boy-girl. The trick is to watch without staring.

FICTION

Nin Andrews and Mary Beth Shaffer

SLEEPING BEAUTY

It was an afternoon in the third grade when I first decided to play sick. The school nurse told me to lie down on the green Naugahyde couch and put my head on the square pillow with a white paper cover that crunched whenever I moved my head. She unfolded the brown blanket and dropped it over my feet, my legs, my arms and up to my chin. It was softer than it looked. But still I could feel it rub against the goosebumps on my arm, which popped up when I thought I might be found out. It was easier to fake sick than I'd guessed. The nurse touched my arm and asked if I felt chilled. She spoke in a gentle voice as if I were as fragile as blown glass. At first I was restless, scissoring my legs beneath the blanket, but then I surprised myself by falling asleep on the couch, despite the phone ringing and the parade of children coming in for Band-Aids, each staring intently at me, lying prone on the couch. It was my falling asleep that convinced everyone there must be something wrong.

That night I took comfort in my parents' worry, their coddling me with hot tea and a warm bath, speaking in hushed tones as if they were in church. I didn't want the hot tea. It was easy to refuse weakly. I let myself be guided out of the tub. When my mother touched my forehead, ever so gently, I felt a light travel down my spine and out from her fingertips. It was wonderful really. "My little Greta, my smart little Greta," my mother sighed over and over, her blue eyes rimmed with red. My mother loved to call me smart, as if it were an incantation or a prayer, as if it were the forecast that everyone needed to know. Or her wish for me to be smarter than I was. But what if I wasn't? Shivering, I snuggled under the covers. I felt warm and safe, listening as she read fairy tales in the rocking chair beneath the lamp: Snow White and Sleeping Beauty, my favorites. I wondered if the poisoned princesses dreamt when they slept for all those years. As I drifted off, I knew why they never wanted to wake up.

Nin Andrews and Mary Beth Shaffer on their process:

After graduating from the Vermont College MFA program in 1995, Mary Beth Shaffer and Nin Andrews collaborated on a series of poems including "Sleeping Beauty," about a girl who was afraid of living in the world and who preferred to stay in bed and dream. As writers they both believe there is a distance needed between the creation of a piece of writing and its completion. By passing their work back and forth, such a distance became a natural part of their writing process.

Tina Jenkins Bell, Janice Tuck Lively, and Felicia Madlock

LOOKING FOR THE GOOD BOY YUMMY

I.

"He just wanted love." For that, he could be disarmingly kind. "He'd say thank you, excuse me, pardon me." He loved animals and basketball and had a way with bicycles. He once even merged two bikes into a single, working tandem. Those were the good times but…"
—A Neighbor

"It always meant trouble when he was with a group. If he was alone, he was sweet as jelly."
—Ollie Jones-Edwards, 54, Neighbor

What of fatherless
Boys, who get their manhood from
Hood-life theatrics.

Nobody taught me to shoot a gun. They just gave me a Nine and told me to show them how BD I could be. Shit, first thing I thought was you can't get mo' down for BD than me. I done stole from strangers, from neighbors, all cause I love 'em. They my folks. My family. My mama. My daddy. My sister. My brother. My everything. I wasn't gon' disappoint 'em! They was mine to protect. That's why I shook up ol' boy, got his nerve coming on my block with no connections.

"Bruh, you BD?" I said. That fool looked down at me like I was some kid.

"Nah shorty. I ain't in no gang." Rolling his eyes, he turned back to conversating with his crew, disrespecting my manhood. I couldn't have that. Decided set or no set, he wasn't BD. I pulled my Nine from my waistband and started shooting 'til I saw old dude get got. Watching him fall slow-mo like that gave me a feeling I ain't never had before. Like playing cowboys and Indians and watching 'em fall with each jerk of my finger. Power, rushing from my fingers, to my brain and back. I was the Man now. No bad ass kid from round the way. No dirty little boy from over to Janie's. No *thing* to be picked up and filed in some other cold place. Naa! I had to show 'em. Least that's what I was thinking when I ran round the block, my Nine spitting bullets this way and that, watching them fools fall. Nobody wanted

Yummy when I was playing with Matchbox cars, dancing like Michael, and wolf-ing down cookies. Nobody cared when I stole Mama J's good knife to scratch BD, six-point stars, and *"On David"*, large as life, on my bedroom door, right by my Michael Jordan poster. All them times, nobody saw or wanted me until now.

II

Shavon Latrice Dean was laid to rest Friday. The 14-year-old girl who dreamed of becoming a hairstylist was killed Sunday night, just yards from her home when she walked into the path of a bullet… The death stunned the city, especially when police announced that the suspected killer was an 11-year-old neighborhood boy, Robert Sandifer.

—Jerry Thomas, Staff Writer ("For 14-year old Shavon, Peace Comes in a White Casket," *Chicago Tribune*)

> *Mama hurt herself*
> *Then me, just a boy searching*
> *For identity.*

Rina, my real mama, was on the stroll about the time the trouble started. She was never round no way. Mama J called her *good for nothing* on account of all Rina's kids lived with somebody else most times, but I loved Rina, even when she burned me. I loved her cause she was all I had for a real mama. Rina couldn't help herself, let alone me. Couldn't go back to Mama J's house cause 5-0 was watching, accord-ing to "K". So, I ended up bouncing round from one homie's place to another 'til they said I was too hot to stay with them. They found me this empty spot, not far from Grandma's, not far from my room where my posters of Michael Jordan, Michael Jackson, and the Tasmanian Devil were. They told me I just needed to hide for this last night 'til they could get me someplace safe. Someplace safe? Before this, anyplace in the 100s was mine to rule 'cause I was down with BD. All I had to do was pull the trigger… they'd take care of the rest, they said. Well, I proved myself. I just thought things would be different after I did. Thought there'd be grins, pats on the back, trips to the Nike Store, maybe a swing set out back of Mama J's for my sisters and brothers. Thought I'd be the man Mama J needed and BD wanted, not hiding out in this dark, stank building where a scurrying rat even stopped to size me up. Had to dump my Nine in the alley not far from where those fools fell and didn't get up. Without protection. I darted at his ass, stomping my foot to let him know I meant business. Rat ran like the bitch he was. In the 100s, we put down rats for practice... Rats and snitches.

Cool air seeped under the busted wooden door that closed but didn't lock. I pulled my jacket tighter, listening to my teeth chatter, night things moan and sirens whine. I wasn't feelin' like a man no mo'. I wanted my grandma, even though "K" told me not to trust her.

"She don't love you, man. If she did they wouldn't a taken you from her to send you to that home on the north side. Stay away from her. She'll just turn you in to 5-o," K had said after I called him on my homie's cell. "Just lay low, son. We got you. Trust that."

I didn't feel his trust, so I booked it to the pay phone on the side of the currency exchange on 95th Street. I called four times, but didn't say a word. The fifth time, I rustled up some nerves.

"Mama!"

"Yummy?"

"I didn't kill no girl, like they saying."

"I know, baby. You ain't did nothing wrong. You need to tell 'em that. You ain't done nothing wrong!"

"Why they lookin' for me? I ain't got nothin' to say. Just wanna come home." Feet pounded the sidewalk. I jumped, dropping the phone. Scared. Not sure of who, just scared. "Mama, help me, please."

"Baby, I'm on my way. Just tell me where." Her voice was tired.

I wanted to wait, but 5-o pulled up on these fools in a stolen car. Couldn't have them spot me and take me in, so I bounced, still trying to get to Mama J, still tryin' to get back home, even if most times I didn't like what happened there.

Running into the night. No moon above me. Just Blackness. Like the night I was born, March 12, 1983, year of the Pig, if Mama J is telling the truth. Mama J was real mad when she'd said, "The day Rina birthed you, even the moon and the stars hid. Should have known you wouldn't be worth a plug nickel, not worth the pain it took to get nor keep you here."

Maybe she was right 'cause pain and fear was double-teaming my ass until I ran into two folks sent to save me. I felt my slumped shoulders rear back with the certainty my boys weren't the bogus bitches Rina and Mama J said they was.

Born on moonless night.
Zodiac pig put down with
Two shots to the head.

III

Police found Yummy "lying on dirt and bits of glass" under the viaduct on 108th and Dauphin Avenue. He wore a green and gray sweat shirt with the Tasmanian Devil cartoon on front, green denim jeans, gym shoes, and a purple plaid jacket.
—Police Report excerpt

Alma Dixon kept the venetian blinds hanging at her window closed to block out the view of her neighborhood. But this evening, she stood at the window peering through the metal slats at the assembly in the yard across the street from her house. As she watched Robert's grandmother impaling candles, then lighting them, into the barren plot of earth that was their front yard, the only word that came to her mind was, "Circus." His grandmother, in her glittering gold blouse, straw hat, too tight white spandex pants, and high-heeled shoes, was bathed in a spotlight of flashing cameras and video floodlights against the evening sky. Moving and bending from candle to candle, she talked to the white news reporters and curious onlookers gathered around her fence about her grandson—how much she loved him and how he was a good boy no matter what people were saying about him. Alma's eyes rested on the bewildered faces of the other small children in the yard, Robert's brothers, sisters, cousins. "A damn circus," she said, and yanked the blinds shut.

Alma walked over to her rocking chair and sat in the darkness. *It's been going on for three days now,* she thought. It started on Sunday when that little girl was killed and those boys were wounded, got worse later that evening when they started looking for Robert because someone said he was the one that shot them. Now reporters and strangers all over the place, police cars with blue lights flashing rushing through the streets and prowling the neighborhood, police knocking on doors and asking questions. Two policemen had come to her door Sunday evening.

"Excuse me, Miss, we're looking for this boy." The policeman handed her a picture of Robert. His mug shot. "They call him Yummy. Have you seen him, Ma'am?"

She had stared at the boy in the photo with the corn-rowed hair, non-descript white tee-shirt, angry dark eyes, and said, "I don't know nobody named Yummy," then handed it back to him.

The officer persisted. "But he lives across the street from you. You must know him."

"I don't know any Yummy."

The other officer handed her the picture again. "Can you take another look, Ma'am? Name's Robert Sandifer. We need to find him. He may have been involved in a shooting."

Alma looked. Reconsidering them, the dark-brown eyes looked more sad than angry. "I don't know any Yummy, but I saw Robert walking down the street early this morning. He was headed in the direction of the gas station. I haven't seen him since then." She gave the picture back and closed her door.

That had been two days ago. They found him. Dead. She took a deep breath and pushed back the tears. She had always hated that name, Yummy. Everyone else thought it was cute. She didn't. It sounded too greedy, like someone who was constantly hungry, who didn't have enough and couldn't get enough. Not enough food, not enough space, not enough attention, not enough love. Another deep breath. The day Robert's people moved on the block the whole neighborhood knew they were trouble. There was too many of them for that little house. Sometimes, there was forty of them, mostly children, living in there. No husbands or fathers, just a whole lot of women and children. You can't have no decent life with that many folks piled on top of each other and only three bedrooms. Her neighbors called them dirty, nasty, noisy, and some other names. The block club had started a petition to get rid of them. Alma laughed, it hadn't worked. She had planned to sign the petition until she saw the boy.

She heard the name before she saw him. Had heard it being screamed through the house by the adults, "Yummy get your little ass over here," laughed in the yard by his siblings and cousins as they played, "Yummy what you get a whipping for," whispered by others in the neighborhood who he had beaten up or stolen from, "I know it was that little son-of-a-bitch Yummy that broke in my car." Yummy. *Who or what was a Yummy*, she had thought.

He was standing on the street across from the corner grocery store leaning on a pole, a little brown thing about 4'7" no more than 87 pounds.

As she passed, he said, "Excuse me, can you get me a Snicker's while you in the store?"

She had looked down at the outstretched dirty palm that cradled the three quarters. "Why can't you go in there and get it yourself since you got money?"

"I ain't allowed in there." He kept his eyes fixed on the ground.

"Why?"

"I don't know. He just say I cain't come in his store no mo'."

Alma looked at him and laughed. "I think you do. Henry Morgan loves money and anybody that's got some is welcome in his store except thieves and trouble-makers. Which one are you?" He didn't answer, just shoved his money back in his pocket and went back to the pole. When she came out, she handed him the candy bar. A smile consumed his face.

"Thank you," he whispered.

"You're welcome, but you got to earn it." She handed him her two grocery bags. "You gonna carry these home for me."

"Yes Ma'am." He grabbed the bags, "They ain't even heavy."

She could have carried them but giving the boy a chore was good for him. As they walked, they talked about how he loved fishing—she did too—why he didn't like school, how much he liked cars, and making things. When they reached her house, she asked him his name.

He shyly said, "Yummy."

"That's not your name. That's some fool name folks gave you for some crazy reason. What's your real name? The name you got when you was born."

"Robert." The sound of it seemed foreign to his ears.

"That's a fine name. It's strong." Alma had smiled and looked straight in those sad eyes. "Do you know what it means?" He had shaken his head.

"The name Robert means 'famed, bright, shining,'" His eyes glowed.

"How you know that's what it means?"

"I have a book with names in it. I'll show it to you sometime. That's your name and that's who you are. You hear me?" He had nodded. Suddenly they heard some-one from across the street calling him.

"Yummy!"

"You better go. I'll see you later, Robert."

"Yes Ma'am." He had laughed then ran across the street.

He would often come back to her porch when he was looking for a quiet place. The noise outside was fading. Alma had hoped they would find him, alive. She had wanted to care for him, teach him who he was, save him from this place. She got up from the chair. It was time to go to bed. She looked over at the window one more time and didn't breathe back the tears. When they killed Yummy, they had killed Robert, too.

Dreams deferred. Real life
Converged. Posters of Disney
Next to six point stars.

IV

"You really can't describe how bad he really was. He'd curse you completely out... broke in school, took money, burned cars."
—Erica Williams, Neighbor (*Time Magazine*, "Murder in Miniature")

"If ever there was a case where the kid's future was predictable, it was this case..."
—Patrick Murphy (Cook County Public Guardian)

"What you've got here is a kid who was made and turned into a sociopath by the time he was three years old."
—A Social Worker

Lisa King couldn't digest the newspaper headline without butterflies sprouting in her stomach: "*So Young to Kill, So Young to Die.*" This was one of those days she hated being a social worker. Her thoughts shifted from the disturbing headline to her infant son resting comfortably in the next room; anxious thoughts flooded her mind, her heart palpitated: Stress. Her doctor recently warned about her deteriorating health: hair loss, added weight on an already obese frame. Her eating habits were horrible. She reached for her Pepsi and O-Ke-Doke popcorn; a healthy selection for dinner. They comforted her as she wrestled with the rising guilt; her 11-year-old client had been murdered. An 11-year-old kid executed, but he was not a normal 11-year-old despite what his mother said. He murdered an innocent girl, had a rap sheet taller than his 4'7" frame, dropped out of school at age eight, stole people's property and caused destruction. Some people called him a monster. Lisa agreed.

Lisa read further, unable to pry herself away. Anger simmered to rage as she remembered her countless attempts to talk to Robert about his criminal behaviors. The pep talks about his life to scare him straight. "Keep walking this path, you will not live to be 18 years old." The placement in special programs he didn't show up for. Interventions with his un-cooperating family. She had driven around looking for him when he was reported "missing," praying that he would be found safe. He died at 11 years old, and she couldn't scream when she heard about his execution on the news. His death would be followed with other causalities that would not be mentioned in the newspaper.

"I can't lose my job over this. I need childcare and..." Lisa stopped midsentence to allow the tears to flow. The reality was that Robert Sandifer's case would be scrutinized by her agency and the Inspector General's Office, his case file examined with a fine-tooth comb. They will question if she had done enough to provide "adequate services." Lisa's supervisor, who also had a family to feed, will not be her advocate because her job will be analyzed as well. Everyone connected to Robert Sandifer will pay a price. It wasn't fair. The media will place blame on the social service agency, stating that he slipped through the cracks. Lisa cringed as she thought about the laundry list of repercussions. "IT'S NOT SOCIETY'S, NOR THE JUVENILE JUSTICE SYSTEM'S, NOR THE SCHOOL SYSTEM'S FAULT," she yelled. She flung the article in the garbage can, and whispered in defeat, "It's not my fault. I tried. Tried my damnedest with every Yummy they send my way."

Lisa reached into the refrigerator for the hot sauce that she poured generously over her cheese popcorn before slumping into a nearby chair.

> *Sand boy sifts from home,*
> *To harm, to nowhere. Seeking love,*
> *Finding crown of thorns.*

Works Cited

Gibbs, N. R. (1994, September 19). Murder in Miniature. Retrieved from http://content.time.com

Thomas, J. (1994, September 3). For 14-year old Shavon, Peace Comes in a White Casket. Retrieved from http://chicagotribune.com

N. (2014, March 9). The Forgotten Story of Robert "Yummy" Sandifer. Retrieved from https://newafrikan77.wordpress.com

Tina Jenkins Bell, Janice Tuck Lively, and Felicia Madlock on their process:

As mothers living in the Greater Chicago area, we are empathetic to other mothers losing their children, specifically their sons, to gun violence. For this project, we brainstormed on topics that would give readers an internal look at the multiple tragedies prevalent in one child's death. Robert "Yummy" Sandifer's story immediately captivated each of us. We chose to tell Yummy's story in the form of a hybrid comprised of fiction, non-fiction, and poetry because so much had been said about him and each form would reflect a different view. We believed the true Yummy was somewhere in the center of all the accounts. We then took the following steps:

We studied other hybrids for a possible structure and individually researched Yummy's life, perusing mug shots, obituaries, news stories, documentaries, and analyses by police officers, social workers, and neighbors. These non-fiction sources served as the "facts" about Yummy and informed our fictionalized accounts. We discussed what we had learned about Yummy and decided who would be the best characters to tell the story of his betrayal then each took a character. The fiction would be presented from two perspectives with Yummy being first person and the neighbor and social worker being in third.

Where to begin the story was a challenge. We considered beginning after Yummy's death, having his ghost narrate the story or beginning with his early years showing what shaped him into a 11-year-old murderer. We finally decided to begin at the point of greatest tension, after Yummy had committed the murder and was running from the police and his fellow gang members. We merged our collective fiction and prose to create a timeline of the murderer Yummy's last hours while providing a glimpse into the 11-year-old's life. We continually revised to achieve a seamless piece. Haikus were inserted last, serving as communal dirges lamenting Yummy's death. The non-fiction facts and haikus were bookends to the imagined "what ifs" of Yummy's life.

Elizabeth J. Colen and Carol Guess

TRUE ASH

If trees could talk, you said. If they could tell us what they saw.

But if you didn't want to talk about it, why would a tree?

We walked in the arboretum as if nothing had happened. Past Japanese Maples, Witch Hazels, Legumes. Through Pinetum and across the stone footbridge. The math of it, was what you said.

We stopped to eat among Hollies and Hawthorns. When you sliced an apple, the red cored curl made me want to ask questions. The thing that had happened was unlikely to happen again, but you needed to be sure, so you carried a knife. You wanted me to carry one, too, but I was clumsy and sometimes fell. Even in the arboretum I liked to wear heels, the kind most women wear at night. It felt safer to wear heels during the day. At night I wore flats, shoes that could run.

When we got back to your apartment, I always cleaned the bottom of my heels with a paper towel. I did this sitting on the floor in my skirt, and sometimes you watched, lifting my hem. After a while I stopped wearing anything underneath my skirt and our walks got shorter.

There was nothing unusual about them, you said.

Who? I asked. We were eating dinner at your place.

The couple, you said. In the arboretum. The couple I saw in True Ashes that day.

I thought you said it happened in Hollies.

God no, you said. Nothing like that.

I sprinkled salt on my salad. Sometimes I ate salty things and sometimes sweet, but never at once. You claimed you couldn't tell salt and sugar apart. But you said that about a lot of things.

I thought about all the couples I'd seen walking in the Arboretum. How the woman sometimes bent into the man as if she couldn't walk on her own. How the man explained the names of trees while she extended her branches.

We're not like that, you said.

But what did you mean?

I wanted to ask what it was that you'd seen. I'd avoided the news for a week after that. You saw it first, from the outside, a stranger. On the cusp of True Ashes, and who knew what they saw.

Maybe trees bend toward us on purpose.

Sunlight, you said. The science of roots.

But maybe it's more. Maybe they feel things.

Would you stop eating plants if you knew what they felt?

I didn't answer, just rubbed my ring across my wrist.

You lifted my hem. Bunched my skirt around my waist and straddled me. My shoes and hands were dirty, but you wanted my mouth, so it didn't matter.

The couple, I asked. What was she wearing?

Did I mention a woman?

I assumed they were straight.

You smirked.

So it was two men. Or two women? Who else could it be, walking in pairs?

\#

The next morning you went to work and I worked from your apartment. It was part of our agreement to trade. Sometimes your upstairs neighbor played music, pot smoke drifting down through the vents.

At noon I walked to the corner store for a sandwich. While I was browsing I noticed a pack of bubblegum cigarettes. I hadn't seen that kind of candy in years. Something about advertising smoking to children.

Can I have these for half? I asked.

The clerk looked at the date on the faded pink wrapper.

Just take them. We don't even carry those here.

I put the pack in my pocket. Bought coffee and a loaf of bread. Walked from the store to the arboretum. Scattered bread, waited for birds.

They swooped down from the sky to land at my feet.

If you would wait. If you would stand very still.

When you came home that night you asked if I'd gone to the arboretum.

Why do you ask?

Because of the dirt.

It was true. I'd tracked dirt through the kitchen. In the movies you liked, girls licked the floor clean.

I scrubbed with a towel while you uncorked a bottle. Then you poured two glasses and we sat on the couch.

#

In the morning you were gone again. I couldn't remember the kiss, if there had been one, how long, mouths open or closed. All I was left with was the dream, but no one wants to hear about that. Everything the color raw umber, everything shaded and drawn. I went looking again.

I liked that the woods had a name here. Arboretum. Sometimes I got glossolalic about it. Sometimes it turned into other things. Our bore eat them. Arrr burr, arrr boar. Eee tomb. A tomb.

What had you seen? I texted you all day. And followed couples. Took pictures while their backs were turned. Them? I texted, with photo. Them? To the pictures you offered no response. Only: stop that. You'll get yourself in trouble. So I stopped that. Was someone taking pictures, I asked. No. Was someone hurt. No. Was there blood. Absolutely not. Well what was it. I took a picture of the sky and you told me: closer. And then the day was filled with meetings, you with your people, me with the trees. Near noon I looked at my watch to see if I could be hungry. The stippled light made my wrist look bark-like just for a second. Then a crow chattered and I was me again.

Did you work today, you asked when you got home. I told you I tried to, but you didn't know what that meant. You took off your shoes and all I could think was that your feet were ugly, but that I liked all of the ugly in you. At ten, like always, you held my wrists behind me and pushed me up against the stove. I liked my hands on you, but you liked them behind me. No, you told me when I tried to get free. That's not how this is going to be. Your face was full of drink and I went stiff until you quit.

What did you see?

What?

What did you see?

But you were out, snoring, sawing zees. I put on the noise machine, turned it to birds and mapped out the park in my head. Everything green, but the ashes were glowing.

#

I went to see my mother in Auburn and sat so long watching talk shows I couldn't get up from the chair. She was talking about men with red hair again.

Why always this I didn't know. And hats. Cloche and fedora, schoolboy and beret. At least it wasn't the shadows. Sometimes she saw people who weren't there. Sometimes my father. Sometimes another one of me. Was I a twin, I started to wonder. I tried to pay attention. Ginger, she said. Ginger? Ginger, their hair. I hit my legs, but they were wooden. I hit them again; they softened a bit. My legs felt filled with water. I felt I could spread out again.

You called to tell me not to come home, that you would be late anyway. I thought it was good to be out in the sun, or, the light like flame on the carpet from the skylight. I let it lead me around the room. I stretched out in it, lifted my face to it. Is it strange, I thought and then texted, that I swear I can feel my hair grow. You never responded. Just two words to say goodnight: sleep well.

\#

What did you see?
What?
What did you see?
Are we back to this again?
Out of the corner of my eye I saw an axe in your hand, but it was just the chain and you led me around, or it was just your two rings catching the light.

Come here, you told me. And I did as you said. I started to touch your face, but you said it tickled. In the lamplight you looked a little green. I couldn't see myself in you.

Close your eyes, you told me. And I was sure I'd never open them again, so I didn't.

Count to ten, you said. But I didn't.

On the bed, you told me. And that wasn't a question. My knees went out from under me. But you changed your mind.

Open your eyes. But they were already open.

On your feet. They felt out of control. I put on my heels.

Out the door. You may as well have collared and leashed me.

I was in front of you all the way, you giving directions. Right at the Hollies, left at the Dogwoods, straight through the copse of Magnolia. They smelled sticky and sweet. Dead blooms blackened underfoot.

Don't turn around, you told me. But I wouldn't have thought of it. Don't speak. I said nothing.

Into the stand of True Ash my heels sank slow as you stopped me. My toes found soil, that damp cold, and began to tunnel down. My legs were striated and hard, hard husk, a cortex, a casing, outer shell. My head felt light and the wind began to move through me. You kissed my shoulder, hand heavy at the back of my neck. You got me down on my knees, but that wasn't low enough. I disappeared in the leaves.

Elizabeth J. Colen and Carol Guess on their process:

Trees bear witness to things people are unable to talk about, excess buried in (what) leaves. Art bears witness to the weight of what's unsaid, and as collaborators, we challenge each other to be braver than our characters.

Sometimes a story serves as an emotional parallel. Sometimes characters have minds of their own. Sometimes the match won't light and sometimes one strike burns miles of green.

In the end, we loved this story so much we built a book around its mystery, still unsolved, still burning.

Dana Diehl and Melissa Goodrich

THE CLASSROOM BENEATH OUR CLASSROOM

Sometimes in the gaps between lessons, those rare moments when no one is whispering or coughing or tapping their marker against the desk leg or humming without knowing it or sharpening their pencil, we hear them. The classroom beneath our classroom.

The classroom beneath our classroom is better behaved than we are. We hear them reciting their times tables in unison, no voice hollering above the rest, no voice speaking a beat out of sync. In the morning they say the Pledge, and they sound like they mean it—not mean, half sarcastic, like we do.

+

Our classroom is on the ground floor, so there shouldn't be a classroom beneath our classroom, and yet there is. The students' voices rise up through the pipes, through the vents. Sometimes when we're doing jumping jacks to test our heart rate, or when the teacher's back is turned and we're testing our limits, seeing how loud we can get before she quiets us, we hear a rapping against the floor—a quick staccato—and we all freeze, imagining the wood of a ruler *slap slap slapping*. Sometimes instead of a slapping it's a thump, a broomstick sound, or the *whack* of the students all closing their books together, loudly.

When it happens, we look down.

I can hear you, it says, that slam below us. *I know exactly what you're up to.*

Sometimes our teacher threatens us with the classroom beneath our classroom. She says, "You think you have it hard with me. I ought to send you to *her* classroom. Then you'll really miss me. Then you'll realize how easy you have it."

We ask if she's ever met the teacher in the classroom beneath our classroom, and she tells us to put our feet on the floor, that there's only two minutes of class yet, that we've lost recess time.

If one of us is misbehaving she'll say, "I'm this close to asking you to leave my classroom. If you can't handle being a fourth grader today, I'll send you downstairs."

Sometimes we feel guilty for being the class that we are. The class that invokes exasperated looks between teachers in the hallways. The class that gets the field trip to the county jail instead of the zoo. The class that teachers swear prompted Mrs. Philips in the second grade to have a stroke when she had us last January.

But other times we love to be that class. Love to be the class that started a petition to stop Miss Thomas from wearing purple eye shadow on Mondays. The class that had a water bottle of vodka hidden under the slide in the playground for a whole month before one of the monitors discovered it. Love to be the class that spits, that hollers, that isn't afraid when a teacher says they're disappointed in us. Love watching that split, like watching a seam come loose, when a teacher gives up on us, gives in, just lets us jump chair to chair or punch each other in the throat, who resigns herself to her desk, behind her computer, rubbing her temples, where she belongs.

+

On the playground, we try to identify the kids from the classroom beneath the classroom. We expect them to be paler than us, part mole creature. We expect them to have inhalers in their pockets and pencil pouches containing only sharpened pencils. We expect them to have hair parted down the middle and T-shirts with the tags carefully clipped off so they're never in danger of popping out.

We find kids who we think fit the description. But they are all friends of our siblings, or neighbors, or kids we know from a different year. No one's heard of the students that learn beneath.

We think about how we've seen the staircase that goes upstairs, but never the staircase that goes downstairs. One day we get curious and look for the downstairs staircase that must exist somewhere between our classroom and the front office. We feel the floors with our hands, for a loose tile, a trapdoor. We stage a food-fight and get the boys in our grade to pee all over the toilet paper in the restroom while an elite team crawls on their bellies toward the teacher's lounge, hunting for clues. We tap the walls, listen for a hollow sound. Maybe it's behind a locker. Maybe it starts on the roof, that one locked door only the buff PE teacher has a key to. We're convinced we're hearing things. Our ears prick up when we hear footsteps.

One day the classroom below us is learning jiu jitsu, and we hear the technique, the lessons, and… it's the voice of a child. A young girl, about our age. It's a quiet voice, it's hard to hear through to one floor when our teacher is trying to get us to understand figurative language, so we have to get quiet. We fold our hands. Our ears stretch around the sound of whiteboard markers. I drop a pencil so I can crawl under my desk to better pick up the sound.

The voice below us says, "A smaller, weaker person can successfully defend against a bigger, stronger assailant by using proper technique, leverage, and most notably, taking the fight to the ground." I can't tell if she is reading from a book or reciting. She sounds strong. I hear a tap against a whiteboard and the scribbling of notes, 30 pencils simultaneously. "In side control, you pin your opponent to the ground from the side of his body." Where did she learn to talk like this? I hear a smart set of footsteps descending what sounds like the south wall of our class-room, and the classroom below us stirs. The girl's voice stops. A door opens and closes. "I'm so impressed," says the teacher in the classroom beneath our classroom. "You're the only class in school who behaves even when I step out. Maybe we'll even get recess tonight. I'll make a special call to the night crew."

I freeze under my desk, my pencil in hand. My teacher taps on my desk, says, "Back in your seat," and I do it, mummified.

+

All week we've been behaving. Our teacher seems pleased, pats us on the heads, says, "You've really grown," says, "I'm writing a note to your parents about this new positive attitude." But really we've just been listening. Waiting for the switch that happens when the teacher in the classroom below our classroom steps out, how the students seem to turn towards one voice, a girl who seems to stand on her chair and say, "We have only this choice. No one is coming for us." She sounds older, her voice deep, serious.

Our hearts strain in our sweatshirts. It's winter. We wonder how cold it is to stay underground. We wonder if they live there. They must, since we've never seen them. The classroom below our classroom is learning how to knit, how to build fires. They ask sharp, inquisitive questions during class. They read all the survival books they can. Now that we've started listening, we can hear so much that we couldn't hear before.

At recess, we convene under the double slide, mittened hands cupping mouths, knees touching.

"We should tell someone," one of us says. "We should see the principal. Demand answers. Those kids are being held against their will."

"No, no," the rest of us say. "All of the adults are in on this. We can't let them know what we know."

The girl's voice had awakened something in us. A desire to turn all of our spit-ting and lying and fighting into something of storybooks, something of heroes.

When the playground monitor walks by us, we lean in closer, digging our knees into the woodchips.

We create a Plan.

It's decided that since I live closest to the school, since I have a ground floor window, since I bike to school, anyway, it makes the most sense that I'm the one to carry out the Plan. I will do it during a full moon so I don't get caught with my headlamp. They will choose the night for me, on my behalf. It is starting to feel like my class is one entity and I am another one, separate, just me.

+

I think about writing a letter before I go. I start one—*Dear Mom, Dear Dad, Dear Classmates*—but throw it out before I get any farther. Writing a letter feels too much like giving up. I slip out my window in a thick sweater, my mother's cellphone in my back pocket, a windup flashlight for once I get to the school. I have our teacher's security pass, which we swiped when we accidentally knocked over all the graded work on her desk, and when we went in a mad rush to "help" her. You'd be amazed what teachers don't notice when we encircle them like a hive. It isn't even that hard.

Outside the grass is frosted and the moonlight hits the hoods of cars, the eyes of cats, the glass windows of the school building. I think about how easy it would be to go back home now, to tell my classmates that I hadn't found anything and leave it there. But then I remember the girl and her voice. The girl who'd given up on rescue, but would be so grateful once it came.

The security key works. I'd half wished it wouldn't. The whole school is dark and my shoes are so loud on the concrete floors I echo. I slip them off. I want to come in stealth. I want to not be known. I have no idea where the staircase is, so I start by going to my classroom. What I know for certain is they're below me, and if they're in there all the time, this is my best bet. I go into the classroom and lay my ear against the tile. I don't hear anything. I mean, I hear the humming of a street lamp outside, I hear my heart coming up for air. The fluids in my ears are making noises. I knock against the ground with one knuckle. Then I think I hear someone cough.

"Hello? Is someone down there?"

I hear a rustling, but that could be anything, could be me hearing my hearing, repositioning my body so my ear is against the floor.

"I hear you all the time," I say, loud enough to be heard below. "I want to meet you. I want to help you."

But it's quiet. Maybe they're all sleeping. Maybe they go somewhere else to sleep.

"If you can hear me, do something. Tap the top of your classroom with a broomstick. Close a book. Cough again."

And while I'm waiting for something to happen, my classroom doors open. And there's a flashlight beam so bright I can't see who's holding it. The flashlight, I mean. I mean, the beam is beaming into my eyeballs, and I can't see, but they seem tall. They're strong when they grab me. "Hey," I shout. "Don't touch me. Let go of me," and I rip myself away, run through the door, am moving backwards, sideways, I can't see because of the beam that blew up my eyeballs, and next thing I know I'm stumbling down the stairs, how can I be stumbling down the stairs, how could they have been here all along, and when I hit the last one, I know it. I'm where the other ones are. I'm beneath the real school.

+

It's hard to tell how much time is passing down here. We don't have clocks. We can't see the sun. It could be four in the morning and we're learning algebra. I don't know algebra yet. Down here, I'm the stupid one, I'm exotic, my skin is so brown.

I keep my eyes peeled for the girl, I keep waiting for her to raise her hand so I can know her by her voice. Maybe this isn't her room. Maybe there is a classroom beneath every classroom, and I've stumbled into the wrong one. When the teacher leaves us to get some coffee—maybe to see some sky?—we don't get out of our seats. Some of the kids close their eyes. Some of them scratch their knees. I lean over to one, say, "What's in her desk? Want to go see? I can guard the door." But she turns me in when Ms. Maypole returns. That's her actual name. She is skinny and smile-less. She stands behind me when I say the pledge. I am learning the meaning of fervor, and not just because I am memorizing the dictionary one letter at a time.

While Ms. Maypole is passing out worksheets, I ask my elbow-partner which is the girl who knows jiu jitsu. Ms. Maypole doesn't have to turn around. "Someone doesn't want recess tonight," she says, and that gives me hope. Night recess means outside, means above-ground, means a chance. I start to form new plans. The playground is surrounded by a concrete wall that no kid has ever been able to climb. I brainstorm on the corner of my paper, pretending to calculate the degrees of angles. I could toss a note wrapped around a rock. I imagine my old classmates waiting on the other side with open palms. Classmates who've been forming their own plans, who haven't stopped strategizing under the slide at recess. Maybe they've left a message for me there, maybe they're tunneling under the walls now, chipping away at tree roots and concrete, passaging my way out.

I behave through trigonometry and phonics and Latin—feet on the floor, eyes on the board, I pretend to be a good kid. When it's time for history, the teacher separates us into small groups. It's the first time I've left my seat since I arrived. In this classroom beneath the classroom, erasers never seem to wear away, pencils are always sharp. My legs tingle as I stand.

In our small groups, we're told to prepare presentations on the make-up of a plant cell. As the others shuffle around the desks, a boy I've never noticed—a boy with blonde, side-combed hair and dark-rimmed glasses and thin wrists–sidles up to me. He murmurs to me without turning his head, "She's not here anymore."

"Who?" I ask, though I know he means the girl.

When he speaks, his lips barely move. "She wanted to get us out. She wanted us to fight, but they caught on. They always do."

"Where did they take her?"

He says that he didn't notice her leave. At some point, he just realized she was gone. I notice for the first time that there are the perfect amount of students for desks in the room. There was a desk ready for me when I arrived. How long was this desk empty before it was mine?

"Maybe she found a way out," I said. "Maybe at recess."

He looks at me for the first time. He looks at me strangely.

And I understand, there is no recess.

When I return to my desk, I search its surface for messages written in eraser that you can only see from an angle, for scratched initials. But the desk's surface is impossibly smooth. I don't even find my own fingerprints.

+

The weird thing is, the thing I can't get over, is that I can't hear them. The classroom above our classroom. I realize now that the thumps we heard from time to time, coming from beneath the floor, had nothing to do with us. I wonder if my old classmates are listening for me. I wonder if somewhere they have their ears pressed to tile, waiting for my voice to rise above the rest. I wonder if I'm in a room that no one else is above.

Dana Diehl and Melissa Goodrich on their process:

When we're in the middle of a writing project, we exist in two worlds at once. Dana-world and Melissa-world. It's unlonely, but super vulnerable. We see each other's writing in its rawest form, before we've edited out our idiosyncrasies. It's amazing how the other solves the problems in a story one of us can't fix. When we hit a wall in our writing, we think to ourselves, "Okay, my instincts aren't working here. How would Melissa do this?" or "How do I match Dana's style, elaborate, blend in?" But mostly it's a lot of, "Wow, I love this, how is she so good?" Mostly it's kind of staring in amazement at the white space someone leaves when they trust you.

It is the most enjoyable kind of work. It's CRAZY fun. It's trust-falling into each other. It's working with someone whose instincts you are in total admiration of, whose jokes you appreciate—who twists and untwists the story you started to write. And it's about letting go of control in the best possible way. It is all the rollercoasters. Once, Melissa was reading aloud an in-progress draft of ours and Dana was laughing at the jokes—the ones *she* wrote. Forgetting they were hers. It was spectacular. It's hard to tell, after a while, where one of us stops and the other begins. We're already daydreaming about reading from the book together. We'll read each other's words. And they'll be ours.

Bryan Furuness, Sarah Layden, Andrew Scott, and
Matthew Simmons

TEMPUS FUGITIVE

Terry Linder

August 27, 2017

Tempus Fugit, LLC
500 West Street
Camden, New Jersey 08105

Re: The Contest

To Whom it May Concern:

In one thousand words or less, here is what I would do if I won the use of the
Tempus Fugitive© for a day: go back in time to cheat on my wife with my wife.

What I have in mind here is to create a "sexual highlight reel" of my marriage—the
sauna on our Smoky Mountain honeymoon, the night she drank Amaretto and
growled, the time she wore a thong, the time I wore the thong, etc.—and maybe
make some new highlights besides. (Don't worry, Tempus Fugit legal team: you
have my word that I won't do anything too weird or statutory.)

As long as I'm replaying my life, there are a few events I'd like to edit, just slightly.
Like the time my wife told me about the only one-night stand she's ever had. The
summer after her junior year in high school, her folks went to Lutherwald for a
church retreat, and she threw a big party. After the party ended, some "old dude
in his thirties" hung around to "help her clean up." Well, you can guess what hap-
pened next. (They slept together.)

She told this story like it was no big deal, and I had to pretend likewise. (How
could I do otherwise, when I'd had a couple of one-night stands myself?) But in

truth I was shocked, and for the last fifteen years, that story has been the pea under my mattress, so to speak. My first thought, when I saw the ad for your contest, was, Hey, what if I traveled back in time to that party? What if I was that old dude?

I would love to be that old dude. I would love doing it with my pre-wife, remembering it, and knowing secretly that I was the one. I will admit that the thought of her sleeping with someone else inflames me. Partly it is a turn-on—that my wife is desirable to other men, that she's a sexual creature, etc.—but it is also a major irritation. Just thinking of her sleeping with the old dude who is not me really bugs me. It feels like a betrayal, or, because technically she hadn't met me yet, a pre-betrayal.

Most guys wouldn't admit to feeling this way about their wives' ex-lovers, but then, most guys are liars. Me, I'm honest. I'll admit that I like the turn-on aspect of that episode, and I don't want to lose that. But if I could be that old dude—well, I could have my cake and eat it, too. So to speak.

The other time I'd edit would be the big fight we had just after getting engaged, when she got mad and drove up to Muncie to sleep with her old boyfriend. Which she did, she later admitted, pretty much to spite me. I would like to travel back in time to assault the shit out of the old boyfriend just as he is taking off his pants. (Don't worry, Tempus Fugit legal team! The courts would not be able to touch me. Though my fingerprints and DNA would be all over the "crime scene," the real version of me, Terry circa 1993, would have an airtight alibi. I was at Bear's Place that night with an ex-girlfriend. A hundred people could vouch for that. My fingerprints and DNA were all over Bear's Place, too, and, I admit, the ex-girlfriend.)

(And, okay, to be fair, I would also time-travel back to Bear's Place, and corner myself in the bathroom until Terry 1993 promised not to sleep with my/his ex-girlfriend. That's one memory I'd like to delete anyway.)

I know this all probably sounds like some macho fantasy to be the only guy my wife has ever slept with. Or maybe it sounds like a way of creating a loophole in marriage, of cheating without really cheating. Or like I just want to sleep with younger, perkier versions of my wife while kicking the ass of her old boyfriends. Well, at the risk of sounding like a shallow jerk, I'll admit that you might have a point there. (Like I said: I'm honest.) But, hey, it's not like I'm asking to use the time-machine to pick up hoochies. At least my fantasies are about my wife.

But none of those theories really get at what this trip is about. What I want is to sleep with my wife forever, for all time. I understand that your technology can not (currently) take me into the future, and I can assure you that is not a concern. I can take care of the future myself, but I need your help with the past. Time's horizon extends in two directions. Love wants to do the same.

Sincerely,

Terry Linder

Marian Wright

Tempus Fugit, LLC
500 West Street
Camden, New Jersey 08105

Re: The Contest

To Whom It May Concern:

I am literally hungry to win the use of the Tempus Fugitive© for a day.

I took it for granted, food. Before the procedure there was food. Now, all I can think about are the feasts of yore: the mutton, the braised root vegetables, the puddings. Check it: I was a lusty wench wielding one of those enormous turkey legs in one hand and a tankard of mead in the other. Every weekend at the Ren Faire, I would replicate the gluttony and fleshiness of a certain class of a certain time. I'd eat good food and drink good drink, and muse that my life was full.

And now it isn't.

I didn't get bariatric, if that's what you're thinking. Hell, my insurance would probably pay for my use of the Tempus Fugitive© before they approved bariatric. (Not that I think I need insurance! I'm sure the Fugitive is completely safe!)

My significant other was getting bored with the Ren Faires. All that historical accuracy. His cell phone kept going off at inappropriate moments, such as when the blacksmith tried to shine up Phil's, my sig-oth's, chainmail. Even on vibrate, the phone clanked his metal like a woodpecker drumming a stop sign. (Why did he even need his phone? Whose call was he waiting for?) So he urged me to think about maybe going futuristic, getting into the slimming suits of the Beam-Me-Up conference crowd. Nobody thought twice about a Vrothling on a cell phone, Phil enthused. "And we wouldn't be gnawing on turkey legs every weekend, either," he added, eyeing my ample waist.

I could take a hint.

Men say they like that extra flesh, the thighs that flatten onto diner booth seats like two pillows stuffed into jeans. They tell you they like your appetite, your taste for the 18-Wheeler breakfast, and the fact that you eat in front of them, not like their last girlfriend who withered away (no doubt saucer-eyed, adorable as a kitten) on salads and diet spring water.

They like it just fine until the day some fairer, thinner wench jangles her way into the Ren Faire. A "Bridget," let's say, complaining about how hard it is to gain five pounds to fill out her corset, and anyway, this scene's getting tired, you know? The conference hotel rooms are where the real party's at, not some dumb field where ticks bite your ass when you have to pee.

Let's say a certain sig-oth giggled. Let's say Phil giggled. (Look, I know what you're thinking: but it wasn't about Phil. Suddenly this was competition, real competition, not a stupid maypole being circled by prancing, bearded men and their boobs-out sidekicks. But I was going to whittle myself into maypole shape.)

Know how serious I was about my dedication to fit into a jumpsuit, and fast? I signed up for the procedure without even doing a consult. My phone demeanor has been described as airy, and even the receptionist at Well N' Good! asked, "Are you sure?" I was.

The form said, "The possibility exists for complication." I signed it, but how could I know? How can I describe what's missing? It's not—it was never—the weight. I know that now. Everything had gone fine at first in the Wellness Gentle Reduction and Acupressure Chamber: soft lights, sandalwood candles, the slightly uncomfortable electrodes countered by the soothing assistant's thumbs digging into the pressure points on my feet. It was textbook, as far as experimental procedures go.

But she was new, and she did me one better than triggering what she called "my metabolism and weight loss chakras." (East meets west, right?) I don't know how familiar you folks are with the map of the foot, but this new trainee needed some serious foot GPS. She spent about ten hours digging into the quadrant that I later figured was associated with taste. Not, like, the ability to select an appropriate mate (though in truth that area could use some massaging), but literally taste buds, flavors, the difference between salty and sweet, sour and bitter. No matter what I eat—from replicating the Ren Faire feasts to pirating the 7-11 snack cake aisle—my mouth responds mechanically. Chew and swallow, with absolutely no hint of pleasure, no hint of anything.

I'm starting to forget what things taste like. What it feels like to be satisfied.

Now I stand next to Phil at Gen Con ("The Four Best Days in Gaming!") and we wear our turquoise jumpsuits and prosthetic high foreheads, and he rests one hand on my jutting hip bone and looks around the room. I put my hand on my other hip, the indignant-yet-sexy pose my character is known for, and I miss the feel of my own flesh. I miss my old body more than I'd miss Phil.

I miss the way my teeth closed around a turkey leg, the crisp, salty skin, the juice dribbling down my chin. Drunk on mead, I had never felt so full. I miss the feel of tart cranberry pie lingering on my tongue. I miss the hit of sugar from pear cake icing, even if it was from a can, just as historically dumb as a cell phone.

If I don't win this contest, I figure I'll just keep eating: choke down enough tasteless food to get my own delicious, fleshly body back.

But I'd love to return to life before the procedure. I'd love to be standing next to Phil on the Ren Faire Exposition Grounds when he gave me the once-over after giving Bridget the once-over. I really want to taste this bitterness, you know? It would be a waste, the perfectly good honey wine I'd toss into his face. But my waist? That's worth saving.

In anticipation,
Marian Wright

Tempus Fugit, LLC
500 West Street
Camden, NJ 08105

August 7, 2017

Dear Tempus Fugit:

I must admit my hesitation to communicate with a company named after a Yes song. And I'm not fond of New Jersey, either. Two strikes, Tempus Fugit.

I want to go back to a time when my girlfriend and I decided to move out here to California. I'd played in bands for years and got into the business of booking and promoting them. I soon owed money to nearly everyone, and club owners weren't exactly forthcoming with cash. So we split. She trusted me to make things right.

If you're going to fail, you should fail big—so my girlfriend (a woman I lived with for seven years) quit her job and we sold our possessions and drove west. I'd decided, hey, I'm in the music industry and people already hate my guts, so why not get paid for it?

My car broke down in the desert a few days later. An old man stopped to help. He put us up for the night and fed us, and let us stay there the next day while the car was repaired, even though he had to leave on business. But before he left, he changed my life forever. This industry is all about connections. Who you know. I've made tons of money signing bands long before anyone has heard of them because friends I've made, people who attend shows in dive bars and swap tapes and CD's and MP3 files to spread the good word, clue me in to what might break out in a big way, and then my fine ear does the rest. This old guy in the desert had connections, too, and tempted me with the chance of a lifetime. When we reached Los Angeles, I had a job waiting for me at C—— Records. One of his clients was the head honcho, rest his greedy soul, and he took me on as his protégé.

That trip broke us to pieces. The fine print on an offer like that might have made clear the dangers a couple like us were up against, that we were on a precipice and only the slightest nudge would cause us to fall forever. The woman I should have married returned home. I stayed here, where I've been getting rich for nineteen years. I've lived through race riots, an earthquake, the rise and fall of Limp Bizkit and Britney Spears and plenty more not worth mentioning. I've made it through each new challenge. I only have to ask, "What's the morally precise path?" and then mosey down the opposite direction. It's hard to be good. I've had to become part of this world.

Thanks for reading this far, Tempus Fugit. We're both in the business of selling empty dreams, and I know you'll agree that it takes a toll. Now that I've put down the words, I realize how wasteful it is to dream of changing the past. I can't deliver on my promises, and neither can you, but at the heart of this wicked business is one clear truth: I can't stand the thought of being broke and hopeless and powerless again, not even for a day, even if it means I get to see her again.

Sorry for wasting your time. I'll leave my name off, if you don't mind. It's the least I can do, a trait my girlfriend would surely recognize.

[Postmarked in Burbank, CA]

——————————————————————————

Tempus Fugit
500 West Street
Camden, New Jersey 08105

Dear Sirs,

Hello to one and all who read this, both in the Tempus Fugit corporation, and members of the various news media outlets to which I have also sent this note.

My name is Luke Banks of Escanaba, Michigan and I am a targeted individual. To any of the others out there who, like me, are members of the TI community, I would like to say hello, I pray for you, and I want you to know that you are not alone. For those unfamiliar with this situation, I would refer you to the website targetedindividuals.com, whereon you will find many details, and many personal stories of tragedy, of harassment, and of psychological warfare engaged in by our government to discredit and destroy individuals like myself for a) discovering some sort of sensitive information or also, b) simply because they can.

One assumes your mailbox has been vigorously pelted with notes and contest entries from individuals interested in petty, personal desires—love or sexual conquesting, or moments where a better-made decision could lead to a life of higher self-esteem. I can understand how one of these entries might fit into the brand narrative you are developing for your company, might position you better in the time travel consumer market, and therefore might attract you to them over my entry. I must ask, though, that you throw those considerations aside, individuals of the Tempus Fugit Corporation.

This is important. You must pick me. Tempus Fugit, there is a life to save, and it is the life of a president of these United States.

Tempus Fugit, you must allow me to go back in time and kill my father.

We are all familiar enough with the "facts" of the John F. Kennedy assassination that I feel like I need not dwell. November 22, 1963. Dealey Plaza in Dallas, Texas. Half an hour after noon, shots were fired.

But this moment, this moment when a projectile sped through the air and dismantled the skull and ripped through the brains of a sitting American president is also the moment when "facts" lose clarity. When the world—your world, my world—becomes a less real, less comfortable, less explainable place. When our reality is sent tumbling and whirling into a confused, messy, dissonant place. A place none of us can live in. We have never recovered from this.

There is a way, though. You must send me back to that year. You must send me back to Dallas, Texas. You must arm me and allow me to make all this right.

"But," I can hear some of you saying, "your name is not Oswald. Lee Harvey Oswald killed the president."

I trust that the more learned among you will set this group of people—this, one imagines, small and exceedingly naïve group of people—straight so I can move on.

I had, for all the years of our cohabitating together, what most would characterize as a chilly relationship with my father. I was, I suspect, an unwanted child, grown from the occasion of an unwanted pregnancy, caused by an accidental conception from a not thoroughly prepared for act of love between my parents. (There is a part of me that suspects one of my birth parents was, in reality, not involved in the conception—either some other man provided the sperm while my father was away on business, or some other woman provided the egg and womb in which I grew—some woman my father maybe met while he was away on a business trip.)

But this is a conversation I had had with my therapist (my Judas) back when I trusted him. There was something about my dad being away a lot during the '60s. Something untoward. Something about the fact that he refused to talk about it. I really wanted to look into it, I told my therapist (my Judas). Really start digging around. Ask mom. Find his old letters. Go through that mess of a basement he left when he died in the mid-'90s.

It was soon after this conversation, this admission to my therapist (my Judas) that the headaches began. And the ringing phones at 2am—the ones that were never anything other than hang-ups. And the whispers at work—I was employed at a graphic design and screen printing workshop—that implied things about me and my sexuality (none of anyone's business, thank you) and my lackluster performance of my duties (lies, one and all).

When confronted, the therapist (my Judas) claimed I was paranoid. But I was not paranoid. I discovered within the vortex of my new life's struggles a web of connections. My therapist (my Judas), a new coworker days after I had talked to my therapist (my Judas) about my father's consistent absence, a seeming endless parade of cable trucks in my neighborhood. A cell phone tower on the roof of the bar across the street.

Google is a magical thing. One day I put all of the strange circumstances of my life together in Google's search field, and connected each symptom (placed between quotation marks) with a plus sign.

"sudden headaches" + "rumors at work" + "harassing phone calls" + "hang-ups"+ "trouble with digestion" (don't ask).

And there I found the key. I found my fellow targeted individuals.

I will dispense with the long story of my conversion. Suffice it to say, I was skeptical. But it all fit. And it all related to my father.

Why had the government chosen to destroy me? What could my father have been involved in?

Kennedy, Tempus Fugit. My father killed Kennedy. The biggest conspiracy of them all.

One day, looking up government conspiracies on the internet, I did a random image search, and found a photo of a man sitting on a curb, looking down. He is partially obscured by a light pole. Next to him is a man in white with a dark complexion. It's my father. I know it.

Following the image back to its source, I found out that the man was the one called The Umbrella Man. I see him now, tapping his lucky umbrella as he prepares to leave for the day. "Always be prepared for anything," he'd say. Some think the umbrella held by The Umbrella Man carried a poison dart in a flechette device of some sort, and said dart immobilized the president. I think it killed him outright. I think it carried a small explosive shot that forced the president's head back and to the left, and blew out his brain.

Don't ask me how that was the photo to come up. I really don't know. The coincidence seems uncanny, I realize. Like I said, though: Google is a magical thing. Google wants this to happen for me. Google wants me to go back and kill my father before he can kill the president. All the fog that surrounds us now, all the haze that allows the government to do what it wants, all that mesmerizes us and pacifies us, it all offends Google. Google is our collective unconscious, and with every search we make and every web page we visit because it offers us a link, Google gets closer to helping us burn away the fog created by a government working in secret and for its own ends.

Google wants me to save the president. Google wants me to kill my father. Please, Tempus Fugit, pick me.

Luke Banks
Escanaba, MI

Bryan Furuness, Sarah Layden, Andrew Scott, and Matthew Simmons on their process:

Like most of my ideas, this one started off as a joke. I heard about some company holding an essay contest. People were supposed to write about how it would change their lives to win a turkey fryer. This struck me as funny. I mean, it's a freaking turkey fryer, not a trip in a time machine. I was like: Ha ha ha, heh heh, hmmm...And then I (Bryan Furuness) made three of my friends write "essays" to win a free trip in a time machine.

Carol Guess and Kelly Magee

WITH KILLER BEES

I'm at the post office, in line, trying to mail a package for Mother's Day, when the pregnant lady two people in front of me just keels over. Everyone stands there for a minute, waiting to see if anyone's going to do anything, to see who will step up. No one does, so I shout, "Protect her head!" because that's something I've heard people say on TV. Still nobody moves, so I shove the guy in front of me out of the way and stand at the pregnant woman's feet. Her eyes are open. She's on her back with her knees in the air, wearing one of those awful jumpers women in late pregnancy sometimes wear, a jean skirt with overall straps and pockets with smiling sun patches sewn on. She looks me right in the eye and says, "They're coming."

"Who?" I say. I consider kneeling beside her, but something about the way she's staring at me, unblinking, keeps me on my feet.

Her resolve breaks for a moment, and her face tenses in fear.

"I don't know what they'll do to me."

"Who?" I say again. I'm wondering what asshole knocked up a crazy lady and left her alone in a post office. She doesn't have a ring.

"The little ones," she says.

I look up at one of the postal workers, who I strongly suspect is trained to respond to emergencies but who is just standing there like he's not. My cousin was a mail carrier for years, and at his main office alone there have been stabbings and robberies and four—count them, four—women in active labor trying to get their last errand done. One was carted off in an ambulance.

"Call 911," I say, and the postal worker says, "Already done."

"Help is on the way," I say to the woman. Now other people are coming to their senses, gathering around her, putting a folded coat under her head. One guy actually goes to the counter and tries to buy stamps.

"It's too fast," the pregnant woman moans. "They won't make it." And just like that, she sort of pops. That's what it looks like. Her belly deflates, and a thing emerges that shatters and lifts and disperses weakly into the air. I say, "Holy hell," and someone else screams and this old lady behind me says, "Bees."

"What?" I glance at her package, addressed to an APO.

"That woman just shat out a whole mess of bees," she says.

I look up. We all do. The air trembles.

"A swarm," somebody says.

The bees look contained for a moment, injured or something, clumped together and hovering around a high window, maybe as stunned as we are about why they are in the post office, or how they just came out of this woman. We seem to all remember the woman at once. She's still on the floor, but now tears stream out of her eyes and into her hair. This man—one of those who was nowhere to be found when she collapsed—starts shaking her shoulders, saying, "What the hell just happened? Lady, pay attention. What happened?"

She closes her eyes.

"I'll tell you," she says.

#

I was having trouble getting pregnant, so I went to the healer. Western medicine, with its catheters and petri dishes, its injections and specimens, wasn't working, so I thought, Why not try something ancient? Something smarter than the present? I'd heard great things about acupuncture; friends swore by Rolfing. I found Health Keepers online—first appointment free—and drove myself because my ex and I had split up after the third year of trying. The doctor told me to call her Dipping Bird and diagnosed me with rage-based infertility. I said I didn't feel mad. She said the mind will sometimes mask the body's response to trauma, and that my body was reacting to the trauma of first being with, then being left by, my ex. A body filled with rage has no space for a baby, she said. She prescribed a wildflower honey fast, said it would promote opening and slow extraction. Rage wasn't the kind of thing you wanted to purge. The honey fast would draw it out so I could safely excrete it.

I asked how long before I could have a real meal.

She said to come back when I started to believe I didn't need to eat.

I went home with my bucket of purified honey and complimentary dipper and thought about rage. I didn't feel rage, not even in a repressed kind of way. I felt lonely. I felt tired. I felt nauseated over the big gulps of honey Dipping Bird had dosed, but that was it. My ex had been broken up over our split. I felt pity, but not rage.

Still, it worked. Like a charm, some might say. Each day I grew a little lighter. I woke up feeling happy. I put myself back together, went out dancing in the evenings. On the toilet, what emerged from my body was like tar. I could tell it was the rage. I took a little more of the honey each day, began writing poetry and smiling at strangers. I started to believe I didn't need food anymore. I went back to Health Keepers.

Dipping Bird said this was a fragile time, the intermediate period, during which I ought to be careful about the company I kept. I told her about the dancing and the poetry. She looked at me sternly. "Very careful," she said.

I wish I could say I followed her advice. I trusted her enough by then. But the thing about rage is that it can keep you alert to danger. Without it, you might let down your guard. You might, at a country line dance, lock eyes with the man wearing the biggest cowboy hat you've ever seen. The one with the sloe eyes and the obscene belt buckle. Your rage won't be there to remind you not to follow him to his car, to enjoy the weight of him on top of you until you ask to get up and can't, and he won't, and you try, and he forces, and you push, and he pushes back, and pushes, and you understand that rage is strong and sweet will not save you.

His rage will be there. Will get inside you. Will multiply in the space it finds in your body.

I was too embarrassed to tell Dipping Bird, tried doubling up on my doses instead. Thinking to flush him out. But instead—well, you see what happened. You see what is happening right now.

#

She's still on the floor. The whole post office has gone silent listening to her. Then the old woman with the APO package groans and says, "You mean for us to believe that you got pregnant with bees because you ate too much honey?"

A couple of people laugh, though it's not funny, and anyway, nobody can explain what just happened in a way that anyone's going to believe.

"I just wanted a baby," the woman says. She goes to rub her belly but it's flat now, which she is only just realizing. She sits up, perfectly fine, no blood or fluids. She searches for a pair of eyes to focus on, lands on me again. "I've had some testing done," she says, and I kind of look around, hoping she'll find someone else to receive this news. "They are not ordinary insects. They are dangerous."

"What, the bees?" the old lady says. "How come they're just sitting up there?"

"I don't know." The woman stands, dusts off her maternity jumper, which now hangs loosely off her shoulders, and resumes standing in line. She holds a stack of envelopes, and the one on top is addressed to a farm. I tap her shoulder.

"What are we supposed to do?" I say. She shrugs.

"Can't you smoke them or something? To make them less dangerous?"

"You could try that," the woman says.

The bees are getting louder, and a few people have glanced up at them and left without mailing their packages. But most of us don't want to lose our spot in line. We don't want to have to come back tomorrow. As long as the bees stay put, we're okay with them being up there.

But they don't stay put.

"Ouch," the old lady says, and we see one of the fuzzy bodies tumble off her.

It seems the bees are waking up.

The swarm unravels, a long loose thread on hemlines and letters. Before its whip can sting, I run.

When I reach my car, I sit panting in the hot box of my Honda, texting Mazie because who else would I tell?

Me: *u wont believ wht hapnd @ po*
Mazie: *TRY ME*
Me: *kiler bez came out of lady*
Mazie: *POST OFFICE ALWAYS CRAZY MONDAY*
Me: *pregnant wit bez!*
Mazie: *NEED CREAM AND BREAD*

At the grocery store I buy cloverleaf honey. I forget onions and go through the line twice. When I get home, Mazie's painting her nails. She's wearing heels and a short black dress.

"Sorry," she says, disappearing into our bedroom. When she comes out she's wearing the fluffy bathrobe I gave her on our 12th anniversary.

"Nice robe," I say, smiling.

"Thanks," she says, texting.

"Fridays are mine now."

"I know. I forgot."

I put the groceries away and start chopping onions. "Rice or quinoa?"

"I already ate."

The honey jar shines like it's lit from inside. I turn off the stove and walk out the door.

#

When I get home it's after midnight and the onions smell raw. I'm afraid Mazie won't be in bed and I'm afraid she will, so I sleep on the couch.

In the morning I wake to the sound of coffee gurgling in the pot. Mazie's sitting at the kitchen table, reading *People*'s annual Most Beautiful People issue.

"You're beautiful people," I say.

She starts to cry.

At first I'm glad. I want to say, "What did he/she/they do to my beautiful wife?" I want to remind her that this arrangement was her idea and she can stop any time. I want to ask her to wear her black dress just for me.

"Mazie, what happened?"

She closes her eyes.

It's always like this now, Mazie with her eyes closed, me watching her too closely, looking for signs. Signs that she's about to leave and signs that she's about to stay.

"Please tell me it wasn't some guy in a cowboy hat."

"I told you. I'm into women right now."

"Was her name Dipping Bird?"

"Cindi. With an *I*."

"Does she have a partner?"

"I don't know who she has."

I tell her about the scene in the post office, about the swarm of bees rising from the woman's skirt. I describe each bee in detail, giving it a name and a particular pattern. I describe them as if they weren't all alike.

Mazie's crying again. She gets up and pours two cups of coffee. Fixes mine with clouds of cream. Then she sits with her eyes closed, fingers wrapped around her cup. It's always like this now, Mazie with her eyes closed, changing. I wait for her. I stay the same.

I think maybe she's in love with Cindi.

I decide to start sleeping with that woman.

With bees.

#

Tracking her down is easy enough. I plug in a few words and news swarms my screen. Everyone's version of the story is different. It's a hoax, a prank. She's gone off her meds. She's an environmental activist calling attention to the plight of the bees. She's an alien host. She's possessed. She's a clown. She's an actress in a DIY film. She was hired by the post office to boost sluggish sales.

But I was there and I know what I saw. She gave birth to bees on that dirty tile floor.

Easy enough to find her address. She's on Facebook. She tweets. I park two blocks away. It's not stalking; we're polyamorous. Mazie sees other people and now I do, too.

Except no one answers my knock. Except as I stand on her stoop I get the feeling I'm being watched. Then I hear it: an unkempt sound. A buzzing, a slur. The window shakes. They're inside, pressed against the glass. The whole house vibrates. I call her name.

"Gina!"

"Who is it?"

"It's me!"

"It's bees?"

I hear her inside, rattling the door. I try the knob, pull with all my weight. "Push," I shout. "Give it all you got."

Years later, our daughter refuses to believe that we met mid-swarm, that she was conceived in that danger.

The bees she's seen are artificial.

Carol Guess and Kelly Magee on their process:

We wanted to start before "Once upon a time." In the gray, grainy space of an ultrasound, hanging from the fridge by magnets shaped like bananas, or posted to Facebook with the caption, "How I Spent My Summer Vacation." We wanted to go back before the princess leaned out of the castle window, tossing her hair around like she owned the place. We went back and back and back, before girl, before baby, before birth, to the fantastic realm of imagination. What if, we asked ourselves, each other, what if humans and animals could make a third, wild thing? The feral inside us felt kin to our creations.

Ron Horning and David Lehman

from LAND OF OPPORTUNITY

Monday, 2:38 P.M.

When she left the meeting, her recently whitened teeth bared in a smile to conceal the grumble in her belly (from having skipped breakfast) and brain (from the mixture of confusion and disappointment that the prospect of orders reliably provoked), the woman formerly known as Grace Hopkins and now recognized as Angela Mavis went to the ladies' room, took a perch in the stall farthest from the door, sat down and counted to sixty, then waited another minute and a half before flushing the toilet. This time out could land her in the elevator with one of the meeting's other participants—all of whom had impressed her as pains in the you know what. She hoped not. After washing her hands she appraised herself in the mirror above the sink. Not that she had to. She knew she looked stylish in her belted blue raincoat from Bergdorf's with the orange and red paisley scarf that her brother Nigel had given her when she visited London the month before. On her right wrist was her most valued possession, a Piaget watch that her last husband, Jordan Bird—the legendary Credit Suisse trader who was a familiar face on financial shows—had bought to celebrate the initial returns of a delightfully legal scam involving credit swaps, delayed debentures, a bond ladder, and two other "products," he called them, that made her eyes glaze over, try though she might to look brilliant to herself and interested to him. It was a silver watch with a circular dial, a black face with silver notches for the hours, and a thin crimson alligator strap. When the elevator door opened, she slipped into one corner and sneaked a quick peek. Two thirty. Time enough to stroll over to the Waldorf for her three o'clock. Damn these heels. Why hadn't she thought to bring a pair of flats and change shoes in the ladies' room? But then she'd need a bag larger than her signature black mulled leather envelope. At least no one else from the meeting was in the elevator.

Grace Hopkins had been no different from Angela Mavis in one respect: she loathed meetings and the timewasters that unfailingly surrounded the round table on the fifth floor where the committee on reappointments at her last university convened each month. She was Oxford educated and capitalized every chance she could on the inferiority complexes of Americans in the presence of a veddy plummy accent reeking of sherry in the Junior Commons Room of Trinity or Balliol. At Cornell she had chaired the Department of Western Studies and taught an overenrolled lecture course on Democratic Theory in the Phallocentric State, with readings from Plato, Saint Just, Marx, Engels, Lenin, Mencken, T.E. Lawrence, Sartre, Althusser, Che, Debray, and Bin Laden. At one time she had loved her old job, the teaching part of it certainly, but also the annual conventions in less militarized cities, when you could get to them—San Francisco and Miami were special favorites. She had even enjoyed her colleagues, trying as some of them could be. But she could not abide the committee meetings, and especially the committee on reappointments, where she had to put up with wankers from departments such as Exercise Science, Computer Game Theory, and Gambling Arts. You could always count on some overweight old fart insisting on proper channels and some gasbag woman urging everyone to reopen a discussion closed a month ago until the committee chair, a widely respected Asian American authority on explosives, urged caution if only because the group mission was primarily advisory and lacked the authority to make whatever decision the group had debated for the last two hours.

At the Waldorf she cleared security and went directly to the newly resuscitated Wedgwood Room, where Felix Edge waited for her, a tea setting and a tiered tray of delectable pastries, savory and sweet, on the marble top of their table for two.

"Ah, there you are," he said, and stood up when the woman he called Grace loped into the room with a smile while expertly navigating the perils facing a pedestrian: dessert trolleys, tall expressionless waiters in rusty tuxedos, bus boys and girls from around the world; a photographer with an old flash camera and a flower girl making the rounds, among other defunct nightclub blandishments; above all, the crisscrossing columns that served no architectural function but permitted the management to post signed photographs of notables who had eaten brunch, taken tea, or enjoyed dinner here. Most long gone. The white borders of the publicity stills were closer to yellow, and the different colored inks of the signatures had turned various shades of sepia. Except one: Donna Summer's silver glitter still sparkled, probably poisoning the air.

Like Felix's green eyes. At least he dressed better than her current associates with their tweeds the color of an afterthought. Today she admired the smooth nap of his dark blue wool suit and the way he buttoned the neck of his light blue broadcloth dress shirt without wearing a tie, his face very white, his hair, combed straight back, ivory blond.

"Sorry I'm late."

"No worries."

"You're looking well."

"Bicycle training."

"Good for you. I can never keep to a proper regimen."

"You look lovely. It comes to you naturally."

He's flirting with me, she thought, wondering what Felix wanted. Gay men were such terrific flirts; at least with her they always had been.

"I do have a sentimental attachment to this place. Formed in Peacock Alley, though."

Felix grinned. "I remember." He poured a cup of orange pekoe tea in her cup, refilled his, and offered her a warm scone with clotted cream. "Do you miss teaching?"

"I miss the students," she said, taking a bite. "And it was difficult to accept the curriculum changes at the end. We were about as far from the quadrivium and the trivium as it was possible to get without colonizing outer space. I had a student, a bright young woman, whose program one fall consisted of Beginning Yoga, Wine: A Global Bender, From Punk to Jihad: The Influence of L.A. Noir on Third Generation Hip Hop, and Diversity and Disney Princesses." Felix laughed on cue. "The wine course was for just one credit, but she dropped it anyway and I never found out why. Enough about me, as they say. Last I knew you were working for the toy company. Bring me up to speed."

"The fact is, I do less and less for the company. Sometimes they bring me in but that's usually when the decision is so major that anyone left out of the loop will feel dissed."

"How about the new Barbie?"

"Yes," he said. "The new Barbie is a good example of the new corporate decision making process, which isn't that different from the old one, although if you're old enough to know that, you're not young enough to fully appreciate the progress. The decision to change Barbie came from the top and was then reinforced by the most arrogant and talented people in the design, concept, and market research departments. The objection to good old basic Barbie—had been for years—was that no girl in America had the body of this blonde anorexic goddess except good looking girls who dyed their hair blonde and starved themselves. In all fairness to the company, there were millions of them and many more millions who were more than willing to pay for the ideal. But when the objection reached critical mass, that is to say the bottom line, the obvious solution was to multiply the options, retaining a few unifying elements but varying the model as to body type, skin color, hair curly or straight, and hair colors including red, brown, and black. In other words, the only real change in options was body type, or size. The other variations, and plenty more, have been available for decades."

"I followed the story. You never forget your Barbies, even if you're English."

"Then you know the new one made the cover of *Time*."

"Did you work on the makeover?"

He almost grimaced. "Technically, yes. Practically, not so much. Which is exactly what everyone else involved would say if they were honest."

His phone rang. The main theme of Schubert's Unfinished, first movement. Felix took one look at the screen and picked up.

"Really?" he said. Suddenly he was on his feet excusing himself. "It's important," he mouthed. She nodded, mouthing back "Of course," and settled into her second cup of tea and—did she dare?—another half scone, this time with loganberry jam, the real Tiptree article from home.

At a table next to theirs, a little behind her, a waiter was seating a tall grumpy looking man, a frowsy woman in her late 50s, and a much younger woman who wore diamond shaped glasses and clutched a reporter's notebook and a small recording device.

Yesterday on the phone Felix had spoken vaguely of "an opportunity" he might tempt her with. Now she wished he had got to the point more quickly. She wondered whether it might have something to do with her orders, which she expected to come directly from Patel and to be, in his manner, simple to an enigmatic degree. The last time she had been told to stand in front of the steps leading to the Metropolitan Museum and to act as if nothing out of the ordinary was taking place during the annual Freedom Day parade down Fifth Avenue. Dress had been optional, but she was proud of her figure and had worn just the right skirt and sweater. No pantsuit for her! Meanwhile, the assassination had taken place in front of the Frick Lounge. She hadn't even heard the shots, but she heard about it a few minutes later. No one was arrested, and no one knew why the deputy and his substitute assistant had drawn fire.

Grace gave in to temptation and eavesdropped on what Groucho and Frowsy were telling the younger lady, evidently a reporter, at the next table. The waiter had come over to take their orders. The reporter asked for a cappuccino and a gluten free banana muffin, but her guests—familiar faces—were more particular about their orders. For him, a plate of toast and a rasher of bacon, which he specified as "crispy but not too crispy—I like to see it put up a bit of a fight before crumbling." For her, two soft boiled eggs and a cup of Prince of Wales tea, "with two teabags," she said firmly, "and a little pitcher of cold milk on the side."

Ah, now Grace knew why she recognized them. They were TV veterans who had starred in an independent British feature called *The Old Couple* about a Manchester widower who begins to see a lot of a Liverpool widow; eventually they marry, she falls ill, and he nurses her back to health. The film was a breakout hit, nominated for several Golden Globes, including one for each of them, and the two actors were on the last leg of a victory lap that had taken them from New York to Hollywood and back, entertaining troops along the way with the help of translators into sign language, Arabic, and Chinese.

When the waiter slid off, the couple resumed their conversation. Groucho commented on the beggars in wheelchairs and Frowsy shook her head about the "cancer of income equality," a phrase, Grace thought, that the old bitch must have picked up at a cocktail party over here, because no one in Britain talked that way.

Now Groucho, in his deepest bass voice, said solemnly, "Yet here we sit in a veritable temple of Mammon, in the city that neither sleeps nor stops stuffing itself."

To which his companion rejoined, "While people are dying of hunger, and others beg in the streets."

"Yes, and some of those beggars ate fifteen minutes ago."

Their meals arrived, the waiter disappeared, and the woman made a face. "I said soft boiled eggs," she said, "not bloody raw. What about your bacon?"

"Satisfactory," the man—Miller, wasn't it?—said, adding, "And then there's global warning."

The actress, Hannah something Newton, munched thoughtfully on her crumpet before speaking. "There must be an ordinance in this city requiring that you be no more than five feet away from food at any time."

"And all this," Miller said, chewing on his bacon, "whilst half the planet is starving."

"At least it's the right half."

At this moment Felix returned and took his seat, looking grim or striking a pose.

"So," he said, "about the elephant in the room."

"My dear, I have no idea what you're talking about. Surely not Barbie. Yes or no, why did you ask me to meet you in this recycled fun house today?"

"Well, Angela—"

"Excuse me?"

"Darling, that's why we're here. You won't receive your next set of orders from whomever you expected to hear from, and I certainly don't want a name. Nor do I myself have the orders, and as soon as we finish our tea and you know what to do next, you'll be Grace again to me, and we'll talk about toys and teaching as if this conversation never happened and we had just met on a gunboat on the Nile. Compris?"

"You are so Continental, Felix."

"Only when I want to be. The occasion and the setting begged for acknowledgment."

"Quite right about the setting. I'm sure there was a time when you could hear plenty of French here." Donna Summer smiled again. Long before disco but maybe during her brief reign also. "It's the occasion I need explained. Besides not knowing what it is, I'm not sure I know you. I mean, are you still Felix when you talk with Angela?"

"To you I am as much Felix now as I will be when you're Grace again. Remember, we don't know who else is in here apart from our friends peering down from the pillars."

She leaned forward. "In case it matters, the two next to us are English actors, I recognize them from British TV. I'd read they were over here to drum up business and press the flesh, and I listened to them while you were away on the phone."

He let his glance drift to her right. He needs glasses, she thought, or contacts, but he's too vain to get either.

"It doesn't matter, so far as I know, but on the other hand I don't know. Thanks for mentioning, and I'll keep this short. You have a new contact."

"What happened to—" She stopped. Why mention Patel?

Felix shrugged as if he were about to yawn. "Doesn't matter, does it? Maybe nothing. Maybe he or she simply changed names. Maybe that's whom you'll see at your meeting tonight. That's why I asked you to meet me today. I called Grace, but I don't know whether Angela lives in the city or not."

"We both do. I wouldn't call it heaven after Ithaca. More like purgatory, a purgatory at the end of a tunnel. How about you?"

He ignored the question. "I have to go," he said, rising and pushing back his chair. "But you're meeting your new friend at a super exclusive rendezvous—not a bar, mind you, although there is a bar—situated in what was once a gentleman's apartment above Grand Central, then devolved into a late capitalist saloon, and has been rehabilitated recently for special purposes." A flashbulb went off in one of the room's far corners, and Felix smiled. "Like this place."

"More directions, I hope."

He put the smile back in the drawer. "Of course. Go to the covered driveway outside the western stairs from the terminal concourse, the ones that lead to Vanderbilt Avenue. To the right of that entrance is another smaller entrance with a guard. The soldier will let you in. Then security and an elevator. Your friend will be waiting for you when the door opens on the only other floor serviced by the elevator. You're expected at six, so you should reach the driveway by five forty five. Security's tight I was told."

They locked eyes.

"Felix," she said. "When will I see you again?"

"The next time, dear." He paused. "Dear Grace. If you don't call me I'll call you. Do you always carry the old number?"

"Always. And thanks for tea."

But Felix was gone.

Angela looked at the savory pastries left on two tiers of the tray and considered an anchovy toast. Her tea was cold. She poured it into Felix's empty cup and refilled her cup from the sleek chrome canteen wrapped in a heavy white linen napkin and leaning against a large black stone plugged into the wall. The fresh tea steamed, but the prospect of drinking it alone changed her mind. And did she really want to spoil the sweet after scones, cream, jam? Time to go home and rest up for who knew what or whom.

Ron Horning and David Lehman on their process:

We had written a book of poems called *The Unexamined Life* plus a few stray poems before, during, and after, but none of these orphan poems suggested another book length manuscript, and only a book would give us the necessary space and freedom. Maybe we didn't want to repeat ourselves with poetry; maybe we had written as much poetry together as we could; maybe we had to do something else first before we could write another book of poetry.

One way out of this impasse would be to write a book of prose, or at least to start one, but however logical that might seem now, we didn't recognize it for a long time, and even then we approached it with an idea, or a thought, the irrelevance of which became obvious as we started exchanging and elaborating upon the tranches of a novel that seemed to have been waiting for us.

We had decided to incorporate as many as possible of the clichés that grate on both our nerves, but the goal of satirizing the common language disappeared quickly as we wrote ourselves into a mystery about some of the people who speak that language, or who would speak it in the future we were inventing for an imaginary New York City. We still don't know what happens next.

CREATIVE NONFICTION

Anne-Marie Akin and Laura Jones

SOUTHLANDIA

The South that's forever in my bones is not a place of ideas or history. It's a place of sounds and smells, it is sticky heat, it's all senses and little sense. The South that calls me home tugs at my body, not my mind. I left a South ruled by the Bible and the belt. And I left a South heavy with the weight of history: the battle of Shiloh, the wrong side of the war; Jim Crow and poll taxes and Martin Luther King crumpled on the balcony.

Of my south then, my mid-south home, I will start with my eyes closed, because I can find my way around with just my nose. Early morning and dusk are the best times for such a tour. Out the front door, to the right. A mysterious piney perfume hovered at the base of the giant cedar tree that bordered our neighbor's house and ours. It was an otherworldly place to hide. The filtered light was bluish green, cool and dim and fragrant. Way on the other side of the house, in the side yard, the magnolia. When she bloomed nothing else mattered, her velvety lemon-jasmine so insistent you almost felt and heard it.

Further South, forty-five minutes down highway 78, a mimosa tree in Aunt Mary's backyard, smelling like cotton candy reborn as a flower. The sharp tang of sticky pine-tar as I shimmied down a leggy pine, and the acrid burning scent of the gasoline my uncle used to remove it from my hands and knees. I was a tree-climber. In our old house we had a pecan tree in the backyard, and I used to scramble to the top of it in minutes. I've climbed them all, and rested my head against their branches, and inhaled their bark, and flowers or fruits: pecan, crabapple, pine, magnolia, crepe myrtle, cedar, sweet gum, oak.

*

Florida is not the place most people think of when they think of the South. They conjure up palm trees and beaches on Christmas. Salt smells, sailboats gliding through darkness, a bridge lifting, moaning, to let them pass. But my Florida, Central Florida, is completely different. There were deserted back country roads, long stretches of single lane dirt or concrete that swung through farms and horse ranches, past abandoned boys' schools, or Christian camps, hidden deep in the back woods. Cold springs that bubbled up clear from the bottom. Fountains of Youth like the ones Ponce de León searched for during Florida's original incarnation. The marine world beneath is its own clear universe: plankton, fish, snails, and lone, slow manatee, like numb cows floating through the chilled fresh water. In the corners of these springs, like at the lakes, alligators or water moccasins hid in mysterious high grasses. Locals would point them out. "Don't swim over there," someone would say. "That's where the gators live. If you do swim, take a dog. They prefer dogs to eat."

How do you find this world? Travel out I-4 from Orlando, land of misbegotten, fantasy worlds—Sea World, Disney World, the Wizarding World of Harry Potter—pass the lesser galaxies—Wet 'n Wild, Legoland, WonderWorks, Madame Tussauds. Leave behind life wrapped in plastic, built from fiberglass and spackle, dream landscapes of color and automation. Leave behind the strip malls and $5 tee shirt shops.

Head up the highway past yet another round of amusement facades. Dolly Parton's Dixie Stampede, and the Holy Land Experience, a Christian theme park in possession of an exact replica of the tomb where Jesus was buried. Every day at 5 o'clock Christ is recrucified there to the horror and delight of visitors, hung up like a sopping wet towel in the streets of a cardboard Jerusalem. The farther north you drive the more the land turns to what it was before they all got here. Hot stretches of liquid green pastures, rippling with humidity, reptiles and weeds. Trees garlanded in ash-gray Spanish moss and thin, reedy grasses, shrubs gone ecstatic with flowers, and clouds hung like set pieces in a clear blue sky. Out here, there's not much besides poetry, and poverty, and the poetry of poverty, everywhere you look.

*

To get to Memphis from Chicago, it's a long straight drive south through cornfields repeating themselves beneath a flat unwavering sky. It's one of the most boring drives imaginable. And yet somehow in that stretch of I-57 that takes you from Chicago to Cairo, probably around the time the flat suddenly becomes a hill and gully descent towards the Mississippi River, the world changes from North to South, and the accents change with the landscape, from flat Midwestern nasal vowels to a twangy drawl that Southern Illinoisans swear is Southern, and that as a child in Memphis I doubtless called Yankee.

If I'm the only one in the car (oh who am I kidding, even if I'm not) at some point I begin singing "Going Down to Cairo" at the top of my lungs.

> *Going down to Cairo*
> *Goodbye, and a goodbye*
> *Going down to Cairo*
> *Goodbye Liza Jane*

I always sing it fast and twangy and I get louder on the "black them boots and make 'em shine" part. For those of you not from around these parts, I should probably tell you that Cairo is pronounced Kay-ro. If you need to back up and read again with a corrected pronunciation, go ahead. I will wait. The right vowel can make all the difference.

*

The southern accents I'm used to are different than that. Rangy, misguided, loose. What some might call "cracker." The term "Florida cracker" comes from the cowboys that once rode cattle up the state, when it was used for its range and open feeding, early on. These are the sounds you're most likely to hear in my small town of Eustis, Florida, population 20,000, soaking wet.

But there are other sounds, too. Before you get all the way up to my little town, you'll pass one even smaller: Eatonville, the country's first incorporated black town, following emancipation. Just 2,300 folks. Small as it is, it's layered in history. The writer, anthropologist and folklorist Zora Neale Hurston lived and wrote in this tiny place, and the stories she collected there inscribed her own life. Hurston didn't write much in the autobiographical "I," but the Eatonville folktales told in her 1935 book *Mules and Men*, somehow transcribed her experience and that of being black at that time in history, all the mysteries, the fears, the role of nature and community. To read these tales now is to hear them hum with not just sound, but meaning. They're a portal to a world comprised of signs. Hurston's love of story was born of Eatonville and the townspeople who held what she called "lying sessions." Stories of "God, Devil, Brer Rabbit, Brer Fox, Sis Cat, Lion, Tiger, Buzzard[1]" and all the rest. These stories comprised her, and in her autobiography *Dust Tracks on a Road*, it's hard to see where Hurston's own story begins and these stories end.

*

Cairo, Illinois, and the rest of the state, I had always believed, was above the Mason-Dixon line. My Uncle was a truck driver and he used to talk about driving up to Cairo. Now I'm a Chicagoan, Cairo is down. When I was a child and people talked about the North (boorish Yankees) and the South (home), they spoke of anything-above-Tennessee as being "above the Mason-Dixon line." It turns out that line, demarcated by Charles Mason and Jeremiah Dixon back before the Declaration of Independence, was way East, keeping Pennsylvania out of Virginia and Maryland, and biting off a little chunk of Delaware. There is no Mason-Dixon line for me to cross over when I travel from Chicago to Memphis.

But there's *something* there. I feel it. I see it. I hear it. My heart simultaneously leaps up in joy and fills with a dull thudding anxiety. Usually the first rumblings of joy happen as the hills begin to bubble up, there are pine trees growing beside the highway instead of cornfields, and the blood in my veins feels the tug of the Mississippi River, slow and inexorable, so powerful it can't be swum. The bridge is enormous, you drive over one more hill and then there it is, looming in the distance, a long high bridge of steel arches, and if I'm alone in the car, when I drive up the quarter mile of ramp it takes to get onto the bridge proper, I roll down my window and holler like Bo Duke. If my kids are in the car, I holler at them instead: "Look, y'all look, it's the Mississippi River oh look!" And just like that, my accent is there, the second "look" has two or three extra syllables for emphasis.

*

In the summer of 1987, I was a high school junior. Eatonville celebrated its 100th anniversary—its centennial—as the first black incorporated town. For months, we heard on the five o'clock news how they planned a grand parade down Main Street. Then one night the news reported the unthinkable: Florida's own Klu Klux Klan had petitioned to march in the Eatonville centennial parade. Their stated excuse? They claimed they wanted to show their support for black towns, separated from whites. It wasn't an aggressive act, they said, but one done in solidarity with Eatonville's cause. We could feel the fear and anger smoldering up the highways and backroads from 30 miles away.

Immediately, public debate cropped up over what should happen. Many people said they shouldn't be allowed to march. Said they were stealing the focus of a peaceful event meant to commemorate African Americans and all they'd survived.

The KKK's presence would instead place the emphasis on their hatred, their history of oppression and violence. Some even suggested canceling the whole thing, even if it meant the KKK had won. The town council debated it, but in the end, it was determined the parade would go on and that the KKK's participation was a first amendment, free speech issue. Everyone had the right to march in a town-sponsored parade, provided they'd filed the necessary paperwork, which the KKK had done. Eatonville had no choice. The KKK would march in their parade.

*

Is it the bridge? Is it the water?

It will be three more hours until Memphis, we will have to slip through a corner of Missouri and then wend our way through more flatness, Mississippi River flatness, passing soybean and cotton fields beneath an unforgiving sky, past ugly fast food marquees through dusty West Memphis, Arkansas, and then again "oh look girls look, there's the bridge!" the second Mississippi crossing is right in front of me, wider than the first, I have a moment of panic where I try to remember am I supposed to take I-40 or I-55 and then I drive up onto the huge M-shaped bridge that is lit at night, I see downtown Memphis winking in the sun with it's low-rise skyline, a sign in the middle of the bridge says WELCOME TO TENNESSEE, I holler one more time, and I am home.

*

The man down front called out: "If anyone here is ready to absolve themselves of their sins, come forward now."

His small, dark moustache twitched nervously on his lip. His black curls hung on his forehead, too immature for his pot-bellied frame, his button-down white dinner shirt and polyester pants. He stood before a makeshift wooden cross they'd borrowed from the church downtown. For two straight hours, we'd listened to testimonies of how the Lord had saved and redeemed sinful lives. Now it was our turn; the uninitiated. We were here to be saved. That's why the faithful had brought us.

I watched the aisle in the makeshift revival tent intently, fighting the urge to walk forward. Then fighting that urge to fight. Part of me felt perpetually sinful, and this was a solution offered, a balm. I was sixteen years old; I had a girlfriend. I sported short hair; I was awkward, ill-spoken, I never fit in. For those reasons alone I was circumspect, never mind my high school lover. The furtive gropings performed in her mother's car on the dark, abandoned lanes near orange groves and the smoking Minute Maid plant.

I stood up and walked down the row to the altar. Someone had laid out a length of white tarp, so that it resembled a matrimonial aisle. The preacher, who in his spare time was my high school algebra teacher, laid his hands on my bent-over head. I felt my silk straight hair soft and lank running like water beneath his callused fingers. "You are absolved, sister," he said. "In the name of Jesus. You are saved."

Outside, the tents billowed in the night breeze, kicking up small swells of sand. My faith reared up but felt impermanent, like these tents, hastily assembled pavilions so like a traveling circus. I all but expected gray elephants to lumber by. The preacher/teacher and I climbed back into his scuffed minivan and headed home, driving silently in the dark.

*

One of the jokes about the South is this: you may not go to church on Sunday, but you know which church you don't go to. We didn't go to Christ United Methodist Church. This rankled my Grandmother no end. She was a charter member of the church, had helped found it, had been in charge of training Methodist Sunday School teachers all over the South. My mother, who had married my grandmother's only son, was a great disappointment to her. Once I asked Mama (on Grandmama's behest) why we didn't go to church. "Oh," shrugged my mother, rushed and distracted, not listening really, the way mothers do, "Oh, I don't have anything to wear to church."

*

In Eatonville, the parade went on as scheduled with all the townspeople standing by on the street and watching it pass. There was the local Eatonville High School marching band. There was the mayor. Various displays of the town's great history had been cut out of cardboard. All that the people had accomplished in 100 years. Men and women stood on the sidelines and cheered, while their children waved small flags. It was as though the KKK wasn't coming at all, as though no one had seen them line up at 7 in the morning, with all the other participants, down by the Publix grocery store, in their parking lot.

Then it was time for them to march by. Whether from fear of reprisal, or just lack of follow through, their sorry group consisted of just three country white boys and a couple of hand painted signs.

And the crowd? They simply turned their backs and let them pass. There was no violence, no confrontation. They just refused to give those boys their attention, as though there was nothing about them or their cause worthy of Eatonville's time.

It was the greatest protest I'd ever heard of. One for the history books. Put that in the folklore along with Brer Rabbit and Brer Fox and all the great tales Hurston heard spun at the local country store. If I could've listened, I'm sure I would've heard Zora laughing from her unmarked grave.

*

Memphis is a city built on a bluff, inside a primordial forest. It sits high above the flood plain; a good three hundred feet above it, on the Fourth Chickasaw Bluff, where the Wolf River meets the Mississippi. Near the center of the city, in Overton Park, are 170 acres of virgin old growth forest. (The forest stopped an interstate in its tracks.) Trees are everywhere in Memphis, tall, climbable, shade trees. So even though I grew up in a city, I grew up in a forest. Or under the faint shadow of one. And underneath the forest, under our feet, three trillion gallons of pure soft artesian water. Until that water was discovered, around 1890, Memphis was a filthy, disease-ridden place, home to cholera and malaria and two yellow fever epidemics.

Call out to the senses. The musty mossy scent of old stone cemetery, something soft and brown-green, not decayed but not living either, a stillness. Sweet yellow honeysuckle vines, waiting for us to suck the tiny drop of nectar from the bottom of each blossom and toss it, discarded, to the ground. We never ran out of flowers. And cooking smells: you could tell the time at my grandmother's house by the smell of sizzling cornmeal as the cornbread batter was poured into hot muffin tins: 5 PM. At 5:10 I would be pulling the heavy iron pans out of the oven, flipping each piece of cornbread over with a fork to cool, and begging to eat just one.

Church smells: air conditioning and Estee Lauder, grape juice, soap. Talcum powder, spray starch, and the spotless smell of a clean conscience. But the smells I miss are mostly cooking smells and green growing things. I grew up in a city but the wild was always there, singing at the doorstep, calling out my name.

[1] Hurston, Zora Neale. "Dust Tracks on a Road" from *Southern Selves: A Collection of Autobiographical Writing.* New York: Vintage Books, 1998.

Anne-Marie Akin and Laura Jones on their process:

Southlandia, the collaboration between southerners Anne-Marie Akin and Laura Jones, began as a joke. Akin, who hails from Memphis, teased Jones, a native Floridian, saying that, to Akin's mind, Florida was not the south. This wasn't anything Jones hadn't heard before. To settle the bet, the two began an investigation: they decided to research and write into four areas they believed defined their own personal experience of the south—dialect, race, religion, and provincialism—to see what similarities and differences emerged. Separately, they each wrote four essays, but read southern writers like Dorothy Allison, James Agee, and Belle Kearney together. They dialogued continuously about their project.

Dialogue has always been a fundamental part of their relationship. They met at an SGI Buddhist conference in 2011, and like to say they haven't stopped talking since. Their ongoing connection has inspired Akin, a songwriter, to write an album of songs, and Jones to write five novels. They both believe there are no other "ears" quite like the other's.

For the final *Southlandia* draft, Jones merged both partners' writing, and Akin applied her editorial eye to polish. Akin and Jones would like to thank Michael McColly, graduate writing faculty at Northwestern University where they completed their MFAs, for supervising the independent study that made *Southlandia* possible.

Jennifer Atkinson and Gillian Parrish

DREAM TEST: A RENGA OF DEVOTION

1.

Remember how in San Juan de la Cruz's sublime, erotic, surreal canticle of devotion, in which the I climbs what seems to be a spiraling dark stairway (upward? downward?) looking for the Beloved? When they finally do find one another, the I's naked breast blooms under his Beloved's resting head. Such tenderness! And then the Beloved strikes him, leaving him senseless—no, more like beyond the senses—lost in forgetfulness among sugar lilies.

2.

It is a quirk of saints that start to finish, they are lost. Lost in thunder and thorns. In dull light of latrines, in kitchen-swill, in stables, sweeping away the work of years. Lost in the locust wilderness, bewilderment of honey. Lost in bellies of beasts, in billows of flood or fire, as if fire is some kind of fun and water the leviathan tide between stars. For saints are nothing if not carried away. It is the work of saints that they are always leaving, and they like to leave for good. Left the palaces, the plum-ripe places. The red shoes, the lutes and the dancing. Left the child and mother and every last wish. For they even leave the one true love, standing there in the garden. Just as the hyacinth bloomed. Left the leavings of the ones they left, a book half-read, the ribbon-bound lock of hair. Left themselves for dead. They follow amnesiac flickers, fall towards a dream or death of a dream. Not knowing what they do. Saints are satellites tuned to the color of rain. Saints hum. They stutter, shout, they sing. Of bees, of blood, of frozen ground, of mansions, arson, nothing left. All in answer to some call that they can never quite believe. Calling in the voice of noon, the pollen-filled heart, the midnight ghost of a flea. Called in the voice of winter, so even the grass is crooning. Dog-call and mockingbird, who's there? Some half-word half-heard strung between belly and breastbone. Something speaking the language of stars. In the dark wood they sat down. Sat down in the charnel ground, hospital, wrong side of town. In tar pits, in thickets, in lotus-blossom lakes on fire. In prisons, in burned ruins. At the snow line, sat down. At their backs, the green seam of glaciers. In front, it's always the ends of the earth—the desert, the cliff and long fall to the sea. How they floated for days, not knowing. Bellies full of moonlight. Roaming the boneyard outside the city walls. For saints are far from our protection. And anyway, they know how to die well. For it is a trick of saints to die a lot. Death on the mountain-peak-meadow-parking-lot-corner-of-main-street. Death like a dove or death like a door kicked in. Tornado-train-roar coming down, pulling the walls apart. All the air whooshed out and the world is a wheel. Death a red sun a white sun shock of the dark. The one they found stunned at dusk, who stood all day at the well; beside her, the broken jar.

3.

In the longed-for bewilderment of honey and blood, the saint, devoted to her devotion, to her attentive forgetfulness of everything else, everything other than the whoosh of the wheel crossing this exact moment, stops. Never mind the track the wheel leaves in the dust. Never mind the cart and its cargo of butchered meat. Never mind the cart-driver dozing, the bullock pulling, the dogs by the road hoping for a stumble. The saint is oblivious. She is gone, plucked from the onwardness. The minutes and hours deepening before her, piling up like unbreaking breakers, like a glassy wall of not-yet-collapsing waves. Gone and right there by the road, by the well, in the shade of the swaying cobra's hood. Gone and as here as a child playing in the dirt, creating the world from acorns and stones. Has she died or woken up elsewhere?

The saint has turned the real realer. She's reeling. Shadows fall at acuter angles, the trees' leaf-tips sting even at a distance, the rainy scent of the heartwood stuns her to sharper alertness, and the saint can taste the fruit that hasn't yet burdened its branches—maroon, beety, granular on the tongue. The moment is too present, too physical to endure. And yet this is what the saint has prepared for, thought she wished for. For this the saint has stood, has knelt, has lain down. For this the saint has sought out the dark, the snowfield, the stony shores. For this—this *this* there is no word for.

It's as if thunder has reverted to silence or silence to thunder. The serrated knife of lightning has struck, has punctured the clouds and it's pouring down milk. The saint trembles like a wren held in the hands of something awful. Maybe it's not death. Not death like a door or a dove kicked in. Not death like a sun or a cave. Not death like a sister or a swoon or the winter solstice. Not an end. Not a start. Not the spark or the ash. What?

4.

And what if, she said, it's more like a bell? Gone and gone and gone and gone. An iron hook out of the mire (at the cost of your skin)? What if it's the rock in the road, the spit in your soup? Hide-and-seek in the midnight wood, alone? All that could be. But maybe not. Maybe devotion is a question riddled with questions, riding the shadow of a doubt. Stop the clock and bar the door. ('Where the [angels] stand ready at all six times of day and night, ready and waiting. And if you have both faith and longing then they'll all come rushing towards you.') But bruised but bells but bank accounts. And what of that sweet burn we thought we wished for? That cat-piss cinnamon scent, the certain myrrh we wanted from moth wings and flames? Now it's no metaphorical fire, but the plastic stench of a household burning. What's real can be hard on the body, the pinch of seared sinus, lungs near collapse. How now the faraway looms too large. Too close too hot too sharp too fast. It pushes, tests the edges. The woman hopped up, the snake in her lap. The one who fed on nettles, turning his skin thin green. All of us learning to fall. Yearning for something like dawn. Laid down on the road, the river of bones, laid down in the grasses in the tents in the fields. Turning to slow beasts, to servants, the ones who stand by. Turning to dreams realer than days: Cut down, the heart cut out, pine wind in a cool grove. Shot in the forehead, throat, the heart. Cried out but no sound came. Woke to the unreal room, the air the color of a bruise. Now I'm like a word crossed out. Something indelible bleeds beneath the skin. Bleared, for I am in question.

5.

In not-quite absentia. I as thin as a stinging hair on a nettle leaf, as delible as a lion's tongue, a spore on the wind, a dying word, a breath-wobbled flame; I as breakable as dry bone, as lithe as smoke, as live as noise in the throat of the bell, as light in the well at noon. I is in question.

Not there and not not-there either. Shifting, re-sorted, a last word's molecules of CO_2 having been spoken, die into the dark, disperse and persist in new breath, new sound—reborn in/through/as the language and bodies of bodhisattvas and ravens, cormorants and Christs, prophets and servants, sex- and aide-workers, reborn in/as a thousand thousand thousand selves—part and parcel, whole and slivered, gone and more present than ever. Again and never and still.

It terrifies I—the promise of severance from the body—and the process hurts. The final cutting of I from it, cell from cell, that last dispersal and re-allotment of breath might not hurt, but the aches and burns I feels on the flesh, blood, bone, and nerve-strung body's way to that moment sure does. And what of the synapse between nerves, that raveling smoke-thread of I? What happens to that emptiness when the thread snaps?

6.

[In thunderous silence sat.]

[Else held up a flower.]

But since we must speak here, let the words be of a flower's blur and binding. Bound in flesh in breath in birth in death in the daily devotions to bread and speech and dreaming. And since we hurt and ache and burn and break, we are in question. We wonder, whisper, shout, we sing and light the candles, cry out, pour out the black tea for all who need protection.

7.
And who does not?

You eat bread, drink tea, steam fogs your glasses. For that moment your attention is undivided. A holy moment, devoted to that very moment. You turn, smear a roll with butter and jam for a child who wolfs it with joy, then lets the dog lick her fingers clean. A holy moment, devoted to pleasure in its quick passing.

What is it that makes a moment holy?

You break the loaf, pull a bit from its core, dip it in the juice and eat. For the moment your attention is undivided. A holy moment, devoted to that very moment. You turn and offer the bread to the one beside you, who takes some, dips, eats, and passes the plate to the one beside him. A holy moment, devoted to passing.

Is it the pure attention, the devotion itself?

Gustave Sobin writes in *Luminous Debris* that in second century Gaul devotees of Aphrodite wore tiny mirror amulets around their necks, glass disks, silvered to make them reflective, and framed in lead. The mirrors were just one eye wide, meant to catch and hold the glance of the goddess. Looking in, whose eye would the seeker see? Who would look back at whom? Whose spider lashes, whose bright tears, whose pupil shrinking to a pinprick? Whose gaze would behold and whose be held? It takes two eyes to complete a full parallax view: with her tiny light and lead mirror held up to one eye like a monocle, what would the devotee see before her?

What if half your vision were a god's? How would the world look? How would the bread taste then?

8.
'What, it will be Questioned,' wrote that god-eyed devotee Blake, 'When the Sun rises, do you not see a round Disk of fire somewhat like a Guinea?' O no no, I see an Innumerable company of the Heavenly host crying "Holy Holy Holy…"

Could we wake to the sky like a song, the celestial singing of rain and buses passing?

In the most perfect meditation, keep the senses open wide. (Say *Ah*.)

Hearsay that the Hasids say everyone is born for the sake of a minute. A particular event you must be present for. Something you were born to do or to watch happen. Trouble is, you don't know what or when. Waiting, not knowing and ready. Each moment a test of attention. Need not say love.

> Dream test. Test of the garden gate. Dinner table test. Test of the black dog barking. Test of pass the salt. Mountain tests. Test at the corner store. Test of sort-the-seeds. Sex test. Test of milk and honey. Broken bones test. The alchemical kitchen test. Bite-the-tongue test. Test of the irritating friend. Spin-the-straw-to-gold test. Wishing test. Test of the perfect lover. Test of home. Test of exquisite kisses. Death test.

Fistfuls of peonies test. Test of never enough.
White-knuckle tests. Tests of poxes and pills.
The arrows-to-flowers test. Test of October sky.
Half-moon test. Death test again. Test of the dark
wood. Breadcrumb test. Test of more salt, please.
Bitter tests. And sweet.

9.

And what does passing that volley of tests gain? A guinea of gold, a scruple of
salt, a wish come true, a day's reprieve. And another worksheet of sums and
problems, after which another test, the test of submitting to tests. Set the table,
set the bone, set the tea aside to steep...

You know you ought to feel grateful, joyous, alert with expectation always
because every moment is that one—holy, holy, etc.—but sometimes words are
sodden bread, bread is tasteless cotton. Sometimes the scent of lilies is laced with
rot, and not in a good way. You know a saint would not falter. You know the
right answers to the test but can't quite see why to fill in the scantron bubbles.
Yes, the lit-up silence before and after the thunder is holy. Yes, the thunder is
holy. And so is the hail that flattens the wheat and ruins the crop. And so is the
moment after that and the day and the day and the day. You know you shouldn't
give up. "Keep your hand on the plow, eyes on the prize, etc." But where are the
singing angels? the host of celestial busses? Where is the A for acing test after
test? Where is the hacker's triumphant breakthrough into encrypted, classified
files? Is the secret password *surrender*? Or *willfulness*? Willingness or will.
Willingness *and* will.

Devotion is entering a cavern with a single candle stub and walking deeper and
deeper into the darkness until, in time, as you knew it would, the candle gutters
out. What will you do? Go on walking further inward? Stumble back through
the maze of cavern chambers to the entrance and open air? Sit down and wait
for rescue? Sit down and curse the foolish pride that led you in? Sit down and let
the darkness settle like dust on your lap?

10.

Devotion is watching the fire go out.

Laid thus low.

Gone in the gut, gone my oh my only flower. Cut down my heart cut out.
World-without-end. What could be could be such splendor, endless. Lost in
this dissolving world. Thunder is nothing but thunder. No reward or rescue.
Nothing but love and death here. Folly of tests and the terrible things we
do. As our angels fall and fail us, flail and fall. Angels with their eyes on the
prize. Angels, you see, don't see us. And the terrible pearl and heedless swine.
Heartblood poured out, for you for you for you and you. Though some are so far
from protection—*this seat of desolation, voyd of light.* Devotion can be walking
away from devotion. Knowing only you don't know. No host of celestial busses.
No cavalry is coming. What's real is hard on the body, bleared. Have you
died or woken up elsewhere? Somehow you're kinder when you've died. (And
sometimes there's a breeze that smells like rain.) No more tests to take. No more
sums or bubbles. Nothing to do but wait here ('No end to this') no spark no ash
no little flame, you're gone, you can't go on, you'll go on.

Jennifer Atkinson and Gillian Parrish on their process:

In a year of hard travel, Gillian reached out to old poet friends to write collabora-
tive lyric essays in a renga-like mode of oblique linking that allowed for a con-
templative conversation on topics ranging from war to home. For one of these
"renga essays," she approached the poet Jennifer Atkinson to circumambulate the

question of devotion, given some shared interest in the Buddhist tradition and Jennifer's mystic Christian works, seen most recently in her *Canticle of the Night Path* and *The Thinking Eye*. Their collaboration, which unfolded across oceans over email, draws on stories from each tradition, with glimpses of saints or siddhas crossing water, walking to wells in Samaria or India. Jennifer opened the series with the first entry, followed by the third, fifth, seventh and ninth. Gillian's are the even numbers, in which she weaves in other voices, starting with Blake's "ghost of a flea" in the second entry. In the sixth, "In thunderous silence" is drawn from the Vimalakirti sutra, a text that, in a similar vein to the more famous Flower Sermon, enacts the gap between naming and knowing. The last entry contains a scrap of *Paradise Lost* as well as an echo of Beckett's *The Unnamable*, which grapples with doubt and faith in language, with questions of speech and silence.

Elizabeth K. Brown, Luther Hughes, Caroline Kessler, Ryan Masters, Gabe Montesanti, and Sylvia Sukop

OF BREATH: AFTER MONTAIGNE

I'd practice Bhastrika Pranayama, otherwise known as the "bellows breath." This breathing exercise involves a deep, diaphragmatic inhalation and a fast, forced exhalation. I used to work with this breath until I was light-headed. I'd even include a couple of kumbhakas—holding the breath in at the top of an inhale or out at the tail end of an exhale for a few seconds—until I would essentially blackout. The blackouts were brief, with my body in a heap on the floor. There'd be a pins-and-needles sensation in my limbs. Blood would rush to my head. I'd slightly lose my peripheral vision and hear a ringing in my ears. It was a kind of high. My body felt completely empty, and in that emptiness was the peace I was searching for.

A dear friend of mine is a scuba dive instructor. The last time I visited her in Annapolis, she showed me a video of three women freediving in an attempt to sway me. "It's like yoga in a way," she explained, "because you have to learn to control your breath. You know, get out of your head."

The body's breathing apparatus is the only physiological function that is both voluntary and involuntary. It lies at the boundary between the conscious and the unconscious.
—Stephen Cope, *Yoga and the Quest for True Self*

I once booked a session with a rebirthing coach. We met in her living room, a large space free of all furniture, and she instructed me to lie flat on my back on the thin cushion she had set out on the floor on the far side of the room. I didn't exactly know what I was getting myself into. And Sue, my teacher, told me that was perfect. Knowledge, she said, can sometimes get in the way. The session consisted of breathing in a circular pattern. Inhale to exhale to inhale to exhale to inhale, without pausing at the top or the bottom: something we all do without thinking. The moment between an inhale and an exhale is thought by some to be a place of emotional repression. The breath retention, *kumbhaka*, is the place where uncomfortable emotional experiences take refuge, sometimes for our whole lives. The circular breathing was disorienting at first. It felt out of control, the way I imagined hyperventilating would feel, but Sue was there to coach me through it. She had to remind me more than once that the point was not to breathe *fast*, just to breathe *continuously*. To slow down. "Let the body breathe itself," she said.

According to the book *Kripalu Yoga: A Guide to Practice On and Off the Mat*, there are many ways to breathe. Most of us breathe in a way that is restrictive and does not fully utilize the body's capacities. Especially in the western world, where the size of a woman's waist is given great importance, we tend to practice what is known as reverse breathing, where the inhalation is visible with the movement of the chest. The rib cage expands slightly, instead of the belly softening and relaxing outward as it should when the diaphragm presses down to create space for the lungs. We like to keep our tummies tucked, and in doing so, we short ourselves.

In 1975, French Dr. Frederick Leboyer published, *Birth without Violence*. The book outlined the traumatic experiences by which babies were ushered into the world in modern hospital settings. In it, he listed the many ways that modern birthing practices were detrimental to a baby's initial experience of the breath. According to Leboyer, prematurely cutting the umbilical cord was the greatest offense. Robbing a baby of its primary source of oxygen before it was able to receive oxygen from its own lungs created a near-death experience at the very onset of life.

There are many enemies of the breath. Clothes that pinch the waist. Clothes that are too small. Belts. Neck Ties. High Heels. Even the body can be an enemy to itself. It can stipend the breath when it is needed elsewhere—the heart being the main factor. Heart attacks occur when oxygen cannot reach the heart in a timely fashion, blocking flow through the coronary artery. If blood cannot reach the heart, the heart throws a tantrum against the body. The body responds in failure and shuts down parts one by one. Suddenly, or not so suddenly, the body will collapse from lack of oxygen: a lack of breath.

This, however, was unknown to me when my father collapsed outside the house. I was five years old, and *Big Poppa* by Notorious B.I.G. was gassing the living room. It was my father's favorite. The entire day, he was dancing, popping his shoulders up and down, flirting with my mom as she smiled that southern belle smile, tossed her head back and laughed a honey voice. Soon, my father began walking in and outside the house, claiming it was too cold or too hot. I looked at the television, breathed a deep sigh, let the oxygen fill my insect lungs. As the breath fled my nostrils, my mother's voice flooded my ears: *Call 9-1-1*. I turned and found my father, collapsed outside on the ground.

When the doctor came to us in the hospital waiting room, they said it was a heart attack. That was the first time I heard of a heart attacking anything. I only knew hearts in the sense of Valentine's Day: cutting hearts over and over for my friends and parents. I thought hearts meant love. I thought love fueled the heart and the body.

As I grew older, I realized love didn't fuel the heart or the body the same way as kinky, meaningless sex. I was introduced to the phenomenon of erotic asphyxiation in college, where a group of my female friends hung maps of the college in our suite to document the buildings in which they'd fucked. The game included a series of naughty challenges, one of which was breath control play. The concept was new to me but I was aware of the basic principles of bondage, dominance, and submission, so it seemed like a somewhat natural progression.

"When the brain is deprived of oxygen, it induces a lucid, semi-hallucinogenic state called hypoxia. Combined with orgasm, the rush is said to be no less powerful than cocaine, and highly addictive."
—George Shuman, *Last Breath*

One of my friends reported her experience with hypoxia as exhilarating. The orgasm had been toe-curling: her best climax to date. She recounted her partner's hands pushing down on her throat as he thrusted so that her air only came in short bursts. Part of the appeal, at least in her opinion, was the uncertainty about when she would be able to seize her next breath.

What my friend failed to appreciate was the breath itself. There are dozens of cases of deaths resulting from erotic or auto-erotic asphyxiation. Albert Dekker, ironically best known for his role in *The Killers*, is one of these cases. His death occurred in 1968 when he was discovered kneeling naked in his bathtub with a rope around his throat. Blindfolded, handcuffed, and gagged, Dekker's body was branded with explicit phrases drawn in red lipstick.

One serial killer best known for his application of asphyxiation is Randy Kraft, sometimes called "the Scorecard Killer," who killed 67 people between 1971 and 1983. All of the presumed victims were male, and many of them were enlisted in the marines. In all cases the men were bound and sexually abused before Kraft killed them with either strangulation or asphyxiation. Based on what we know about Randy Kraft's sexual life, he had never displayed any violence toward any of his romantic partners. After ending a relationship with a man named Jeff Graves, Kraft started seeing a 19-year-old baker named Jeff Seelig. The two regularly sought out hitchhikers and brought them back to their apartment for sexual threesomes. Still, Seelig maintains that Kraft never displayed any violent tendencies in his presence.

A year or so after I began lifeguarding at the local community pool, I watched a little boy go down the slide and slip under the surface of the water. He didn't come back up. A tingling sensation lit up my muscles so that the water had no temperature when I jumped in to save him. He came up sputtering, heaving, gasping, clutching my body as the only thing that was keeping him afloat. It didn't register that he was also choking me.

For weeks after the rescue, I could not unhear that child's raspy, uneven breath. It rattled around in my mind. When I considered asphyxiation as sexual gratification, there was only fear. There was only Albert Dekker hanging by a rope in his bathtub and Randy Kraft dumping a body on the side of the freeway like roadkill. There was only that child and his little arms wrapped around my throat in an attempt to keep breathing. It took days to reground myself: to intake air and expel it.

"I took a deep breath and listened to the old brag of my heart. I am, I am, I am."
—Sylvia Plath, *The Bell Jar*

This idea of re-grounding, of using the breath to be centered, of echoing the pattern Plath indicates—"I am, I am, I am"—seems like a particularly human impulse. What other animal needs to focus so intensely on one of the things that comes most naturally? Perhaps there are underground conventions of wasps, beavers, and raccoons learning how to exhale their breath in a more efficient way, or to get more oxygen into their blood, but I doubt it.

Chanting *kirtan* is a practice that comes from the *bhakti* yoga tradition, often defined as the yoga of devotion or love. *Kirtan* involves singing or chanting the names of God in a call-and-response fashion, usually in Sanskrit, although sometimes in Hindi or Gurmukhi, and occasionally in English. David Newman, a *kirtan* artist and *bhakti* yoga educator, explains that *kirtan* means "to praise that which is exalted" (the divine). *Kirtan* stems from a Sanskrit root which means "to cut through," he says, so kirtan is also a "practice for cutting through the idea of separation for connecting to our hearts and connecting to the moment through sound."

Instead of chanting "I am, I am, I am," the focus turns outward. Perhaps one doesn't quite understand the Sanskrit, even as it's explained to mean something like "victorious one" or "love" or "god of beauty," making it easier to chant the syllables which contain this obfuscated meaning. To focus on the syllables is to forget the self. Chanting what is essentially a vibration seems far more useful than focusing on the breath. And by useful, I mean, able to get me out of my head and into my body; out of my incessant, swirling thoughts about the past or the future and into the present; out of anxieties and worries about things I cannot control and into the *now*; out of obsessing over my ego and into a meaning(less/ful) vibration of sound. We are, after all, just creations of sound and light. We are all vibrations, set to a certain frequency we may not even be conscious of, waiting to be tuned to a specific pitch by a steel tuning fork.

"No more words. In the name of this place we drink in with our breathing, stay quiet like a flower. / So the night birds will start singing."
—Jalāl ad-Dīn Muḥammad Rūmī, *Night and Sleep*

If you take the night shift with someone in the closing days of their life, you get to know breathing all over again. The person you are caring for—old or young, parent or sibling, or someone who has no one besides you—will finally fall asleep after you've given them their middle-of-the-night meds, changed out the batteries on the pump to their PICC line, adjusted their pillows and blankets, perhaps said a silent prayer. You'll lean in to kiss their cheek (it's not the right time for hugging, you save that for goodbyes) and you'll turn out the light (with your breath if candle, or by winding down the wick in a kerosene lamp, flicking the switch for hospital fluorescent, or reaching under the bedside lampshade that years ago was a present from you, with real baby's breath, iris, and freesia pressed between translucent sheets, quiet flowers nightly illumined).

You might then sit on the one chair in the room, or you might lie down on the floor at the foot of the bed on a sleeping bag where you won't sleep, and, eyes open, you'll listen with the alertness of a nocturnal animal. You'll be extremely tired but you'll appreciate this spacious time, this wordless communion, drinking the same air in different rhythms. Your fear will recede which is surprising in the dark—your fear about what comes next and whether you will be ready, whether the one you love will be ready. What takes its place is an urgent desire to remember everything that has happened that day. You reach for the notebook you placed there earlier, with the pen in the gutter where you last left off. Despite knowing you can't possibly remember and record it all, despite that deflating sense of defeat before you even begin, you sit upright with the notebook on your knee, pen in one hand and flashlight in the other, and you press the rubber nub, careful once it's on to keep the bright beam aimed down at the page. The tip of your pen scratches against the silence, like a furtive squirrel burying or digging up the thing that could not be immediately consumed.

The patient stirs—is it your fault? You pause. You turn off the flashlight. Some nights they wake up restless, suddenly burst with strange energy and dire but indecipherable warnings. ("We're in a bad place: *Malkeeyum*. We have to move."). When they want out they want out, never mind the snow piled high as the wooden porch, the late spring thunderstorm, the snare of the PICC line or oxygen tube, the rules of the crowded nursing home. Talking them out of it never goes well. Logic loses at this late hour.

Tonight, they fall back to sleep. Their breathing becomes once more the focus of your attention. You've been told the ever-widening interval between exhale and inhale is normal at this stage. Not freediver wide, but 15, 20 seconds of empty lung, lung no longer lunging for breath but resting in its absence. The yogis mastered this with disciplined practice, to the dying it comes naturally.

And the Lord God formed man of the dust of the ground, and breathed into his nostrils the breath of life; and man became a living soul.
—Genesis 2:6

I am a parent now, and I use breathing exercises to calm both my children and myself. Like every gift my father gave me, I worry that my heart is slightly damaged. At times I lie still and it races. Other times, I come home from jogging and I have to search for its beat. I feel nothing at all, nothing but cold sweat. I lie on the couch in those moments and listen to my own breath, controlling it, shaping it. I make it a bird that flies away from me and then flutters back. Then it's a spray of colors that paints the morning blue and purple. It's important to turn fear into beauty, before fear turns into anxiety, which turns to pain, which turns to an early death.

The same Hebrew word for "spirit" is also the word for "breath." So, these mornings the breath I'm trying to control is like some sort of demon, the grinding of whose teeth gives off that low-frequency death rattle that besets my days. I am afraid of the delicacy of breath, how thin and insubstantial—yet vital—it is. A heart at least has walls and valves, it pumps, it beats, it throbs. It has the combustion of life working in it. The breath is invisible. Like a spirit or an idea, but one whose absence breaks you.

Worst of all is when death touches children. Even the idea, the spirit of death—that invisible wind with the stink of death on it. My son only knows about the death of bugs, which he can only equate to the breaking of toys. Bugs don't die; bugs just stop working.

I don't understand why we tell children that people have to die, like it's not a natural function of the body, but rather a verdict. Every night when my son was an infant, I snuck into his room while he slept. I would wet my fingers and put them up to his nostrils. If I felt the cold of his breath on my wet fingers, it meant he was okay; that we were okay.

It was as if each night I was having a verdict read to me through the breathing of my child. And all those years ago my father heard that verdict in the silence of his heart, but was granted reprieve. Now I wake early so that I can breathe in some concentrated, controlled way. I sit, mindful of the invisible thing moving through me, listening to what I have come to think of as the gavel-pound of my heart.

Elizabeth K. Brown, Luther Hughes, Caroline Kessler, Ryan Masters, Gabe Montesanti, and Sylvia Sukop on their process:

"Of Breath: After Montaigne" came into existence in an MFA course at Washington University in St. Louis called "The Art of the Essay." Kathleen Finneran, the instructor of the course, postulated that one way to achieve a meandering, surprising essay each week was to write it collectively. We used the exquisite corpse process, adding to the piece and passing it on to the next writer within twenty-four hours and with no verbal communication. The order in which we received the essay was determined randomly by Finneran; the student whose name appeared first in the list could choose the subject of the piece, and the student whose name appeared last could choose how to end it. Eight collective essays were born during the semester, each of which was inspired by a single essayist.

Page Delano, Ellen Geist, and Katt Lissard

LOVING MAO

We all used to have red hair, but now Page is blonde. Red was an iconic color for us back in the 1970s and 80s. We were Reds. We carried red flags. At a demonstration in DC after Mao died, we wore red Mao buttons. Red expressed our desire for radical change, to transform the system from its roots seeped in exploitation, poverty, war, sexism, racism—to create something new.

We'd been inexplicably drawn to each other at a conference for leftist artists in New York City in 1987. We started meeting at a café near Washington Square Park. Although we talked about our politics, lives, loves, and most of all our writing, it took a while to reveal that our pasts not only included common ideals and activism, but that we'd been in the same organization at different times, in different places, doing different kinds of work: Page in West Virginia organizing miners and their wives, Ellen in Pittsburgh among factory workers, and Katt in the projects of the South Bronx, East New York, and Spanish Harlem.

It took even longer for us to begin writing about that time and giving group readings of our work under the title, *Red Heads/Red Tales*. This is a compilation of some of our pieces.

Page: My brother has a huge poster of Chairman Mao in his studio on Greenwich Street—the man in the Mao suit with the mole on his face, greyish, and a pinkish red hue to the whole thing. The studio, in the front of his loft, faces the Hudson River. For the first year he lives here there is nothing between him and the river but a fenced in grassy lot, waiting apparently for progress. The loft, up two long flights of stairs, resides in the egg and cheese district, where you can buy huge wheels of Swiss cheese, the size of a car tire.

> Ellen: We were very poor. By choice, you might say. Some of us were from Scarsdale, Shaker Heights, and Georgetown, but we never talked about that. I wasn't from any of those places. My father always said we were "lower middle class," but we were probably more in the middle than he

cared to admit. Some very few of us were not poor by choice; they were true workers. We had met them at Kenner Toys, at General Hospital, and at Frigidaire. We prided ourselves on adopting every nuance of the workers' lifestyle/values/habits of mind. I myself adopted a southern accent, which I can slip into to this day. We decided to like country-western music. We were going to organize a Marxist style revolution in America and we were going to the workers, like "Peasants marching off to war,"—a quote we liked from Mao Tse-Tung. We liked Clint Eastwood movies. We no longer liked Shakespeare, Beethoven, Romantic Poetry, although my husband had a penchant for Abstract Expressionist painting. I sold all my works of world literature during college where I became involved with the most extremist group I could find, the one that was serious about organizing a Marxist style revolution in America.

> *Katt: It's 3:00 in the afternoon, just before Halloween, and I'm alone in a dirty beige-colored, very chilly jail cell hoping the party's lawyer might finally make an appearance and get me out of here. I was arrested in the South Bronx the day before yesterday, in Lincoln Hospital, in the employee cafeteria to be exact. And until this morning I wasn't sure which precinct they'd taken me to because my ride from the hospital with New York City's "finest" was purposely circuitous and threatening. Or maybe I just couldn't accept the obvious: Fort Apache, the South Bronx, is no place you want to spend the night.*

My friend who went to California after college to work with the Peace and Freedom Party, comes east. Valedictorian at Sarah Lawrence the same year as Hillary Clinton spoke to her graduating class at Wellesley, she'd been working at a cardboard box factory in Oakland. From my apartment on East Second Street, fifty-eight dollars a month, water heated by a coal furnace, adjacent to the 19th century Marble Cemetery, sanctuary for trees and birds, we explore First Avenue. She finds the store on 11th Street that is hard-core Maoist, selling Red Books and Mao pins and pamphlets. The book store people are more intense than my friend Allie; humorless, as if the revolution will be here tomorrow and they're ready for serious shit. Allie is friendly to them nonetheless, and I buy a Red Book and the Selected Essays. I already have *On Contradiction*, which I used in my philosophy class when I was a freshman, where we read Hegel's *Phenomenology of Mind*, along with Marcuse's *Liberation*—I saw Marcuse speak at the New School. It's a big deal, the kind of thing one might make up, but I heard him.

We were not Russian-style communists. We denounced the Communist Party USA as a Soviet Puppet. We were America's Maoists and we were purists—we wanted real communism, as Karl Marx had envisioned it, the communism I fell in love with in college, tracing down from Hegel, the true spirit of history, where everything is equal and one is a worker in the morning and a poet in the afternoon. When I took a Marxism class in college, it made absolute sense to me and I set about trying to find a group that was serious about it. The group that seemed most serious, however, were Stalinists and wanted me to quit my advanced poetry seminar. I didn't quit the seminar, but I did stop writing poetry. Everyone else from the seminar went to the Iowa Writers' Workshop, where, remarkably, most of them became rather well-known figures in the poetry scene, while I went on to graduate work at Delco Moraine making wheel cylinders for cars. It was very challenging to learn to keep up with the assembly line and at first I was covered in oil, but eventually I learned. I hated Stalin, but gradually I made the adjustment. I don't know how or why I did this. My entire collection of literature became whittled down to two works of fiction. One was *Barricades in Berlin*. You probably have never heard of this book. It is about May Day in Germany before the war. I have no idea anymore if it's any good, but I suspect it is not any good. The other was *The Mother* by Maxim Gorky, which is indeed a good book.

Later on, I was assigned to sell our newspaper at poetry readings. We were trying to broaden our strategy from just organizing the working class to including the "Petit-Bourgeoisie." I would sit in the back of the room watching others read poetry and tears would roll down my face.

As a departure from our main work selling the party's newspaper and agitating about overthrowing the system, our team has been experimenting with other forms of following Mao's famous dictum: "Create Public Opinion ... Seize Power!" I'm the cause of our recent forays into street theatre. It's obvious theatre isn't going to bring down U.S. imperialism, but we've been having a lot more fun and our paper sales have increased. So, those higher up the leadership chain of the organization have given us their blessing to continue.

For the past month, we'd been performing a pre-election mock debate. But I proposed a different idea for the illegal hospital show—focused on it being 1984, the most symbolically fraught year imaginable, combined with the ongoing farce of Reagan, actor-turned-president, ready to reprise his "role of a lifetime" for the ruling class. What does it mean, I wanted us to ask, the confluence of George Orwell's grim, prescient dystopia and the bright, blatant stagecraft in the White House?

For a while, after SDS and our take-over of the administration building, and my leave of absence from college, I can move from one political context to another, to mix all these things: I have my labor history group, my Lower East Side Women's Liberation Collective, and the Alice Kramden Printshop in Greenpoint, for which we bought (at auction) an offset printing press, which we place in a loft in a factory of sewing shops on Metropolitan Avenue. The World Trade Center is visible from the street, right near the L train, the Lorimer Street stop, yet we are socially and culturally *far* from Manhattan.

What if the new neighbors upstairs, the skinhead band from Seattle with swastikas tattooed on their arms, are really undercover working for COINTELPRO—what if they're behind my arrest, somehow? Maybe not. But what if the party's lawyer can't find me because I'm here at Fort Apache, not where they'd expect me to be? That must be why the cops drove all over the place before they brought me here.

There were two of them.

"So, you're a Communist?" the large, pasty one, who'd taken the passenger seat, said over his shoulder as we started off and he shuffled through the arrest paperwork he'd begun filling out at the hospital. "Friend of Joe Stalin and Mr. Chernenko and Chairman Mao, huh? Don't think people should have the right to vote? Bet she loves Fidel."

"Fuck!" the younger one, who was trimmer and almost handsome, exploded from the driver's seat, slamming his palm on the steering wheel, "I hate the Communists!" He looked Hispanic but had no accent. "I hate Castro!"

Ah, I thought, great, a Castro-hating Cuban guy with a temper.

"Me, too," the pasty one agreed. "I hate every Communist dick-head on this planet."

"The women too!" the younger one insisted.

"The women're the worst. But they give good blow jobs, right? Right?" he repeated, turning to me. "You give good blow jobs, Mao-lover?"

From this loft we plan to print pamphlets for working class women, to organize them. The Working Class and Class Conscious Women's Workshop invites me to join them. I'm the token *class conscious* woman. For a while all this works, my unemployment checks continue, and then—I begin to congeal, to harden, to want definition, and the people I am drawn to have harder lines, are less sympathetic to other groups. I begin to love Mao in a practical way. He is not Che, not John Brown, not Rosa Parks or even Malcolm X. He is Chairman Mao.

Eventually I was fired from the factory for stopping production. We marched through the factory shouting "Mao Tse-Tung did not fail, Revolution will prevail!" and throwing Mao buttons. Mao Tse-Tung had died and we stood with the Gang of Four. After that march, the workers thronged outside the factory as we left and one pulled a knife on me while I was arguing with him. We were always getting into arguments with workers who wanted to kill us. There wasn't that much respect for the law and many workers owned guns and were quite willing to use them, although most of the fights were verbal and fist. I never saw myself as brave and didn't like to get into fights. I don't know how I did this, how I woke up at 5 in the morning and put on a down overcoat and snow pants and stood in the freezing cold trying to sell communist newspapers at factory gates to workers who wanted to kill me. I believed in what I was doing. I sublimated the personal to the political.

I knew they were trying to scare me. But sitting there, looking at the backs of their heads, I realized I'd noticed something strange when they arrived at the hospital, something lodged in my sub-conscious that now, trapped in the back seat, came into focus . . . It's their badges, I reluctantly acknowledged, my skin puckering with goosebumps. Their badges were covered up with black tape, their names and numbers hidden.

Could that be true? I shifted in the seat to see if I could get a glimpse of the big cop's badge. I did, and for a moment I thought I was going to wet my pants, the rush of fear was so intense, and completely and involuntarily physical. My god, I thought: it's dark out (it was only 6:30, but a cloudy fall dusk); I'm in a car alone with two unidentifiable cops; we're driving on unnamed back streets; and no one knows where I am.

Mao is in the *Red Book*, in the *Selected*, and the pamphlets, *Mao on Art and Literature*, *Talks at the Yenan Forum*, the multi-volume *Collected Works*. You can read Mao with Engels, with Marx, with Lenin, and even with Stalin. Mao is the great Helmsman; he tells you that to know the taste of a pear you must eat a pear. I have always loved pears. I love practice. I love contradiction. I love dialectical materialism, the way the words themselves have a material quality.

"Hey!" the driver was saying, his voice high and agitated, "Answer my buddy's question—do you Communist whores give good blow jobs?"

"You know," the pasty one said in a between-us-boys tone, "we could just take a little drive, do whatever we want and get rid of her. Who will know? Unless we take her in and process her, no one's going to know we have her."

"The rent-a-cops at the hospital'll know."

"Yeah, but they gave us all the paperwork—this here is the only record."

"Party's over, Mrs. Mao!"

I want to do working class organizing. I want to galvanize, radicalize, use my skills of organization, learn from the working class. I was a feminist but I was interested in class, and the Alice Kramden Printshop was not enough. There are fights in the women's movement about class. Betty Friedan loves Rita Mae Brown, but it is a secret, or at least she wants to spend a few nights with her. The Lavender Menace wants women to dance with women. I go to a dance but it doesn't work. Friendship is politicized. Romance is politicized.

> We worked very hard, day and night; we stayed up all night writing leaflets, and spent all day passing them out. I remember once we were driving through the park with a stack of leaflets and someone swore we were being tailed by undercover cops, and I chewed up and ate about fifty of those leaflets, god knows how I did it, chewed and swallowed them, so if we got stopped, the cops wouldn't find them. We worked very hard, we stayed up all night, we ran around all day, and I was the most dedicated. Even if I couldn't be the most brave, I could be the most dedicated.

>> *Their game had a dark, nasty edge. Where was I anyway? On some completely derelict side street in the South Bronx where the torched-out buildings all looked alike, their missing windows covered with sheets of tin the city bolted over the gaping openings, each painted to evoke a version of bright, happy home—red flowers in a vase, green polka dot curtains, an orange and white cat on a ledge eyeing a yellow bird in a cage.*

>> *I'm not easily frightened. My stance with the police has always been stoic, a stony silence I can maintain for as long as it takes. I assume an admittedly ridiculous mantle of moral superiority I trust to protect me—they're the arm of the state, after all; I'm with the good guys. But there was something unsettling about these two men, something I'd never encountered before.*

>> *"My lawyer will be looking for me," I said, loathing myself for opening my mouth, especially to say something so cowardly and privileged.*

>> *"Son of a bitch, Lady Mao has lawyered up!" The big, pasty cop turns and looks at me, his eyes bright, predatory. "Fine, Lady, fine... We'll take you over to the Fort, but I'm going to keep your little file for myself."*

>> *In the days following my eventual release from Ft. Apache (it took a bit longer than the party's lawyer anticipated, since my passport*

and arrest report had gone missing), I think a lot about why noth-
ing happened to me that night in that car. Ultimately, I know I
was spared by the thing I'm most trying to escape—my class, my
place on the food chain, the fact that I'm not isolated and alone in
an indifferent city.

I quit not so long after swallowing those leaflets because I was pregnant with my second child. I thought, I can't keep living like this or my baby will never make it. That wasn't the only reason. There were many reasons I quit. I wrote them all down and handed in dozens of resignations, I didn't want to just quit, I wanted to explain my ideas. I was reading Simone de Beauvoir and Doris Lessing who I hadn't read since college.

I was reading, and I was also thinking I just wanted to be normal and not part of world history. I thought: if I could just go to Seders, if I could just write, if I could just spend time going over letters with my son, if I could just visit my family, if I could just go on hikes to outdoor places, then I would be happy.

I am not so sure about necessity, nor about historical inevitability, because I have studied history. I love the feel of causality, of the tricky elusiveness of meaning. I love *knowing* the damage caused by the Versailles Treaty, that Germany rearmed in defiance of all the restrictions against it, that the reactionaries felt stabbed in the back and hated women, that Weimar Germany was culturally exciting and radical, but fascism triumphed with historical reasons. I respect these measured assessments. I've studied Rosa Luxemburg. I love her, even if she doesn't fit in the litany of Marxism-Leninism-Mao Tse-Tung Thought. And May 1968, and the Cultural Revolution, the American athletes raising fists in Mexico City, the Tet Offensive, Chicago—we are part of a great sweep of history.

Page Delano, Ellen Geist, and Katt Lissard on their process:

The idea of writing a collaborative group memoir came out of a conversation about what might be interesting to a larger audience about the kind of commitment and level of involvement the three of us experienced at the times and places where we were active: the coalfields of West Virginia and a factory in Pittsburgh in the 1970s, the housing projects and low income neighborhoods of New York in 1980s. Here we offer some parts of the process of how we became "Reds," and what that meant in our day to day lives, private and public. Each of us writes in a different primary genre and rhythm: Page is a poet, Ellen writes fiction and Katt is a playwright. We were involved in exciting and risky activities, open and above board about our political views with everyone we met. We chose to reject the class identity we were born into and immerse ourselves in the working class, in the case of Page and Ellen, or, in Katt's case, into Lenin's "real proletariat"—essentially giving up or disguising our previous identities in the spirit of our goal to change the world.

Jacqueline Doyle and Stephen D. Gutierrez

IMAGINARY FRIENDS

A friend of mine just learned from her much older brother that she had an imaginary friend in kindergarten. She's agitated when she tells me. "I mean, is that normal?" And can't believe she forgot her so completely. "Who was she? How is it possible that I don't remember her at all?" I'm jealous that I never had one.

My husband Steve had an imaginary friend when he was five years old. "What's it like to have an imaginary friend?" I ask him as we stride along on our evening walk. It's dark and he holds a small flashlight at his side, which he switches on and points downward when a car passes. There's a sliver of moon overhead in the sky.

The friend's name was "Steve." Steve—my husband Steve that is, the flesh and blood person walking beside me—writes fiction and creative nonfiction. Sometimes it's hard to tell them apart. Two recurring characters in his fictional stories are a lot like him. One is named Walter. The other is named Steve. I never made the connection to his imaginary friend before. I guess because he's never talked much about him. Now I wonder whether his phantom companion became his character.

We pass under a streetlight and for a moment Steve's face is illuminated before his corporeal being becomes incorporeal again. I reach out and touch his arm in the dark to make sure he's still there.

"What was 'Steve' like?"

Steve thinks for a while.

"'Steve,' as far as I can remember him, was an ideal friend, a lot like me, only better, only perfect," he says. "I was excruciatingly embarrassed by my big ears as a kid, not just large ears but ears that stuck out at an acute 90 degree angle from my head. And I got called names, of course. I learned to withdraw. But 'Steve' didn't need to! He had regular ears. He wore a striped shirt like I did, a blue tee shirt with red and yellow horizontal stripes, but 'Steve's' looked better on him, spiffier, brighter, newer. 'Steve' didn't act better than me—he was me, only not me. I haven't thought about him for years."

Steve grabs my arm. "Watch out for the pothole, Jackie!"

* * *

I'm curious. I do some research, scanning the Internet and our university's online databases, arrested by a scholarly article here, an anecdote there. I learn that some children see their imaginary friends and can describe them in vivid detail, as Steve can, while some only hear them. Most know that they are imaginary, but some do not. Children develop language skills with their imaginary friends, improvise play scenarios, work out anxieties and fears, develop their identities, and find comfort with them. Writers are twice as likely to have had childhood imaginary friends as the population at large.

I'm particularly interested in imaginary friends as doubles of the writer, though of course they're not always doubles. One writer friend tells me that her imaginary friend in preschool was a dinosaur. Another tells me that hers, named "Amy," was not a friend but an enemy. In Poe's seminal tale, William Wilson is dogged for years by his whispering double and unwelcome companion, until he finally plunges a sword through his heart. Borges seems ambivalent at best about his imaginary friend. As Borges and the other "Borges" stroll through the streets of Buenos Aires, the other "Borges" usurps Borges' experience to write about it. "Little by little," Borges writes in "Borges and I," "I am giving over everything to him, though I am quite aware of his perverse custom of falsifying and magnifying things." Or maybe the other "Borges" writes that. Borges admits he's not sure.

* * *

Steve's interested in the research, but it's not completely matching up with his childhood experience of "Steve."

"I don't know," he says. "We inhabit our doubles to escape, but we don't always like them. They're not exactly friends. Maybe they inhabit us. We're possessed by them."

"So 'Steve' is more of a daemon than a companion?" I ask.

He pauses. "'Steve' is a smiling version of hell."

* * *

Steve's Take on Imaginary Friends. One notion that seems missing in the scientific studies is that we *hide* in our doubles; they don't seek us out so much as we create them to inhabit them without the discomfort of being, and then we blame them for existing as if we didn't call them forth in the first place out of great need. Relieved of our psychological burdens, which are heavy, we both rejoice in the displacement of those burdens and reject their projection—is that the right word?—in the form of these frightening, annoying creatures who pester us exactly because we want ourselves back, our old bedeviled selves who we couldn't live with in the first place.

* * *

The sky grows brighter as the moon waxes. Tonight the tree branches cast intricate shadows on the street, and seem to intertwine with each other. Steve and I walk through ourselves and each other's thoughts and memories in the deepening twilight, retracing the same steps through our sleepy neighborhood that we do every night. We pass a subterranean storm drain and hear water rushing under our feet. We pass a gated driveway where three tiny dogs yip their combined greetings and warnings, a cacophony of indignant chihuahuas. We pass a dark cabin surrounded by a thicket of tall bamboo trees where the deafening din of tree frogs fills the air. The sound recedes as we walk on and becomes background noise to a quiet so profound that we can hear the faraway whoosh of the freeway.

I'm nosy about other people's lives, and peer into their lighted kitchens as we walk by. Someone's living room is illuminated by the eerie glow of a large screen TV. Once in a while a shadowy figure looms in the darkness on the street. Someone passes with a beagle on a leash. Someone trundles his recycling and green waste bins to the curb.

"Cool that we're both in *Tattoo Highway* at the same time," I say. The latest issue of an online literary zine has just come out with creative prose from both of us.

"I know. It's great."

"You know everyone's going to think the professor character in your story is you. That you had a breakdown and ended up in the mental ward. He looks like you. He dresses like you. He sounds like you."

"So what. Let them think that."

"But it didn't happen. You don't care what your students think?"

"No."

The streets are filled with yellow leaves, wet and slippery from yesterday's rain. It's cold tonight, and I pull up the hood on my sweatshirt. We both teach at the same university. I know it doesn't matter what our students think, but they're so curious about our personal lives and I'm so private. Since both of us have published creative nonfiction about my breakdown (which was, shit, more than twenty years ago), they probably know already. I hid "Meeting the Virgin Mary" in a combined scholarly and literary journal that I thought nobody would find. Steve's "The World Came Crashing Down on My Wife" came out in a literary journal too, but was just reprinted in his latest book. I don't know how many copies students have brought to him for personal inscriptions. A lot.

"Your new story looks like nonfiction," I say. "It's not labeled fiction or nonfiction in the table of contents. Your professor story."

"It's a story."

"Partly my story."

"Well yeah," Steve says. "But I know what the hospital was like because you were there. The weird vibe in that group therapy room."

"Why put yourself there?"

"I don't know," he says, thinking about it. "It fit. The professor tells the other patient right up front that he exaggerates."

A city bus glides by, the interior lit, not a soul aboard.

That is, we've seen the bus before, but maybe tonight it is a phantom bus. When I write creative nonfiction, I try to hold on to the facts. Occasionally an imaginary (but not entirely imaginary) bus intrudes.

"So why do you exaggerate?" I ask him.

Steve stops in his tracks.

"I don't exaggerate. I write the truth. If it's not recognizable as experience, it's only because experience is paltry and needs to be revealed. By 'exaggerating,' I get at what's behind the curtain."

He resumes walking, and begins to gesticulate as if he's in an imaginary classroom.

"The carpet at the hospital you stayed in stared back at you when you looked down at it, a tight, gray, woven pattern, very mild, very calming, very drab, very exciting. I wanted to fall to my knees and eat it when I saw a thread sticking up.

"And you say I exaggerated in my story? I held back! I wish I had the courage to exaggerate! Look, my double, peering at me from the around corner! His face just popped out from behind the wooden fence! A terribly hideous repulsive face! 'Steve,' with a mask on! I want him gone! I can't leave him to roam the streets! Where has my sweet, innocent 'Steve' gone? He was a sweet boy. I loved him. He loved me."

I slow down and Steve falls in step with me.

"I think I got more love from him than I did from my family at the time."

I understand that, but I'm not sure why Steve's double now wears such a repulsive mask. Steve can't really enlighten me either.

"He was there. He just popped up. He needs a double, too. Shit! We're all in pain."

* * *

Jackie's Dream: That night I dream I'm in a forest clearing under a bright, not quite full moon. The night is clear, the sky awash with stars. Trees tower on all sides of me, dark and stately. I can hear tiny animals rustling in the fallen leaves and underbrush, the soft hoot of a faraway owl. I am face to face with what seems to be a man clothed in a cape made of twigs and leaves. He holds two large staffs made from branches, planted firmly in the earth, and wears a deer head with antlers that masks his face. We don't speak, or if we do I don't remember what passes between us.

* * *

More than once we've encountered deer on our walks. A lone stag with outsized antlers. Two does prancing delicately down Seven Hills Road. One time a doe and two fawns. They paused to gaze at us with startled eyes. We all held our breath as they looked at us, and we looked at them. And then with a few graceful bounds they disappeared.

I love Thoreau, and reread him every year when I teach my American literature survey. Near the end of *Walden*, he writes, "I fear chiefly lest my expression may not be *extra-vagant* enough, may not wander far enough beyond the narrow limits of my daily experience, so as to be adequate to the truth of which I have been convinced. *Extra vagance!*...I desire to speak somewhere *without* bounds; like a man in a waking moment, to men in their waking moments; for I am convinced that I cannot exaggerate enough even to lay the foundation of a true expression."

And it was like that, the deer. There's just no way I can describe the beauty, the deep hush of that encounter.

Maybe she can describe it, the imaginary friend I have acquired in middle age. The other Jacqueline, who sits up late at her computer, her face illuminated by the glow of the screen. Maybe she can return to the darkness, the sliver of a moon, the wind that ruffled the tops of the tall trees, lifted the dry leaves on the street and sent them skittering. And then the extraordinary stillness, the three deer poised for flight.

* * *

Steve Muses on Thoreau and *Extra-vagance*: Extraordinary to read this *Walden* passage! I don't dare compare myself to Henry, but I think I was trying to say the exact same thing.

The world is magical and has nothing to do with reality. I do not know what that means, only that it sounds good, and I will not veto it on the basis of its logic. I cannot defend the statement. It makes no sense, it is cheap, easy, trite, and yet it is grand, true, eternal!

The deer are just deer, but what deer they are! Dear deer! They go bounding off in the night, and we both stand deer struck.

I think Thoreau would say, "Deer me," but with such emphasis that the deer would absorb the speaker and render him helpless to resist even if he wanted to. "Deer" is a verb engulfing Henry, and Henry is pawing at the ground with antlers on his head, head bowed, smiling happily for the first time in many, many years.

The deer are magnificent.

* * *

Jackie Muses on Her Imaginary Friend: "Thus my life is a flight," Borges writes in "Borges and I," "and I lose everything and everything belongs to oblivion, or to him." The extraordinary grace of the deer in flight brings me back to the Borges line, apparently the subtext of my reflections all along.

The chord that Borges touches in me has something to do with loss. How much will be lost if I don't write it down. How urgent my writing feels because I began so late in life. "I am destined to perish, definitively," Borges writes, "and only some instant of myself can survive in him." How important that instant of myself and its connection to the larger world seems in the face of mortality. How my new imaginary friend Jacqueline, the self who writes, feels separate from the self who experiences. Vital, dark and light by turns, multi-vocal, ephemeral, yet eternal. How I don't always trust her as she waits, eager to cannibalize my experience and everyone's around me in order to make it her own.

"Jackie," she whispers, when I sit down at my desk. "Jackie." And again. "Jackie."

Like a ghostly revenant, my other self returns to rescue my past from oblivion and populate my pages. Imaginary friend, imaginary enemy, she reassembles my scattered experiences, usurps them, transforms them, and writes them for me. She remembers, she reimagines, she recounts.

* * *

I share my thoughts with Steve.

"Yes," he says, as we reach the halfway point on our walk. The moon is out, plumply yellow. The thick shrubbery and trees make this block a forest.

"Exactly! And they destroy, they overturn, these imaginary friends of ours. They demand an audience when we haven't learned to speak yet.

"'Speak, bastard, speak,' they say.

"'No,' we reply, meekly, so they tear open our throats and rip out our vocal cords and stuff them in their mouths and speak for us."

Steve continues with the royal "we," or "majestic plural," and I'm not sure I agree, but I'm caught up in his vision anyway. The dark woods lining the road seem enchanted and unfamiliar.

"We are rendered mute in their presence, everything life-giving in us is taken by them, and they want even more, our immortal souls. 'You have not been good enough for the earth,' they say, with their eyes, their mad eyes, and then they begin to laugh, and howl, and dance in a little circle with antlers on their heads and encased in too tight, horizontally striped shirts till we drop in obeisance and beg forgiveness for all we've done wrong in our lives. 'Please, please.'

"But they only lift our chins, romantically, and kiss us. 'It is all a bad, bad dream,' they whisper, and they disappear as quickly as they appeared. In a flash, they are gone, the smell of deer hangs heavily in the air, above, in a tree, a striped tee-shirt entangled on a branch makes me want to jump and grab it."

Steve suddenly leaps in the air. He seems to swipe at the moon.

A city bus passes without stopping. It shifts gears on the hill.

"Remember the night we got on the bus?" Steve asks me.

"You mean the night we thought about getting on the bus?"

"Whatever," he says

* * *

Now I remember. We did get on the bus once. It was like stepping into that Edward Hopper painting. The artificial light inside the bus, the blackness outside. We were looking from the inside out, and from the outside in. There was a little kid in a striped tee shirt huddled in the back. Was his name "Steve"? It must have been way past his bedtime. I wanted to comfort him but he disappeared as the bus became a diner, and there we were, Steve and I, drinking coffee at the counter in silence. The bus driver was there too, taking a break in one of the booths. She looked a lot like me.

Jacqueline Doyle and Stephen D. Gutierrez on their process:

Steve and I have collaborated before (in stories published in *Timber* and *Jelly-fish Review*), both times alternating back and forth, finding our rhythm, editing each other's sections somewhat, but basically preserving a braided structure. *The construction of my non/fictional character "Steve" was Frankenstein-ish, which is a good way to describe collaboration, only instead of one mad genius, it's two doctors working different shifts on the same monster you hope turns out to be presentable, and alive. More than anything, alive!* "Imaginary Friends" was completely different. It grew out of a series of discussions we had on our evening walks. I was doing some informal research on imaginary friends, and quizzing Steve about his childhood imaginary friend "Steve." We tried alternating sections but the essay became more and more confusing. *Jolt it! Payoff is the living thing. The risk in collaborating is losing the juice that might go into a bigger, better, more fearsome, personally inscribed monster.* I took over the revision (and another revision after it was published in *Grist Online*), incorporating some of what Steve had written into his dialogue, labeling other sections. *Jackie rocks in a different way than I do, so learning her motions—ha!—is in effect good for the creative body, the nimble mind. Can't hurt. Can help.* In the end, we found collaboration more difficult than writing something ourselves. But it's great to see the monster stand up and lurch forward, ready to conquer the world. *Why not?*

Denise Duhamel and Julie Marie Wade

13 SUPERSTITIONS

Always return a kiss under the mistletoe.

Kiss the boy who is with you now but always looking for someone better. Kiss him even when you know he has been kissing someone else, late nights in her father's race car stacked on bricks in the yard. Kiss him later, for nostalgia's sake, after he has left the girl whose father was a race car driver and moved on to the girl who will become a teenage mother. Kiss a different boy because you are kind, and it seems unlikely anyone else will. Kiss one man because he remembers you as a child, and you are forgetting yourself. Kiss another man—the one you will almost marry—because he was born near Christmas, and because he was an orphan, and because you can picture him, chubby and dark-eyed even then, his unruly curls blowing in the parentless wind. *Is love a kind of pity, too?* Kiss a girl when you are a girl, then try to forget about it. Kiss other girls when you are a girl, but only in your dreams. Kiss a woman when you are full grown—the one you will marry someday—and marvel at how small her mouth is, soft as a plum. Then, do away with mistletoe altogether and make love on the living room rug.

Something old, something new, something borrowed, something blue.

My mother saved her wedding dress—the same one I was obsessed with as a girl. I would stand at the closet unzipping the garment bag to touch it. As a teenager, I tried it on a few times when she was working at the hospital, her white frills exchanged for her no-nonsense, white uniform. I was a budding feminist and would never have admitted to anyone my desire. I publicly announced I thought marriage was stupid to anyone who would listen. In the 1950s, my mother and father both said they'd never marry, which is why their friend introduced them to each other. My father, a rose in hand, took the bus, and my mother felt her "never" change to "maybe." When I finally gave in, deciding to marry at thirty-one, I admitted that I wanted to wear my mother's dress. When we unzipped the bag, we found the fabric yellowed and brittle. The beading fell to the floor like dust. I should have seen this as an omen. Instead, I scrambled for a new dress and borrowed my mother's pearls. There was a blue bow on my bra and my dead grandmother's handkerchief in my purse. I had all these things and still my marriage ended thirteen years later.

An apple a day keeps the doctor away.

I come from Washington, where apples are lucky already. Everyone knows someone with an apple tree. My uncle owns orchards in Chehalis and Yakima. Red Delicious is the most famous, but Braeburn tastes the best. My grandmother lives to be ninety-six and insists the secret of longevity is apples, though she prefers them as cobbler or cake, squeezed into cider, sauced with cinnamon. "A little sugar never hurt anyone," she smiles. My mother teaches elementary school. Her students bring her shiny red apples like you see in picture books. The apple is long life, is good health, is knowledge. *Later, though, Mother puts the apple into Snow White's hand, and then it's poison!* (Rae Armantrout)

Step on a crack, break your mother's back.

A child prone to guilt, I was careful on my way to school and back. Head down, I avoided fissures in the sidewalk, bits of concrete sprouting grass. Hopscotch was especially complicated—I tried my best to chalk pink squares close to any crevices so my sneaker would land in the unbroken middle. I grew up with uneven sidewalks and potholes. I grew up with a chipped linoleum kitchen floor, squares not that much bigger than the length of my foot. I grew up thinking that even *imagining* something nasty was a form of sin. Each winter, at St. Joseph's church, the crumbled steps slicked over with ice. When I fell, my mother scooped me up.

Cross your fingers.

As a child, I favored imagination over truth, which is another way of saying I liked to lie. If I wanted a wish to come true, I pronounced it as though it already had. "My father is a private detective," I told everyone who asked, even though he was just a run-of-the-mill salesman who sat at a desk calling his customers. He used to be a traveling salesman, which was really true, but I pretended he went on missions like a spy. "The FBI used to hire him for contract work," I told the two girls in third grade who were too pretty to be my friends and spent all their time together anyway. On Parent Night, someone's mother called my bluff. She asked my father about his work in the field—if it was dangerous. "Not unless you put your head inside the plastic bags!" he laughed, because what he mostly sold was packaging for supermarkets and retail chains. Another girl, less pretty and more knowledgeable, taught me a trick. "You can say anything," she grinned, "as long as you cross your fingers." I kept them that way in my pocket, permanently pressed. When a pretty boy asked me, "Do you want to go roller-skating sometime?" I smiled and nodded my head.

Never walk under a ladder.

Short on cash one Christmas, Sally turned her ladder into a tree. She decorated it with mini bottles of whiskey and vodka she had pocketed as a flight attendant. She hung her boyfriend's cigars as ornaments. I declared the tree was art, though Sally knew even less about art than I did. She said she was shallow, but I knew that wasn't the reason she abused laxatives. She was weighed in at American Airlines, a company that demanded their female employees have a "trim silhouette, free of bulges, rolls, or paunches." Sally wanted to climb the corporate ladder, sit behind a desk, so she never again had to flirt with fat men in first class.

Women on board bring bad luck.

No siren, I boarded with my breasts and mons pubis, past the golfers, the hunters, and the adventurers. They had a way of looking at me but at the same time through me, as though I did and did not exist. Women have always boarded this way, say our foremothers, who ignored the topless women on the bow, the mud flaps on truck tires. *Get thee to a nunnery, to the kitchen, to the bedroom*—all ways of saying *Get thee to steerage!* I passed a man whose T-shirt read *Cool Story Babe Go Make Me A Sandwich.* He smiled, clueless as a nonswimmer without a lifejacket wandering into a rip current.

Never open an umbrella inside.

Even if you are pretending to be Don Lockwood in *Singing in the Rain* just after kissing a pretty girl goodnight. Even if you are pretending to be Mary Poppins blown in by a strong wind to Number 17 Cherry Tree Lane. Even if you are pretending to be Marta from *The Sound of Music* who tells the governess she will be seven on Tuesday and wants a pink parasol. You have quoted this line so often your parents believe you actually *want* a pink parasol, ruffles and all. Now you have it. You open it in the parlor and twirl around. It only takes a moment for what is breakable to break.

At the end of a rainbow is a pot of gold.

First you have to pick which end, north or south. Then you must run, pedal, or drive as fast as you can, the rainbow fading before you make it even halfway. There's nothing to do but wait for more rain and hope for concurrent sun. You buy a few lottery tickets and try your luck at the casino. You pick up an extra shift when you can. You go to college, play the stock market, or attempt to write a bestseller. But these are just ways to occupy yourself until the day you haul that heavy kettle to the bank, until you outsmart everyone. This is also known as capitalism, the American dream.

Black cats.

When a black cat crossed my childhood path, I scooped him up in a basket. A black cat outside the house brings bad luck, but a black cat inside the house is cause for serendipity. That Halloween, a ready-made costume—small witch with her shy familiar. When I grew up, I fell in love over crème brûlée at a restaurant called Le Chat Noir. Later, my love and I crossed two black cats' paths and brought them home from the rescue. It was nearly Halloween, and the attendant said, "We don't usually allow adoptions like this so close to the holiday." Two pairs of eyebrows arched. "Kids have their pranks," she sighed—"and Satanists have their *rituals.* You can't be too careful these days." For us, the rescue made an exception, though for all they knew, we were two tall witches carrying our familiars home in a crate. For many years, we lived in many houses with two black cats. One grew a long white hair from his paw, which, if plucked, promises a lifetime of happiness. We didn't pluck it. We were happy enough. When the laws changed, my love and I married at Le Chat Noir. We wore black dresses. The white streak in my hair glistened impossibly in the moonlight.

Evil energy is repelled by salt.

When I was going through my divorce, afraid my husband would return to do me harm, a psychic told me to put a teaspoon of salt in front of my door and on the windowsills. I did as she said, throwing salt over my shoulder, trying not to cry over all that had been spilled. Did it work? He never came back to harm me despite his cruel emails and his lawyer's ridiculous demands. How I love sprinkling salt onto my scrambled eggs, a steak, or steamed broccoli. My husband had always preferred soy sauce, the way it ran to a plate's edge, the way it stained the cloth napkins he left behind.

Broken mirror.

I'd like to break all the looking glasses, smash them to shards, grind the smithereens to fine sand, and take it to the seaside with me. I'd like to make my own hourglass from the silver seeds, repurpose an omen with a more poetic way to keep time. The vanity mirror can save her vanity. The compact can stay small, doting on appearances. I'm tired of women primping before office building windows, of the men who conjure mudflap girls on their arms. What better luck than to send back the looking glass like a spoiled entrée, or better still—to fling it like a Frisbee so the roadside glitters with white light?

The number thirteen.

When you are born on the thirteenth, it's hard to be afraid of the number. I love thirteen anything—blackbirds, donuts (a baker's dozen), teenagers on the verge. Even though most elevators don't stop on the thirteenth floor, it doesn't mean the floor is not there. You can rename or you can embrace, which is what I've chosen to do. Judas, Schmudas—my favorite dinner parties have thirteen guests. In Italy, right next door to the Vatican, thirteen is a lucky number, like our seven. Consider our alphabet—thirteen times two. Each deck of playing cards has thirteen clubs, diamonds, spades, and hearts. When we play, let's make the Queen the wild card.

Denise Duhamel and Julie Marie Wade on their process:

"13 Superstitions" belongs to a series of collaborative essays we wrote using numbers and subheadings as a way for us to explore certain topics. We started with the concept of debunking widely held (but unjustified) beliefs, made a list of thirteen—which seemed the obvious choice—superstitions and then took turns writing about each. Our process is to send each other "chunks" of writing back and forth so that our writing often reverberates or plays off of what comes before…

Tracy Jane Gregory and Susan Gregory

MOTHER-DAUGHTER BONDING: AN EXPLORATION OF STUPID

Mother

Age 6 – Early 1960s
I am playing on the school playground. Three teenage boys pass by and ask me if I want to see their wieners. I am scared and say no. "Well, here it is," shouts one of the boys. He pulls a hot dog out of his pocket and waves it in the air. I run home.

Age 16 – Early 1970s
I am walking to work when a fat, forty-something-year-old man asks if I want a ride. I am stupid and say yes. During the ride, we are silent until the end. I turn to thank him, and he slides his hand up my dress. I scream and run into my building. After work, my mother tells me, "It serves you right for getting in the car."

Age 19 – Mid 1970s
I am walking home from work, and I cut through the park to catch my bus. A good-looking twenty-something-year-old man is sitting on a park bench. He smiles at me and says hello. I smile and say hello back, but then I stupidly look down. His hand is in his pants. He's jacking off.

Age 22 – Late 1970s
I am working at a car dealership, and I am still stupid. At the end of my shift, my manager, Dick, calls me into his office. He looks me up and down and tells me a filthy joke. For the next few weeks, I start wearing clothing two sizes too big. He still calls me over. I try making an excuse, "I'll be late for my bus," but this makes Dick mad. "When Dick calls you, you come!" He grabs me by the coat collar and drags me to his office. I ask him what he wants, and he tells me a filthy joke. I leave crying and never go back.

Age 30 – Mid 1980s
I am working in an office where my husband also works. Every morning, two married co-workers talk to me at my desk. They tell me about the porn they watched

the night before and ask if I'd like to watch the next one with them. I say "no, thank you" every time, but they ask again and again. I complain to personnel, and the couple stops speaking to me. I am finally getting smarter.

Age 38 – Early 1990s
I am in a grocery store parking lot holding my 18-month-old daughter while putting groceries into my car. I look up and see two twenty-something-year-old men standing next to me. One of them grabs his crotch, looks at my daughter, and shakes his junk around. "She's gonna be one hot mama when she gets older." I am sick. I want to puke.

Daughter

Age 10 – Late 1990s
I am walking with my mother to Wienerschnitzel to buy a hot dog. We pass a parked semi-truck. The driver honks his horn and whistles. I ask my mom who the man is whistling at. "Not at me, I can tell you that much."

Age 15 – Mid 2000s
I am instant messaging with my boyfriend's twenty-something-year-old friend. He asks me to have sex with him, and I tell him no. He takes a screenshot of the conversation and uses Paint to switch our screen names, as if I am the one asking him for sex. He sends the image to my boyfriend and calls me a slut. My boyfriend believes him. I am stupid and convince my boyfriend not to dump me. We stay together for another two years.

Age 17 – Late 2000s
I am at my first college party, and I meet a boy. He says he likes me. For the next two weeks, we talk in his dorm room and watch movies on his bed. He never touches me until one night when we can hear his roommate at the door. The boy jumps on top of me and sticks his tongue in my mouth just as his roommate walks inside. I leave crying and never go back.

Age 20 – Early 2010s
I am studying abroad in England, and I meet a seventeen-year-old Swedish boy. We go to a dance club and get drunk with some friends. I black out, and when I

come to, my friends tell me the Swedish boy had my arms pinned to a wall and his hand up my dress. They wanted to tell him to stop, but they decided I probably didn't care. I am stupid and believe them.

Age 21 – Early 2010s

I am staying the night in a hostel, and I am the stupidest I have ever been. I walk in my shared room and a thirty-something-year-old Colombian man sits cross-legged on the floor. He is naked minus a towel wrapped around his waist. He asks if I am alone, and I say yes. He slides his towel to the left, revealing his flaccid penis. I try to leave the room, but he stands up and blocks the door. I try stepping around his body, but he moves closer to me. "You have beautiful eyes," he says, and I push him. He slips, and I run out the door. I find a new room and stay inside it all night, not even leaving to pee.

Age 23 – Present day

I am working in an office where my brother also works. Every afternoon, a forty-something-year-old coworker talks to me in my cubicle about his motorcycle and drinking habits. I ignore him, but he comes back again and again. One day, he asks me to watch a video of a Barbie and Ken doll having sex. I say, "No, thank you," and he laughs. "It would probably remind you of your brother anyway." He stays in my cubicle and plays the video at maximum volume. I can hear the moaning, and I want to puke.

Tracy Jane Gregory and Susan Gregory on their process:

Our collaboration between mother and daughter started with an attempt to define "creepy." Tracy, after having a man holler at her on a run, decided to collect stories from people about their own creepy interactions. She started "The Creepo Project," a Tumblr page that shares submitted stories ranging from street harassment to questionable Tinder conversations. When Susan, Tracy's mother, submitted a few stories of her own, we realized our stories sounded eerily similar and decided to combine them in poem form.

The writing process started as a phone conversation that involved sharing moments of harassment with each other, becoming an act of bonding and catharsis as many of our stories had never been voiced before. We then had the strange task of deciding which harassments were worthy of including, deciding to keep the poem (somewhat) light and to have at least one harassment per decade. We wrote and edited through Google Docs while continuing to discuss our changes over the phone. As two women with dark senses of humor, we often found ourselves laughing at the idea of someone overhearing mother and daughter discussing sexual harassment so lightly: "...and then he put his hand up my skirt. Yeah that sounds good!" While we attempted to place some humor within the piece, we ultimately decided to keep the poem documentary with little emotional reflection and use first person. This allows the reader to more easily place themselves within the poem, showing the commonality of sexual harassment.

Meghan McClure and Michael Schmeltzer

from A SINGLE THROAT OPENS

Which is worse for the addict:

  a) time
  b) distance
  c) substance
  d) no substance

All four choices are the addict's one problem. Choose any answer, and you're right. Nothing is acceptable to them. Nothing is fine.

Not the time it takes the addict to drive and see his grandchildren. Not the distance from his bedroom apartment to the nearest convenience store. Not even the short steps from the couch to the kitchen. Not the six packs stashed in the trunk of the car. Not the single throat open, drinking as fast as allowed. Not the empty noose of an empty ring. Not six of them. Not twelve.

∴

How do you solve for the addict? Separation as an answer, a solution, separation as the liquid the drunk dissolves in. How time splits the drunk from his drink, allows sobriety to sneak in second by second. How distance divides. Substance, no substance, which is no longer as separate as it once was. Time and distance have narrowed.

Now, there is never no substance; there is just the appearance of no substance. I've looked carefully. I've counted empty cans. I've smelled beer in the air like the worst cologne, intoxicating and sickening. How to separate the man from the drink when you no longer know him sober.

∴

I've wished for a test, a question, anything I can ask or give my father to see if he is really an alcoholic. I've wanted a test that was rigid, not rigged. I've questioned a thousand different ways trying to alter the answer.

Step 1: Admit you have a problem, that you are powerless over alcohol.

Thirty-six years later and I am ready to admit I have a problem; I am powerless over alcohol.

The problem is denial. No matter what he does—drive drunk, shake when he's sober, steal my liquor and replace with water—I hold on to almost.

Look, I say to myself, *he almost seems better. He almost stopped for a few days. He is nearly sober. We're almost there.*

I am powerless over alcohol. I've given up ((my father) to the bottle). I am ready to watch him wither, dissipate into a bottle like a genie called home.

∴

"When the intoxication is platonic or noble as in the case of a poet ... meaningful life is possible."[1]

I disagree, but I don't know with which part the most: platonic, meaningful life, possible. It is hard to believe any of it. But intoxication, yes, this I understand well. However, it is never platonic. Intoxication is nudity, intimate and impersonal. The way drunks at a bar will point at a stranger and yell, "I love this guy!"

Love—another thing hard to believe. But I will always choose love, despite love. Even when the addict chooses otherwise. Even when alcohol intoxicates the stars more than poetry.

∴

Dear M_____,

I've written this letter from the island of make believe; I hope you receive it and send help. My hands are shaking; they tremble because I grieve.

Always,
M

∴

Other Reasons Your Hands May Shake:

Maybe you used a water bottle to spray the desk lamp bulb, that brightly burning star. Maybe you liked the sizzling sound the mist made when it evaporated. Maybe you thought you could spray it, and the small sound would grow large and proportionately more pleasurable. Maybe the most minute supernova occurred, and a star-shard flew past your hand. Maybe you sat at your desk, shocked, your hands trembling, your finger bleeding from the thinnest cut.

Maybe two boys attempted to mug you. And you felt torn in three, equally sad, angry, and frightened. Maybe they stole nothing no matter how scared you were. Maybe you said, "I hope this makes you feel like a man" because you have a smart mouth. Maybe you were punched in the face. Maybe because you had a bloody lip. Maybe the taste of blood. Maybe anger more prominent than fear now. Maybe the slap to your face and still you stood there, defiant but not fighting back because they were boys, just boys, and boys like this don't need another fist. Maybe because you saw stars. Maybe because when you looked at their hands they weren't shaking at all, but you wish they had been.

Maybe it's the medication, a side effect. You've read the label over and over and nowhere does it say tremors. But you know it must be. You check online and check the websites and triple-check the bottle and nowhere does it say shaking. And you read the bottle and read the bottle and then you finish a bottle and then another and soon there is all this glass around you. After four glass bottles you are able to think of course not, the doctor would have told you about shaking, you asked him last time, and so you put down the bottle and you feel fine, you feel fine, and you are swaying in the kitchen because you feel so good you want to dance and look your hands are so still you can hold them in front of your face so still and you feel fine, you feel fine, you feel fine.

∴

All the alcoholics I know shake from rage. I'd like to pretend I know what it's like to get that drunk, to let my rage take over. But I keep it caged and lull it with a few sips here and there. My cage rattles.

It would be so easy to say, it must be _____ that leads them to drink. But genetics and history muddle it all up. Studies say maybe there are genes that make you more likely to fall into a bottle, other studies say maybe there aren't. But when we are born, we are born into more than genes, we arrive in the pain of the history of our shared blood.

There is no measurement for addiction. On Google it looks like a lot of research groups are trying to come up with standards and tests. But even if there were a test, an addict wouldn't take it. Or they'd know how to answer so they don't end up in rehab. The way I knew how to make my personality test tell me I would make the best doctor. If you aren't the problem, you should be the solution, right? Or maybe there is some middle ground where you are both.

I imagine the test like this, in an otherwise empty, dimly-lit room, (drug of choice) on the only table in the room with a pen and stack of paper:

> #1: Please map your genome on the following blank pages using only black ballpoint pen.
>
> #2a: Have you ever felt hurt, trauma, or pain of any kind?
> #2b: Do you ever wish you could erase that feeling?
>
> #3: Date, time, and location of first encounter with your drug of choice. List every subsequent usage and reason for usage.
>
> #4: Define addiction.
>
> #5: List any and all factors that may play a role in your usage.

#6: Go back, you didn't list them all.

Please put pen down, someone will be with you as soon as you've answered all questions as thoroughly as possible, until then, feel free to explore the room.

∴

I can shake it all off like a bad dream. The shakes are in my control, just like I know how to let the glass sit on the table long enough to collect a puddle beneath it before I take another restrained sip. I can shake off the thought of addiction like a sweater tied around my waist, lost in a crowd in a foreign city. If I run hard enough or read deep enough or shower long enough, I can forget about the things that tie a man's hand to a cheap beer can, I can forget all about the whisky tucked into a boot, I can forget.

Can we drink to forgetting?

∴

Addiction works through endless escalation. For example, my father brings weekly gifts for my daughters. At first it was simple: three gummy bears wrapped in tin-foil, a couple mints. Then he added spare change. Then he began to bring fruit: bananas, Gala apples, blueberries. Now every Tuesday there is a plastic bag, one for each girl, identically filled: some candy, mints, fruit, snacks (chips, granola bars), and a small toy.

Addiction requires no substance, only something to escalate, something to build until it crumbles under its own weight.

Gravitational collapse. *Our body produces alcohol; the stars seem to need it*, you said. You're right.

∴

I wonder if Elizabeth Bishop knew about addiction? Her poem "One Art" reads like a manifesto on tolerance. Lose keys, cities, loved ones. You build up to any loss. Write it like disaster.

I forget what else I want to say. I forget where we were going. I forget farther and faster.

∴

There is a point in the night where you lose track of how much you drank. You forget the shot between the two mixed drinks. You forget the second drink was a double.

Double down. Double vision. Doable, this life, under the influence.

And it's *under the influence,* isn't it? Never *over.* Never *influenced.* It doesn't end. It never passes.

Once empty, you push with one finger the bottle like a pillar, and it falls, pins you to the ground.

Our hands shake. The earth shakes. Write it. My father, my disaster, trembling, drunk and falling. Never fallen. It never ends.

"Not even happiness feels this good."[2]

And the peal of empty bottles sounds almost like laughter.

---

1. Jagadguru Sri Shivarathri Deshikendra http://jssonline.org/jss/meaningful
-life-is-possible-through-noble-saatvik-intoxication/
2. from Craig Morgan Teicher's "Drunkenness" (An appropriate ending. Where it all began.)

Meghan McClure and Michael Schmeltzer on their process:

On the surface, the collaborative process between Meghan and I may seem very simple: I'd spend one week writing as much as I could then pass it off to Meghan. She'd spend a week with it then pass it back, etc. And on many levels it was very organic, the writing shaping itself into forms and exploring topics we wouldn't have thought of on our own. By choosing an agreed upon subject for *A Single Throat Opens* (alcoholism) it was as if we mutually agreed on the soundtrack but each took turns making up the lyrics. Every week was a surprise, and that surprise allowed us access to different notes or harmonies, different rhythms. It allowed us to often sing in what others have called a "third voice," a literary voice that was neither completely mine nor Meghan's but still uniquely our own.

Brenda Miller and Julie Marie Wade

HEAT INDEX

Alcohol

> In the 16th century, shipping companies often paid sailors in rations of rum. The sailors (always wary of the bosses) learned how to see if they were being ripped off: they poured samples of the liquor on small piles of gunpowder and set them on fire. If the gunpowder ignited, this "proved" the rum hadn't been watered down. If not—well, then there was hell to be paid. From this drunken history, we get our current system of alcohol proofs: 100 proof (50% alcohol), 80 proof (40%), and so on. When my boyfriend drank, he preferred 100-proof vodka. We didn't need gunpowder to prove its efficacy—to make everything around us explode.

Ardor

> The word "ardor" stems from a Latin word, *ardor,* which means "heat" or "burning." It's come to mean a fiery passion most likely short-lived. Flames that burn hot, burn out, they say. Yet when we're in the throes of it, ardor masquerades as love—wants to be the steady burn of hardwood rather than the flash fire of kindling.

Bikram

> This style of yoga takes its name from founder Bikram Choudhury, a controversial figure who claims his series of 26 Hatha postures restored him to full mobility after a crippling accident in his youth. Critics insist this story has not been verified. Bikram studios, of which thousands now exist worldwide, are heated to a minimum of 104 degrees to mimic the climate in India. One paradox of such high

temperatures is that they aid in deepening each stretch, but they also deplete the body completely. At a certain point, your muscles become loose, hyper-flexible, but you become so dehydrated and light-headed that you are barely able to move. At Bikram Yoga Harlem, the teacher is a hairless, shiny man in a Speedo whose rib cage ripples like a waterfall. He takes the towel from my hand when I attempt to wrap it around my ankle. "Use the heat instead," he says. "Bend into it. There are no modifications allowed in Bikram."

Blush

I've been watching (over and over) a video that's gone viral on Facebook. A high school girl is filming her classmates one by one; she frames them in her lens, then says: "I'm taking pictures of things I find beautiful." These teenagers have hair dyed orange, piercings in their noses; some are transgender; some have acne and braces. All of them look neutral or wary at first, dressed in a way that shows great attention to persona. Lots of make-up. Tortured hair. And then, at the word "beautiful," their faces bloom in unguarded pleasure. They blush, the capillaries of their skin dilating with heat. They put their hands to their mouths. Some of them begin to cry.

Boiling Point

Sometimes called the "saturation temperature," it's the degree of heat required to vaporize a liquid. Water boils at 100 degrees Celsius, 212 Fahrenheit. I have to take the chemistry teacher's word for it, since I can never make the corresponding equation come out right. When he asks me to stay after class, I plead poetry as my defense for poor performance. "Poets aren't empiricists," I explain. "We're interested in describing more than proving." It must take a tremendous amount of self-control for Mr. Nowak not to roll his eyes. His own boiling point is set higher than most adults I know. "You see, I'd rather describe the sound the tea kettle makes when she reaches that heat than work the numbers to explain her whistle-song."

Can't take the

Harry S. Truman is thought to have coined the phrase as early as 1942. Known as a plain-spoken President, he reportedly told his White House staff not to quibble over their appointments: "I'll stand by [you], but if you can't take the heat, get out of the kitchen." During long Pennsylvania winters, we always sought refuge in the kitchen, baking all day or simply heating the cast-iron skillet inside the oven—to deepen its seasoning, we said, but really to warm our hands. In Florida, when temperatures dropped into the 40s, we tried to turn on the heat, but nothing happened. A quick call to maintenance explained the problem: "This building isn't wired for heat," the plain-spoken super said. "Given how rarely it's needed, Management decided it wasn't worth the expense."

Dead

When I ran track, I tried to come in second because I thought the red ribbon was prettier than the blue. I'd match my opponent stride for stride, then pause a second on the final step so she could split the streamer at the finish line. Soon, though, the competition stiffened: twelve runners instead of six, the fearsome gun instead of the pleasant whistle. I moved to the back of the pack. A contender no more, my mother cried from the stands, "You're dead in the water out there!"

Desert

Once upon a time a fair maid lived with an evil prince in a trailer by an enchanted lake. This lake sprung up in the middle of the desert: sapphire-blue water against fiery red rocks. The water was cold and deep, held ghosts of drowned junipers and coyotes. Sometimes, at night, the maid could hear cries of Anasazi women reach her from thousands of years away. One day, the evil prince took her out in a motor boat and drove her deep into an isolated side canyon. She had little food and water. She had a tent and a sleeping bag. He left her there to have what he called a *vision quest.* By day the heat grew steadily, enveloped her in its embrace. A dry heat. The water lapped against the shore, but she didn't dare go in. A raven traced a cat's cradle against the sky. Called her a new name. Wanted her to be transformed.

Discussion

When he told me was leaving, things got a little *heated.* I repeated the word *why?*, my question marks growing loud and harsh. Our words had friction, threw sparks. It felt like arson. We lived in a log home in the middle of almost-nowhere, surrounded by woods. It wouldn't have taken much to start a wildfire.

Exhaustion

What comes after "heat cramps" but before "heat stroke"—this mezzanine of heavy sweat, rapid pulse, the body overheating the way car engines do. Caused by—prolonged exposure to sun, too much exertion at high temperatures, not enough water. Even Jacuzzis and saunas can be culprits if you stay in long enough. Every September I ran the high school jogathon on the hottest day of the year. Sister Rosemary brought her sun umbrella to the track. Other teachers drank lemonade and fanned themselves with packets: our math homework and essay exams. In the single hour, I could do six miles, but I wanted to reach seven. Think of all those pledges—one dollar a mile, five dollars, ten. Think of all those silly girls who wore visors, took water breaks, chewed on ice. Think of all those girls who shamed themselves by walking. Not me. I wouldn't stop, even when Sister Rosemary suggested I was "dangerously red." Every year I missed the award ceremony. Home in bed—an ice pack on my head and feet, the Mercury relentless in its rise.

Fever

The body fights fire with fire. In response to inflammation, the hypothalamus resets the body's core temperature in order to burn out intruders. The hypothalamus sits deep within the brain, manning the controls—a small organ, ringed with nerves. It monitors signals from throughout the body and regulates just about anything: thirst, hunger, mood, carnal desire. It craves *homeostasis*, the status quo. Imagine it hunched over a switchboard, directing input and output—a little bit here, a little bit there. It remains cool. It never takes a coffee break or chats at the vending machines. It never gets out of hand.

Geothermal

Once upon a time there was a girl who lived in a valley where hot water burbled up from underground. She was a very pretty girl, but not the fairest in the land. Still, she worked hard every day: weeding the garden, cleaning the hot tubs, answering phones at the front desk and making reservations for honored guests who wished to partake of the magical waters. She was a gatekeeper; occasionally she needed to escort an ogre from the property. She lived in a shack with a man who was not a prince. But when she disrobed in the bathhouse at dawn, the waters claimed they loved her. Water poured over her neck, her arms, her breasts. Her skin grew soft, luminous. She became a queen, a woman who glowed with power.

Hell

All we know is that it's supposed to be hot—a raging furnace, a lake of fire. Later, we learn "Hell hath no fury like a woman scorned," an idiom not to be confused with "She's hotter than Hell." Perhaps Hell, like God, is in the details. Or perhaps anger and attraction are closer than cousins after all. Maybe we don't always want the heat of wanting. Maybe it burns us up to burn for the beloved this way. Anne Carson writes, "Love, as you know, is a harrowing event." *Hellish*, we call it, the aching descent into desire.

Hot & cold

Like fever and chills of the heart. So many strong verbs: to waver; to oscillate or vacillate; to toggle between possibles or straddle a line. More recently and politically: to flip-flop. The phrase evokes mood rings and pendulums, the fickle lover and the bar room tease. Perhaps even the Magic 8-Ball. From the Greek, *peripeteia*, a reversal or intention or outcome. A twist, a recursion. In other words, as it's often construed: to be wishy-washy, to send mixed signals, to give false hope, to change—that most daring maneuver—your mind.

In

When an animal is ready to mate, she's *in heat.* Her hormones put her into estrus—eggs plumping up, uterus thickening, all cylinders firing. Breeding females are called *bitches,* but it's not meant as an insult. I once fostered a nine-month-old Shepherd as she gave birth to eight puppies. She'd gone into heat as a stray, and from the looks of the litter, more than one male sniffed her out. Though I knew it was all simply biological—that the dog, Becky, wouldn't feel any shame—I wept when I thought of her on the streets, beset by males, trapped.

Index

It turns out that the old adage "It's not the heat, it's the humidity" is true. The heat index, created by weatherman George Winterling in 1978, calculates how poorly sweat will evaporate in humid conditions, thus creating the *perception* that you're hotter than you actually are. He first called it the "humiture." He predicted the landfall of Hurricane Dora in Jacksonville, Florida in 1964—the early years of televised weather reports. George was innocuously good-looking, in the way of meteorologists. Someone you could trust: photogenic for the camera—blond hair, a craggy nose, bright eyes—but not what one could call *hot*.

Journey to the Center of the Earth

In the Jules Verne novel, Professor Otto Lidenbrock, his nephew Axel, and their guide Hans descend one volcano in Iceland and eventually resurface through another volcano in Italy. Even with my limited understanding of world geography, I find this premise ludicrous, not to mention miserably hot. "But isn't it exciting," my father prods, "all the adventures they have underground?" I hate the way adventure stories are always written by men about other men and boys. I am a girl, I am a reader, but I want to have adventures, too. "It would be more exciting if there were a girl in there—doing something," I say. "Doing anything."

Miami

In winter, all of South Florida revolves around The Heat. Their games are broadcast at every taco shack along the beach, in every bar and probably every boardroom, too. Boys wear oversized jerseys that fit like dresses. Swaddled to their knees, it becomes difficult to shoot, let alone leap to the hoop like Duane or LeBron. When we first moved here, I thought I was seeing signs for a Pentecostal church, a holy white halo filled with righteous fire. "Naw, that's the logo for the Miami Heat," a Super Fan touting the image on his t-shirt explained. "And if you think that's neat, you should see Burnie, the team's mascot." Then, as if it was something people said every day: "He's great. He's an anthropomorphic fireball."

Of the moment

Adrenaline is an archaic drug. Whoever designed us figured we'd need a little boost to help us spring into action against threat. Saber-toothed tigers, say, or an unfamiliar man bearing a club. Our bodies actually sense danger a split-second before our minds can register it, so we're primed for fight or flight before we really know it. Evolution failed to phase out this reflex, so even in the absence of real threat, our hearts start beating fast, our faces flush, and we begin saying things we won't mean the next day, or even in the next hour. We call it *the heat of the moment.* You see it in cartoons: the boss man with steam geysering from his head, or the woman with exclamation points flying from her mouth like daggers.

Of the night

When Ray Charles sings it, you know salvation must be near. *Seems like a cold sweat/ Creeping cross my brow, oh yes /In the heat of the night/ I'm a feelin' motherless somehow…* We have to drop deep into darkness before the morning comes. Sometimes we call it "a dark night of the soul." It's a theme for the movie of the same name. In it, Sidney Poitier gets to slap a white man: the first time such a retaliation in public was permitted. He gets to say: *They call me Mr. Tibbs.* It's 1967. Lots of things are on fire.

Packing

It's hard to know who is really "packing heat" and who is just posturing. The phrase seems to proliferate: music videos and video games, the songs they play in spin class, *Law and Order,* every action movie from *Die Hard* to *Mad Max: Fury Road.* Do women pack heat? Even when they carry guns, the phrase seems decidedly masculine, as if it doesn't even apply to them. Then, a student of mine—a woman, older than I, a mother of three—confides she always carries a gun. "It's not something I advertise, but I do have a concealed weapons permit." I'm speechless. Perhaps my lip turns down, suggesting a question or a judgment of some kind. "Yeah," she says, "I just feel safer knowing I have what the bad guys have."

Pre

I never follow recipes. Perhaps this is my small rebellion in a life
otherwise spent heeding the rules. I mix cake batter and pour it into
a Bundt pan, say, or I arrange winter vegetables on a roasting tray, but
then I'm ready—ready to slip these encumbrances inside the oven and
be done, wash my hands and wipe them on my pants since I have never
invested in an apron. I'm ready to head back to my book or my desk
with its papers fluttering like so many pairs of wings. Forget about
pre-heating or setting the timer; I'm certain I'll smell the edibles when
they're done.

Steam

It's a kind of heat, but it's also a kind of song—a show tune—which
is the kind of song I like best. Before I ever saw *The Pajama Game*
performed on stage or screen, I saw Georgette Franklin—sweet
Georgette!—transform herself into a slinky, sexy diva and belt out this
number on *Mary Tyler Moore*. Her boyfriend Ted is embarrassed. He
doesn't want Georgette showing off her body that way—skimpy black
leotard, transparent tights—or is it her talent that he wants her to
hide? Carol Haney has a version of the song, as do Shirley MacLaine,
Patti Page, Doris Day, Ella Fitzgerald, and Liza Minnelli. Every singer's
version is different, but all of them begin with a visceral-sonic pop-hiss-
fizz, an erotic onomatopoeia: *I've got ::cling cling:: fsssss steam heat.*

Wave

When I was four years old I got my tonsils out. No big deal, but when
my parents brought me home, the city was in the midst of a heat wave.
Temperatures soared over a hundred degrees day after day; we had no
air conditioning, so I sat sweating by the screen door. The nights were
no better: the house gathered heat that radiated inward. I ate ice cream
and whined *it's so hot.* I had a fever. I whimpered and slept fitfully, the

covers kicked off. I kept hearing the words *heat wave,* and imagined the heat like a tsunami, the crest curling but never quite smashing down. The water just keeps building and building until it floods.

White

Dare you see a Soul at the 'White Heat'?" Emily Dickinson asks. In blacksmithing, white heat represents the temperature "at which a body becomes brightly incandescent." Heat loses all color at its uppermost limit, a heat so bright it blinds. It might be, if we squint hard enough, the light of heaven. Dickinson uses the forge as an analogy for creative and spiritual expansion; we become malleable, melted, misshapen in order to become something useful, enlightened, or beautiful. We must dare to lose ourselves, become *hot,* and disappear.

Brenda Miller and Julie Marie Wade on their process:

When *Rappahannock Review* announced "Heat" as a theme for their summer 2016 issue, we got to work. We'd been collaborating for about a year on essays that revolved around simple topics—telephones, cameras, cars, etc.—so this word immediately conjured many ways to approach the subject. Brenda began by looking up the phrase "Heat Index" and decided this would be the perfect way to organize the piece. Individually, we brainstormed associations with "heat," especially as they might appear in an index: including "boiling point," "can't take the," "geothermal," "hot & spicy," "of the moment," "wave," and so on. We exchanged our entries as we wrote them, drawing inspiration from each other's writing. To complete the final piece, we decided to alphabetize the entries as an actual index, so the entries do not occur in the order they were written but now create their own narrative thread. In the final version, our "Heat Index" begins with "alcohol" and ends with "white." Some of the entries switch back and forth between our voices; in other parts of the essay, entries by the same author are stacked two or three deep. One result of writing together so closely over the past two years is that it is sometimes hard to recall which of us wrote which entry!

CROSS GENRE

Amy Sayre Baptista and Carlo Matos

LETTERS FROM *THE BOOK OF TONGUES* OR THE BOOK OF INÊS DE CASTRO

Pedro,

This world lacks precision, has become a place of blunt objects since you traded your knives for a crowbar, your fangs for dentures, my danger for poor sleep. I've forgotten, my cruel one—though you are said to be the most just of the three Pedros—how to taste my will, how to test for blood, how to feed my wiles. I fear, most of all, to guess, to underestimate, to risk my night logic on the simplest of things. You never overestimated anyone—that was your strength. What shabbiness this business of seeing the splitting world from a glutton's breast pocket with his insufferable mask of simplicity, or in a Wasp Eater's skirt with her devotee's terrifying complexity, or a demon's marsupial pouch never so dark as the mouth we shared: disappointing like finding the devil doesn't exist and that you already knew, disappointing like the savage making of virtue.

Inês,

I hate the taste of wasps, a carapace licked clean as finger bones left in the sun. Who could love such a lesson in fear—the ruination of figs, the soft, inturned flesh spotted with black seeds, not wasps, I know, but wasps to my tongue nonetheless? We were never very hopeful people, but I should have been willing to sacrifice my fear in order to make a promise or break one like Eve masking her knowledge with a fig leaf, a promise like a yearning broken and wingless and surrounded by fissured flesh and not the hard enamel of my penetrating teeth; antipodal like when I warmed to the sound of your voice refracting off the bedroom wall like a mother's: not yours, not mine, not any we ever actually knew but the kind painted on caves sealed for centuries by earthquake and volcano blast. Like your confidence that winged towards a dream where looking the part was the part, where a costume or a crown was not for hiding or revealing but seeing and scarring-up all that is left undone.

Pedro,
You said once you believed the human soul survives in handwriting. Do you
still? After everything? Here in the dust of Alcobaça, I taste you. I try not to
swallow too quickly, even a woman so long in the grave aches with loss revisited.
I am but lung and illumination trying to grow the heart back inside me. I am
so very tired, my love. But the taste of you is here with me. The flavor is mixed
with the city of Leira, salt, yes, salt from the sea, and the ochre blood of ancient
Lusitanian's cremated remains grown into the bark of trees. Trees for paper.
Paper from the water mill sewn into a book for a ship captain's log, and me
sailing away from you tasting the pages. Speaking in tongues, I've covered the
world with my words, when all I really wanted was you. You before that terrible
red Sunday. I am so very tired, my love. Forgiveness exhausts demons. You taste
of it all, the entire life. I can't really be anywhere and not find you with me. A
body once lived here. A spirit's body is slow to return: tingle in the scalp, the
flex in my foot, and a tongue in my mouth, a longitude. A heart once lived here.
Would you lay with me, as we once did, by the sea? In the tomb you built me, let
the dust of our bones mimic sand. And you my love, would you be the sun?

Inês,
Failure is growing up with too many rules or too few and still doing the right
thing, is an incomplete object horrid and waiting to happen on the lips of
the man you met at 15 or the woman who did not blink, is the great lie that
our hands are an ample reservoir against the long run in the sand: serious, a
rictus at the end where even anger flounders. You are right, a promise should
be massive, should be many times the failure of an old train wreck, should
be found standing in the mirror measuring itself. Sadly, nothing is absolute.
Thankfully, nothing is absolute. I was just trying to protect you, the girl who
understood clearly that escape and exile require staggering along backroads in
constant danger. Could I have finished stranger? Could you have opened a gift
from someone who hurt you? Could you … be someone else for a night? Maybe
we were simply waiting for the found to be lost, for time to stand still where no
one leaves and no one will. Everyone else turns away when they see a monster,
could you bear my countenance? What if I commanded it? I know it's a small
step from too good to you and too good for you, like loving the violin but not
the fiddle, but the truth is everyone thinks they're the good guy—belief its own
kind of maybe.

Pedro,

There should be a word (in Galician, maybe) for the way you buckle—a word with shoulders as broad and ill-fitting as Lisbon's, a compound, polyglot word that means I am missing a past that is still in the present from a future that, like all futures, never quite manages to arrive. This word would start with "x" or "z" and be both a noun and a verb. It would be a contronym—*pois não, pois sim*—or maybe a secret word we pass along the aqueduct of the monastery of Santa Clara-a-Velha. Or it might simply be a sad, 12-stringed Portuguese guitar kind of word pretending to be fun but cleaving to the shapeless, unquenchable, and crashing yearning you had at 15 when you wanted something (so bad) but didn't know what, like revenge which doesn't simply happen but must be made, crafted, forged and tempered. Tell our son to be a good man but not a fool; the line is thinner than you think.

Amy Sayre Baptista and Carlo Matos on their process:

Our collaboration started when Amy came to me one day and asked if I'd be interested in working with her on a series of persona poems based on the tragic love affair of Prince Pedro and his doomed beloved, Inês de Castro. Amy had written one poem that memorably starts out with the line, "Unbury me, reverse the dirt"—a poem describing the day Pedro, now king of Portugal, exhumed the corpse of his lover and had her coronated, just before he killed two of the men that had murdered her on the orders of the late king, his father—and I was caught. Originally, we had intended them for performance purposes. We thought it would be fun to write poems back and forth in the voices of these two bizarre and wonderful characters; however, the project very quickly grew beyond those bounds. We worked on a shared Google doc and pieces flowed. New voices demanded to be heard, new grudges grew from old ones, and we lost track of what was history and what was myth, what was Amy and what was Carlo. It was the kind of ecstatic experience that gives rise to something that neither one of us could have written alone. By the time we were done, we had a book-length manuscript titled *The Book of Tongues*, the story of a dead queen and the tongue that has not stopped speaking for 600 years.

Andrea Blancas Beltran and Melissa Matthewson

FIRST, DISLOCATE

If there is to be a season, let it be summer and let it be
full of storm—the kind that disrupts the afternoon, all
shifted light and pressure, abbreviated and quick, the air
condensed and dark. We must learn again the face of each
year's rain. How it pools, or doesn't. How it changes the
sky. The lightning tonight, so far over the ridge tells something
of the dark. Of unlearning. For so long, there's been
only one way to live. And now, I am an exile of sorts, a
new national in an inherited country. What it means to
discard a life into memory: tossed weeds on the fractured
grass, wine spilled on the tile, lips I'll never know again in
that certain sweetness that always tasted like home.

ring finger heavy
with absence, I cut angles
into what's still green

Andrea Blancas Beltran and Melissa Matthewson

AN OCCASION OF RINGS

Our rings rest on the sill: one slanted to the wood, the
other flush. How long they've been empty of fingers or
skin or bone. What to do with these silvers of love,
resistant to corrosion even in the window light, native to
the alluvium of some river far from here, this slope, this
mountain. And what if we let them go back? Into sand,
under rocks, never to tarnish, washed to the ocean or
pushed to shore. Maybe a day will come when a child will
find one near her pail and fit it to her thumb taking home
an imagined story to her jewelry box, the plastic doll
spinning to the dance of sugar plums and soldiers, the salt
still in the creases of her hands.

and even the dirt
that buries forget creates
fossils from touch

rainbow, double rings.
before the storm is over
one arch disappears

Andrea Blancas Beltran and Melissa Matthewson on their process:

We decided in the summer of 2015 to begin a collaborative haibun project after a lecture given by Tyler Brewington at Vermont College of Fine Arts in which he encouraged participants to explore collaborative writing. We felt a shared project would ease our mutual anxiety over experiencing the rumored post-MFA writing slump. Tumblr was the space where our collaboration lived and we called our private blog *the unlearning*. Andrea began with a haiku as a jumping off point, which we later scrapped, and Melissa responded with prose. We went back and forth like this over a six-month period. We both tried to respond within a week, but sometimes weeks went by before either of us responded. We had both agreed at the beginning of the collaboration that we wanted the process to be free from obligation, so the lapse between responses allowed for a certain longing to surface. Once we felt the correspondence had found its natural ending, we let the writing sit for a couple of months and revised it the next spring. The revision process allowed for an even greater synthesis of our work as we combined the haibun project into one document and revised the work equally, then compared notes on our separate revisions. We revised one final time. Once we felt the writing was ready we submitted it to Artifact Press, who accepted and published it as a limited edition letterpress chapbook titled *(un)learning* during the summer of 2016.

Mel Bosworth and Ryan Ridge

from SECOND ACTS IN AMERICAN LIVES

- - - -

There are no second acts in American lives.
—F. Scott Fitzgerald

SITCOM STARS STORM THE BEACH

At nightfall we ran aground. Faint stars and fainter tails of comets like bullwhips. Passengers fainting face-first onto the sand. I thought, turn them like this. Good. Make it more like the movies. We eureka-ed the MDMA powder with vacuum-like precision and soon enough our hands joined like people who join cults joined and afterward we said a little prayer that tonight would outshine the notion of night and that we would survive to tell the tale to some fat network execs and maybe even add a scene or two in our inevitable biopics. Now the fainters were up and the bonfire was lit and just as the orgy was about to shift into the next gear we heard the sound of the sky slicing, then gulls crying, and then we watched a helicopter white-knuckle it onto the beach. Out of the black bird popped a famous film director renowned for wearing dual eye patches when he directs. Good. We are actors, dammit, children who never ceased believing. Give us direction.

<<< *** >>>

RECOVERY

After draining the toilet, I put everything in the toilet. I drank a bottle of cough syrup and went outside. The cat spoke to birds. The birds spoke to bees. The bees spoke to me. They swarmed in proximity to my head and said, "A culture of rampant sexual repression and misogyny promotes chaos and leads to collective violence and insanity. The veil will soon be lifted. The fourth dimension is upon us, a realm of pure consciousness constituted by a democratic and communal mind. See you there. Don't be late." The bees dropped to the ground and died and then came one of those epiphanic moments where everything was clear and the trajectory of my future crystallized in a single thought: store. I went to the store and picked up a forty of Olde English, a box of menthols, and a Shake Weight. "Health kick?" the clerk asked. I nodded and left without paying. Yes, I had all the instruments now for an absolute and total recovery.

<<< *** >>>

LAST DECADE

The year the world split open and bared its teeth. The year sharks grew wings and erupted from saltwater. The year the Taffy Strangler hung himself forever to avoid trial. The year the skydivers landed on the moon on television. The year you could recognize the astronauts by their epitaphs. The year the wild horsemeat was all the rage. The year the dog walkers walked themselves and house cats hacked the Internet with their minds. The year the pursuit of happiness led to indefinite detainment. The year the humanities became the roboties. The year the nines rolled over and the clocks stopped at midnight.

<<< *** >>>

WHAT GOES AROUND

I'd been working the graveyard shift at the town graveyard for six weeks when bones began to sprout like flowers around the headstones. The bones grew into new people, people who didn't know the people they once were. With their new fingers they traced their old names. I brought them blankets. I fed them soup and gave them Gatorade. I taught them math and science and literature, what little I knew. I told them I loved them and I meant it.

<<< *** >>>

Mel Bosworth and Ryan Ridge on their process:

Ryan: "If I start a piece, Mel will finish it. If Mel starts a piece, I'll finish it."
Mel: "If I start a piece, Ryan will finish it. If Ryan starts a piece, I'll finish it."
And on and on it goes. Back and forth. Forth and back. We both edit everything for continuity and voice and continuity of voice. To date, we've written a collection of stories this way and we're working on a sequel. A selection from the sequel just won the Editor's Prize at The Cupboard Pamphlet and will be published in the fall of 2018. Literary collaboration probably isn't for everybody, but we're not everybody. We're probably nobodies. We don't care. We have fun, which seems to be a rarity anymore. Fun.

Justin Lawrence Daugherty and Jill Talbot

ON LEAVING: A CONVERSATION

A confession: I think it is always me who causes the leaving. A scene: she lies in my bed. I've moved from an apartment we shared, and she is between that place and her next place, hundreds of miles away. She asks, can we just try again? I tell her that's not what she really wants, that she's the one who ended things. I'm lying when I say this: I don't know that we're who we want each other to be. A fear. I won't unlearn how to ask her to leave.

~

I've been wondering for weeks how to respond—to you, to endings and unlearnings, to the way I keep finding ways to use the word "beleaguered." I read a story of yours, lingered on that line about *taking trips to get away from what we have to run from.* I imagined you in an airport, seated on a stool of some bar at an under-construction gate. I don't know why. A scene: he cries in a chair of the last apartment we shared, announcing his ~~desertion abandon~~. Maybe the word is "bewilderment."

~

It's been months, but I still wake up to find my arms reaching for her, to press my nose to her hair. In that story, there's the impulse to lock oneself away from the world until it becomes remade and we emerge into it the same, the world altered. That's not the way. What we face is our own fear of movement. Do you ever wonder if you asked him to go? I visited her in Boston, and each night I lay on the couch, and she said goodnight, and she would leave the bedroom door open. Invitation is not what that was, but instead a lie she told. An open door can sometimes be the strictest prohibition.

~

I think of a question in Anne Carson's "The Glass Essay": *Why hold onto all that?* Then: *Where can I put it down?* I think of your question, how it reads like a reckoning. My ~~wondering memory~~ unknowing (yes, that's it) rummages through the living room where he and I lived fifteen years ago. I open a closet door and stare at his workboots (I do that often). Or I'm (again) waiting at a window in the dark, holding my breath for his headlights to pull into the drive. Or I'm shuffling to the kitchen to stop the sink's drip, listening to loss with each note of the water's cadence. It's unnerving, standing inside the aftermath before the event even arrives. But I haven't answered your question.

~

Leaving is a question. A question of: *How did it come to this?* And: *What will you do now with what you hold?* I don't know if I want you to answer. My unknowing: waking up to a new daily unraveling. My unknowing: seeing in the unraveling something we expected all along. The bed I sleep in is the one we shared. It is too small, too closed in. How a thing changes in the aftermath. How that leaving is embedded. I lie down and the bed forgets her contours, her shape. A fear: I will stop feeling the unsettling.

~

I wrote this stanza years ago—months after he left:
I've seen ticket stubs in wallets, the way these words will be folded up in a drawer with leadless pencils, the matchbook with one match left. Statues of paper pinned to bulletin boards, tucked into frames. A suffocation, this poem, a memory of something we saw once, like the man missing his train.

I keep going back, revising the lines:
I've seen ticket stubs in wallets, the way these words will be settled in a drawer with leadless pencils, the matchbook with one match left. Faded receipts folded between book pages. Such suffocation, a forgotten secret, a memory of something we saw once, like the man missing his train.

What changes—memory or its meaning?
He used to tell me I mumbled (or sometimes sang) when I wrote. He'd come to the door and listen before understanding I was somewhere else. Maybe that's one way to ask someone to go.
One afternoon during those days in Colorado, I checked our account and found a charge from a gas station in Oklahoma. I didn't even know he had gone.
Such mystery misery fear—the distance that arrives only after so much has been lost.

Justin Lawrence Daugherty and Jill Talbot on their process:

JT: *Let me know if this works as a beginning.* These are the words Justin wrote to me in an e-mail on the day he sent the first section of "On Leaving." That was November 16, 2016. Usually when Justin or I send each other a segment, we respond within a day or two, sometimes within the hour, as if our words tremor across the distance until an answer settles them. Our responses are reactions, all instinct and echoes. When I typed, *I've been wondering for weeks how to respond,* I realized my words were a response to a new reality, new questions, to an anchor on a cable news show who used the word "beleaguered." I wrote to Justin, asked if we might approach this political landscape subtextually.

JLD: So often, for me, what I compose in response to Jill feels like a reverberation. It's not simply *response*, but it carries her words as they hit me and echo, ricochet. We were writing to each other, but also writing the sort of concussive feeling of the post-election moment. The crossing out and eventual landing on *bewilderment* feels like the heart of the essay to me, and it drove me in writing in response.

Craig Foltz and Quintan Ana Wikswo

THE HEART IS AN ORGAN WHICH MUST BE BLED

1.

No wonder the damselflies scatter when we confer. We have become linked organisms, but still, notice how we move away from one another. Our mother removes all the photographs from the house. *It is time*, she says. This is when we begin to forget what we looked like.

"Here," she says, "take this basket of fruit." She holds out her hands. They are empty. "Place these restraints on your elbows and knees."

Restraints are a precursor to exodus, and the lack thereof. Elbows and knees are appendages that must be at times tucked in, but at others spread out. We are still learning our new selves.

I think, *How funny we must look.*

2.

Before the transformation, the suitcases contained the definitions of who would be permitted to depart. Surely not ourselves—surely some form of acquired or imposed self, with interests and abilities determined by lottery. Surely not those who signal failure via paired cerci and other pinching weapons.

This suitcase has been forced to relinquish its romance and now is programmed to broadcast the message: anyone too awkward to meet our criteria will be carefully trimmed off with a sharp blade and a straight edge. The slick snip of the skin closing neatly on itself, containing its orderly inhabitants.

3.

Our mother can no longer tell us apart. We were born and reborn in seawater, on a subtropical coast of rocky outcrops and narrow, sandy inlets. The water of the ocean was warm and had deep, nutrient-rich currents which brought the small shoals of baitfish in closer. Despite manifestations of desire and arborescent shapes we were often controlled via tiny invertebrates and involuntary memories. Our mother spent the late afternoons under some mysterious spell in which her eyes would track the sun until she claimed she couldn't look away. When we looked into her eyes our reflections appeared upside down.

To us, she was haltingly adorned with strands of hair, vanishingly present. To others, she was a sturdy woman with nervous habits who wore a crucifix like a belt around her neck. Many years later she became known as the woman who impaled herself on a fence post by leaping from a great height. That was before we embarked on our gloomy little killing spree. It was before we hid lilacs and other aggressive species away as sources of future content.

Sometimes we wore the same clothes as one another. Other times we responded to the same name. The functions of certain pronouns became confused and difficult to pin down. For years, she cradled us in her wide arms, until one day there was a tinge in her voice that hadn't been there before and, after that, everything changed and became indecipherable. Twinned, but unable to cohere. We referred to each other as Sasha. Gender neutral, but identified by opposing demographics.

Two syllables are all that is required to start an exodus. SAH-shuh. We hear our names pronounced like corpses, or future archetypes. There is a user manual of course, which helps describe the shape of a curve, or the tilting of a planet. It tells us how to pronounce the words, but for whatever reason, we have chosen to stay mute.

Somebody, we can't be sure who, joins us who claims that they can travel in and out of time. We can't move backwards, we think, but neither can we move forward or stay put. This is archaic knowledge, time travel. Time has been suspended until further notice.

4.

The person who joins us moves into the back room, the one whose doors open out onto the ocean. She begins to convey something about these things—time, architecture, the changes in our bodies but loses momentum halfway through. I ask you to tell her that you have given up blood.

You say, "I have given up blood."

Without a clearly understood and readily operable engine of conveyance, we wait. We wait for her to tell us one or even two things: a half-fragment from a salvaged manual. A scrap from the days before, to site the way.

Instead, she says, "Let's pretend that dusk is dawn. Let's suppose that ambivalence is our default position." We agree to her terms, but what we think that means is she will get to wander freely, while we will be suspended in limbo, waiting to say something which cannot be contained in a sentence. "I have never wandered freely," say her lips, and the angle of her jawline.

5.

Paradoxically, it is at this exact moment when the entire ocean recedes, revealing pools of squirming marine invertebrates and shimmering piles of ooze unaccustomed to the harsh rays of the sun. Hidden is a temporary state, and remains so whether or not the secrets are sensed. Syllables are insignificant until they rise above the horizon, glowing. It was at this moment when we replaced all the pronouns in the text with the word "we".

It was here that we drafted the manual and here that we studied methods of torture and pain tolerance.

Our mother once relayed the story of how we came to emerge from the swampy undergrowth of estuarine environments. Mangroves from which the other participants were extended downwards. But we rose upwards. Our mother, to her credit, always planning for an emergency, envisioned a world for us in which we could live underwater, among the waving crests of sea grass.

6.

I ask you, "Did we even have any friends growing up? Can you remember any of their names?"

"They had names like Feather and Willow and Red Skull and Tui-Belle."
The vocabulary of a diaspora fails precisely because it does not accommodate occipital function and thus we are unable to replicate the things people actually talk about.

7.

The corpses begin to float to shore. Sometimes we want to wind the clock back to a time before we would approach the glossy blades of kelp with trepidation. I say, "It's hard to believe we used to approach these areas without the apparatus of documentation."

More simply put, friends and confidants are in short supply. As their corpses drift towards land, we traffic in endocrines.

Here is a face I recognize. Another carcass tumbles through the waves and washes up on shore.

8.

Our father was on the scene back then too. He was a keen boatsmen and taught us that only via safety lines and points of anchorage could we be lowered. He said, "Karabiners must be shaped like a pear and serve as a proxy for coral environments."

Our memories of him are clouded and lack distinguishing characteristics. Sometimes we remember his face draped in a mustard-colored beard. Other times he had no beard at all. We recall the navy blue rain slicker he wore, even in bright sunlight. But then, one day he just completely disappeared. He was erased, replaced by biomes of flesh near the high-tide markers. Back then, the water was very warm, and one could walk right in without noticing.

9.

We enter through the front door of the house, but are greeted by unfamiliar smells; faintly citrus. Although we have been absent for weeks, the air seems as if it has been recently disturbed.

Our lips exchange root verbs and other granular material. We allow our bodies to become vapor. We allow the particles of our body to circulate in the air, towards the ceiling. We allow a text to become a grouping of dark clouds; the beach, covered in black beach balls.

Each time another body washes up on shore, we wave sheets of smoke beneath the entrances to our home. This is a ritual that is not discussed.

10.

We drink seawater and it tastes just like blood. We concoct poisons in the sleepout and test them on the person who has joined us. Their body undergoes temporary transformations in which it is possible to reconsider the utricle and the effects of vertigo. It is possible that even decommissioned people sense their adversaries; that they *want* to be colonized.

You say, "It's true, the absence of syntax will tear us down until we become tedious and esoteric."

We discover another object. A body wrapped up in a navy-blue rain slicker.

The one we call Sasha says, "I don't want to touch it." And nobody knows what that means, but we all understand how it feels.

11.

A narrative is suggested and then curves back on itself. But there are complications. We appropriate from the narratives of other stories. We leach details from hardwood ash and manzanita pine. Language, despite what the authorities tell us, is still public property. Disk florets are concealed until dusk.

At night, our eyes open. One of us is incredibly downcast, but is unable to pinpoint the reasons behind this sadness. The grief is seeping. Even the people who have been decommissioned insist it is present. You point towards their sad, final resting places, "It's in *this* way that adjectives compete for space."

12.

The year is 1994. A year on continual repeat. Our mother shepherds us into a lively room full of martyrs. She tells us, "We are going to party until the power goes out." On the steps of a house, another habit: she brushes her fingers against the leaves of a shrub. Our lips are tinted blue and suggest words that have not yet been invented. Hominy. Anise. Piloncillo.

We know where the people who will not survive the night are stored. These are the ones past their use-by date. The ambient temperature is just low enough to delay decomposition. Organs are harvested and blood is streaked across their faces. Before they are marched away one of them looks me in the eye and says, "Somebody must have set us up."

It's Sunday. Our mother has a craving for pozole and Bloody Marys. Her mouth moves in slow motion, says, "In this context only very small things can be classified as creatures."

We were listening to Pavement back then. We saw Mudhoney open up for Sonic Youth at an all-ages fairground.

Perspective unearths beautiful objects but will not satisfy critics.

To deter escape, we dug pits beneath all the windows on the bottom floor. These pits were covered with brittle palm fronds and filled with large shards of broken glass.

The smoke from the doorways settled comfortably in the hollows.

13.

To the left is caution. To the right, a thinly laid array of palm fronds and bamboo shoots. The quality of light is distracting, but in a nonspecifiable way. Let's not pretend that fear is not involved here. When night falls, there is less light to discern the particulars.

Our vocabulary is replete with indications of signs. When further analyzed, those indications reveal themselves as meaningless. I say, warily, "The meaning may emerge over time."

We consider keeping records. Organizing the meaninglessness by alphabet and taxonomy. Or is that what we have decided to leave behind? We decide to proceed despite the terror of rampant ignorance.

And in that way, parts of speech begin to adhere to one another until something delicate emerges from the debris. It makes a brief appearance in our line of sight, but then, just as quickly, it disappears.

After a long journey, we reach the edge of the wilderness. The wilderness is full of contaminants and provides an audience for our designs.

14.

The year is 1987. The color is red. Our mother takes her crucifix to the sandstone wall and presses it in up to where her elbow used to be. Her other hand turns into a schwa. With it, she sweeps all the piles of umber dust into an envelope and folds. She can't help but scurry around the place, verifying specs.

She invites the man in, in the hope that he will offer up more than he did before.

But he offers nothing, outside of this cautionary observation: "The moon prevents transmission."

She believes in context, and she believes in the moon, but how the two beliefs will get them to a site where they emerge as whole selves seems elusive. She follows the man along the shoreline, avoiding the nets and straight lines. She begins a ritual chant that he supposes surrounds what they are leaving behind. He can hear the latches on the suitcases popping open, like bivalves.

The man has an unsettling shape, plunging and farfetched, in which the body is inscribed with branchy signals and mass-produced trinkets; small objects displayed for attraction.

After all these years he is only recognizable by the sound he makes. He has a mustard-colored beard and long water-resistant jacket which nearly reaches the ground.

15.

You bring the person who joined us into the living room and say, "In the ancient cities, it was preposterous to assume we could stand at the edge of the unknown and hurl a spear without it continuing into the unknown. But everyone argued that there was a solid wall, and the spear would recoil back and maim the person who hurled it. This is true of galaxies beyond the Milky Way in particular. They are isolated behind a seawall of one's own conception. There is no seawall. And yet this empirical evidence, recent in human history, is resistant to our emotions in this situation."

The person who joined us hesitates to hurl. Behind her, the empty suitcases.

Leaving the shoreline wasn't as difficult as we expected. There are holes in either side of the skull for just this purpose. The lances were not particularly painful, and the rotation on the linear axis provided an opportunity for our plans to develop further. A rotary fan blade began to take shape on our collarbones. In the beginning, we might have considered these to be injuries. Enigmatic wounds. But the evidence is incontrovertible: our velocity increased as a result. There was no seawall, just a thicket of negating verbs that could be averted with the careful use of antidotal numbers.

We hurl spears across the great chasm of letters. Only the spears are returned, defanged of their meaning.

16.

Here's what we remember about our former lives: There was a black box on a black floor with black wires and cords protruding from it. There was a black book with black paper and words written in black ink. There were black clouds floating above a black beach covered in black beach balls. Exposed black rocks poked above the wash of frothing waves. We had ten million words which could be used to describe darkness. The syllables were draped in deep shade.

Color identification has been suspended until further notice. These bulletins are now widely posted.

It was with this in mind that it seemed best if we headed back to the coast, that thin band of green on maps where a light mist from the ocean blankets the houses each morning, but now that we had left, you wouldn't have it. You say, "There is no green but the green in our memory."

Finally, the person we called Sasha decided to take us against our will.

17.

We are going to a very specific place, only we have no map. The map doesn't exist. You say, "Say something sweet." But then, just as quickly, "No, stop. Pretend I didn't say that."

We continue to travel in the direction of the coast and its variations of shamanism. Every surface is covered in the veneer of peace, love, and understanding, but underneath the surface something disturbingly evil. I enter a taco shop but leave before eating because I believe someone has spiked the salsa with hallucinogenics.

There are ghostly shapes in the air which we can sense but are unable to manipulate. What happens when we drive the lance through our skulls and become the vehicle of exodus, well, you couldn't say. Sophists and fortune tellers conclude the same: It is a violent and contemporary point in time.

There are many, many corpses in our wake. We are moving faster than ever before, but appear to be frozen in time.

A mark placed on the flesh signifies carnage, but also growth.

Something about the setup appears artificial, as if it were manufactured in a land far, far away, and then smuggled into our bodies late one night while we slept.

I tell you, "I'm attracted to the patterns generated by incidental human behavior." In lieu of human contact, you fiddle around with your injuries when no one is looking. We all do. Very soon, I think, we will be decommissioned as well.

Someone, we can't be sure who, addresses us in a way to indicate that there is only one. The syllables collapse on themselves. And this is how we end up together, curled around a color both of us would struggle to describe.

Craig Foltz and Quintan Ana Wikswo on their process:

There was a point in time, a place marked by (two or) three garish X's, where we discussed a few high-level nodes and nexi—form and function options, themes and the like. Later versions of the text included references to a set of unwanted items. A grove of chestnut trees. A tower of chronometer needles. Amphorae shards.

Structure as "an organizing principle," it turns out, is kind of a drag. To people who say, *I wouldn't want to climb in your head*, we say *Visible light is only one kind of wavelength.*

Perhaps, one of us once said, the ocean is just another barrier keeping us from arriving. Perhaps birds and constellations and air currents are all that we ever really needed to guide us. Maybe growing trees signal more than some mysterious, chromosomal rearrangement.

We note that one of us provides a public service by dipping their body in diesel fuel and getting the artists they respect the most to shower them in lit matches. Another one of us resides in a former sea—now a bed of diverse soils typically containing the bones of sea-dwelling dinosaurs. Is an ossuary calm? Do the forms of these selves disturb you? We think not.

Having forgotten the form, the shadow remained. Having dispatched the intruder, the ghost returned. When the dust finally settled, neither of us could actually determine which words / sentences had come from ourselves, and which ones had come from the other side of the ocean. Or ossuary. It was in this way we gravitated towards our penchant for remaining loudly undetected.

The Brothers Grandbois

STOOL PIGEONS

It isn't clear what ate him, though it's quite clear what he ate. The stool tells the story: a man ate humble pie before a terror taco. The storyteller wasn't *his* stool (that told of love and pancakes, not to mention forceful ejection), but the stool of what ate him. So what was it? Our methods of deduction failed us (as his bowels had failed him) and came to feel like withered instruments, waving in our hands as if on a vast and thoughtless sea. Johnson reacted in typical fashion and went to sleep. Kinte pulled out the bologna sandwich his wife had packed him, and Polacheck came down with a fever and asked to go home. I took a seat on the stool. Not *that* stool, of course, and not your run-of-the-mill lab stool either, but a custom job, noted for its sensitive arrangement of legs. When one's own legs dangled among them, an impression of childlike playfulness was sure to follow. Snowball fights always did wonders for releasing schoolyard tension. What did it matter now that the world was without snow? Stealthily, I retrieved a pair of rubber gloves from Johnson's kit. *Shit-ball fight!* What followed was a shrewdness of apemen in lab coats, flinging feces—though the feces weren't their own. And then it happened: Polacheck exploded a shit-ball against Kinte's forehead, and the man, quite unexpectedly, went rigid as an obelisk. The *eureka!* moment dawned, for in the surfaceless smear across Kinte's forehead, we could see everything we would ever need to know.

MISTAKE

What I find most ignoble about the whole affair is the way he stood in his plaid robe at the edge of the lake, waiting for the migration of the cranes. When I asked about it, he didn't even lower his binoculars. "The reason I've gathered you all here today…" It was quite plain whom he was addressing, though their long-necked ears were still too far out to hear. "People confuse you with herons," he went on, "yet your necks in flight are outstretched, not pulled back." It was then I realized I'd made a horrible mistake. Outstretched. Pulled back. Yes, my fly was undone. *Zip zap!* I concealed the long-necked bird by a swift interlocking of teeth. If there's a hell, it's having to stare at that old thing, my wife used to say. Cold. Disapproving. Of course, her flowering turkey-wattle was nothing to write home about either, but these things are neither here nor there, much like the home we used to share and unlike the cranes who were now, apparently, both here and there. Was it some trick of the glass? The old professor had, after all, flipped the binoculars around. "Never mind the past!" I shouted, willing him toward the other side of it. The binoculars were lowered, and the birds, as if on cue, craned their shafts in our direction. A barrage of beak-tipped arrows from across the lake, where our castles and our queens apparently wished us well.

The Brothers Grandbois on their process:

To begin a piece, one of us will write several possible opening lines. The other will choose one to work with and add a sentence or two. Much like a campfire story-telling game, it goes back and forth from there until an ending is reached. Along the way, each of us has total freedom to edit as he sees fit, including by adding interstitial material, moving things around, or reworking the whole piece. Lines that have been cut are often pasted at the bottom of the page until we're certain of their fate. Series of word or phrase choices are sometimes suggested in square brackets beside a questionable word or phrase. We don't discuss where we see the piece going. The words on the page do the talking. Sometimes one or the other of us gets carried away and adds too much material, which tends to take over the story and close down the possibilities, so we try to keep our contributions fairly short. If a piece ends up in a ditch, it's left there to rust, though we may give it a couple shoves before moving on. It can be helpful to have more than one piece going at a time. For years, Daniel has used lines and phrases found in books with which to converse in his writings. This is a two-way version of that process. The longtime collaboration of our childhood friends, The Clayton Brothers, may have informed us as well. They responded back and forth to each other on the canvas.

Carla Harryman & Lyn Hejinian

from THE WIDE ROAD

We have left our broken house in ecstasy, traveling out of the city. We walk in a vaporous valley with our bovine heads bent toward the plain where it is said it is possible to measure desire. We can't wait to see the grass that grows there. Our wish makes us thirsty.

> spilled from an empty pan
> the patch of rice
> left behind
>
> —running to risk
> the rain

Time and again the curly yellow weeds were clawed with clicks by bicyclists who dodged us where we walked, thriving with modesty. Tree and grass seeds scattered in the increasingly firm air. There is no analogous flattened happiness to that of curious and receptive travelers. Indeed, the morning bowed informally to us from the wide road which was filled with things to be coupled and compared.

> many thoughts remain
> in a soft head

How was it that we could still hear the slurping of deep kisses as clearly as when they first occurred and were recognized as the structure for much that was to come? We remembered our thrill upon discovering, for example, that two halves could be reversed.

> we find it delightful
> to go to another place
> while we still sleep
> in this one

>   one this
>   in sleep
>   is still
>
>   where will
>   we fit nips

We wrote these lines with inconsolable dispatch, after leaving the apartment in which we had spent our first night. WELCOME was the official instruction hanging from its door. A stranger had knocked with a deep and sylvan racket just above the peephole at its center, and we, sleepy from our exertions but hospitable in the hope that hospitality would be offered in return, had taken the shiny knob in our fingers and had opened the door.

We could say no more than this:

>   in a perfect circle
>   rises the warm spring night
>   but it gains an enormous length
>   before it sinks

Spreading our legs we invited the stranger to enter and make himself comfortable.

>   only my shadow
>   will come to you
>   tonight to beg
>   for a little flesh

**

Love opens life's warm seams. Do you realize that we're clothed in skin inadequate to any other destiny? No one was there to hear this question. The mother's breast is still unveiled but no one watches the scene with fatherly interest.

The morning light, forming pearly drops of mist, sprayed against our mouth. We inhaled the heady emanations of the eucalyptus trees whose ragged bark and pungent buttons were drawn into the breeze. A young unhaltered mare approached the trough under the trees nervously, shying with contradictory impulses, prancing backward and tossing her head. Then she thrust her head forward and curled her lips around a column of water deep in the trough beside the fence.

We opened our shoulder bag and wrote in our book:

> hidden under our open eyes
> the cleft
> is coterminous with our destination

We set aside our rifted introspections in order to get to the motel by nightfall. The shoulder of the interstate is not safe after dark. So without pausing for thought we found ourself by 8 p.m. facing a salad bar under an enormous antlered clock at Al's Lockhorn Cafe. Across the street the reflection of the word EAT from Al's neon sign was flashing on the windows of the Recluse Motel.

> ah! night lights
> pushing through to the bed
> — almost at that height already

We know that sex is sometimes an escape from other more indigestible knowledge. The lights flash again and we have no appetite but one. Again, like anyone, we're miserable from the news of the day.

> flapping around the air-conditioned room
> newspaper brushes our skin

We kick the sheets off.

> legs open
> the street

The curtains are drawn a little, and as long as we can see the source of the rumblings, we can remain relaxed.

> herds of jellyfish
> surround a waterfall

**

Sex is an incitement, urging us to elapse. Or wrap. Or glare. Uninspected, undressed, and unreconciled as we are, we continue to watch for the flickering which had been an anchorman. It is the passage of time that allows us to become moral, and as we wait we watch the wriggling of the sunlight across the floor and onto the futon where we are resting as it expands until we succumb to its elusive but warm pressure on our naked breasts which we call Me and Not-Me.

Just as the tips of bare magnolia twigs make little ovals in the wind, just as the eyes of a frog can see in every direction, just as common gossip wavers this way or that, just as mothers in their sleep hear their babies' crying from all sides and come awake in an instant, just as a horse may be taken to represent certain forms of meditation, and just as desire provides its own genesis and sex its own explication, just so we sprawl in the flickering sunlight.

The sunlight is applicable to our situation, or, shall we say, we make it so.

> all labor is respectable
> in the saving

Masturbation is equivalent to a pamphlet.

> militants, flirts
> in their fortress,
> the author
> with foamy criteria

Forever!

**

We knew we were angry about something; many things point to it. As for the anger itself, it is located sometimes in the torso, resembling a dahlia rooted in the stomach but blooming against the ribs where they form a cage behind the breasts, and sometimes it's in the skull, like a copious sweat worked up by an idea. Or so it seems upon introspection.

One has to introspect *something*.

> assuming abrupt control, assuming
> magnification, the authentic Aphrodite
> is relatively large
> and ambiguous

You titles of men, do not touch us! Not the samurai but the scowl produces our choice vocation, our literate licks. However, we confess for the sake of our love of the camel and its open sway that sometimes, while havoc has hold of our priceless repose, we call upon Joyce's multiple styles for proof that we can say modestly, "once sprawled in the flickering sunlight." We do. For the love of *Arachnida* and sticky lines. Or is it that we had just written "within the grip of" amidst the clamoring semi-tropical shrubs, clasping ourself to ourself in the dampness?

> obscure Macoute
> participation in
> Haitian election

Dampness, thicker than rain, fades within our pungent, dilettantish mouth tasting of affinity and finality. The end and the beginning of money meet. Obscure Haitian—

> not fitting
> or water
> funny bursting
> under earth
>
> earth fitting
> water
> not under or
> funny
> bursting

or under earth
fitting bursting
not funny water

earth
water
under
funny
or
not
fitting
bursting
not water
earth

or bursting
under fitting
funny

++

May 12
Dear Lyn,

It seems to me that this may be the right moment to start a correspondence; I think we need to take a break from accumulating fragments. The difficult aspects of sex or sexuality may have to do with the way the fragmented form has evolved to this point. In addition to our eagerness to work in the most obvious genre that traveling used to suggest, the letter, a correspondence might give us more thoughts about the fragmentation that thus far has constituted our excursion. Might I consider this insert erotic?

But it is odd, funny to be writing to you about our work-in-progress as a part of the work itself.

In one of our recent conversations you mentioned your resistance to violence in Bataille and to "dark sex," and this I think creates a fruitful tension between us:

we have to negotiate our individual experiences and our thinking about, or feelings for, the "erotic" in order to write anything together at all. Some of the tension is explicit, even judgmental, and other aspects of it go unstated; in a sense they remain eroticized.

We have arrived at a site where anxiety over sexuality is connected to forms of non-erotic, political violence within the frame of our pleasure-laden writing. Yet, the writing's disposition toward pleasure does not disappear when the Haitian elections are referred to, but the language changes key. The word "Macoute" is eroticized in our use of it, because part of the "landscape" of the writing is "sound" and the sound of the word exceeds its social meaning—or acts as an indication of another kind of meaning in which terror and sexuality entwine in fantasy. Yet the morose affect of "Macoute" in the poem is a sign, or symptom, of both protest and disappointment in what seems to be a hopeless situation—the invisible power operating outside the narratives of the news. How often are the U.S. interests in controlling such nations as Haiti made apparent to us through the media?

In bits of the material leading up to this correspondence, I have been attempting to show, rather than to explain, the imagination's vulnerability to and working with the associations between mediated images, narratives, documentary, cultural knowledge, and fantasy.

Here fantasy, as gendered, is related to the feminine projection of power onto men—through an autobiographical lens. When I was around twelve, I saw a news documentary on Papa Doc, the Haitian Dictator. He and his "Macoute" thugs were "scary guys." In the girl's mind it is easy for the scary guy to become associated with scary adult male sexual power/desire. Power and desire of the other are sites of projection. Here "the other" is also an ethnic other; his opposite would be those Haitians who oppose and/or are suppressed by the power of the Macoute. How does this information impress itself on the mind of a twelve-year-old white girl in California?

As an adult, I have read about the history of the Haitian political struggle as well as about its culture with great interest. But in what capacity could or would I go to Haiti? Not as a tourist.

Yet the passages related to Haiti in *The Wide Road* initiate a tour (this sounds frighteningly militaristic); what I have done is read and respond to an American newspaper's representation of current events, absorbing these into the erotic undertow of our imagination.

Right now I am imagining a bright flashlight shining on a body, my own or anybody's; the body in this frame becomes "just a naked body"—the same as, or close to, a dead body. Then I think: expose, exposition. Then: detective, police novel, and genre.

Oddly, I just now recall that there is an actual experience related to the image of the body exposed with a flashlight. I was in a building occupied by anarchists in Paris, sleeping next to a young man. The police came to arrest us for illegally sleeping in the building. One of the police, a white person of about my age, turned his light on me while I dressed. I kept telling myself "just put on your clothes, you're just a body to him. It doesn't matter, I'm just a body." By convincing myself that what was happening didn't matter and that I was only matter, I was removing myself from the place where I could be violated or threatened. But the distant feeling I communicated, by having removed myself from my physical body, brought out the sadism in the cop, who then attempted to belittle me for sleeping with "Chinois." He informed me that my transgression would make my babies dirty. It was this comment that terrified me; it was then that I became fearful of not knowing what would happen next. If he could say anything, perhaps he felt that he could do anything too.

What do you make of these thoughts that link colonial/post-colonial violence, sexuality, fantasy, and autobiography?

Love, Carla

May 15
Dear Carla,

Here is a nonviolent scenario: A bends to B, B bends to A—both are wielding power and both are submitting to it in a game of pleasure, A or B on top, B or A wiggling and waving. But power at play with pleasure is not violence: "I silence your moaning with violins."

I'm side-stepping your question—but not the challenge it entails. I'm giving myself time to think, to fantasize, to range through my own associations. We live in an aftermath condition—or aftermath is the condition in which what you are calling our fragments (the intentionally under-explicated bits of some implicitly vaster story, only semi-contextualized expository asides, and the very asidedness of our attention and the dubious duplicity of our personage) become, at least for me, a topography. At one point in the writing, I crafted a gnomic phrase; it was some meta-comment like "we will not know where we will go." It deserved the rejection / deletion that it received. But it did point to a tension between power and play, intention and open inadvertency, willfulness and willlessness that pulls at this extended foray into erotic adventure and pastoral contemplation; the work has multiple centers of gravity. Your question demands an understanding of the resulting topography; I'm on the verge of asserting the undesirability of that.

Power at play with pleasure is not violence: "I silence your moaning with violins."

The situation becomes ominous when *pleasure* is at play with *power*.

Or am I getting too metaphysical? I think so. A metaphysical conceit is a poor substitute for the linkages that constitute mattering.

"My dear, you are a genius in a pink and black harlequin suit."

"My dear, take my high-powered flashlight."

Various caricatures come forward into the light: there is the squeamish cowpoke with a quirt, the sentimental general with a lapdog, the revolting torturer with perfect teeth, the 8-year old girl in the dark. The girl is tossing in ersatz feverishness, coddling a pretend broken arm, indulging in a fantasy of hospitalization or imprisonment where passivity is mandatory, culpability impossible: whatever pleasures she will experience won't be her fault and her endurance will be heroic. I can remember much of this; it came to me when I learned of the Holocaust. The sentimental general presses the prongs of a red hot fork into the paws of his lapdog. That happened in the aftermath of monotheism, the aftermath of the Inquisition, the aftermath of colonialism.

Invention directed toward the repression of invention as well as the repression of alterity has provided "dark sex" with some disturbing instruments and eroticism with disturbing instrumentality. Cruelty, the use (inevitably eroticized) of torture as an instrument of power, the violence to optimism that even milder misuses of power produce, the defamation of the very notion of power so that creative uses of power are perceived as threatening, even monstrous—our gender, fantasy-life, the soil underlying concrete highways and crushed by cars, etc., have been devastated by these.

Submission, even to violence, does have its place in the realm of the erotic, but the violence in the sex is not necessarily inflicted violence, it can also be violence that is very precisely, even meticulously, withheld, as the prolongation of an otherness that occurs only in and as sex.

The sound "Macoute" is, as you say, eroticized in our use of it, and I don't think glibly. Among other things, we are pointing to the pleasurability of round and percussive sound; the play of lips and teeth and tongue involved in making it; the aesthetic triumph of referent over reference; the danger inherent in the drift of signifiers out of context.

But, Dear Carla, a letter should *open* with the setting of a scene. It should show the letter-writer in her scene so as to produce an inviting passage through which the writer brings the reader in. This may be considered erotic. Dear Carla, I have just closed the windows. Outside, the wind is blowing and I can see the branches of the neighborhood trees leaping and shaking, though whether they are trying to get into or get out of the wind and sunlight it's impossible to say. Now that I'm paying attention to the scene, I notice that I'm not sitting up straight. I should do so. I'm wearing black socks, my favorite black pants, an old and comfortable long-sleeved purple thermal shirt, and I've wrapped a blue and white long scarf around my neck.

There is a calculator on the desk along with assorted papers, and Bataille's *The Impossible*. Opening it at random, as a bibliomancer might, I come upon this phrase: "his guiding concept." For me, *The Wide Road* has multiple guiding concepts, and apart from those that might be more obvious, compassion and animal exhaustion (death) are among them.

People are still fighting to be people; why do they hold animals in contempt?
Love, Lyn

**

Sometimes we accept the enormous situation of the subject-object, wherein we exhibit (but I could say *embrace*) some of our capacities.

> praises
> praises
> porosity

Carla Harryman and Lyn Hejinian on their process:

Composition of "The Wide Road" began somewhat spontaneously one evening. We rapidly—ecstatically—came up with a thematic substrate and a loose formal architecture. It would be an erotic picaresque narrated by a "we" who embark(s) into a sexy terrain by which "we" isn't intimidated at all. We don't remember who wrote the opening paragraph. Basho's *Narrow Road to the Far North* provided us with a compositional frame: prose and poetry (reflecting our different literary emphases, though both of us have written both), event and response, reflection and action, formality and sassiness. The basic compositional rules were simple: one of us wrote something (there was no rule as to how much or how little) and the other added to it. We sustained this "trade off" or "call and response" method throughout the composition of the first draft, but we also made changes to the text that were occasioned by public readings of it. For these readings, we would move text around, mingling what we had written such that it would be difficult to discern who wrote what, and we would frequently keep those changes intact. At a significant point, we "broke through the fourth wall" and embarked on an epistolary exchange. Some of this material was written over the course of a week we spent together in the country. We returned a year later to the same place for a week of collaborative revisions. In a third year, we met again, completing the final draft. Belladonna realized the work beautifully, and we end this note with thanks to the Belladonna feminist collective.

Tom Henthorne and Jonathan Silverman

THE NOISE OF COLLABORATION

Their project started out of the boondoggle of one of the authors' other projects: the six-year odyssey to publish the dissertation. Jonathan, a new faculty member at Pace University in NYC, was presenting a paper comparing Henry Roth, the immigrant Jewish writer, to De La Soul, the rap group, in front of the Dyson Research Group, an informal group of professors at Pace, who got together to discuss works in progress. Jonathan, in his own mind, was also testing out the work as a possible new conclusion to his dissertation, a sprawling comparison of three historically marginalized groups in the early part of the twentieth century: African Americans, immigrant Jews, and women and their efforts to use their writing as a way of negotiating mainstream success. Jonathan had struggled to make this a viable book, especially in finding a suitable frame/point of reference. This new comparison, he thought, might be a way of connecting the work of the 1920s to the present day, through the organizing principle of audience: both Henry Roth in writing in the 1990s in his weird and majestic *Mercy of Rude Stream* and De La Soul in *De La Soul Is Dead* had incorporated audience expectation into their works. They both understood that their follow ups—Roth 50 years after his canonical *Call It Sleep* and De La Soul after its auspicious (soon to be canonical) debut, *3 Feet High and Rising*—that they would find it difficult to negotiate the response of audiences expecting them to produce similar greatness.

Another professor, Tom, had worked with Jonathan on a draft, and so Jonathan's natural anxiety of being an untenured faculty and presenting material was somewhat diminished. But when the presentation took place, Jonathan's fears were renewed—no one quite knew what to make of his piece. Besides some reactions to his unapologetic use of informal language, including—gasp—use of contractions, people didn't know where you could place such an essay. At that point, Jonathan thought that a useful and interesting exercise would be to send it to many journals, print the responses to the essay, and a revised copy of the essay as a way of showing the process of revision and response and audience in the academic world.

But then Tom made a suggestion that led to a whole different project. He suggested that they randomly apply to an MLA panel, by first counting the amounts of calls for paper, then choosing at random a number corresponding to the panel they counted, and then see how the academy would write the paper in much the same way that Jonathan thought about doing for his own paper. Tom and Jonathan would write the abstract together and then a paper and revise it according to the feedback it received under the peer review system. Thus was the generation of a defining collaboration, one that was largely unfulfilled, but one that took an unexpected direction, both delightful and worrying at the same time.

Jonathan went to the Internet to find a number generator. Tom had some difficulty counting the calls—then he left the brochure as numbered in California. But finally they succeeded in randomizing the selection project. The first number generated a call for papers on Arnold Schwarzenegger whose deadline was too soon, and frankly Tom and Jonathan thought this project too easy, given their cumulative knowledge of popular culture. The second generated a call for paper on the Spanish *comedia*, a subject that neither Tom nor Jonathan knew anything about. They began.

The narrative of the paper

Not only did Tom and Jonathan want to write about their subject without any previous knowledge, but they also wanted to do so in 24 hours, once they settled on a text and an approach. Why 24 hours? They wanted to simulate the intense pressure of writing a paper for a conference; also, it was stupid. Sometimes when they talked about doing work together, they tried to outdo each other in terms of what weird thing they would try.

In order to begin the process, they both set out to read Calderon's works. Unfortunately, their college library, though it had versions of Calderon plays, it did not have recent publications; most translations were from the 1950s and 1960s, and they knew there were better ones. Nonetheless, they read some of his plays and figured out an angle from which they wanted to make their argument—they found a passage in *El Magico Prodigioso* that seemed ripe for explication (or as Tom observed, exploitation).

The play, in English roughly, the *Wonder-Working Magician*, is about the temptation of a secular philosopher by the devil, who first puts a spell on him to make him fall in love with a local virtuous woman, and then makes a deal with him for his soul. The play ends up with both the philosopher and woman killed by authorities for their religious beliefs, his newly found and hers steadfast, and their romantic, unconsummated entry into heaven.

In the passage where the devil tempts the scientist/philosopher, much is made over the devil, who is tempting a scientist to sign over his soul (see Dr. Faustus), and his successful efforts to move mountains. The move is supposed to suggest the ill-gotten power of Lucifer, but they noted that the stagecraft in this play—the moving of mountains—might have had a similar effect on Spanish audiences as blockbusters have on modern ones.

Now they just had to write the abstract. Fortunately, Tom had a free meal at a Mexican restaurant, Red, which is where they had brainstormed their approach. A few days later, with the deadline approaching, Tom and Jonathan forced themselves to come up with what they thought would be an acceptable abstract/proposal, which they did in three short sessions within a single afternoon.

Tom contends that this abstract in a sense wrote itself, given their experience in academic discourse and writing proposals—they knew all the conventions (It included the theorist Slavoj Žižek, Spanish in the title, cultural history). They sent it out, and a month or so later, they got their rejection.

Why? They did like the abstract they wrote. But they suspected that their approach may not have been new or that Calderon already had literary admirers that trumped their approach. Whatever the reason, they moved on.

Still, they didn't give up and set their paper-writing plan in motion. They figured they would try to spend a night at school trying to write this. Then as a pattern of their usual one-up-themselves goofiness, Jonathan suggested they try writing the paper at a casino, which further muddied the possibility of doing the work.

So on a May afternoon, they headed to Mohegan Sun via Metro North and a special bus, carrying photocopies of Spanish history, theatre history, and work about Calderon, as well as a copy of his play. On the train, they outlined the argument and divided up the workload.

Here was the basic outline on which they collaborated:

1. They would use the abstract as a basis for an introduction and re-write the introduction later after they wrote the conclusion (2 or so pages).

2. Jonathan would write the historical and theatrical context, researching the declining Spanish empire as well as the state of Spanish theatre at the time (2 to 4 pages).

3. Tom would do a close reading of the play and passage (4 to 6 pages).

4. They would collaborate on the conclusion (2 pages).

They would then add and subtract from each other's work when finished. They were not this precise at the time, they confess, but in looking back at their notes and writing at the time, this is how it seemed to be working out. When they got to the casino, they could not take their backpacks with laptops in but were free to take in their notes. They worked steadily throughout the afternoon, in between breaks for Keno and horse racing betting. Jonathan bought a "bottomless cup" for coffee.

At one point, they had to decide whether they were going to stay up all night or get a hotel room. So they put 75 on a 2 to 1 roulette bet—and won. Had they not hit it, they might have actually finished the paper, Tom suspects.

The paper writing went relatively smoothly, except for the conclusion. Jonathan worked in American Studies, an interdisciplinary discipline that often invites speculation; Tom was an English studies scholar, whose work was more theoretically sophisticated than Jonathan's, but it also stuck closer to the text. When working on the paper at Mohegan Sun, Jonathan's inclinations were to turn the discussion to larger conclusions. For example, the idea of moving mountains having a double meaning in the politically-charged world of Spanish drama, where Calderon was a court (read government-controlled or at least influenced) dramatist, immediately raised connections with the political landscape of the time.

Jonathan thought about the way George Bush wore a flight suit and landed on an aircraft which said, "Mission Accomplished" as well as the Disney's retreat on backing Michael Moore's *Fahrenheit 9/11* and CBS/Viacom's presentation of the Reagan mini-series. The analogy Jonathan drew was that the ideas of spectacle and power always have double-edged meanings when they come from the government, which exerts its power directly (the coverage by networks of the Bush landing on the aircraft carrier) and indirectly (behind-the-scenes maneuvering that pressured Disney and CBS to drop/move their respective narratives). Plus the connection between the fading empires of Spain and US, especially given American Studies' recent emphasis on empire studies, would have been hard to resist.

Plus audiences like to watch spectacle, as those in Spain would have. The Spanish comedias were not unlike American popular culture. So watching the mountains move, even if by the devil, would have had some appeal, as watching something like *The Day after Tomorrow* or *Independence Day* might have for us.

They did some more work on it the next day and agreed to work on some more at a future time. That time never came.

The conference

Tom and Jonathan knew, given their schedules and commitments, that they would probably not finish this without some incentive. They looked at first in vain for an appropriate conference, which in their case meant, one that could be funded and did not conflict with other conferences. So they applied to a graduate conference at Brandeis University, and they were accepted, though not before receiving a note from the conference organizer: "Also, this conference is a graduate conference; I notice that you're an Assistant Professor. Some of our early calls for papers did not make this clear. If you'd like to withdraw your abstract because of this, please let me know." Uh, no. It was better for Jonathan and Tom's purposes to be in this particular group, though not exactly for the reasons they thought—a lower bar—but because of their audience.

As the conference approached—as a running joke (Jonathan thinks), Tom kept asking what date it was—their anxiety about producing the paper increased (Jonathan thinks). A week before the conference, as they prepared for another marathon session of writing, Tom approached Jonathan with another idea—going meta about the paper.

The reactions

Jonathan was relieved but also reassured that they actually had a paper. As they had described this project, the reactions had become a story in themselves. Because of who they are, they talked a lot about the project to friends and colleagues. And their world was displeased with the project.

From the beginning of this project, the most interesting aspect was not the paper but the reactions to the paper, which ranged from amusement to outrage.

It's hard to know where to begin, but Jonathan's favorite reactions were from his colleague and officemate Steve, his collaborator from another project, Meghan, and his chair, Walter. Steve said, when hearing about the project, "you'll never be able to present at another MLA again." Meghan said, "you are mocking the entire discipline of Spanish drama," and Walter pretended not to hear about the project, but then eventually said, "You cannot work on a work in translation."

Tom's friend, Beth, who asked or stated, Tom forgets, "Can you do that? You can't that." And the third was a chair in another department, rolling her eyes and presumably thinking, "that's what they do in English." They heard from their colleague, Tricia, who called the project "arrogant." Others were more generally amused, like Martha, but when hearing about their project's shift in course at the last minute, essentially called them cowards.

Two more positive responses came unexpectedly. One from a colleague Mark, who is generally bemused at the whole academic project; he said, in essence, one needed about six weeks to master a field (albeit with a touch of irony).

The other was from a friend of Jonathan's co-author of a textbook, Dean Rader, Brandon, a physicist. As they were walking back from a delicious burrito lunch in San Francisco, Jonathan told Brandon about their project. His reaction was unexpected; he compared their randomization project to current science projects on the subject of noise.

Essentially, their random choosing of subject was the equivalent of us creating noise within the academic community. Noise has an effect on organisms, he explained. Just by putting out noise it affects an organism's health and vitality. And he gave them the example that they are giving shoes with random pressure points for people who have lost their balance and purely through these pressure points, people are able to walk better.

Now Tom and Jonathan wondered what the result of this noise was. People were talking about their project and getting really mad because they were pressing some button in them that was making them react. And they were learning a lot about this course of knowledge through those reactions. And that was the noise they were creating.

Their reactions to other reactions

Jonathan and Tom presented the material at the conference, and if you listen to the tape, the narrative they tell sounds almost like a comedy routine. The thing is—they didn't mean to be funny. Both have reputations of being funny, but the project's absurdity was not meant to generate laughs, though it didn't mind gathering them. The reactions from the crowd after were different from those from colleagues—one divinity student asked them "do you think of yourselves as Martin Luther?" They guessed they could only have meant as a type of truth teller or revolutionary (neither of them is particularly good at religious or world history), but the fact is that Jonathan and Tom don't think in orthodoxies more generally—except academia is a system that enforces it, and so their goofy rebellion was more a nose ring of the body of their academic work than theses nailed to a door.

They liked to think that this project is a form of noise, that what they did had a good effect in drawing attention to scholarship, but that is something could be self-justifying. What they think they learned was that perhaps they could not fake it the way they wanted to, or more accurately, they did not have the same interest in faking it as they did before. Jonathan liked the project as it collected data from interested bystanders, a sort of a big rubber band of academic discourse that grew but had an undefined center. In the end, Tom was comforted by the rejection from the MLA, but he could not help but wonder, that if they had generated a topic closer to their expertise, could they have succeeded?

Tom was more concerned with the way the academic discourse produced knowledge and was less concerned with the negative reactions the project provided. One of the reasons was that Tom was in a better place professionally than Jonathan; he had just received tenure when this project began, while Jonathan, though he received his Ph.D. only a year after Tom, was only in his first year on the tenure track.

But Tom also is more cynical about academic generally, finding the rules and practices of academic arbitrary and somewhat limiting. So the reaction to the project concerned him less. Indeed, he did not as readily tell the story as Jonathan, who at first was seeking approval, then became engaged with even the negative responses.

What did they learn about collaboration? As frequent collaborators with each other and other scholars, Jonathan and Tom began with a healthy ability to propose ideas and not hold on to them closely. They were able to work together on a project in which they were not experts. But in the end their academic disciplines—one an interdisciplinary field that rewards speculative and cross-genre and period thinking and the other more traditional—shaped their work more than either of them might like to admit.

Postscript

Fast forward eight years. Jonathan was now a tenured professor at another university. Tom was a full professor. They never worked on the piece again, but in frequent interactions, they talked about it. Ultimately, Jonathan learned about disciplines in a way that shaped his own understanding of audiences. It led him to think more about the way academics think more closely about their responses than they might themselves imagine. Jonathan and Tom disagreed about what the project meant, but they agreed that it meant something, even if only that a paper that gazes at itself learns more than what the paper itself means.

Tom Henthorne and Jonathan Silverman on their process:

The process piece in many ways is embedded into the essay itself—it is the story of how we collaborated. We discussed the piece as we wrote—our offices were across the hall from each other. We wrote separately and together, and it would be difficult to separate each person's contribution from the other. Because much of the material of this piece was actually presented at a conference before it was written, a good part of the collaboration took place as we practiced the presentation. We streamlined the writing, took out awkward transitions, weeded out sentences that didn't work. In that sense, the practice for the presentation was a crucial part of the collaboration and writing process.

We also describe the intellectual contributions we each made. In that sense, the paper is also a document of the way we *differ* in terms of how we look at the project specifically and academia more generally. Rather than trying to reduce the disagreement when talking about the project at large, we describe it. Often in collaboration, the idea is to speak with a unified voice that represents compromises in content and tone. We do think the piece is unified in style and tone, but we hope it accurately reflects our differing opinions about the subjects of academic discourse, as well as our agreements.

Rebecca Hart Olander and Elizabeth Paul

from HOW THE LETTERS INVENT US: A CORRESPONDENCE

"WHERE YOUR TREASURE IS, THERE YOUR HEART WILL BE ALSO"

citation from the "Book of Matthew" on Chopin's memorial at Holy Cross Church, Warsaw

It is said Chopin feared being buried alive, asked that his stilled heart be excavated from his body, transported to his homeland after his death in Paris. The pianist must have also wanted his emotional core in Poland, similar to the Hmong, who bury placenta under the birth house so the soul can find its way back after death, and stop its restless wandering. If the border guards had lifted Ludwika's skirts, they would have found the jar of amber liquid and tender organ, bound by duty to her brother's whispered deathbed wish. We do strange things when faced with mortality, and nothing can quite quell our deepest fears. I remember a fetal pig floating in a jar, bathed in formaldehyde, in my basement for a time as a child. Was it a requirement for one of my mother's nursing school labs, Anatomy & Physiology 101? A way of looking inside a fellow mammal in order to understand the self? How I hated going to sleep in my bedroom upstairs, knowing it was below me, in the open grave of washing machine and cleaning supplies, swimming through my dreams. The pig was likely bound for dissection, unlike Chopin's preserved organ, extracted from his body but kept whole, a relic entombed in Warsaw, bobbing in a bath of cognac in its crystal vessel. Chopin's body rests in the Parisian Père Lachaise Cemetery, and I visited his grave there when backpacking across Europe the January I was twenty, the tomb graced by the muse of music, Euterpe, weeping over her broken lyre. Now I'm remembering the tiger maple piano my mother paid for in installments, bought for the potential in my long fingers, the piano that got water damage after our next move, sitting dormant then, more furniture than instrument. An elephant in the room, that rippled albatross, reminding me of dreams that didn't come true. The longing to own beautiful things. The abandoned lessons. Is anything sadder than an unplayed instrument?

—Rebecca

Rebecca Hart Olander and Elizabeth Paul

NO APOLOGETIC ADJUSTER

In his last five years, Matisse could no longer sit at his easel, but propped up in his bed or chair, he painted with scissors, creating cut paper collages with the aid of assistants who arranged his colorful jungle, circus, ocean shapes on the white walls of his bedroom. My mother at some point stopped sculpting and turned first to still lifes and finally watercolor, consulting books for beginners like *Painting with Freedom* and *Pouring Light*—a portrait of grace I didn't understand at the time but now perceive with unexpected pleasure as though discovering a smuggled masterpiece beneath a lesser picture of malaise. What other heroic adjustments go unnoticed in their moments, glossed over with platitudes—making choices, slowing down, tightening one's belt, building a career, putting the children first, getting used to married life, moving on without them? With a piece of charcoal lashed to a fishing pole Matisse sketched faces on his ceiling. Of his bedroom walls decked in paper fruit and flowers he said he'd made himself a garden to go walking in. No apologetic adjuster, all his phases, gropings, discoveries, and transitions in impressionist, fauvist, pointillist, monumental, languishing, distilled evidence for the sake of art and all to see. I would apprentice myself to such an artist, learn to live without arriving, thriving even on the redoubtable rebirth, in the end embracing just another new beginning.

—*Liz*

Rebecca Hart Olander and Elizabeth Paul

OF MOTHERS AND MATISSE, THE HONEY AND THE BEE

What would I lash myself to the mast for, and what sirens would be too tempting to listen to, drawing me from my daily bread and the multiplying calendar pages? To what art would I pledge my openness, say *you are bee* and *I the lumbering bear,* fly out and collect all that beautiful yellow dust, return it to me, unburdened as a Polaroid shaken by the wrist, showing what is possible. In the small square, a picture starts to form, like a body rising up from a murky pond. I'd hitch my wagon to that star, the shooting kind, that trails out in the far night but glows all the brighter before its diminishing. My mother had to give so many things up, her own poems tucked in notebooks, a handful of chords, that camera stolen from our apartment, only its long lens left behind. Did she push her journals under the bedframe in storage boxes and case the guitar so I could write my own verses? That thought is a bitter kind of honey. In my room at seven, a jungle mural, tree trunk growing up the seam where two walls met, a panther in the tall grass, toucan on the branch. Like Matisse, I lived in a constructed jungle, while upstairs my brother inscribed his wall with urine, peeing behind his bedroom door like it was some kind of fire hydrant and he was some kind of wild. We all want to make our mark. My grandmother painted violets in a darkened corner of a forest, my aunt collaged felt into landscapes tinged with twilit tones, and my mother, the way she tended her garden, pulling each weed like redoing a stitch in a patchwork quilt, wasn't that, after all, another kind of poem?

—Rebecca

Rebecca Hart Olander and Elizabeth Paul

OF ALL POSSIBLE FORMS

Everyone had choices we'll never know. They could have gone otherwise, done otherthing, become otherhow. Unless not. Mustard seeds sprout mustard plants. But not if they're tendered in the hand instead of given to the earth. They have to drop and find the good earth to grow. But the good earth is everywhere. Of all possible forms, it took that of a sphere, an edgeless eternity endlessly spinning, dizzy and alive and as everywhere at once as motion can make a thing. On the walls of our bedroom was a pattern of rainbows, a garden of arcs and reveille of colors, marshalled, in order, and at bright attention. Red to violet, they lined up and stayed still—the things we were learning when dogs were scary and stairs a danger and the days turned like circles from school to home. How to pet the cat. How to test the water, feed the rabbit, gently touch the lady bug. An epic acquaintance and intimacy with the world. These are the things it had. It had clouds and rainbows and rain and sun and dirt and worms and lightning and thunder and shapes and numbers and streets and people and cars and parks and colors and animals. That's what they told us as if they knew for sure, as if there was one book, and everybody had it, as if it was written on the inside of everybody's eyelids. But it wasn't. So how else could we have learned the world? From the ocean or our dreams or the stars with their certain perspective that of all the forms the earth could have taken, it took the form of a sphere, a wholeness, self-containment, seamless kind of equity—one for all and all in all—or perfection? So should we be surprised to find ourselves in circles, picking up where our mothers left off, returning to our own beginnings, accepting the book, passing it on, questioning every word, and accepting it again, every black dot on the lady bug, how to pet the cat, thunder shapes and lightning worms, rooms with rainbows, tendered in the hand, lined up and stayed still, good earth, gently touch, knew for sure, mustard seeds, dropping, spinning?

—Liz

Rebecca Hart Olander and Elizabeth Paul on their process:

Rebecca Hart Olander and Elizabeth Paul attended Vermont College of Fine Arts together from 2013-2015, Rebecca concentrating in poetry and Liz in creative non-fiction. This selection is from *How the Letters Invent Us: A Correspondence*—their eighteen-month collaboration, written during their final semester at VCFA and continuing over the following year. The project components are hybrid in nature, borrowing from the epistolary tradition, the prose poem form, and the terrain of creative nonfiction.

"We had few rules," writes Rebecca in an afterword meta-correspondence reflecting on the project. "We decided whoever got around to writing first would do so, and then we'd go from there. That we'd respond within two weeks, and that the only requirement was to be sparked in some way by the other's words. That we wouldn't talk about it along the way... We said we wouldn't name each other, but at some point there became address, a modest use of 'you' and of our given names, and at another point, these became letters." Liz replies, "I think that's what I'd registered when I remarked once on 'how the letters invent us,' because the form was also our friendship... We let our responses say everything that needed to be said, trusting them to get at the heart of the matter. They did well for us, like a third friend at the table."

Justin Rovillos Monson and Leigh Sugar

from OMNIS CELLULA E CELLULA

INTRA NOS (INTER NOS)

we begin where we end: two BODIES for bruising and a shiver where they never
met but divided into separate CELLS of folding-in-on-themselves-safety in a
boundary walls teach as truth: a BODY is a BODY living or dead even just a
mass distinct from other masses.

Mia notices CELL fragments along the avenue
                of the americas   they move and shift inside her BODY
she wants to cross the street   Tino's fingertips have a smooth
CONSTITUTION
                from dragging them against walls   he tries to see
what LAW vibrates ceaseless beneath brick
                Mia failed architecture school   her walls always held
a CONSTITUTION of holes   *you must learn our* LAW *of opacity*
                a teacher's scolds penetrated her skin   Tino
tethers himself
with a beaded bracelet   blood and wood
                and fishing line remind him he's inside a BODY
Mia and Tino wonder about each other's words
                the other's BODY   CELLS   the space between

PROCRUSTEAN SYMPHONY

LAW gave them walls and the road to nowhere between their vibrating CELLS
which are questions and not rooms or anything that can ever join [together]
beyond this CONSTITUTION which was never theirs [together] only
separate governing BODIES under which they each organized independently
into lit bone-houses of   spit of   silt of   skin.

Mia worries for the bees.

Mia worries for anything that fits

       inside a human fist.

         inevitable separation and division and regeneration.

as sum.   as a monk

    in a small room.   a small room that separates the monk

       from other monks   from the hallway.

    what hides

a CELL inside a BODY hides inside.   not the room.   the verb. as in:

      please do not look.

               please, look

as in: *before I forget*   *I am here.*   what hides

   a BODY inside

a CELL hides inside.   into a gripping CONSTITUTION.

  into native tongue.

     a device translates electricity from light.   in a container

         as supplicant to wet LAW.   as

      bonehouse.

     inseparable regeneration and division and separation.

         inside a delirium plan.

       anything unable to read palms

        Tino fights.

          Tino fights for heat.

TELEOLOGY OF SMALL ROOMS

Mia meets a monk outside his small room.

why don't you leave this place? Mia asks the monk.

what am I missing? the monk asks Mia.

do you feel trapped in there? Mia asks the monk.

do you feel trapped out there? the monk asks Mia.

do you want to stay in there? Mia asks the monk.

do you want to stay out there? the monk asks Mia.

you are stuck in there, Mia says to the monk.

> > *you are stuck in here,* the attorney says to Tino.

> *you are stuck out there,* the monk says to Mia.

> > *I'm not stuck in here,* Tino says to the attorney.

> > > *do you want to stay in here?* the attorney asks Tino.
> > > *do you want to stay in here?* Tino asks the attorney.
> > > *do you feel trapped in here?* the attorney asks Tino.
> > > *do you feel trapped in here?* Tino asks the attorney.

> > > > *who do you miss?* the attorney asks Tino.

> > > *when can I leave this place?* Tino asks the attorney.

> > > > Tino meets an attorney inside a small room.

INTER NOS (INTRA MUROS)

these BODIES of CELLs, the walls between which regenerate, ad infinitum,
a meaning to a BODY governed by LAW, an echo in a constellation of
CONSTITUTIONS –

Tino bows to the electricity in his CELLs from a CELL in a BODY
        of replica CELLs   he stacks clouds on top of clouds, *this is how*
you string BODY *and tongue into a thousand nights*   his sentence a
   container
        separate from Mia's life of walls between walls
of questions to monks or any BODY inside a honeycomb of what bleeds a self
        into another or doesn't.   Tino prays to the LAW of heat
that anneals a BODY.   he learns in a police state
        a BODY is nothing if not walled, a response without call.

Mia, a bioluminescent container for crumbling walls, dances
        in a dim room.   bombs implode in distant lands then seep
        into her
turns.   Tino traces CELL walls
        his fingers drip blood   he beats a bassline
that pours – so many CELLs one body can't contain.   he drops
        to his knees, still only inside his own BODY.   from an airplane,
        Mia takes notes
on the BODY: where will it go, this BODY governed
        by LAW, traced across a trillion skies, this open CELL of skin.
Tino, the heat by which walls crumbled and will, in time, anneal
        defuses CONSTITUTION under the spinaltap of LAW in his CELL.
Mia buzzes inside the strange geometry of the BODY's curve.walls
        vibrate and bend.   a CONSTITUTION turns itself away from
        LAW
            to translate cruelty   into holes   of light.

Justin Rovillos Monson and Leigh Sugar on their process:

Writing in physical separation, "omnis cellula e cellula" is a reflection of our ongoing inquiry into how bodies—individual & collective—create, resist, and converse with institutions (economic, political, carceral, and beyond). We construct our work via letters, and the resulting poems reflect this back-and-forth: What is inevitably omitted when two people communicate only through written correspondence? What life is revealed through the cracks in these omissions? What creative universe is possible in the gulf that exists between two lives unfolding in parallel worlds (prison and the "outside" world)? In our work we seek to explore boundaries between the written & the spoken, between connection & loneliness, and subvert those boundaries created by systems that exist to separate people. Each poem is at once thesis and question: Where does language fit into our bodies, between them? What is this cluster of words and meanings? Better, what can they do?

CONTRIBUTOR BIOGRAPHIES

Kelli Russell Agodon's most recent book, *Hourglass Museum*, was a Finalist for the Washington State Book Awards and shortlisted for the Julie Suk Prize in Poetry. She's the cofounder of Seattle's Two Sylvias Press where she works as an editor and book cover designer. www.agodon.com / www.twosylviaspress.com

Anne-Marie Akin has an MFA in creative nonfiction from Northwestern University. She is a 2017–18 Jubilation Foundation Fellow, a faculty member at Chicago's Old Town School of Folk Music, and a songwriter for Carnegie Hall's National Lullaby Project. Her work has been published in *The Bitter Southerner, Mothers Always Write, Pass it On,* and *About Place Journal.*

Maureen Alsop, PhD is the author of four poetry collections: *Apparition Wren, Mantic, Mirror Inside Coffin*, and *Later, Knives & Trees.* She lives on an island in the Coral Sea. Together, Maureen Alsop and Hillary Gravendyk's collaborative poems have appeared at *VOLTA.*

Kimberly Quiogue Andrews is the author of *BETWEEN* (Finishing Line Press), winner of the 2017 New Women's Voices Series chapbook prize. Her work in various genres appears or is forthcoming in *The Shallow Ends, The Recluse, RHINO, The Normal School, West Branch, BOMB,* the *Los Angeles Review of Books, ASAP/J, Textual Practice,* and elsewhere. She is Assistant Professor of English and Creative Writing at Washington College.

Nin Andrews is the author of many books including her most recent poetry collection, *Miss August*, which was published by CavanKerry Press in May, 2017.

James Ardis published the chapbook *Your Arkansas: A Strategy Guide* (Gauss PDF) in 2016. His writing appears in *Heavy Feather Review, Rivulet, The Rumpus, Crossing Genres,* and a personal Tumblr page dedicated to hypercapitalist *Everybody Loves Raymond* posts.

Cynthia Arrieu-King is an associate professor of creative writing at Stockton University. Her books include *People are Tiny in Paintings of China* (Octopus Books, 2010) and *Manifest,* winner of the Gatewood Prize as selected by Harryette Mullen (Switchback, 2013). Her poems will appear this year in *Poetry, TriQuarterly*, and *Crazyhorse.* cynthiaarrieuking.blogspot.com.

Amy Ash is an assistant professor at Indiana State University. She is the author of the poetry collection *The Open Mouth of the Vase* (Cider Press Review, 2015), which won the 2013 Cider Press Review Book Award. Her collaborative work with Callista

Buchen appeared in various journals, including *Heron Tree, Spiral Orb, Stone Highway Review,* and *BOAAT.*

Jennifer Atkinson is the author of five poetry collections. The most recent one, *The Thinking Eye,* was published by Parlor Press/Free Verse Editions in 2016. *Canticle of the Night Path,* won Free Verse Editions' 2012 New Measure Prize. She teaches in the MFA and BFA programs at George Mason University.

Devon Balwit teaches in Portland, OR. She has six chapbooks and two collections out or forthcoming, among them: *The Bow Must Bear the Brunt* (Red Flag Poetry), *We are Procession, Seismograph* (Nixes Mate Books), and *Motes at Play in the Halls of Light* (Kelsay Books). Her individual poems can be found in *The Cincinnati Review, The Carolina Quarterly, Fifth Wednesday, The Aeolian Harp Folio, Red Earth Review, The Fourth River, The Free State Review, Rattle, The Inflectionist Review,* and more.

Amy Sayre Baptista's first chapbook is the winner of the Black River Chapbook Competition and is forthcoming from Black Lawrence Press. Her writing has appeared in *The Best Small Fiction Anthology, Ninth Letter,* and *Alaska Quarterly Review,* among other journals. She performs with Kale Soup for the Soul, a Portuguese-American artists collective, and is a co-founder of Plates&Poetry, a community table program focused on food and writing.

Tom Barlow is an Ohio Writer. Other works of his may be found in anthologies including *Best American Mystery Stories 2013, Best of Ohio Short Stories #2,* and *Best New Writing 2011,* and many periodicals including *Hobart, Temenos, Redivider, The William and Mary Review, Anomalous Press,* and *The Sonder Review.* His novel *Meet You Yesterday* and short story collection *Welcome to the Goat Rodeo* are available on Amazon. www.tjbarlow.com.

Tina Jenkins Bell writes long and short fiction as well as plays and is a fan of haikus. Currently at work completing edits on her novel-length manuscript, *Mud Pies,* some of Ms. Bell's shorter works have appeared in various anthologies, including the recently released *Revise the Psalm: Work Celebrating the Life of Gwendolyn Brooks.* A Chicagoan, her stories expose the tender spots that breach and challenge familial or cultural relationships, identities, and other factors.

Andrea Blancas Beltran is from El Paso, Texas. Her work has recently been selected for publication in *Southwestern American Literature, A Dozen Nothing, Glass: A Journal of Poetry, Fog Machine, Gramma, H_NGM_N, Pilgrimage,* & others. She's the associate editor for *MIEL.* Her chapbook *Re-* is forthcoming from Red Bird Chapbooks.

Molly Bendall is the author of five books of poetry, most recently, *Watchful* from Omnidawn in 2016. Her work has appeared in *New American Writing, Lana Turner, Denver Quarterly, Volt,* and other journals. She teaches at the University of Southern California.

Mary Biddinger is the author of five full-length poetry collections, including *Small Enterprise* and *The Czar* (both from Black Lawrence Press). She teaches at the University of Akron, where she edits the Akron Series in Poetry. *Partial Genius*, her first book of prose poems, is forthcoming from Black Lawrence Press in 2019.

Kimberly Blaeser is a Professor of Creative Writing and Native American Literature at UW—Milwaukee and MFA faculty member for the Institute of American Indian Arts in Santa Fe. Anishinaabe, enrolled at White Earth, she is author of three poetry collections, most recently *Apprenticed to Justice*. Blaeser was Wisconsin Poet Laureate for 2015–16.

Sarah Blake is the author of *Let's Not Live on Earth* and *Mr. West*, both from Wesleyan University Press. An illustrated workbook accompanies her first chapbook, *Named After Death* (Banango Editions). In 2013, she was awarded a literature fellowship from the NEA. She lives outside of Philadelphia with her husband and son.

CL Bledsoe is the assistant editor for *The Dead Mule* and author of sixteen books, most recently the flash fiction collection *Ray's Sea World* and the poetry collections *Trashcans in Love* and, in collaboration with Michael Gushue, *I Never Promised You A Sea Monkey*. He lives in northern Virginia with his daughter and blogs at NotAnotherTVDad.blogspot.com.

John Bloomberg-Rissman, a mashup ethnographer, has been working for the past 15 years or so on *Zeitgeist Spam*, which is turning into a life project. Three parts have been published so far. He is also co-editor, with Jerome Rothenberg, of *Barbaric Vast & Wild: Poems for the Millennium Volume 5*.

Andrea Blythe writes speculative poetry and fiction. Her work has appeared in *Drunk Monkeys, Literary Orphans, Diode Poetry Journal, Linden Avenue,* and other publications. She serves as an associate editor for Zoetic Press and is a member of the Science Fiction Poetry Association. Learn more at: www.andreablythe.com

Mel Bosworth is the author of the novel *Freight* and the poetry chapbook *Every Laundromat in the World*. A former series editor for the *Wigleaf Top 50* and assistant editor for *The Best Small Fictions,* Mel is the curator of the *Small Press Book Review*. He lives in Western Massachusetts.

Traci Brimhall is the author of three collections of poetry: *Our Lady of the Ruins* (W.W. Norton), *Rookery* (Southern Illinois University Press), and *Saudade* (Copper Canyon), as well as the collaborative chapbook *Bright Power, Dark Peace* (Diode Editions) with Brynn Saito.

Elizabeth K. Brown is a nonfiction student in the MFA program at Washington University in St. Louis. Her work has been published in *Brevity* magazine.

Callista Buchen is an assistant professor at Franklin College. She is the author of the collection *Look Look Look* (Black Lawrence Press, 2019) and of the chapbooks *The Bloody Planet* (Black Lawrence Press, 2015) and *Double-Mouthed* (dancing girl press, 2016). Her collaborative work with Amy Ash has appeared in various journals, including *Heron Tree, Spiral Orb, Stone Highway Review,* and *BOAAT*.

A graduate of the Helen Zell Writers' Program at the University of Michigan, **John F. Buckley** lives and works in Ann Arbor with his wife and ninja. His publications include various poems, two chapbooks, the collection *Sky Sandwiches*, and with Martin Ott, *Poets' Guide to America* and *Yankee Broadcast Network*. His website is johnfbuckley.net.

Michael Burkard's books of poetry include *My Secret Boat, Entire Dilemma,* and *Envelope of Night*. He has received fellowships from the National Endowment for the Arts, the New York State Foundation for the Arts, and the Guggenheim. He is an Associate Professor of English at Syracuse University where he teaches in the MFA Program in Creative Writing.

Elizabeth Jane Burnett is a UK poet and academic who curates ecopoetics exhibitions. A collection on wild swimming, *swims,* as well as *Dictionary of the Soil* are forthcoming.

Anders Carlson-Wee is the author of *The Low Passions* (W.W. Norton, 2019). He has received fellowships from the NEA, the McKnight Foundation, and Bread Loaf. His work has appeared in *The Kenyon Review, The Nation, Ploughshares,* and *The Best American Nonrequired Reading*. Winner of the 2017 Poetry International Prize, he lives in Minneapolis. www.anderscarlsonwee.com

Kai Carlson-Wee is the author of *RAIL* (BOA Editions, 2018). A former Wallace Stegner Fellow, he lives in San Francisco and teaches poetry at Stanford University.

Tina Carlson is a New Mexican poet whose poems have appeared in many journals and blogs. Her book *Ground, Wind, This Body* (UNM Press) was published in March 2017. She was featured in the Nov/Dec 2017 of *Poets and Writers* magazine.

Brittany Cavallaro is, with Rebecca Hazelton, the author of the collaborative chapbook *No Girls, No Telephones* (Black Lawrence Press). Her first collection of poems, *Girl-King,* was published by University of Akron Press. She is also the *New York Times* bestselling author of the Charlotte Holmes novels, a series for young adults.

Travis Cebula lives in Colorado with his wife and trusty dogs, where he writes, edits, photographs, and teaches creative writing. He is the author of six full-length collections of poetry, including *The Sublimation of Frederick Eckert.*

Christopher Citro is the author of *The Maintenance of the Shimmy-Shammy* (Steel Toe Books) and a recipient of a 2018 Pushcart Prize. His poems appear in *Ploughshares, Best New Poets, The Missouri Review, The Iowa Review Blog, Gulf Coast,* and *Crazyhorse.* He lives in Syracuse, New York.

Ben Clark grew up in Nebraska and now lives in Chicago, where he works as an editor for *Muzzle Magazine* and Thoughtcrime Press. He has two collections of poetry: *Reasons to Leave the Slaughter* (2011) and *if you turn around I will turn around* (2015).

Brian Clements is the author of several volumes of poems, most recently *A Book of Common Rituals* (Quale Press). He is co-editor of the anthologies *An Introduction to the Prose Poem* (Firewheel Editions) and *Bullets into Bells: Poets and Citizens Respond to Gun Violence* (Beacon Press). He lives in Newtown, CT and devotes much of his time to gun violence prevention awareness and activism.

Cathryn Cofell is a fierce arts advocate, helping to launch the Wisconsin Poet Laureate Commission and its endowment, *Verse Wisconsin,* the Wisconsin Fellowship of Poetry Chapbook Prize and a long-standing reading series in Appleton, WI. She has a collection called *Sister Satellite,* six chapbooks, and a poetry/music CD to her name. www.cathryncofell.com

Mackenzie Cole work has recently appeared in *Pacifica Literary Review, Ghost Town, Sonora Review, Atlas and Alice,* and elsewhere. They have poems forthcoming from *Passages North* and Black Lawrence Press. They live in Missoula, Montana, where they received their MFA from the University of Montana. Keep up with them at deadfallsandsnares.com.

Elizabeth J. Colen is most recently the author of *What Weaponry,* a novel in prose poems. Other books include poetry collections *Money for Sunsets* (Lambda Literary Award finalist in 2011) and *Waiting Up for the End of the World: Conspiracies,* flash fiction collection *Dear Mother Monster, Dear Daughter Mistake,* long poem / lyric essay hybrid *The Green Condition,* and fiction collaboration *Your Sick.*

Michael Collins is the author of two chapbooks and the full-length collections *Psalmandala* and *Appearances*, which was named one of the best indie poetry collections of 2017 by Kirkus Reviews. He teaches at NYU and The Hudson Valley Writers' Center and is the Director of Studies at Why There Are Words Press and curator of the New York City branch of the national Why There Are Words Reading Series. Visit notthatmichaelcollins.com.

Juliet Cook is a grotesque glitter witch medusa hybrid brimming with black, grey, silver, purple, and dark red explosions. She is drawn to poetry, abstract visual art, and other forms of expression. Her poetry has appeared in a peculiar multitude of literary publications. You can find out more at www.JulietCook.weebly.com.

James Cummins is curator of the Elliston Poetry Collection at the University of Cincinnati. He lives in that undiscovered gem of a city with his wife, the poet Maureen Bloomfield.

Kristina Marie Darling is the author of twenty-seven books, which include *Je Suis L'Autre: Essays and Interrogations* (C&R Press, 2017) and *Dark Horse* (C&R Press, 2018).

Justin Lawrence Daugherty lives in Atlanta and holds a Ph.D. in creative writing from Georgia State University. He is the author of the novel *You Are Alive* (Civil Coping Mechanisms).

Jon Davis' most recent books are *Improbable Creatures* (Grid Books, 2017) and *Preliminary Report* (Copper Canyon Press, 2010). A recipient of honors from the Lannan Foundation, the NEA, and the Academy of American Poets, he directs the Low Residency MFA at the Institute of American Indian Arts in Santa Fe.

Kendra DeColo is the author of *My Dinner with Ron Jeremy* (Third Man Books, 2016) and *Thieves in the Afterlife* (Saturnalia Books, 2014), selected by Yusef Komunyakaa for the 2013 Saturnalia Books Poetry. Her poems and essays appear in *Waxwing, Los Angeles Review, Gulf Coast, Bitch Magazine, VIDA*, and elsewhere. She is co-host of the podcast RE/VERB: A Third Man Books Production and she lives in Nashville, Tennessee.

Page Delano is Associate Professor at Borough of Manhattan Community College/CUNY. Her 1960s activism turned into seven years among coalminers in West Virginia, and later, poems, including *No One with a Past is Safe* (Word Press). Her current project is a study of American women in France during WWII.

Matthew DeMarco lives in Chicago. He is a recipient of the Eileen Lannan Poetry Prize, for which his work has appeared on Poets.org. His poems can also be found in

Opossum, Columbia Poetry Review, Ghost City Review, Landfill, and elsewhere. Poems that he wrote with Faizan Syed have appeared in *Dogbird*.

Natalie Diaz was born and raised in the Fort Mojave Indian Village in Needles, California, on the banks of the Colorado River. She is Mojave and an enrolled member of the Gila River Indian Tribe. Diaz teaches at Arizona State University and the Institute of American Indian Arts Low Rez MFA program. Her first poetry collection is *When My Brother Was an Aztec*.

Dana Diehl is the author of *Our Dreams Might Align* (Jellyfish Highway Press, 2016). She earned her MFA in Fiction at Arizona State University where she served as editor of *Hayden's Ferry Review*. She has taught fiction at Arizona State University, the National University of Singapore, the Arizona State Prison Complex in Florence, and BASIS Primary.

Cat Dixon is the author of *Eva* and *Too Heavy to Carry* (Stephen F. Austin University Press, 2016, 2014) and *Our End Has Brought the Spring* (Finishing Line Press, 2015). *The Book of Levinson* (Finishing Line Press) was published in July 2017. She is the Managing Editor of The Backwaters Press. Her website is www.catdix.com.

Tyler Flynn Dorholt is the author of *American Flowers*, a book of poems and photographs (Dock Street Press), and numerous chapbooks, including *Modern Camping* (Poetry Society of America), and two from Greying Ghost. He co-publishes and edits the journal and press *Tammy*, and lives in Syracuse, NY with his wife and son.

Jacqueline Doyle's recent publications include a flash chapbook, *The Missing Girl* (Black Lawrence Press), and stories and essays in the *Gettysburg Review, Hotel Amerika, Superstition Review,* and *Post Road*. Her creative nonfiction has earned three Notable Essay citations in *Best American Essays*. She teaches at California State University East Bay.

Denise Duhamel's most recent book of poetry is *Scald* (Pittsburgh, 2017). *Blowout* was a finalist for the National Book Critics Circle Award. Other titles include *Ka-Ching!; Two and Two; Queen for a Day: Selected and New Poems; The Star-Spangled Banner;* and *Kinky*. She teaches at Florida International University in Miami.

Alicia Elkort's poetry has appeared in *AGNI, Arsenic Lobster, Heron Tree, Menacing Hedge, Rogue Agent, Stirring: A Literary Collection,* and *Tinderbox Poetry Journal,* among others. She lives in California and will go to great lengths for an honest cup of black tea and a cool breeze.

Chiyuma Elliott is an Assistant Professor of African American Studies at the University of California, Berkeley. A former Stegner Fellow, Chiyuma's poems have appeared in *Callaloo, The Collagist,* the *PN Review,* and other journals. She is the author of *California Winter League* (2015) and *Vigil* (2017).

Craig Foltz is a writer and photographer whose work has appeared in numerous journals and galleries in both the northern and southern hemispheres. He has released two books with Ugly Duckling Presse. He currently lives and works on the slopes of a dormant volcano in Auckland, New Zealand. Visitors are encouraged. These days he has marshaled all of his creative efforts on collaborative endeavors. Send proposals to craig.foltz@gmail.com.

Kate Hanson Foster's first book of poems, *Mid Drift,* was published by Loom Press and was a finalist for the Massachusetts Center for the Book Award in 2011. Her poetry has appeared in *Comstock Review, Harpur Palate, Poet Lore, Tupelo Quarterly* and elsewhere. She was recently awarded the NEA Parent Fellowship through the Vermont Studio Center.

Bryan Furuness is the author of a couple of novels, *The Lost Episodes of Revie Bryson* and the forthcoming *Do Not Go On.* He is the editor of the forthcoming anthology, *My Name was Never Frankenstein: And Other Classic Adventure Tales Reanimated.* He lives in Indianapolis, where he teaches at Butler University.

Elisa Gabbert is a poet and essayist and the author of three collections: *L'Heure Bleue, or the Judy Poems* (Black Ocean, 2016), *The Self Unstable* (Black Ocean, 2013), and *The French Exit* (Birds LLC, 2010). Her work has appeared in the *New Yorker, Boston Review, Pacific Standard, Guernica,* and many other venues. She lives in Denver. Learn more at www.elisagabbert.com.

John Gallaher spends a lot of time one the other side of the road from a cornfield, though some years it's soy, and now and then, fallow, but no matter how far out he lives, he continues to get all the same TV stations everyone else gets. Radio too.

Ross Gay is the author, most recently, of *Catalog of Unabashed Gratitude.* He teaches at Indiana University in Bloomington.

Ellen Geist is an author of fiction and mini-memoirs. An expert in early childhood through adolescence learning and educational technology, she's developed products and white papers for educational publishing companies. Her fiction has appeared in magazines and journals, including: *Painted Bride, Women in Judaism, River Styx,* and *The American Voice.* Sadly, Ellen died in March 2018—her collaborators aim to continue sharing her work in *Red Heads/Red Tales.*

Jennifer Givhan is a Mexican-American writer from the Southwestern desert and the author of three full-length poetry collections: *Landscape with Headless Mama* (Pleiades Editors' Prize, LSU Press, 2016), *Protection Spell* (Miller Williams Poetry Prize Series, U of Arkansas Press, 2017), and *Girl with Death Mask* (Blue Light Books Prize, Indiana University Press, 2018). Her honors include NEA and PEN/Rosenthal Emerging Voices fellowships.

Benjamin Goluboff teaches English at Lake Forest College. In addition to some scholarly publications, he has placed imaginative work—poetry, fiction, and essays—in many small-press journals, recently *Unbroken, Bird's Thumb,* and *War Literature and the Arts.* He is the author of *Ho Chi Minh: A Speculative Life in Verse, and Other Poems* (Urban Farmhouse Press, 2017). Some of his work can be read at www.lakeforest.edu/academics/faculty/goluboff/

Melissa Goodrich is the author of *Daughters of Monsters* (Jellyfish Highway Press). She received her MFA in Fiction from the University of Arizona, and her fiction has appeared in *The Kenyon Review, American Short Fiction, Gigantic Sequins, PANK,* and others. Find more at melissa-goodrich.com.

Anne Gorrick is a poet and visual artist. Her latest books are *An Absence So Great and Spontaneous is it Evidence of Light* (forthcoming in 2018 from the Operating System) and *The Olfactions: Poems on Perfume* (BlazeVOX, 2017).

Joshua Gottlieb-Miller, a PhD student at the University of Houston, serves as Digital Non-Fiction Editor for *Gulf Coast.* His poetry has appeared in *Four Way Review, Grist, Pacifica Lit Review,* and elsewhere. Together, Maureen Alsop and Joshua Gottlieb-Miller's collaborative poems have appeared in *Verse Daily, Contrary, Inertia, Switchback, A-Minor, Baltimore Review,* and elsewhere.

Daniel Grandbois is the author of several books of fiction and poetry, including *A Revised Poetry of Western Philosophy* (Pitt Poetry Series, 2016). He lives on a mountaintop in Colorado and wishes his brother would join him.

Peter Grandbois is the author of eight previous books, the most recent of which is *This House That* (Brighthorse Books, 2017). His poems, stories, and essays have appeared in over one hundred journals. His plays have been performed in St. Louis, Columbus, Los Angeles, and New York. He is a senior editor at *Boulevard* magazine and teaches at Denison University in Ohio.

Hillary Gravendyk (1979-2014) was an Assistant Professor of English at Pomona College in Claremont, CA and a native of Washington State. Her poetry appeared in journals such as *American Letters & Commentary, Bellingham Review, Colorado Review,* and *Sugar House Review*. Her chapbook, *The Naturalist*, was published by Achiote Press in 2008 and her full-length collection *Harm*, came out from Omnidawn in 2012. She leaves behind many devoted colleagues, friends, family, and beautiful poems.

Susan Gregory is a former accountant who graduated from California State University Fullerton with a BA in Business Administration. She writes poetry for personal enjoyment and has not previously been published. She is the mother of two grown children and lives with her husband and their dog in Orange County.

Tracy Jane Gregory is a cross-genre writer, collage artist, and musician. She is a graduate of University of Washington Bothell's MFA program, an editor at Letter [r] Press, and an English Tutor at City College of San Francisco. She currently lives in San Leandro, CA. Find her publications at tracyjanegregory.com.

Carol Guess is the author of numerous books of poetry and prose, including *Darling Endangered, Doll Studies: Forensics,* and *Tinderbox Lawn.* In 2014 she was awarded the Philolexian Award for Distinguished Literary Achievement by Columbia University. She teaches in the MFA program at Western Washington University.

Michael Gushue is co-publisher of the nanopress Poetry Mutual, and co-curates *Poetry at the Watergate.* His books are *Gathering Down Women, Conrad, Pachinko Mouth,* and—in collaboration with CL Bledsoe—*I Never Promised You A Sea Monkey.*

Stephen D. Gutierrez is the author of *Elements; Live from Fresno y Los* (American Book Award), and *The Mexican Man in His Backyard.* A recent essay in *Fourth Genre* was nominated for a Pushcart; an essay in *Waccamaw* was a Notable in this year's BAE. He teaches at Cal State East Bay.

Brenda Mann Hammack teaches creative writing, children's literature, folktale, and women's literature at Fayetteville State University. She is also a teaching artist at Poetry Barn. Hammack's first book, *Humbug: A Neo-Victorian Fantasy in Verse*, appeared in 2013. Other work (poetry, fiction, and photography) has appeared in *Menacing Hedge, NILVX, Hermeneutic Chaos, Rhino, Anthropoid,* and *Papercuts.* Hammack serves as managing editor and web designer for *Glint Literary Journal.*

Shrode Hargis' work has appeared in *Bat City Review, Cream City Review, Harvard Review, Fugue,* and elsewhere. He currently teaches at Delgado Community College in New Orleans.

Carla Harryman is the author of twenty books of experimental poetry, prose, and performance writing. Recent works include the epistolary essay *Artifact of Hope* (2017) and a volume of performance works, *Sue in Berlin* (2018), published by PURH in French and English editions. She lives in and around Detroit.

j/j hastain is a collaborator, writer and maker of things. j/j performs ceremonial gore. Chasing and courting the animate and potentially enlivening decay that exists between seer and singer, j/j hopes to make the god/dess of stone moan and nod deeply through the waxing and waning seasons of the moon.

Rebecca Hazelton is, with Brittany Cavallaro, the author of the collaborative chapbook *No Girls, No Telephones* (Black Lawrence Press). She is the author of two books of poetry, *Fair Copy,* from Ohio State University, and *Vow,* from Cleveland State University. Her poems have been published in *Poetry, The New Yorker, Best American Poetry*, and the Pushcart anthology.

Kathleen Heil is a dancer, writer and translator of poetry and prose, whose work appears in *The New Yorker, Threepenny Review, The Guardian, Beloit Poetry Journal*, and many other journals. More at kathleenheil.net.

Lyn Hejinian's most recent book is *The Unfollowing* (Omnidawn Books, 2016). Belladonna will bring out her prose work, *Positions of the Sun*, in 2018. She teaches at the University of California, Berkeley, and is part of the UC Berkeley Humanities Activism coalition, formed immediately after November 8, 2016.

Derek Henderson is alive and well in Salt Lake City, Utah, where he lives with his wife, his kids, several cats, and a pug. He is the author of *Thus &* (if p then q) and co-author with Derek Pollard of *Inconsequentia* (BlazeVOX). He teaches English at the Walden School for the Liberal Arts in Provo, Utah.

Tom Henthrone was professor English at Pace University in New York City. He was the author of *Conrad's Trojan Horses: Imperialism, Hybridity, and the Postcolonial Aesthetic, William Gibson: A Literary Companion, Approaching the Hunger Games Trilogy*. He died in 2014.

Jeannie Hoag's work has appeared in *notnostrums, GlitterPony, Invisible Ear, Divine Magnet*, and elsewhere. Her chapbook *New Age of Ferociousness* was published by Agnes Fox Press in 2010. She is a librarian in New York, NY.

Leslie E. Hoffman is an independent copy editor who moonlights as a poet. Results of her midnight sojourns have appeared in *The California Writers Club Literary Review*; *Caesura, The Journal of Poetry Center San Jose*; *Helen: FNS*; and Nevada State College's *300 Days of Sun*.

Grant Holly is a writer, coder, bad-ass welder and machinist who has developed a mild allergy to Java and .NET; a love for Python, Javascript, and Go; and an admiration for SQL. He finds the beauty in language, mathematics, and poetry. He's been known to reply "No" to required meetings and plays in a rockabilly band.

Ron Horning's poems and prose have appeared in magazines and newspapers as well as three recent collections: *From Philip Drunk to Philip Sober* (Color Treasury, 2014), *Blind Date* (Untitled, 2016), and *Two Poems and a Letter* (Untitled, 2017).

Amorak Huey, a 2017 NEA Fellow, is author of the poetry collection *Ha Ha Ha Thump* (Sundress, 2015) and two chapbooks. He is co-author of the textbook *Poetry: A Writer's Guide and Anthology* (Bloomsbury Academic, 2018) and teaches writing at Grand Valley State University in Michigan.

Luther Hughes (@lutherxhughes) is a Seattle native and author of *Touched* (Sibling Rivalry Press, 2018). He is the Founder & Editor-in-Chief of the *Shade Journal* and Associate Poetry Editor for the *Offing*. A Cave Canem Fellow and Windy City Times 30 Under 30 Honoree, he has work published in or forthcoming from *Columbia Poetry Review, Vinyl, BOAAT, Tinderbox Poetry Journal*, and others. Luther is currently an MFA candidate in the writing program at Washington University in St. Louis.

Karla Huston, Wisconsin Poet Laureate (2017–2018), is the author of *A Theory of Lipstick* (Main Street Rag, 2013), as well as eight chapbooks including *Grief Bone* (Five-Oaks Press, 2017). Her poems, reviews and interviews have been published widely, including in the 2012 *Pushcart Best of the Small Presses* anthology.

Laura Jones is a journalist, nonfiction and screenplay writer, with a background in film and television production. She has an MFA from Northwestern University, where she won the 2015 AWP Journals Prize in nonfiction. She currently teaches at Central State University, and her work has been featured in *Creative Nonfiction, Fourth Genre, About Place Journal, The Gay and Lesbian Review,* and *The Oklahoma Review*.

Megan Kaminski is the author of two books of poetry, *Deep City* (Noemi Press, 2015) and *Desiring Map* (Coconut Books, 2012), and many chapbooks, including most recently *Providence* (Belladonna*, 2016). She is an assistant professor in the University of Kansas' Graduate Creative Writing Program and an Integrated Arts Initiative

Faculty Fellow at the Spencer Museum of Art. She also curates the Taproom Poetry Series in downtown Lawrence.

W. Todd Kaneko is the author of *The Dead Wrestler Elegies* (Curbside Splendor, 2014) and co-author of *Poetry: A Writer's Guide and Anthology* (Bloomsbury Academic, 2018). A Kundiman fellow, he is co-editor of *Waxwing* magazine and lives in Grand Rapids, Michigan, where he teaches at Grand Valley State University.

Persis Karim is a poet, editor, and professor of Comparative Literature at San Francisco State University and the inaugural chair of the Center for Iranian Diaspora Studies. She is the editor of three anthologies of Iranian diaspora literature, most recently, *Tremors: New Fiction by Iranian-American Writers*. Her poetry has been published in numerous publications including *Callaloo, Reed Magazine, HeartLodge, The New York Times*, and others. www.persiskarim.com.

Ariana-Sophia Kartsonis lives in Powell and Tipp City, Ohio. Of late, she's writing short stories, essays, and hanging out with her lovely husband on Aggy Road Farm for the important chores of growing garlic, herding barn cats, and petting goats.

Mary Kasimor has been writing poetry for many years. Her work has appeared in *Big Bridge, 2River, Glasgow Review of Books, Nerve Lantern, 3 AM, Touch the Donkey, Posit, Yew Journal,* and *Otoliths*. Her recent poetry collections are *The Landfill Dancers* (BlazeVox Books, 2014) and *Saint Pink* (Moria Books, 2015). She was also involved with a political chapbook project (Locofo Chaps). She has also been a reviewer of many small press poetry collections.

Diane Kendig's five poetry chapbooks include the most recent *Prison Terms*, and she recently co-edited the anthology *In the Company of Russell Atkins*. A recipient of two Ohio Arts Council Fellowships in Poetry as well as other awards, she has published poetry and prose in journals such as *J Journal, Under the Sun*, and *Ekphrasis*. She blogs at "Home Again": dianekendig.blogspot.com.

Caroline Kessler is a poet and community builder. Her work has been published in *The Susquehanna Review, Sundog Lit, Profane, Superstition Review*, and elsewhere. A graduate of the MFA in Creative Writing from Washington University in St. Louis, she is also the co-creator of The 18 Somethings Project, a writing adventure. carokess.com.

Lissa Kiernan is the author of *Two Faint Lines in the Violet* (Negative Capability Press, 2014) and *Glass Needles & Goose Quills: Elementary Lessons in Atomic Properties, Nuclear Families, and Radical Poetics* (Haley's, 2017). She is the founding director of the Poetry Barn, a literary center based in New York's Hudson Valley.

Annie Kim is the author of *Into the Cyclorama*, winner of the Michael Waters Poetry Prize and a finalist for the 2016 Foreword INDIE Poetry Book of the Year. Her poems have appeared, or are forthcoming, in *The Kenyon Review, Ninth Letter, Pleiades, Mudlark, Crab Orchard Review*, and elsewhere. A graduate of Warren Wilson's MFA Program, she serves as an editor for *DMQ Review* and works at the University of Virginia School of Law as the Assistant Dean for Public Service.

Dean LaTray was born on an April morning on the headwaters of the Missouri River in Montana. He grew up in the foothills of the North Moccasin Mountains under endless blue skies, and has been exploring the world ever since. He now lives in the San Francisco Bay Area, near the blue Pacific, and often reads poetry.

Sarah Layden is the author of *Trip Through Your Wires*, a novel. Her work appears in *Boston Review, McSweeney's, Salon, The Humanist*, and elsewhere, and she is a Lecturer of English at Indiana University-Purdue University Indianapolis.

David Lehman is the author of *Poems in the Manner of…* and *Sinatra's Century: One Hundred Notes on the Man and His World*. He edited *The Oxford Book of American Poetry*. He lives in New York City and in Ithaca, New York.

Dana Levin's most recent book is *Banana Palace* (Copper Canyon Press, 2016). Her work has received many honors, including fellowships and awards from the NEA, the Whiting, Rona Jaffe, and Guggenheim Foundations. She serves as Distinguished Writer in Residence at Maryville University in Saint Louis.

Susan Lewis (susanlewis.net) is the author of ten books and chapbooks, including *Zoom*, winner of the Washington Prize (The Word Works, 2018). Her work has appeared in *Boston Review, The Brooklyn Rail, Diode, The New Orleans Review, Seneca Review, TAMMY, Verse*, and *VOLT*. She's the founding editor of *Posit* (positjournal.com).

Rae Liberto is a queer poet and nurse living in Oakland. She is obsessed with dreams, bodies and dark spaces of the mind. Her work has been featured in *Sinister Wisdom, Foglifter Journal, Dryland,* and *Lavender Review*.

Sarah Lilius is the author of four chapbooks including *GIRL* (dancing girl press, 2017), and *Thirsty Bones* (Blood Pudding Press, 2017). Some of her publication credits include the *Denver Quarterly, Court Green, BlazeVOX, Bluestem, Tinderbox, Hermeneutic Chaos, Stirring, Luna Luna Magazine, Entropy,* and *Flapperhouse*. Her work has been nominated for a Pushcart Prize. She lives in Virginia with her husband and two sons. sarahlilius.com.

Ada Limón is the author of four books of poetry, including *Bright Dead Things*, which was named a finalist for the National Book Award in Poetry, the National Book Critics Circle Award, and The Kingsley Tufts Award. Her fifth book *The Carrying* is forthcoming from Milkweed Editions in 2018.

Katt Lissard teaches in Goddard College's Graduate Institute and is artistic director of WSI, an international theatre project in NYC and Lesotho (wsimaketheatre.org). Recent publications: *Venus in Lesotho: Women, Theatre and the Collapsible Boundaries of Silence*, (Palgrave-Macmillan); and *Imaginary Intersection: Thomas Mofolo, Gertrude Stein and W.E.B. DuBois* (Tydskrif vir Letterkunde/South Africa).

Janice Tuck Lively writes fiction and nonfiction that celebrates and examines the joys and struggles of women's lives and their ability to overcome obstacles. Her work has appeared in several literary journals and anthologies. She is an Associate Professor of creative writing and literature at Elmhurst College and was a 2016 Pushcart Award nominee.

Tony Lopez is an English poet best known for his book *False Memory*, first published in USA by The Figures, 1996. He grew up in Brixton, South London, and was educated at Essex University and Gonville and Caius College, Cambridge. He worked as a pulp fiction writer in the 1970s and later taught for many years at Plymouth University where he was appointed the first Professor of Poetry.

Mark Luebbers teaches English at Cincinnati Country Day School in Cincinnati Ohio, and wishes he had stuck with the piano lessons when he was a kid. His poems have recently appeared in a number of journals, including *The Apple Valley Review, Blue Line, Kudzu House Quarterly, Indiana Voice,* and *Bird's Thumb.*

Jennifer MacBain-Stephens lives in the Midwest and is the author of three full-length poetry collections: *Your Best Asset is a White Lace Dress* (Yellow Chair Press, 2016) *The Messenger is Already Dead,* (Stalking Horse Press, March 2017,) and *We're Going to Need a Higher Fence,* tied for first place in the 2017 Lit Fest Book Competition. Recent work can be seen at or is forthcoming from *The Pinch, Prelude, Cleaver, Kestrel, decomp,* and *Inter/rupture.* jennifermacbainstephens.wordpress.com

Pushpa MacFarlane "breathes" poetry. She reads poetry on radio and community television, records videos, designs poetry blogs, and is published locally. She has designed two poetry anthologies: *Remembering* and *Third Thursdays*, from Willow Glen readings in San Jose. She has presented World Poetry segments at two San Jose poetry festivals.

Sarah Maclay's most recent collection is *The "She" Series: A Venice Correspondence*, a braided collaboration with Holaday Mason. A 2016 City of LA Literary Fellow and 2015 Yaddo resident, her poems and criticism appear in *APR, The Writer's Chronicle, FIELD, Ploughshares, Poetry International,* and have been awarded the Tampa Review Prize for Poetry. She teaches creative writing and literature at LMU.

Felicia Madlock writes across genres: novels, poetry, and children's tales. Ms. Madlock is author of six dynamic books: *Back on the Block* & *Sins of the Father* (novels); *When Love Cries, Forever,* & *Black's Blues and Red's Tears* (a collection of poetry) and *Selfish Raine* (a children's tale). Her work reflects the emotional turmoil of the human heart and the resiliency of the human spirit.

Kelly Magee is the author of *Body Language,* winner of the Katherine Anne Porter Prize for Short Fiction, and *The Neighborhood,* as well as several collaborative works including *With Animal,* co-written with Carol Guess. She teaches at Western Washington University and can be found at kellyelizabethmagee.com.

Holaday Mason is the author of two chapbook and four full length collections—*Towards the Forest, Dissolve, The Red Bowl: A Fable in Poems,* and *The "She" Series: A Venice Correspondence,* a collaboration with Sarah Maclay. Nominated for three Pushcarts, widely published, she is also a fine art photographer focusing on the beauty of aging & the human in nature & a psychotherapist in private practice since 1993. www.holadaymason.com

Ryan Masters currently working on a memoir about the death of his first child. His work has been mentioned in the *Best American Essays* series.

Carlo Matos has published ten books, including *The Quitters* (Tortoise Books) and *It's Best Not to Interrupt Her Experiments* (Negative Capability Press). His poems, stories, and essays have appeared in such journals as *Another Chicago Magazine, Rhino, One,* and *Handsome,* among many others. He currently lives in Chicago, IL, is a professor at the City Colleges of Chicago, and is a former MMA fighter and kickboxer.

Melissa Matthewson's essays have appeared in *Guernica, Mid-American Review, Bellingham Review, River Teeth, VIDA Review, Essay Daily,* and *Sweet* among others. Her work has earned an AWP Intro Journals award and has been listed as notable in Best American Essays. She holds degrees from UC Santa Cruz, University of Montana, and Vermont College of Fine Arts.

Meghan McClure lives in California. Her work can be found in *American Literary Review, Mid-American Review, LA Review, Water~Stone Review, Superstition*

Review, Bluestem, Pithead Chapel, Proximity Magazine, Boaat Press, and *Black Warrior Review*, among others. Her collaborative book with Michael Schmeltzer, *A Single Throat Opens*, was published by Black Lawrence Press and her chapbook *Portrait of a Body in Wreckages* won the Newfound Prose Prize.

Kyle McCord is the author of five books of poetry including National Poetry Series Finalist, *Magpies in the Valley of Oleanders* (Trio House Press, 2016). He has work featured in *AGNI, Blackbird, Boston Review, The Gettysburg Review, The Harvard Review, The Kenyon Review, Ploughshares, TriQuarterly,* and elsewhere. He is married to the visual artist Lydia McCord. He teaches in Des Moines, Iowa.

Kevin McLellan is the author of *Ornitheology* (The Word Works, 2018), *Hemispheres* (Fact-Simile Editions, 2018), [*box*] (Letter [r] Press, 2016), *Tributary* (Barrow Street, 2015), and *Round Trip* (Seven Kitchens, 2010). He won the 2015 *Third Coast* Poetry Prize and Gival Press' 2016 Oscar Wilde Award, and his poems have appeared in numerous journals. Kevin lives in Cambridge, Massachusetts.

Joe Milazzo is the author of the novel *Crepuscule W/ Nellie* and *The Habiliments*, a volume of poetry. He co-edits the online interdisciplinary arts journal [out of nothing], is a Contributing Editor at *Entropy*, curates the Other Peoples Poetry reading series, and is also the proprietor of Imipolex Press. Joe lives and works in Dallas, TX.

Brenda Miller is the author of six collections of personal essays, most recently *An Earlier Life* (Ovenbird Books, 2016). She co-authored *Tell it Slant: Creating, Refining, and Publishing Creative Nonfiction*, and *The Pen and the Bell: Mindful Writing in a Busy World*. She is a Professor of Creative Writing at Western Washington University.

Tyler Mills is the author of *Hawk Parable*, winner of the 2017 Akron Poetry Prize (forthcoming in 2019) and *Tongue Lyre* (SIU Press, 2013). Her poems have appeared in *The New Yorker, The Guardian,* and *Poetry.* She is editor-in-chief of *The Account* and teaches at New Mexico Highlands University.

Justin Rovillos Monson is a Filipino-American poet currently serving a prison sentence in Michigan. He was the recipient of a 2017 Kundiman mentorship with Paisly Rekdal. He is not a fan of prison.

Gabrielle Montesanti is an MFA nonfiction student at Washington University in St. Louis. She is a Pushcart Prize nominee and currently serves as the Nonfiction Editor at *Stirring: A Literary Collection.* Her work can be found in *Sinister Wisdom, The Offing, Crab Creek Review,* and *Devil's Lake.* She is currently at work on a full-length manuscript about roller derby.

Alicia Mountain is the author the collection *High Ground Coward* (University of Iowa Press), which won the 2017 Iowa Poetry Prize, and the chapbook *Thin Fire* (BOAAT Press). She is a queer poet, a PhD candidate at the University of Denver, and an assistant editor of the *Denver Quarterly*. Mountain earned her MFA in poetry at the University of Montana. For more, check out aliciamountain.com.

Erin Mullikin's poems and short fiction have been published in *elsewhere, Ghost Ocean, Arts & Letters, Phantom*, and *Best New Poets 2014*, among others. She is the founding editor of the online literary journal *NightBlock* and the small literary press Midnight City Books.

Rachel Neff has written poetry since elementary school and has notebooks full of half-written novels. She earned her doctorate in Spanish literature and recently completed her MFA. Her work has been published in *JuxtaProse Magazine* and *Crab Fat Magazine*. Her poetry chapbook *The Haywire Heart and Other Musings on Love* is forthcoming from Finishing Line Press.

GennaRose Nethercott is the author of *The Lumberjack's Dove* (Ecco/HarperCollins, 2018), selected by Louise Glück as a winner of the National Poetry Series. Her other recent projects include *A Ghost of Water* (an ekphrastic collaboration with printmaker Susan Osgood) and the narrative song collection *Modern Ballads*. She tours nationally and internationally composing poems-to-order for strangers on a 1952 Hermes Rocket typewriter. www.gennarosenethercott.com

Aimee Nezhukumatahil is the author of four books of poems, most recently, *Oceanic* (Copper Canyon, 2018). A collection of nature essays is forthcoming from Milkweed. She is Professor of English in The University of Mississippi's MFA program.

Dustin Nightingale is the author of *Ghost Woodpecker*, a chapbook from BatCat Press. His poetry has been or will be published in journals such as *The American Journal of Poetry, new ohio review, Cimarron Review, Portland Review,* and *decomP*. He lives in Hartford, Connecticut.

Margaret Noodin is an Associate Professor at the University of Wisconsin-Milwaukee. She is the author of *Bawaajimo: A Dialect of Dreams in Anishinaabe Language and Literature* and *Weweni,* a collection of bilingual poems in Ojibwe and English. To see and hear current projects visit www.ojibwe.net.

Isobel O'Hare is the author of three chapbooks as well as *all this can be yours* (University of Hell Press, 2018). Two of their poems appeared in *A Shadow Map* (Civil Coping Mechanisms Press, 2017). They received an MFA in Poetry from Vermont College of Fine Arts.

Rebecca Hart Olander's poetry appeared recently in *Yemassee Journal, Radar Poetry,* and *Mom Egg Review,* and her reviews have appeared in *Rain Taxi Review of Books, Solstice Literary Magazine,* and *Valparaiso Poetry Review.* Rebecca lives in Western Massachusetts where she teaches writing at Westfield State University and is editor/director of Perugia Press. Find her at rebeccahartolander.com.

Daniela Olszewska is the author of five collections of poetry. She lives in Chicago.

Martin Ott is the author of seven books of poetry and fiction, including *Underlays,* Sandeen Prize Winner, University of Notre Dame Press and Forward Indies Finalist. His newest poetry book *Lessons in Camouflage* will be published in 2018 by C&R Press. His work has appeared in fifteen anthologies and more than two hundred magazines, including *Harvard Review, North American Review,* and *Prairie Schooner.*

Christine Pacyk is a poet and educator living in the Chicago Suburbs and who holds an MFA in poetry from Northwestern University. She was recently named a finalist for the 2017 Claire Rosen and Samuel Edes Foundation Prize for Emerging Artists. Her work has appeared in *Jet Fuel Review, Beloit Poetry Journal, Kettle Blue Review,* and *Crannóg Magazine,* to name a few.

Gillian Parrish's recent work has appeared in *Faculty Focus* and *Volt*; a book of poems, *of rain and nettles wove,* is available from Singing Horse Press. She is the mothership of *spacecraftproject,* an arts and literary journal that comes together through conversation and coincidence.

Elizabeth Paul's chapbook of ekphrastic prose poems, *Reading Girl,* was published in 2016. Other work has appeared in *Cold Mountain Review, The Carolina Quarterly,* and elsewhere. Liz served as a Peace Corps volunteer in Kyrgyzstan and currently teaches ESOL and writing in the Washington, D.C. area. Find her at elizabethsgpaul.com.

Michael Peterson's poems have appeared in *The Kenyon Review Online, Boston Review Online, Fence, Western Humanities Review,* and elsewhere. He is the recipient of fellowships from Yaddo and The MacDowell Colony. He is completing his PhD as an Elliston Fellow in Poetry at the University of Cincinnati.

Derek Pollard is co-author with Derek Henderson of the book *Inconsequentia* (BlazeVOX Books). His poetry, criticism, and translations have appeared in *Best of the Net, Colorado Review, Drunken Boat, Edgar Allan Poe Review, Pleiades,* and *Six Word Memoirs on Love & Heartbreak,* among numerous other anthologies and journals. He is Assistant Editor at *Interim.* More information can be found at: dpollard.squarespace.com.

Ethel Rackin is the author of three collections of poems: *The Forever Notes* (Parlor Press, 2013); *Go On* (Parlor Press, 2016), a finalist for the National Jewish Book Award; and *Evening* (Furniture Press, 2017). Her poems, book reviews, and collaborations have appeared widely in journals such as *The American Poetry Review, Colorado Review, Hotel Amerika, Jacket2, The Kenyon Review, Verse Daily,* and *Volt.* She is a professor at Bucks County Community College in Pennsylvania.

Stella Reed is from Santa Fe, NM. She teaches with the WingSpan Poetry Project bringing poetry classes to residents in shelters in Santa Fe. You can find her poems in the *Taos International Journal of Poetry and Art, Bellingham Review,* and *The American Journal of Poetry.*

Virginia Smith Rice is the author of the poetry collection, *When I Wake It Will Be Forever* (Sundress Publications, 2014), and a poetry chapbook, *Whose House, Whose Playroom* (Dancing Girl Press, 2017). Her poems appear in *The Antioch Review, Baltimore Review, Cincinnati Review, CutBank, Denver Quarterly, Massachusetts Review,* and *Southern Poetry Review,* among other journals. She is poetry editor at *Kettle Blue Review,* and associate editor at Canopic Publishing.

Ryan Ridge is the author of four books, including *American Homes* (University of Michigan Press, 2015), which was the Michigan Library Publishing Club's inaugural book club pick. Ridge received the 2016 Italo Calvino Prize in Fabulist Fiction judged by Jonathan Lethem. He lives in SLC, UT and edits *Juked.*

Jay Robinson is the co-author of *The Czar.* He teaches at Ashland University and The University of Akron. He's also the Co-Editor-in-Chief/Reviews Editor for *Barn Owl Review* and helps edit The Akron Series in Contemporary Poetics. Poetry and prose have appeared in *32 Poems, The Laurel Review, Poetry, Whiskey Island,* among others.

Andrea Rogers is a postdoctoral fellow at Georgia Tech, where she teaches writing. She is the recipient of the 2015 Agnes Scott Writers' Festival Poetry Prize, judged by Tracy K. Smith, and two Academy of American Poets awards. Her poems have been published by *The Adirondack Review, District Lit, Negative Capability Press,* and others; her band, Night Driving in Small Towns, has appeared in features by *Rolling Stone* and NPR.

Sarah Lyn Rogers is a Pushcart-nominated writer from the San Francisco Bay Area and was formerly the Fiction Editor for *The Rumpus.* She is the author of *Inevitable What,* a poetry chapbook focused on magic and rituals. For more of her work, visit sarahlynrogers.com.

Stephanie Rogers was educated at The Ohio State University, the University of Cincinnati, and the University of North Carolina at Greensboro. Her poems have appeared or are forthcoming in journals such as *Ploughshares, Pleiades, upstreet, New Ohio Review*, and *The Adroit Journal*, as well as the *Best New Poets anthology*. Her first collection of poems, *Plucking the Stinger*, was released from Saturnalia Books in October 2016.

Kathleen Rooney is the author of eight books of poetry, fiction, and nonfiction, as well as a founding editor of Rose Metal Press and a founding member of Poems While You Wait. She is also the co-editor, most recently, of *Rene Magritte: Selected Writings*, and her second novel, *Lillian Boxfish Takes a Walk*, was published by St. Martin's Press in 2017.

Bonnie Roy has written poems, translations of poems, and essays about poems for publications including *Contemporary Literature, Jacket2*, and *Jubilat*. She lives in northern California.

Tony Ruzicka primarily writes about potatoes, tea, and meat substitutes for a living. He lives in the Ozarks with his wife and daughter, in the town where they were all born.

Brynn Saito is the author of *Power Made Us Swoon* (2016) and *The Palace of Contemplating Departure* (2013), both from Red Hen Press, as well as *Bright Power, Dark Peace* (Diode Editions), cowritten with Traci Brimhall.

Shannon Salter has had work published in *Birdfeast, The Bitter Oleander, Denver Quarterly, Juked,* and *Word Riot*. She holds an MFA from the University of Nevada, Las Vegas, where she is currently a part-time instructor in the English Department.

Elizabeth Savage is a professor of English at Fairmont State University and poetry editor for *Kestrel*. She has two books of poetry, *Idylliad* and *Grammar*, and a new chapbook, *Woman Looking at a Vase of Flowers*, from Furniture Press.

Philip Schaefer's debut collection of poems *Bad Summon* (University of Utah Press, 2017) won the Agha Shahid Ali Poetry Prize, and he's the author of three chapbooks, two co-written with friend and poet Jeff Whitney. He won the 2016 *Meridian* Editor's Prize in poetry, has been featured on *Poetry Daily, Verse Daily*, and through the *Poetry Society*, and has work in or forthcoming in *The Kenyon Review, Prairie Schooner, Guernica,* and *The Cincinnati Review*. He tends bar in Missoula, MT.

Michael Schmeltzer was born in Japan and eventually moved to the US. He is the author of *Blood Song*, a Washington State Book Award finalist in poetry, and *A Single Throat Opens*, a collaborative exploration of addiction, family, and childhood. His work can be found in *Black Warrior Review, Water~Stone Review, Mid-American Review, Poetry Northwest,* and *Split Lip Magazine,* among others.

Andrew Scott is the author of *Naked Summer: Stories* (2011), which was named a Notable Collection by the Story Prize. His fiction and nonfiction, including author interviews and book reviews, have been published by *Esquire, Glimmer Train, The Writer's Chronicle,* and many other outlets. He lives in Indianapolis and is a senior editor at Engine Books.

Maureen Seaton has authored nineteen poetry collections, both solo and collaborative—most recently, *Caprice: Collected, Uncollected, and New Collaborations* (with Denise Duhamel, Sibling Rivalry Press, 2015). Her awards include the Iowa Poetry Prize, two Lammys, the Audre Lorde Award, an NEA fellowship, and two Pushcart Prizes. A new collection, *Fisher,* was released from Black Lawrence Press in 2018.

Katherine Debella Seluja's work has appeared in *bosque, Intima, Iron Horse Literary Review,* and *Santa Ana River Review,* among others. Her first collection, *Gather the Night,* focuses on mental illness and is forthcoming from UNM Press in 2018. Katherine is currently working on a collaborative poetry project in response to the 2016 presidential election.

Mary Beth Shaffer is a fiction writer who has published her work and collaborations in the *Indiana Review, Quarter After Eight, Diagram, Iowa Writes,* and the anthology *Saints of Hysteria.*

Martha Silano's most recent book is *Reckless Lovely* (Saturnalia Books). She also co-edited, with Kelli Russell Agodon, *The Daily Poet: Day-By-Day Prompts For Your Writing Practice.* She edits *Crab Creek Review* and teaches at Bellevue College. marthasilano.net

Jonathan Silverman is an associate professor of English at UMass Lowell. He is the author of *Nine Choices: Johnny Cash and American Culture,* the co-author of *The World Is a Text,* and the co-editor of *Remaking the American College Campus.* He has served as the Fulbright Roving Scholar in Norway.

Matthew Simmons (@matthewjsimmons) lives in Seattle. He is the author, most recently, of the story collection *The In-Betweens* (Civil Coping Mechanisms, 2016).

Leigh Sugar is a writer and movement artist based in Brooklyn, New York. She is an MFA candidate in poetry at NYU, where she is the 2018 Veterans Writing Workshop fellow.

Sylvia Sukop holds an MFA from Washington University in St. Louis and has received fellowships including PEN Center USA Emerging Voices, Lambda Literary Emerging Writers, and a Fulbright to Germany. Her essays are published in *Creative Nonfiction* and *The Southeast Review*, and in the anthologies *Strange Cargo* (2010), *LAtitudes: An Angeleno's Atlas* (2015), and *Emerge* (2016).

Paige Sullivan completed her MFA at Georgia State University, where she served on the staffs of *Five Points* and *New South Journal*. In addition to essays and book reviews, her poetry has appeared or will soon appear in *Tampa Review, Arts & Letters, Ninth Letter,* and other journals. She lives and works in Atlanta.

Sarah Suzor's collection of poetry, *The Principle Agent*, won the Hudson Prize, and was published by Black Lawrence Press. Her collaboration with Travis Cebula, *After the Fox*, was also released from BLP in 2014. She is the owner and founder of INK, LLC., which provides assistance to writers who are looking to write new manuscripts, or re-vamp their existing manuscripts. She lives in Venice Beach, and teaches writing workshops around the country.

Faizan Syed is a psychiatrist in training located in Queens, NY. He was awarded the Folger Adams Jr. Prize and the Graduating Poet's Award from the University of Illinois. Faizan's work has appeared in *Montage Literary Arts Journal*, and collaborative work with Matthew DeMarco was published in *Dogbird*.

Jill Talbot is the author of *The Way We Weren't: A Memoir* and the editor of *Metawritings: Toward a Theory of Nonfiction*.

Molly Tenenbaum's books include *Mytheria* (Two Sylvias Press, 2017), *The Cupboard Artist, Now, By a Thread*, and the artist book/chapbook collaboration with artist Ellen Zeigler, *Exercises to Free the Tongue*. She teaches at North Seattle College.

Molly Thornton writes from the femmiverse, influenced by female friendships, queer love, and life's gritty magic. Her work appears in *The Leveller, The Seattle Globalist, Lavender Review,* and *baldhip magazine*. She is a Lambda Literary Emerging Writers Fellow.

Julie Marie Wade is the author of ten collections of poetry and prose, including *Same-Sexy Marriage: A Novella in Poems* (A Midsummer Night's Press, 2018) and the forthcoming *The Unrhymables: Collaborations in Prose*, co-authored with Denise Duhamel (Noctuary Press, 2019). Wade is an Associate Professor of Creative Writing at Florida International University in Miami.

William Wadsworth's work has appeared in *The New Republic, The Paris Review, The Yale Review, Tin House*, and *The Boston Review*, among other magazines, as well as in several anthologies, including *The Best American Erotic Poems*, edited by David Lehman, and *the Library of America Anthology of American Religious Poems*, edited by Harold Bloom. He currently teaches at Columbia University, where he is director of the graduate and undergraduate creative writing programs.

G.C. Waldrep's most recent books are a long poem, *Testament* (BOA Editions, 2015), and a chapbook, *Susquehanna* (Omnidawn, 2013). With Joshua Corey he edited *The Arcadia Project: North American Postmodern Pastoral* (Ahsahta, 2012). His new collection, *feast gently*, is due out from Tupelo Press in 2018. He lives in Lewisburg, PA, where he teaches at Bucknell University, edits the journal *West Branch*, and serves as Editor-at-Large for *The Kenyon Review*.

Trent Walters explores spaces like abandoned dollhouse cupboards and dank basements. He is the author of *Learning the Ropes* (Morpo Press). He has lived and worked in Honduras and Mexico. Poems of his appeared in *Asimov's, Mid-America Poetry Review*, and *The Pedestal*. He has poems forthcoming in the anthologies *Flatwater Stirs, Allegro & Adagio*; as well as the magazines *Typehouse* and *Menacing Hedge*.

Jeff Whitney is the author of five chapbooks, two of which were co-written with Philip Schaefer. Recent poems can be found in *32 Poems, Adroit, Booth, Muzzle, Prairie Schooner, Rattle,* and *Verse Daily*. He lives in Portland.

Quintan Ana Wikswo is the author of the collection of short stories and photographs *The Hope of Floating Has Carried Us This Far* (Coffee House Press) and the novel with photographs *A Long Curving Scar Where the Heart Should Be* (Stalking Horse Press). Her work is widely anthologized, and appears regularly in *Tin House, Guernica, Conjunctions*, and more. QuintanWikswo.com

Laura-Madeline Wiseman is the author of 26 books and chapbooks, include *Some Fatal Effects of Curiosity and Disobedience*, twice nominated for the Elgin Award. Her poetry has appeared in *Strange Horizons, Abyss & Apex, Gingerbread House, Star*Line, Silver Blade,* and elsewhere. Her latest book is *Through A Certain Forest*.

David Wojciechowski's first book, *Dreams I Never Told You & Letters I Never Sent*, is out now from Gold Wake Press. His poems have appeared in *Bateau, Better, iO*, and *Meridian* among other places. He teaches literature and writing and does freelance design work for *Salt Hill Journal*, Pleiades Press, and others.

Maggie Woodward is a poet & person who lives in Los Angeles, where she's working on a PhD in Film Studies at USC's School of Cinematic Arts. She is the author of the chapbook *Found Footage* (Porkbelly Press, 2017). She holds an MFA in Poetry from the University of Mississippi. Previously, she served as senior editor of the *Yalobusha Review* & curated the Trobar Ric reading series.

Devon Wootten teaches at Whitman College. His poems have appeared in *BAX 2018, Fece, LIT, Aufgabe,* and *Colorado Review,* among others. He has been supported by Yaddo, Anderson Ranch, and the Fulbright Foundation. Devon holds an MFA from the University of Montana and a PhD from the University of Iowa. He curates bestamericanyou.com and wikipoesis.com

Gail Wronsky is the author, coauthor, or translator of twelve books of poetry and prose. Her latest book, *Fuegos Florales/Flowering Fires,* a translation of the poems of Argentinean poet Alicia Partnoy, won the American Book Award from Settlement House Press.

Anne K. Yoder's writing has appeared in *Fence, Bomb,* and *Tin House,* among other publications. She is the author of two chapbooks: *Jungfrau Happy AHHHHH,* and *Sigil & Sigh* (with Megan Kaminski). She is a staff writer for *The Millions* and a member of Meekling Press, a collective micropress based in Chicago.

ABOUT THE EDITORS

Simone Muench is the author of several books including *Lampblack & Ash* (Kathryn A. Morton Prize and *NYT* Editor's Choice; Sarabande, 2005), *Orange Crush* (Sarabande, 2010), and *Wolf Centos* (Sarabande, 2014). Her chapbook *Trace* won the Black River Chapbook Competition (Black Lawrence Press, 2014), and her recent book, *Suture*, was co-written with Dean Rader (Black Lawrence Press, 2017). In 2014, she was awarded the Meier Foundation for the Arts Achievement Award, recognizing innovation, achievements, and community contributions. Other honors include an NEA poetry fellowship, Illinois Arts Council fellowships, and residency fellowships to Yaddo, Artsmith, and VSC. She is Professor of English at Lewis University where she teaches creative writing and film studies. She serves as advisor for *Jet Fuel Review* and as a senior poetry editor for *Tupelo Quarterly*.

Dean Rader's debut collection of poems, *Works & Days*, won the 2010 T. S. Eliot Poetry Prize and *Landscape Portrait Figure Form* (2014) was named by *The Barnes & Noble Review* as a Best Poetry Book. Three new books appeared in 2017: *Suture*, collaborative poems written with Simone Muench (Black Lawrence Press), *Self-Portrait as Wikipedia Entry* (Copper Canyon), and *Bullets into Bells: Poets and Citizens Respond to Gun Violence*, edited with Brian Clements & Alexandra Teague (Beacon). He is also the editor of *99 Poems for the 99 Percent: An Anthology of Poetry*. Dean writes regularly for *The San Francisco Chronicle*, *The Huffington Post*, *BOMB*, and *The Kenyon Review*. He is an Affiliate Artist at the Headlands Center for the Arts and a professor at the University of San Francisco. In their review of Rader's recent book, *Publishers Weekly* writes "few poets capture the contradictions of our national life with as much sensitivity or keenness."

Sally Ashton is the author of *Some Odd Afternoon* (BlazeVOX, 2010), *Her Name Is Juanita* (Kore Press, 2009), and *These Metallic Days* (Mainstreet Rag, 2005). She is Editor-in-Chief of *DMQ Review*, an online journal featuring poetry and art. Honors include an artist's fellowship from Arts Council Silicon Valley and a residency fellowship from Montalvo Arts Center. She served as the second Poet Laureate of Santa Clara County (Silicon valley), 2011-2013. Work appears in several anthologies including *Fish Anthology:* First Prize Fish Flash Fiction. She teaches creative writing and composition at San José State University and has taught a wide variety of workshops including in *Disquiet: International Literary Program* in Lisbon, Portugal.

Jackie K. White is the author of three chapbooks—*Bestiary Charming*, winner of the 2007 Anabiosis Press Award; *Petal Tearing & Variations* (Finishing Line Press, 2008); and *Come clearing* (Dancing Girl Press, 2012). She is also co-translator of Cesar

Rondon's *Book of Salsa* (North Carolina Press, 2008) and her translations and poems have appeared in such journals as *ACM*, *Bayou*, *Fifth Wednesday*, *Folio*, *Natural Bridge*, *Quarter after Eight*, *Spoon River*, *Third Coast*, and *Tupelo Quarterly*. An editor with *RHINO* for ten years, she is now a faculty advisor for *Jet Fuel Review* and has been the recipient of fellowships at Ragdale, VCCA, and the Mary Anderson Center for the Arts. She is a Professor of English at Lewis University, teaching courses in poetry, Native American, Latinx, and Latin American literatures.

ACKNOWLEDGMENTS

In the spirit of collaboration, the editors would like to acknowledge one another for the absolute pleasure of working together. We would also like the thank Richard Every for his superlative design skills and continual support, and Jim Tsinganos for his graciousness in letting us use his striking artwork. A final hefty thanks to our publisher Diane Goettel; to Michael Anania, Lynne Thompson, Laura Cogan, Oscar Villalon, and Christopher Salerno who so generously agreed to read and blurb the anthology; and, to all the authors who contributed to *They Said* for their exhilarating collaborative camaraderie.

Simone Muench would also like to acknowledge the following:
Much gratitude to Lewis University's Faculty Scholar Award that provided a course reassignment so I could devote time to this anthology, as well as to my student editors who ran *Jet Fuel Review* like rock stars when I was stressed out and playing catch-up. Many thanks to my prior collaborators who've instilled in me a longstanding love and appreciation of collaborative texts: William Allegrezza, Philip Jenks, Jackie White, and Dean Rader. And, to the other collaborators in my life, my family and friends, with much love and gratitude: Richard Every, Kim Ambriz, Lana Rakhman, Hadara Bar-Nadav, Jackie White, Jen Consilio, Chiyoko Yoshida, Jason Koo, Sarah Long, Melissa Grubbs, Jessie Ambriz, Sara Voden, Jesse Muench, Loretta McSween, John McSween, Chuck Crowder, Bill Mondi, Lanko Miyazaki Goldberger, Stephanie McCanles, and Wesley Kimler.

Dean Rader is especially grateful for the excellent work of Caitlyn Miller who was enormously helpful with manuscript preparation before going to press. Without her tireless efforts over the holidays, we would not have made our first deadline.